IMMORTAL
WITH A KISS

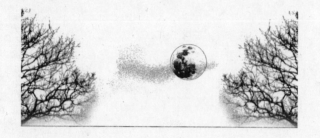

D0292551

Also by Jacqueline Lepore

The Emma Andrews Series

DESCENT INTO DUST

IMMORTAL
WITH A KISS

JACQUELINE LEPORE

WILLIAM MORROW
An Imprint of HarperCollins*Publishers*

This book is a work of fiction. The characters, incidents, and dialogue are drawn from the author's imagination and are not to be construed as real. Any resemblance to actual events or persons, living or dead, is entirely coincidental.

IMMORTAL WITH A KISS. Copyright © 2011 by Jacqueline Navin. All rights reserved. Printed in the United States of America. No part of this book may be used or reproduced in any manner whatsoever without written permission except in the case of brief quotations embodied in critical articles and reviews. For information address HarperCollins Publishers, 10 East 53rd Street, New York, NY 10022.

HarperCollins books may be purchased for educational, business, or sales promotional use. For information please write: Special Markets Department, HarperCollins Publishers, 10 East 53rd Street, New York, NY 10022.

FIRST EDITION

Designed by Diahann Sturge

Library of Congress Cataloging-in-Publication Data

Lepore, Jacqueline.
  Immortal with a kiss / Jacqueline Lepore. — 1st ed.
     p. cm.
  ISBN 978-0-06-187815-2 (pbk.)
     1. Vampires—Fiction. 2. Great Britain—History—Victoria, 1837-1901—Fiction.
I. Title.
PS3612.E64I46 2011
813'.6—dc22

                                                                2010031068

11 12 13 14 15   OV/BVG   10 9 8 7 6 5 4 3 2 1

This book is dedicated to Kate Klemm.
With love and appreciation.

Acknowledgments

I have a great publishing team: Christina Hogrebe at Jane Rotrosen Agency, and Kate Nintzel and everyone else at HarperCollins. Thank you for championing these books and for letting me run with the concept. Your contributions continue to be so very helpful.

I need to express my most heartfelt thanks again to my sisters: Kate, Kay, Krisann, and Lorie—the power group, for sure (real power comes from love).

Thanks to my kids—Luke, Lindsey, and Kelly—who have been so supportive and ingenious in helping to spread the word about their mom's vampire book to whomever would listen.

And again, my husband, Mick, deserves the biggest thanks. He worked almost as hard on this book as I did.

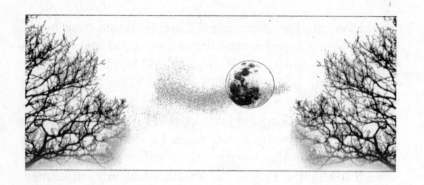

Love-sick Beauties lift their essenced brows,
Sigh to the Cyprian queen their secret vows,
Like watchful Hero feel their soft alarms,
And clasp their floating lovers in their arms.
—The Origin of Society, Erasmus Darwin (1803)

Chapter One

The play of light on a heaving sea is hypnotic. In Copenhagen, the water is like ink. It is cold and it is cruel, and it deserves all the brutal lore it has earned through the ages, of sea monsters and wild, ravaging storms. Even before Sebastian's letter arrived, I had begun to feel more and more acutely how this sea separated me from home. Its slick, turbid waters whispered to me, a summons in every briny breath I took, every frigid sea spray I wiped from my brow. An ache began in my breast, a flicker of something not quite right in my world was just out of reach of consciousness, lurking on the fringes of my thoughts.

I was in Denmark late in that year of 1862 upon the

permission of Dom Beauclaire, a French Benedictine monk and archivist who had become both a mentor and a friend when I'd fled to his monastery last spring. He'd helped me then, and so I turned to him when, with the conclusion of that nasty business in Avebury, I had felt the need to prepare myself, arm myself by seeking out knowledge. This quest brought me across the North Sea to a place where I might learn of matters that would mean the difference between life and death—and even that which was beyond death. For I had only just learned the terrifying and thrilling truth about myself and the very unorthodox life that was, it seemed, going to be in my future.

If what I am about to tell you strains credibility, then best put this book down and settle comfortably into a life of ordinary human things. But if you can believe in that which is outside science, reason, doctrine . . . even sense, then pay close attention to what it was I had recently come to learn. It was—is—my destiny to hunt and kill the undead. In Avebury, I had come to understand that I am Dhampir, a child of woe, a child of suffering—a vampire hunter. Something I did not at all feel equipped to undertake. I cannot imagine how one would.

And so I had fled to the familiar sanctuary of books to find an extensive, albeit haphazard, collection housed among the faded splendor of an old Oldenburg palace the monks had acquired for their peculiar abbey. Stacked in piles under murals of cherubs and noble depictions of Olympian gods, heaped upon shelves lined against walls decorated with chipped gold leaf, stuffed in every nook and cranny lay a collection dizzying in its breadth and depth of very unique, very special, very rare texts.

Here was housed the wisdom and folly of the ages, a veritable history of man's ancient battle against the most powerful forms of evil. Books, scrolls, clay tablets from days beyond history's reach, unbound manuscripts and journals penned in forgotten hands, all crisp with age and reeking with the vinegary scent of dust. Yet this was only part of the vast and secret network of archives maintained by the Vatican.

My twenty-fourth birthday came and went within these walls. It was soon after that a vague tension began to build. I ignored it as long as I could, stubbornly reading until my eyes ran with exhausted tears. My fingers, scored by razor-thin cuts from the aged pages, rifled greedily over vellum inked with ancient words. I pored over the information, filling my mind with as much as I could force myself to absorb.

The sense of urgency, of imminent purpose waiting, biding its time, grew deep and dense inside me as the darkness of winter hunkered low over the city. My impatience surged in increments like a cold tide, even as I was thinking, thinking—the words echoing like a far-off cry at the bottom of a well: *Semper praesum.* Always ready. It had become something of a motto of mine. Or perhaps it was a prayer. And so I read feverishly, knowing I must hurry . . .

For there was a storm coming. As the sky grayed and night encroached on daylight hours, I knew I was too far from home, too far from where I would be needed. I only hoped I would have enough time to make myself ready.

But fate does not wait for us to be ready. It does not ask us to be fully prepared. It requires only that we are willing.

The scrape of the monk's footsteps, like sandpaper on the smooth marble surface of the palace's long central hallway, was startling in the silence. From where I was seated—behind a raw wooden table I'd made my desk in what used to be a ladies' sitting parlor—I saw his tonsured head bowed as he advanced to my doorway, his brown-garbed form dwarfed by the towering windows of the great hall. I think I knew even then that what I'd felt hurtling toward me had finally arrived.

I was going over a Greek translation at the time, and was feeling a sense of unease. Nausea rose against the back of my throat. I had come to learn that the undead sometimes posed as scholars to write false documents to mislead and misdirect hunters. I found I had some talent for detecting this and I sensed it strongly in this document, a boastful, fraudulent account of the purported powers of the Greek vampire known as the *vrykolakas*.

According to the author, there existed a breed of revenant that was not subject to the same limitations as the rest of the undead. I marveled at the lies as I read of communities where vampires lived out in the open, sunning themselves in exotic flower–draped grottos and drinking pomegranate juice, living among their prey like brothers. They were capable, this clever deceiver would have it, of casting both a reflection and a shadow. My stomach roiled precariously at the falsehoods, but there was something in the words, some boast, even a lurid triumph, that had made me forge on.

Upon the arrival of the young cleric, however, I pushed my task aside and struggled to compose myself. Even here, where the brothers knew what I was, I had been careful to remain guarded, retreating into a reflexive secretiveness. It was my habit in any case. Even before I knew about my peculiar destiny, I had been accustomed to hiding my . . . oddities. Having discovered the dark secret of my heritage, I was even more aware how important it was to guard a secret like mine, lest I find myself situated in the Colney Hatch Lunatic Asylum.

"Mistress," the monk muttered. He was middle-aged, tonsured, rather undignified in his brown robe and shuffling boots. "This arrived for you this morning."

I saw at once by the handwriting on the address that it was from Sebastian Dulwich, and my heart leaped with happiness. This man, my closest, dearest friend, had stood at my side and fought with me during my initiation into the world of undead.

I took the letter eagerly, but waited to break the seal and unfold the heavy paper until the last of the monk's hollow footsteps had faded to silence. When I did, a small packet fell onto the table.

I examined it curiously. It was folded and sealed with a wax impression I did not recognize, and though there was no direction or address, I assumed it was also meant for me. I set it aside for the moment and focused upon the expansive, florid script that was Sebastian's hand.

Dearest Emma,

London is dreary, but I am frightfully busy what with soirees, balls and whatnot. I absolutely live for the delicious opportunities to watch the debauches of my peers firsthand. It is so droll to have to wade through the papers to find one's daily dose of gossip, and so I dress in my finest—darling, you should see the gorgeous new coats I've had made!—and find what amusements I can as a spectator of bad behavior.

I am presently engaged in a very interesting intrigue with a groom from the mews, whom I like to dress up in gentleman's clothing and present as my cousin from Yorkshire. The fellow is a crack at impersonating the gentry, accent and all. It has been a fine diversion, but not enough that I do not miss you sorely. At times, dear Emma, I am positively furious with you for refusing my invitation to join me in Town this season.

I am being a bore, but you must be used to that by now. So, then, how is Denmark? Have you met any ghosts? Any demented princes or waifish chits looking a bit damp? No doubt you are in your glory, up to your neck with books, an endeavor which confounds my brain, although I admit, I did enjoy the recommendation you gave me. Lord Byron is as dry a wit as myself and Don Juan a scoundrel I can adore.

Speaking of the great lover, have you had word from our Mr. Fox?

I paused, a little hitch catching in my chest. I had not, as it happened, had a single word since Valerian Fox and I had said our good-byes last spring. That had been five months ago. And I had found the separation much more difficult than I would ever have anticipated.

Ours was a rather complicated situation. What feelings he had for me, I was not at all certain. He'd saved my life more than once. More than that, he'd forsaken a chance to fulfill his most cherished wish, to destroy the evil vampire lord known to us as Marius, to do it. As to my feelings for him . . . I did not think about that much. At least, I tried not to.

No doubt you are anxious for word of our beloved Henrietta, Sebastian's letter continued. *What a dolt I am to delay the good news that she is flourishing.*

My heart twisted in my chest, as if it literally leaped for joy. I adored my little cousin, for a sweeter child could not exist, and it was for precisely this reason of her pure spirit that she had been at the center of the evil events that had taken place in Avebury. It was on Henrietta's behalf I had engaged in my first battle with a vampire. Before this, I had not even known such an evil truly existed. With Valerian Fox's help, I had discovered my powers, and together, along with the aid of the warrior priest Father Luke and my dear Sebastian, we had prevented a terrible fate not only for my precious Henrietta but for many innocent lives.

The child appears to have no ill effects. She often asks for you, and in the most admiring of terms informed me when I was out in Wiltshire for a hunt that she intends to be tall and scholarly like you. Despite her love for you, I doubt my sister-in-law was pleased. You know how her mother feels about your bluestocking ways.

You are wondering about the letter enclosed. Something of a mystery, but you have not opened it yet, have you? You see how well I know you. You have patiently waded through all my drivel, for you are predictably ordered. It is part of why I love you, my dear Emma, and I am glad of it. I confess, my delay has been to give me time to warm up my pen, for I hardly know how I am to go about explaining the pages I have enclosed.

Lifting my gaze to the multipaned window, I drew in the breath I needed to brace myself. My eyes drifted to the glossy blackness of the sea that lay beyond the neglected terraced lawns of the old palace. I thought idly of the terrible coldness of the water, the kind that seizes a body into paralysis. One instant plunge into a rigor not unlike death.

A sense of inevitability sealed itself in my mind as I lowered my head and read on.

The words contained therein are from the journal of a Miss Victoria Markam, an unfortunate young lady whose path crossed mine at a Kensington fete. The night was a bore and my new toy was not with me, so I was rather in my cups, and found plain-faced Miss Markam wandering around quite foxed. Naturally, this amused me, and we together went on a little adventure to pilfer a fine whiskey from the library. She began to drink like a sailing man, became predictably loquacious, and I learned, much to my supreme lack of interest, that she was a teacher. But then she told me she was formerly em-

ployed at a prestigious girls' school in the Lake District. She had fled in the midst of the Michaelmas term and vowed never to return. I assumed she'd committed some indiscretion and been let go, but as she began to speak of the events which precipitated her abrupt withdrawal from the teaching staff, I began to see her fear. She was truly terrified. I began to pay attention.

With some prompting, I elicited some rather bland accounts of shadows and noises about the place, subtle changes in the students and a veil of conspiracy. Mere schoolgirl mischief aimed at a despised teacher, I thought, and was inclined to dismiss my flash of interest until she mentioned the deaths in the village. After this spring, and, I fear, for the rest of my life, that will get my attention, be it proven to be nothing more dastardly than common influenza. I shamelessly plied the woman with more of the single malt whiskey, and pried at her defenses until she told me her dark secret.

The story is this: She had become aware of a group of students sneaking outdoors in the middle of the night. They had grown brazen and secretive, challenging her authority. She believed they were meeting local boys in the woods, and so one night she covertly followed them. The girls eluded her. As she was telling me this, I should add, she was as calm and sober as I unfortunately am now, though by rights she should have been intoxicated into oblivion for the amount of spirits she consumed.

As she tried to find her way home, she came upon what she described as a cache of corpses. "Human bodies cast about like discarded husks." I quote her, for I remember it exactly. She spoke of how pale they were and I could not keep my mind from remembering the unnatural pallor of the victims we saw this spring. She mentioned bruising *and cuts, and quite specifically told me that this damage was done about the neck, just under the ear. She believed they had been murdered, and all in the same manner.*

I was pondering this shock when she delivered another. The Blackbriar School for girls, Emma darling— that was where she was employed, and I know you know the name well. Do you recall lamenting to me that your mother had attended this very school when she was a girl, and it had been your dearest wish to follow in her footsteps but your stepmother had forbidden it?

The mention of my mother landed in the center of my chest like the thump of a fist. I gasped out loud, my jaw jerking open. I had not been prepared for that. My beautiful tragic mother had haunted me all of my life, even more so now that I had learned the terrible truth about her. My hands began to tremble, making it necessary to lay Sebastian's letter flat on the table as I read on.

So there I was, quite overset to realize I was distressingly sober, and I am afraid I made a dreadful decision, one for which I pray you not to despise me. I said, and I quote myself precisely, "I know of someone whose knowledge in these things may be helpful." She grasped my hands so piteously that I was glad I had made the offer of aid.

Soon after, we were discovered. Miss Markam, being the sister of my hostess, was quickly borne away to her bedchamber to sleep off her indisposition. I, being a man, was looked upon with disapproval and left alone with the rest of the whiskey. Not long after, a maid found me and handed to me the enclosed papers which she informed me Miss Markam had torn from her journal and sent to me, with the intention of my making good on my offer of service.

I have not seen nor heard from her since that night, and for all I know she is mad, and I am a fool. But I cannot help thinking that this is what anyone would have said of each of us just a few months ago, when we were chasing monsters about the Wiltshire downs. My mind no longer has the luxury of dismissing the insane.

So I give you these pages. I will tell you I did not read them and not because of any sense of honor or integrity— my Lord, you know me better than that. Quite simply, I am a coward. I will stay here in Town until Christmastide, when I will feast and be jolly with my new man, and I will think no more of this matter, for I have delivered this intelligence into your hands and my duty is done.

I smiled softly despite my troubled mind. Sebastian had a very amusing flourish, and I could imagine if he were here to speak these words, he would do so with gesticulating hands and a moue of disdain worthy of a king. He meant none of it, of course, as the forthcoming lines bore out.

But should you need me, and you have exhausted every other aid and imaginable resource, then I shall be of what little service my humble self can provide. You have but to call.

The reference to himself as humble won a dry chuckle from me, as I was sure Sebastian had intended it would. He signed the letter "With Affection" and then his loopy, bold signature.

So it was Sebastian who called me home.

I did not read the packet of Miss Markam's journal. I placed it in my reticule and began to make arrangements to return to England. In the wake of Sebastian's letter, my thoughts were not of the troubled teacher, or of the young women whose lives were in danger. My thoughts were selfish. Even as I knew I was being pulled by the thread spun by the Fates—those dispassionate witches in whose hands all destiny lies—I felt unprepared, unready. After all, I was no expert, not yet. Despite my experience in the spring and my present studies, I knew relatively little. I was only just discovering the nature and breadth of my talents, and how to use them.

Even more disturbing was that I had not been able to learn anything of the Dracula. In all of the archive, there was nothing save a few mentions and none of those instructive. So elusive was information on the being purported to be the most powerful vampire in existence—who had been somehow connected to the happenings in Avebury—I began to doubt he was anything more than legend.

I would have been mad not to have been afraid. The memory of what I had faced that past spring still held me. I had been thrust against forces so vile and so strong they had defeated mortal men for generations. I still grieved for all I had not been able to do, and for all that had been lost. I had to keep reminding myself that despite my failings I had saved Henrietta. I had kept a terrible force from being unleashed upon the world. I had done battle with a great vampire lord and won.

But in weak moments I would think of the child I had not been able to save, and her mourning mother. I would think of the priest with his broken faith wandering the world looking for answers no earthly source could supply. I would think of Valerian Fox, whose quest for salvation had not ended.

And I would, of course, think constantly of my mother, who I had learned was a vampire. I wanted so badly to save her. Now, here was a link to her, a tie to her past.

I had to go, of course. I was frightened, unsure of myself as yet, but I thought again of the uncaring Fates, furiously spinning their gossamer thread, and I would have been but a fool to tangle them with something as inconsequential as my free will.

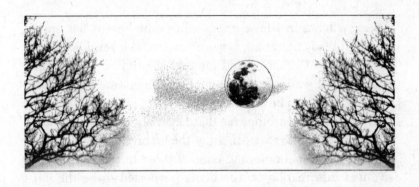

Chapter Two

I cannot describe what it was I felt as I packed my belongings into the old portmanteau that had once been my mother's, one of the few things I had of hers. I could have afforded much better, for my late husband, Simon, had left me a wealthy widow upon his death a year ago. Yet I would not give it up.

When it was crammed full, I summoned a carriage to take me into the city and settled in a finely appointed room at the best inn. It was there, embarked and committed at last, that I finally opened Miss Markam's journal pages.

A newspaper clipping fluttered out as I unfolded the packet, and a scrap of foolscap slipped out with it, bearing Sebastian's scrawl: *Victoria Markam has gone missing.*

A single thump punched a rude blow to my chest. I turned

to the carefully cut piece from the *London Daily Mail*. "Five Dead Near Penrith. Unknown Disease Terrifies Village."

The article, which I read quickly, gave very little detail. Perhaps there was not much to report aside from each of the victims having been struck down with a mysterious malady in which they grew pale and listless. They died within three to five days, suffering from melancholia, delusions, delirium, and severe anemia.

That weird sense of destiny settled more tightly around me. I had seen this plague before. It had been referred to as a wasting disease in Avebury. Valerian Fox, who had much more experience in these things and had served as my mentor, had told me that this was what an unaware population called it when those among them began to expire from exsanguinations. That meant a vampire was feeding. I unfolded the journal pages and adjusted my lamp closer.

Miss Markam's hand was delicate and exact. A schoolteacher's hand, laying out her thoughts in evenly balanced lines as formal and ordered as a document of state.

I am put out with Margaret, her pages began. *She has always been unpleasant, but she is now sly. I am stymied by her recent friendship with Vanessa, who is generally well regarded by students and staff. I am concerned about Margaret's influence on the sweet-natured Vanessa.*

I felt instantly sorry for the maligned Margaret. I had been such a one as she, my quick mind seen as unattractive and suspicious, while my sister, Alyssa, had been our family's Vanessa, the favored one.

I catch them whispering all the time. Even young Eustacia knows something is wrong. She is my little informant, only because she cannot lie when I pin her with pointed questions. I know they go to the woods. Margaret mocks me even though she is only a tradesman's daughter and above her station here. But she acts like the Queen herself, and all the others follow her. I shall speak

The sentence was left uncompleted as the entry continued on another page which was not included. What followed was dated some days after.

The Irish boy was here. I saw him waiting in the copse at dusk. I spoke to Miss Easton about it, but she never sees anything. So I chased him off myself. He was brash and disrespectful, the same gloating manner I hate so much in Margaret. Such arrogance. I wonder if I should go to Miss Sloane-Smith. I fear she will not take my side against the girls. There was that business last fall, and she does not like me.

A pen crossed out the rest of the page, signaling it was of no import. I made out some reference to a chatty tea with another teacher and disregarded the rest. The next entry also had omissions above and below the following: *A young boy in the village has been missing for near a week. He did not return after setting out for home from his uncle's farm. The girls were disinterested in this tragedy, standing apart while the other students could speak of nothing else. Margaret and Vanessa, and now a few others who have joined them, were interested only in whatever secrets keep them constantly whispering like bees until I fear I will go mad with the buzz.*

That was followed by another page, dated soon after this. *I discussed with Ann my concern about the growing problems among the girls. I strongly sense them conspiring something. But she makes excuses for them. She argues they are well-behaved in her class, as if it were my fault they do not treat me well. I fear I am the only one who sees what is happening.*

Another passage on the next sheet read: *A man came in from the fields to find his wife gone without a trace. No one has seen her for a fortnight now.*

I inhaled sharply and tried to assert my rationality. A missing boy, a missing mother and child—these things sometimes had explanations. Women ran off, children got lost or found more entertaining things to do than return home promptly. It was possible these happenings were not the result of dark deeds. It was certainly not conclusive.

I read more of the pages, deciphering the rapidly deteriorating penmanship that chronicled Miss Markam's obsession with the growing circle of girls. I was frustrated with how little she knew, yet her conviction of something somehow wrong rang through every passage. The rancor of her scrawled words made her seem small, a petty tyrant unraveling because her authority was being usurped, and I wondered if that was all that was at work here.

I lay the pages down, rubbing my tired eyes. While I could see there was reason to suspect vampire activity in the area, it also appeared Miss Markam was the sort whose nerves made her brittle, apt to imagine all manner of things. She was prone to drinking in excess, Sebastian had reported. How reliable was her account? And why was no one else at the school in the least perturbed by the great dangers she seemed to sense growing among the students?

I feared weakness regarding my mother had caused me to act precipitously, and I was not certain at all there was anything to be investigated at the Blackbriar School after all.

A nightmare that night took me back to Avebury, to the chalk downs where the hawthorn tree had stood with its grasping branches. Valerian appeared at my side, his angular, sharp-featured face rendered true in every detail. I studied the leashed power of his frame, his dark and inscrutable eyes, the sensitively curved mouth I had kissed once.

Even in the dream, I felt the presence of the bond that had drawn us together. I had never examined that feeling too closely, but there was no mistaking how happy I was to see him again, all my brittle disappointment at his having left me without a word these last months forgiven in an instant.

He, however, remained stoic. "They are in the forest," he told me, and I heard the far-off sound of girlish laughter riding sweet and pure on the air. *Margaret,* I thought at once. She and the other students with whom Victoria Markam was obsessed were here.

I turned urgently to tell this to Valerian. He stood frozen, his rapier-thin body as rigid as steel, his finely tailored clothing hanging on him like a corpse. Behind him a shadow rose, a familiar and dreaded one. A dragon, curled like a serpent, ready to strike. The sign of the Dracula, the feared and mysterious Dragon Prince. I felt its hatred pulsing out to me like rays of heat off a bonfire.

I opened my mouth to scream, but the dragon did not threaten Valerian. It hovered. Watching. Biding its time.

Valerian looked haggard, and I thought: *He is dead!* But his lips moved. He told me to go, and I backed away from him, not knowing if he had been changed at last, if Marius had found him and bestowed the fatal kiss that would make him my enemy.

I ran to the forest, and he called to me again. When I turned, he was beside me, although he had not seemed to move. In his eyes, a world of sadness smoldered as he intoned in a voice dusty and not his, "Do not forsake Father Luke."

I reeled at the reminder. I grieved for Father Luke, the warrior priest who had run in disgrace from his church and from us after we had defeated the monster together. What had happened in Avebury, on that plain where standing stones marked the presence of an ancient and terrible evil, had destroyed him.

The cries from the girls, meanwhile, were pure joy and delight. They drew me away, taking me deep into the shaded forest, away from Valerian, and I was relieved. I did not like his mentioning the priest. *Am I to save all of the world?* I thought bitterly.

The growth in the woods was jungle-like, thick and stubborn, and growing more so as I fought my way through it to the girls. I had almost reached them when their voices changed abruptly from happiness to horror; they began to scream, their cries terror-filled, bone-rattling, turning my veins to runnels of ice. And then I felt him: Marius, the mighty vampire lord.

His voice was in my ear, in my head, saying my name like a vile incantation, like a lover's call. My body crawled to an awful, thrilling awareness. I felt his hand on my neck and his breath lifting the fine strands of my hair. As before, when I'd looked into his eyes not knowing the danger, I felt the rasp of his putrid mind against my quivering soul.

That was when I woke, gasping as my mind scrabbled away from the terrible dream. I felt for the taper on my bedside table. It flared on my first try, even with my hands trembling, and I sat up in the puddle of light until my heart settled. The truth went through me in jagged spikes of electricity, jerking my back straight as I stared into the darkness beyond the sputtering flame of my candle.

I was not only going to Blackbriar for my mother. I had another, equally powerful motivation driving me home to England, to a place where a plague of "pernicious anemia" often meant a vampire was gorging himself. Where there was evidence of a vampire, there was a chance it was Marius. And perhaps I could make right what I had taken from Valerian, for when he had been forced to choose my life or his own salvation, he had made an admirable, though agonizing, sacrifice. I owed him.

Now awake and facing no hope of resuming my rest, I penned a letter to Valerian, informing him of my plans to return to England. I posted the letter along with another to Sebastian, giving him my intentions and asking him to make some arrangements for me with a London employment agency, for despite my misgivings about Miss Markam, my mind was more than made up to proceed to the Blackbriar School.

A week later, I made a surprisingly fine journey to England on a kindly sea. Barely establishing my wobbling legs under me in Northumbria, I climbed immediately into a train car and headed west, across to the brooding Pennines into the heart of the Lake District, then to the jewel known as the Vale of Eden. The train made swift passage through a series of cols around which the fells rose gently like towering swells on a sea of rock, and a day later I arrived in Penrith, where I changed to hired carriage and followed the old Roman road that ran along the Eden River, northward to the isolated moor beyond the majestic Bryce Fell.

The mountain was already whitened by recent snows, reflected perfectly in the clear waters of the Houndclaw Tarn lapping at its base. Next to the lake was the village of Blackbriar, bristling with the charm of cobbled streets and storefront windows crowding its lanes. As I clattered along toward the inn which I had been told was the best to be had in these parts, I peered out the window and saw people going about their business with cheerful smiles.

I had not expected this. If a vampire were here, how was it nothing was in the air, no sense of terror or skittish looks? My limited experience in Avebury had taught me that fear gripped a population in a peculiar way when a vampire was nearby. The fear it brought with it was like a wash of watercolor over everything, an ugly and angry red that cast the most innocent thing in a lurid light. One could sense the creature's presence, even smell it. Or at least I could sense it with the blood inheritance with which my mother had gifted me.

I felt nothing terrible here. As dusk descended, I arrived at the Rood and Cup, my destination, and my doubts renewed at the bucolic picture of the cozy inn. Had I done naught but follow a lark in coming here?

When my hired carriage gained the small courtyard, the innkeeper came out to meet us, offering me a beefy and scarred hand to aid me in my descent down the step.

"Evening, mum," he muttered, but his friendly smile disappeared with startling alacrity as the driver called to him, indicating that my mother's portmanteau needed to be unloaded from the top of the conveyance.

He scrapped the hat off of his head. "Oye," he muttered, his good nature replaced by sloping shoulders and a petulant shuffle. The monstrosity I used for travel was indeed large and unwieldy, and I could well understand why he was not at all happy to have to wrestle it down from its perch and then carry it up the stairs to my room. But when he grabbed a leather strap and began to roughly jerk it up the stone steps, scraping the bottom of the heavy trunk against the ground, I opened my mouth to object. My sharp command was cut off by the sudden appearance of a woman who came bustling into the courtyard like a player taking the stage at Haymarket. Her voice was raised to a shrill, commanding ring. "Mr. Danby, you great oaf! It'll be your hide if you do this lady's property harm. Have a care, and none of your sulking, mind you!"

The man cast a sullen look in her direction. But she, who I suspected knew exactly what reaction she would get and didn't care, had already turned to me, her scowl transformed into a smile. "Well, then, miss, look at you with all the dust from the road on you. Come on, then, and we'll get you to the fire. You're hungry, I'll wager."

"Thank you," I said with a warm smile for both the offer of food and her handling of Mr. Danby. "I'm Mrs. Andrews. I will be needing a room, please."

"Of course you will, dear," she declared. "Look at you, poor thing. You're as beat as a puppy. I'm Mrs. Danby, of course. Now come along. You'll catch a chill in this night air. Nice cup of tea will fix you up, won't it? And I made rabbit stew today. It's what I'm best known for, and my bread's the envy of the county."

I found myself inside the great room, my cloak off before I knew it. "There," Mrs. Danby pronounced, giving the fine wool a few swats. "Janet will have it aired and cleaned."

Janet, a pretty thing of maybe sixteen or so, appeared as if summoned by magic, bobbed a quick curtsy to me, and carried off my cloak as if it were an ermine-lined cape such as the queen would wear.

I found myself in a low-ceilinged bower, beams dark with age overhead and boards worn pale by countless boots underfoot. I could smell the delectable aroma of meat and spices and my stomach rumbled in response. Tables were set up neatly with chairs, although there was no one about as the hour was too early for supper. Mrs. Danby situated me at a table near to the shoulder-high hearth.

"Now, this is cozy, isn't it?" Mrs. Danby's quarter-moon eyes were warm and her broad grin beamed at me, hands clasped as if she found especial delight in seeing to my comfort.

"I'll bring you tea, first. That should warm your bones straight away. Then I'll bring you the stew."

I sighed, smiling my gratitude. "That would be lovely, thank you."

"How long will you be staying, if I might ask?"

"I'm not sure. I am here to see a Miss Sloane-Smith about a newly vacant teaching position at the Blackbriar School."

Her frown drew her entire face into a pucker. "Yes, that business with poor Miss Markam. Who would have thought, a young, strong thing like that coming down with the consumption? Though she was a troubled soul, there's no denying that. Ah, well, it makes one appreciate every day of healthy life God gives you, it does. I suppose it was only a matter of time before they'd be needing a replacement, sad as it is. Well, good luck to you, then. Will you be riding up there tomorrow?"

"That is my plan," I replied, pulling back my trust a little bit. Her mothering had disarmed me—an admitted weakness of mine—but her inaccurate statement about Miss Markam's having died of consumption left me wary. I would do well to keep my guard up.

Her husband was just now bearing my trunk, which was perched safely on his shoulder, up the stairs. Mrs. Danby, who seemed to have eyes in the back of her head, called out without ever breaking her gaze from mine, "That better not have a scratch on it, Mr. Danby. Put her in the yellow room, and get Janet to unpack her things."

I laughed. "It is very old, Mrs. Danby. I hardly think your husband can be held to account for a scratch, when there are far worse already in evidence."

Mrs. Danby twitched a pert smile. "You'll be settled in a trice. I'll have my boy run up with the message for the headmistress to expect you tomorrow, and I'll make sure Colin O'Hara is here to drive you." She stoked the fire with a few brisk pokes before disappearing into the kitchens to bring me my tea.

I looked around me at the pleasant room. Small-paned windows shut out the miserable day. In the hearth, the flames sprung to life, high and bright and greedy, filling the air with the pleasant aroma of wood smoke. The silence was punctuated by the sharp snap of sap popping and the heat and quiet combined to lull me into a state of lassitude that made my eyelids heavy until a reedy voice from the other side of the room spoke.

"Winter is at the door," it said in the silence with a soft singsong lilt that raised a fine prickle of gooseflesh on my arms. I jolted awake to spy a thin old lady bundled in rugs, seated in a wooden chair on the other end of the hearth. I had not noticed her before, for she was enveloped in shadows. She was not addressing me directly, but staring into the flames, and the light cast her ancient features into a ghoulish picture.

For a moment, I thought she wasn't really there. There are times when I've seen and heard things others do not. When I looked at the old woman, I believed I was looking at one dead, for her face was no more than a skull cast in shades of gray and ash, and her body, even swathed in blankets, seemed too thin to support life.

However, I felt the energy of a long-lived will reaching to me. In a second, I knew my sense—the one that came from the blood of my mother—had teased awake something I could not have otherwise understood. She was not a vampire or ghoul, merely an old woman. But she was close to death. Very close.

"Hello," I said. I admit my voice was tentative, for I was still the tiniest bit unsure she was not a shade.

"Winter," she repeated, nodding. "And the Cyprian Queen has come."

"Pardon me?" I asked politely.

She spoke with confidence, not in the airy, uncertain terms of the old when their minds have been lost to dementia. I stayed in my seat, for my legs seemed to have gone numb somehow and I could not rise, although I did have to lean forward and strain my ears to hear better what she was saying.

She whispered, "She stands here at the gate." Her head rolled, as if she were in pain. "She tempts with the glories of passion . . . yes, but her kiss is cold."

"Mama!" Mrs. Danby exclaimed, appearing in the common room. She carried a tray upon which sat my tea, a cream jug and sugar tin, and a stack of shortbread biscuits on a plate, all clattering together as she rushed toward us.

The old woman shot her a glance, her eyes keen and clear of confusion. Mrs. Danby scowled back at her.

"Do not mind my mother," Mrs. Danby said. For the first time, her smile was strained. "I'm so sorry, dear, leaving you with her. I forget she's here. She's so quiet for the most part. I hope she did not say anything to upset you."

"No," I replied quickly. "She was merely musing. I trust my presence did not overset her."

Mrs. Danby humphed and poured my tea. "'Tis kindness itself, you are. You have your tea, then, missus. I'll have Janet—"

The outer door opened to reveal the outline of a cloaked man in the frame of the ancient, stooped portal. I felt a gust of chilled wind whip its way around the room, teasing the flames in the hearth into a spitting flare as the man stepped inside. He paused and clapped his gloved hands together smartly as if to brush off the cold. The door swung closed behind him and sealed us all together in the close warmth of the room.

Mrs. Danby's smile was radiant the moment she saw him. "Well, Lord Suddington, good eve to you. I feared you would not be in this evening." Her tone made her disappointment, should this have been the case, very clear.

The gentleman lifted a hand in recognition of the innkeeper's gracious reception. His steps were long, sure, bringing him out of shadow and close to a table just off to my left. "Good eve, Mrs. Danby." He smiled, his white teeth gleaming as he executed a shallow bow to his hostess. "I was caught up in a pleasant ride today, venturing all the way to Binsby Tarn. It set my schedule back."

His features and bearing were fitting for a Roman statue, with fair hair pulled away from his forehead to a knot at his nape. He was dressed elegantly in beautifully made clothes, a touch of intriguing whimsy in the small flower he wore pinned to his coat. In with him came an air of charged expectation, and of a shivering awareness, a shift in the way air flowed about the room. The fire dimmed, I thought, as if it were bowing in deference to his arrival.

Mrs. Danby's matronly smile blossomed into a blush. She giggled, a delighted sound coming from her ample bosom. "It is rabbit stew tonight. Sit and I'll have Janet bring you wine."

The man's gaze met mine for an instant. He was polite enough not to do more than smile ever so slightly, which was the proper thing to do. After all, we hadn't been introduced. To speak to me without the benefit of a formal presentation would be tantamount to treating me no better than a streetwalker.

His wine was brought by Mrs. Danby herself. She did not forget me, either, stopping to inquire whether I was enjoying my tea and informing me that my dinner would not be long in coming.

Other patrons began to arrive within a few moments. I observed them covertly, my gaze touching on faces and wondering about their simple lives. Smiles were in abundance as they caught my curiosity. Although we were strangers, there was a feeling of intimacy here, for we shared company in this den. I suppose that had something to do with Mrs. Danby's cheerful presence. She was very much in evidence, managing to be attentive to all, but chiefly dividing her time between Suddington and myself. He was clearly a favorite of hers, and I was a traveler to be made as comfortable as possible.

After some time I returned my attention to the old woman, who had fallen silent at Mrs. Danby's chiding and not spoken since. She was still in her chair by the great hearth, staring at nothing, sitting quietly but not, I noticed, completely motionless. She was shaking, despite the blankets tucked tightly about her.

Surely, that close to the fire, she would not be cold. Thinking she might be in distress, I stood and approached her. "May I help you?"

She did not respond to me. I saw then that she was weeping.

"Mrs. Danby!" I called, beginning to move away to fetch my hostess, but the old woman muttered something. I leaned in close, for she spoke barely above a whisper, as if she were imparting intelligence of the most dire nature. "They think she is love. You see, don't you, girl? You see . . . You must tell them."

"I am sorry," I told her urgently. "I do not understand." Half-turning, I prepared to call for Mrs. Danby again.

A claw emerged from under the blanket, fastening itself around my wrist. Her fingers were brittle, the skin like a mere film over vein and bone, but her grip was surprisingly strong.

"Let me go summon your daughter," I said with compassion, resisting the urge to pull away.

Her old face crumpled, and she openly wept. "She is a lie, the Cyprian Queen . . . She is not love, child. She is death."

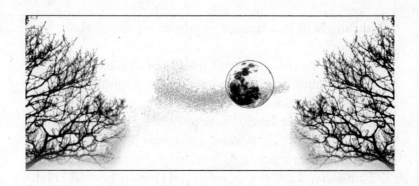

Chapter Three

My heart was beating wildly for some reason I could not specify. I was afraid of this woman. The desire to push her clutching hand away was overwhelming.

Mrs. Danby came into the dining room just then, a savory puff of steam trailing behind her like a friendly dragon. Her pleasant demeanor changed to crossness when she spied me with her mother and she rushed towards us. "Oh, Mrs. Andrews, please forgive me. Has she been troubling you?" She immediately asserted herself between me and the old woman, her back to me. "Come now, you are too tired to sit out," she told her mother. "Into your bed with you now." She glanced over her shoulder at me. "Do forgive her, Mrs. Andrews. She is very old."

"There is nothing to forgive," I assured her. Instinct told me

Mrs. Danby would not appreciate my offering to help, so I resumed my seat.

When I looked up, Lord Suddington was watching me. Upon the connection of our gazes, he rose. I was surprised at how flustered I became when I saw he was headed toward me.

"I am about to be abominably rude, for we have not been introduced." He executed a very low bow. "Allow me to remedy that. I have it from Mrs. Danby's address that you are Mrs. Andrews."

When I was a girl, my stepmother, Judith, had despaired of my manners, for I sometimes abandoned convention when I did not see the sense in it. That was what I did now. It was not done, a woman speaking to a strange man like this, but the truth was I wished to make his acquaintance and Mrs. Danby was busy with her mother and could not do the honors. "And from the same source, I can assume you are Lord Suddington?" I replied.

His smile widened. He was surprised; he'd expected to be rebuked. "Yes. Lord Robert Suddington, madam. Your servant." He clicked a smart bow and, upon straightening, his handsome face adopted a mischievous aspect. "I hope you are not disturbed by Old Madge, the poor creature."

"Not at all." I thought of the type of creatures who had "disturbed" me of late. An old woman was hardly threatening. And yet, she had given me some disquiet, and he saw this.

"May I press my fortune and beg a seat?" He indicated the chair on the other side of the table from mine. "You seem like you may have had a start from the old woman, and could use some company."

I thought about this for a moment, and could see no rational reason to refuse him. "As we are in a public place, I cannot see the harm."

He sat with the same flourish that embellished all his movements, like a dancer aware that his every movement is being scrutinized by a sharp-eyed audience. His eyes locked onto my face. I saw him touch the flower he wore on the lapel of his coat, an absent gesture as he settled into his seat. "I applaud you for your courage. That ancient creature rattles everyone." He laughed, a carefree sound that was very masculine, very sensual. "Even me."

But I thought of how he had remained in his seat. "You must be used to her. I take it you frequent the inn?"

"Yes. And I see her often. A rather strong drawback to the attractions available in this hall, and if not for Mrs. Danby's exceptional cooking, it would be enough to drive me away. It is nothing personal to the woman. I find age . . . well, it reeks of death."

I raised my eyebrows. "That is quite a statement."

He smiled. "Are you going to faint, Mrs. Andrews?"

I realized then he was flirting with me! "I do not believe I shall," I replied primly to cover my bemusement. I applied myself to my tea, which was stone-cold now. I gulped it anyway.

"That is good," Lord Suddington responded without a hint that he had taken note of my discomfiture. "I would not want you to miss Mrs. Danby's rabbit stew."

As if upon a cue, Janet appeared with a tray upon which rested two steaming bowls and two towel-wrapped bundles, which I judged, from the aroma emanating from them as she set them on the table, to be Mrs. Danby's famed bread. She appeared confused for a moment to find Lord Suddington and myself at the same table but recovered quickly, though I thought I saw something flashing and sharp in her eye, a curl upon her lip. Jealousy? I nearly laughed at my fancy—she was but a girl!

"Thank you, Janet," Suddington murmured. He never looked at her, but her gaze lingered on him, and I saw I had been right. There was a naked longing on her young face. She was sixteen—old enough to feel the effects of the man's attractiveness, though he was too far above her station to notice her.

We ate the excellent stew. Steam billowed from the bread as I ripped into the crust. Lord Suddington smiled when I smeared it liberally with freshly churned butter and bit into it, my eyelids drifting to half-mast.

"I do not know when I've enjoyed a meal more," I said as my bowl emptied.

He laced his fingers together in front of his chin. "I am pleased you enjoy the Rood and Cup. It is a good sign you will stay for a while."

I smiled back at him, feeling suddenly very fine. Being sated with good food and the recipient of a very charming man's attention had a heady effect. I was deplorably sensible as a rule, a dull balance to my sister Alyssa's dreamy nature. But I felt somewhat enchanted under the almost intoxicating regard of Lord Suddington.

He asked polite questions, and I replied in kind, our conversation taking on a comfortable rhythm that lulled me further into complacence. I began to notice how mobile and expressive his mouth was, how elegantly his long fingers moved with a restless energy.

We remained at our table as people began to bundle up against the weather and take their leave. I happened to notice a boy slip in, a youth who appeared to be perhaps seventeen years of age. He was handsome and seemed to know it, judging from the sly way his gaze swept the room. I took in the masculine prettiness of his face, the long silky lashes framing glittering blue eyes as brilliant as sapphires. I had little doubt the local maids would find him irresistible, for there was a palpable sexual pride that crackled around him like a compact storm.

Seeing me looking at him, he returned my regard with unapologetic smugness I found somehow insulting. I sensed Lord Suddington stiffen, and I feared for a moment he was going to rise and address himself to the lad.

"Out with you!" Mrs. Danby exclaimed, suddenly appearing, with a pitcher of ale for one of the other tables. "Get on, Colin O'Hara. I told you about using this door before."

"Danby said you wanted me to go up the school tomorrow," the youth said with the lilt of an Irishman.

"I'll speak to you in the yard. You are filthy. Get."

He rolled his eyes. To my utter dismay, Mrs. Danby did not lay her hand on that arrogant cheek. In fact, her tone gentled. "Now, get out of my dining room and come round to the kitchen. I've your supper."

The lad laughed. He exited back through the front door, though not before casting a look my way, his lingering smile full of confidence that I would share his amusement at his having bedeviled the older woman.

I thought of the Irish boy Miss Markam had mentioned in her journal. This must be him. I could see how the swaggering brat had upset her. He was clearly brash and disrespectful.

"Young people," Suddington murmured, eyeing the youth's retreat with malice, "should be taught better. Although the irony of my making such a statement does not escape me as I was unable to resist introducing myself to you against all dictates of propriety. I hope you are glad I did."

I was very glad to have met him, and to have spent the evening in his company. But I felt he was teasing me, leading me to agree with him, and it is just my nature to resist. "Certainly," I replied tightly.

"Your husband, may I be so bold to say, is a fortunate man. Will he be joining you here in Blackbriar?"

I smiled at his obvious ploy. "I am a widow," I told him.

He managed to appear sad and pleased at the same time. "My condolences. I was a cad to mention it. Forgive me."

"Do not regret it, Lord Suddington. You did not distress me."

"Ah." When he smiled, his blue eyes glittered like hypnotic jewels. "Mrs. Andrews, you are most generous."

Janet interrupted us just then and I was surprised to feel a sense of relief. I felt like I'd been allowed to come up for air. As Janet cleared away our dishes and placed a glass of wine before my companion, I noticed how closely she pressed to Suddington. It was a subtle thing, and perhaps unintended, but her breast brushed against his shoulder. He did not register the contact, but lifted his glass up to the light to admire the deep red of the claret before he drank, savoring the liquid like a connoisseur. "Ah. Excellent."

His eyes leveled on me, and I felt a charge leap across the table, as if something very hot and alive snaked between us two. I realized with some amazement I was in the powerful grip of womanly excitement, and I felt the heat of a blush creep up my neck to burn in my cheeks. I feared very much that Suddington sensed my state, for he had the look of a man who was used to having this effect on women, and enjoyed it.

I, I discovered with something of a start, was enjoying it as well.

I made an effort to pull myself together, and I am sure my manner grew cool. We continued to talk, and he took his leave close to ten o' the clock, extending his good wishes for my success tomorrow in procuring the teaching position and expressing his wish that we might see one another again soon.

As soon as he was gone, my fatigue returned and so I asked to be shown to my room. I was taken upstairs to find a very nicely appointed bedroom. The bed was already turned down and my mother's portmanteau lay open, unpacked enough for me to quickly access a light blue night rail and my hair brushes.

I had waited to finish reading the last entries of Victoria Markam's journal, wanting to be close to the origin of action when I came to the heart of what had driven her off. However, as I settled under the fluffy featherbed, my expectation that Miss Markam's account would build to a crescendo was sadly deflated. I plodded through repetitive writings. The mutinous attitudes of the girls grew, along with her despair. She was nearly obsessed with proving them guilty and vindicating herself.

The last entry was not dated, but it seemed to come a good deal of time after the others. The handwriting had deteriorated substantially. I could barely make out the wild scrawl.

> *They think I am mad, although they will not say it. Elizabeth watches me all the time. She hates me, for I have disgraced her. No one wants a raving sister to set the gossips' tongues wagging. London is so far away from the Penines, and still I do not feel safe. I close my eyes and see the bodies. No one believes me. God, I still see them. The small hand of the baby, lying limp with its fingers spread like a tiny star. The blood, brown and old and dried, like rusted necklaces. They'd been cast off like rubbish. The girls had to know they were there. Did they kill them? Is that what they were forever whispering about among themselves? Whispering, whispering. Dear saints, the sound of their hushed voices fills my ears even now. The boy knows. The Irish boy. Maybe he killed those people, and the girls are innocent. Does that mean one of the girls will be next? Who? Not Vanessa. Let it be Margaret. I must stop thinking of it. I cannot help them. I tried. No one listened. I had to flee. I would help them if I could, but they despise me, ridicule me. I tried and*

That was the end; there were no more pages. I felt let down as I folded the excerpts and tucked them in the nightstand drawer, then pinched out the candle. The particular mention of blood on the victim's necks was inarguably evidence of a vampire, but it was disappointing that there was no more firm proof than this. Still, the question remained, buzzing in my veins with a low hum of excited conjecture: Was this the same vampire that had touched the life of a young Laura Newly, my mother?

The following morning, I traveled into the fells forest to meet with Miss Sloane-Smith, the headmistress of the Black-briar School, armed with the falsified documents Sebastian had sent. These were necessary for the ruse I had in mind.

People, I have found, rarely surprise us. One would expect a woman who ran a prestigious school dedicated to the education of young girls from the Quality to have a certain air, a certain look. Miss Glorianna Sloane-Smith surpassed all of my ideas of what these should be.

She was a matron of perhaps two score and ten years, a tall, dignified personage with impressive posture and steel-gray hair pulled into a tight chignon. Small eyes darted sharply behind a pair of wire spectacles. I was sure those clever glances missed nothing. Her dress was high-necked, the penultimate of mod-esty and fashioned of good material and tailoring, plainly cut and in a color so drab it was only a step above mourning.

I suffered a surprising attack of nerves as I was shown into her study and seated on the other side of a monstrosity of a carved mahogany desk. I have never been a good liar and I was going to have to tell a lot of lies now.

With Sebastian's help, every bit of documentation I placed into her hands had been manufactured: references, past expe-rience, even my schooling had been enhanced. According to these papers, I was the epitome of what an instructor in such a well-known establishment should be.

Miss Sloane-Smith perused the forged documents from behind her desk, peering disapprovingly at them, then at me. Her hand lifted, smoothing her hair with the lightest of touches, as if this were meant to keep any errant hairs in place. It was unnecessary; I doubted a lock would dare venture from its bindings. I clasped my hands together on my lap and composed myself as best I could while she read my fabricated qualifications.

"How is it you were made aware of the position?" she inquired, not glancing up.

"My friend is an acquaintance of Miss Markam's sister. He told me of the situation and suggested I apply."

Miss Sloane-Smith pinned me with a discriminating glare. "Did he indeed? And what did he tell you of Miss Markam's sudden departure?"

"Troubles," I replied vaguely. "Although I heard in the village it was consumption. How sad."

I had the most absurd sensation that the headmistress saw right through me. Laying down my papers, Miss Sloane-Smith sat back in her chair. "Her illness was the main reason she was dismissed. However, prior to her collapse, she became distressed about certain things and worked herself into something of a state, which of course became of concern to the trustees of this school. As you can imagine, we take utmost care with our professional staff to maintain the high standards our families expect. Behavior such as Miss Markam's will not be tolerated. I trust there have been rumors, and you may have heard some of these. She was not always discreet, Miss Markam, and I would not like it if any gossip she spread had attracted curiosity-seekers."

"No, ma'am," I replied dutifully. And then, absolutely out

of the blue, I had the most ridiculous urge to laugh. It was not funny, not in the comic sense, but what could be more absurd? Miss Markam's wild claims were *exactly* why I was here.

Miss Sloane-Smith snapped the papers I'd provided and resumed reading them. "There is no place for flighty, imaginative women here. We have a solemn duty to see to the education of the daughters of the finest families of England, and to do this, one must be serious-minded and dedicated. I trust you are the practical sort, with a good head on your shoulders, and mindful of all the things young ladies need to be taught in order to take their places as dutiful wives."

My cheek twitched. "I assure you, Miss Sloane-Smith, I am exactly that." The lie was like cotton in my mouth. How she did not see through me, I could not imagine.

She nodded, frowning at the papers I'd provided her, but I knew I'd passed muster. It was not long before she sniffed and pronounced, "You will do," with an air of resignation.

"Thank you. I will give you my best on every level," I promised, quite sincerely.

She made a point to appear unimpressed. "You will begin at once. We have been without a literature instructor for some time, and require the post filled immediately. I will have Miss Easterly show you the school, where your rooms will be, and the classroom you will be using, all of that." Her critical eye took me in from head to toe. "I trust you have suitable attire. We like to maintain a serious atmosphere here at Blackbriar."

I assured her I did, although I had not given any thought to my wardrobe. My tastes did not run to the somber sort of dress she was wearing, which must be what she had in mind for me. However, I did have a few items. A royal-blue skirt I wore with a white lace shirtwaist was quite plain. Also, my forest-green day dress would do for my new role, and perhaps the lavender muslin, which was made with a high neck and long sleeves.

The rest of my wardrobe would prove too fashionable. I could rework a few dresses, if I had to, to make them functional.

Miss Sloane-Smith rang a bell. "Good day to you, Mrs. Andrews. Ann Easterly will show you about. You may wait for her in the hall. I shall expect you to arrive with your belongings no later than Thursday so that you might acclimate. You are familiar with Dante? Good. You will be teaching *The Inferno*. I suggest you reacquaint yourself with it in the meantime and be prepared to discuss it with the students."

"I will be ready." I rose, adopting a mien of subservience I had often used when my stepmother was alive. I had learned many tricks to appease Judith's need to dominate me. "I feel I must ask, headmistress, although I assure you I am not doing so from salacious motivations. Were the girls much affected by the murders?"

"Murders? I am not aware of any murders."

Deep in the pit of my stomach, a hot coal burned, and I sensed my mistake before my brain comprehended it. "The bodies, madam. The ones in the woods."

"As I've told you, Miss Markam was a troubled woman," Miss Sloane-Smith said comfortably, all but laughing at me. "She imagined some dreadful things before her illness became apparent. One can only assume it was the result of some sort of fever associated with her consumptive disease."

I faltered, made uncertain by her lack of concern. "Then . . . there were no bodies found in the woods?"

The headmistress narrowed her eyes and for a moment her placid face appeared quite cunning. "This is exactly the rumors, the gossip I mentioned a moment ago. Allow me to be quite clear, Mrs. Andrews—definitively *no*, there were never any bodies found."

"But I . . ." I trailed off, the words withered by the realization that I must sound a dupe. Worse, a fool who thrived on such lurid stories.

And now the older woman, with an air of superiority that made that coal of humiliation blossom like a conflagration to flush my entire body with discomfort, confirmed my worst suspicion. "Miss Markam was mistaken. She had a frightening experience out in the woods, where she had wandered due to her illness. Her delirium made her imagine things that were not there." She shifted her weight from one foot to the other, somehow making the slight movement menacing. "The authorities were taken to the spot where she had had her apparition, and found not a trace of anything untoward in the woods. And that is the end of it. Now, I hope you will never speak of this again."

"I see. My apologies, Miss Sloane-Smith. I should not have listened to such a fantastic tale."

She was not appeased by my contrition. In fact, by the way she peered angrily at me, I feared I might be sacked before I began. I'd made a terrible error in pressing the matter so soon, and with the wrong person. As I sat outside her office awaiting Miss Easterly to give me a tour of the school, I wondered how badly I had damaged my position.

But then I realized something. I had almost missed it, what with Miss Sloane-Smith's stern dressing down and the officious, stifling manner in which she had delivered my rebuke. Now that I reflected, however, I thought I'd seen a momentary flash of something cunning in her eyes when she'd slapped down my questions about the bodies, and I knew she was hiding something.

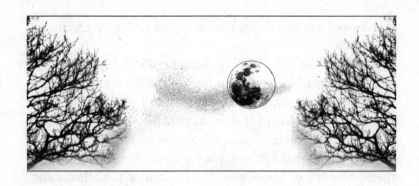

Chapter Four

I waited in the dark hallway, the deep walnut wainscoting surrounding me like a drab monk's cell. Obviously, the place
had once been richly appointed, but the old house had lost its
glory long ago. It was clean, but not charming. The wood was
scored and dull with age. The scuff of girls' shoes showed on
the floors. The place was a demoralized testimony to the violence of impetuous youth rushing here and there within these
walls. I was wildly curious to see the students Victoria Markam
had written of in her diary. Vanessa, Margaret, and what were
the other girls' names?

A woman rushed toward me with an ingratiating smile and
a ready apology for keeping me waiting, which she had not
done at all. She held out a hand. "I am Ann Easterly." Perhaps
a score of years older than myself, she possessed the kind of

unfortunate figure that widens drastically as one's gaze lowers. In her green dress, she gave the impression of an emerald pyramid.

I took her hand. It was frail and cold. "Thank you for taking the time to show me the school."

"It is a wonderful establishment," she said, turning efficiently on a heel and sweeping toward a doorway off the dingy main hall. We entered what I deduced was the dining hall. A faded Renaissance-style mural was the only decoration, its figures looming like ghosts above the long sideboard on the near wall.

Ann Easterly gave me only enough time to peek inside before taking me back out again. "It is quite a modern idea of girls' education," she told me as she marched me down a white-washed hallway leading off to the east wing, "and not without some controversy. We do have the extra subjects here, not just the elementary ones. I teach geography and history."

"Why controversy?" I asked, intrigued.

She made a face. "You know quite well there are those who are against the formation of the female intellect."

"It does make for inconveniences, such as opinions and the like," I said dryly.

Miss Easterly did not laugh. "Our goal," she said, "is to prepare the girls for marriage and the demands of the sophisticated society in which they are expected to travel. The art of intelligent conversation is the aim, conversation others should find amusing but not offensive."

Judith would have loved that sentiment. And although I secretly balked, I knew most people of society agreed with it.

We peeked into the formal parlor where the girls received family on the rare occasion of visits. As we moved on to the cozy, almost masculine library, I became aware that we had a companion shadowing us. After three or so turns through the serpentine halls, I turned to face the spy. "Hello," I said pleasantly.

The girl should have been taken aback, and rightfully embarrassed at being so handily caught up. Instead, she merely stared quite boldly back at me without speaking. It was extraordinarily rude.

"Margaret!" The word burst out of Ann Easterly as if she'd had a fright.

Ah. This was the tormenting, unlikable Margaret. I studied her closely, taking in the long dark hair coiled in fat sausage spirals that reminded me of the perfect coif of a shiny new china doll. I judged her age to be thirteen or fourteen years, just over the cusp of adolescence. Her eyes were deep brown, unnaturally large and fitted with lashes so thick it appeared as if a small tiny moth perched on the end of each eyelid. Her nose was a tiny button, pushed up too much. Under this an exaggerated bow of her upper lip turned the corners of her thin lips down in a look of unhappiness or displeasure. She was almost beautiful—and the resentment that stared out at the world from her lush, glorious eyes gave away all; she knew her features had conspired too hard, missing their mark. And it infuriated her.

"Margaret is one of our brightest students," Miss Easterly said. "I am certain you will enjoy her insights and challenging questions, Mrs. Andrews."

Margaret did not reply. Those large, sullen eyes took my measure. I felt myself respond with something stronger than mere dislike. I mentally recoiled against her, as one would curl the tongue against the hint of sourness in milk just barely turned, that metallic tingle, the unrealized reflex to a foul taste.

"What is this?" a new voice cut in. I saw a reedy woman sweep into the hallway, her pinched, intelligent face frowning fiercely. "Margaret Elizabeth Kingston, where are you supposed to be at this hour?"

"I had to use the necessary," the girl murmured.

"Get along, now, then. You will see the new teacher in class. Go on, and do not pull a face at me, Miss Kingston, or I will see you in detention."

Margaret's mien of rebellion dropped away and she turned, disappearing in a flash. She might hold Miss Easterly in contempt, but she feared this new arrival.

"Thank you Miss Thompson," Ann Easterly said tightly, not meeting her colleague's gaze. "I was just showing Mrs. Andrews the school."

Miss Thompson addressed herself to me. "You are taking Markam's place?"

I inclined my head. "I am to start the end of this week, I believe."

She gave a sharp nod of her head. "Agatha Thompson. Mathematics." She looked me over with approval. I felt at once the force of her personality, the kind of strong-willed, no-nonsense sort Miss Sloane-Smith had described as the ideal for Blackbriar instructors. "Welcome, then. And do not let the girls intimidate you. They are good girls from excellent families, but of course they are spirited, coming from impressive pedigrees as they do. That is a fine thing in its place, but we must have order here at Blackbriar. I find a firm hand best." Her look to Miss Easterly was almost chiding.

"Indeed," Miss Easterly said with an injured air. "If you will excuse us, we must continue our tour."

We were about to leave when Miss Thompson surprised me by suddenly grabbing my hand. I started, and when I looked at her face, I saw something hidden in the plain, sturdy features, something I did not quite fathom.

"Have a care in the school, Mrs. Andrews," she said. "This house is old, and we are isolated up here on the Fell. Be sure never to go out of doors at night."

"Certainly, I shall not," I assured her. "Why would I do such a thing?"

"No reason," she said, but I thought of Miss Markam. Was that her meaning?

After a beat of awkward silence, Miss Thompson added, "There are wolves hereabouts." She abruptly dropped my hand and took her leave.

"Let me show you the music room," Miss Easterly announced. I was then taken next to the conservatory (ever since the Great Exhibition, all ladies of quality were expected to know their flowers) and then the informal parlor, which was used daily and contained neat rows of embroidery baskets bristling with colorful thread and handkerchiefs proudly sporting carefully stitched monograms.

Mrs. Eloise Boniface, the dance instructor, met us in the hall and introduced herself. She was surprisingly old and plump and was dressed severely in widow's weeds, but her smile was warm and welcoming.

"Mrs. Boniface has been here the longest of us all, even longer than Miss Sloane-Smith," Miss Easterly said.

The dance teacher bobbed her head proudly. "That is true. Nearly thirty years. Dear me, it always surprises me."

I immediately wondered if she'd known my mother. I wanted to pull her aside that moment and ask her, but Ann Easterly led me away, this time at last to the classroom in which I was to teach.

I was happy to find it brightly lit by large windows with eastern exposure. It contained a desk and chair for me and long tables with chairs for the girls. Along the wall, bookshelves teemed with novels and collections of sermons, poetry—Spenser and Tennyson, Milton, a volume of Keats—and a good many of Shakespeare's plays, which was surprisingly modern, I thought.

"I would love to teach this," I said, grasping a copy of *The Merchant of Venice*. "I adore Portia's speech on the quality of mercy. Do you know it?"

"Unfortunately, no," Miss Easterly said. "But Miss Sloane-Smith chooses the assignments. You must speak with her."

I caught myself up. I was not here to share the passion of good literature. But I had been a lonely, isolated girl and books my only friends. And I had loved the fiery, rebellious Portia—she whose life had been trapped so singly by her father's death wish. I had believed I, too, was blocked from finding happiness by thoughtless adults who did not understand me. I always loved how it was she—a woman—who finds the wisdom to save her beloved Bassanio from having to deliver a pound of flesh to Shylock. How clever she had been to determine that the moneylender could indeed collect his debt if he could do so without extracting a drop of blood.

Shakespeare understood the profound metaphysical value of blood, its precious worth, its sacred embodiment of life. The remembrance of that sobered me. My heart squeezed lightly and I carefully put the book back in its place.

Noises from the hallway alerted me that the class period must have ended, and indeed I saw several students crowding at the doorway to peek in at me. Word had apparently traveled swiftly that the new teacher was in her classroom.

"I see I am going to be the object of some curiosity," I observed to Miss Easterly calmly.

She whipped her head about, a startled bird, then nodded, smiling nervously at the girls. "Oh." With an effort, she did a poor imitation of Miss Thompson's severe tone. "Vanessa Braithwait and Marion Tilman, get on with you." She waved a shooing hand at them. "You girls should be in the conservatory with Miss Brown."

The girl with the pre-Raphaelite curls spilling down her

back, a face like a Madonna, and the long, lithe body of a prima ballerina had to be Vanessa Braithwait. She stood poised like a painter's model, her features composed in soft lines as she gave me a shy smile.

"Yes, ma'am," replied the plump, plain-faced girl with stringy brown hair, who stood beside her. She did not seem petulant as Margaret had, but neither did she seem in any hurry to obey Miss Easterly. No one did, it appeared.

The girls left in their own good time. I stared after them, Vanessa's height and swanlike neck making her head visible above the throng in the hall. My breath caught as I noticed the thing trailing after her.

A few other girls darted to the doorway to take a peek at me but I kept my eyes on Vanessa. My heart stopped for a second or two. The sound of Ann Easterly's voice, straining to bear some authority as she sent the new wave of students away, faded as a pricking sensation that had no physical cause rode lightly along my skin, and my gut twisted.

I had seen this before. I can describe it only as something oily and foul, the stain of evil, no more than a smudge of darkness in the air. It was the mark of the vampire that only I, as Dhampir, could see, and it curled like a finger around the graceful curve of Vanessa's neck. I knew without a doubt she was in terrible danger.

Dinner at the Rood and Cup that evening was quail, baked with a crisp skin, the succulent flesh underneath running with savory juices. Mrs. Danby served it with baby carrots sweetened in brown sugar and red-skin potatoes as soft on the inside as custard.

Lord Suddington, dressed in a formal waistcoat and again sporting the elegant touch of a flower pinned to his breast, begged to join me. We chatted amiably while we dined, and he showed himself knowledgeable on topics ranging from horticulture to the theater. He had traveled to the United States, he told me, referring to the young country by the gentrified term of "the colonies" and laughing at himself when I caught him at it.

I relaxed with him, and pleasant lull of his male attention wove a spell around me. I'd never been a woman to whom men paid much notice, perhaps because in my younger days I was usually paired with the irresistible confection that was my younger sibling, Alyssa. But then Simon, my late husband, noticed me, and I found that I was not unattractive, nor unwanted. Then there was Valerian.

I started somewhat at the topic I had been so determined not to reflect upon. I realized I had not been entirely successful. While Valerian was not always in my conscious thoughts, he had not gone far, only to the back of my mind. There the memory of him was ever present, along with the dull sadness at all that separated him from me.

The dining room was busier tonight, and my dinner companion never failed to introduce me to the locals who came by to say hello to him. One young couple, a man of my age with a frothy young wife on his arm, paused to converse. I was amused by their reverent obsequiousness to Lord Suddington. Me, they ignored, until Suddington mentioned my appointment to Blackbriar's teaching staff.

The wife regarded me with an arrogant sort of pity that made my blood boil. "Oh, dear. You are to be congratulated, I suppose, although it must be a dreadful thing, having to earn one's living."

Before I could defend myself, Suddington's eyebrows forked dangerously. "Miss Sloane-Smith runs an excellent school. Its reputation is known down into Kent and all the way up into

Scotland. As I am on the board, I am intimately aware of the great service she provides for the children of the best families from all over England."

"Some think her too exacting," the wife countered. I saw she was looking for entertainment, the way some nasty children pull the legs off an insect and watch its mortal struggle. "I heard she is a taskmaster indeed."

"Well," I said in a blithe tone, with an eye on Suddington's growing ire, "one must have discipline."

Suddington shifted his gaze to me, somewhat surprised. I remained sanguine. After all, I was quite used to dealing with her sort of woman.

My serenity drove the couple off, the wife in something of a huff. "Heavens, what a witch," Suddington muttered, his eyes following her retreat. And then his mouth moved, and I believe he whispered something. I did not hear it, but I would wager it was not pleasant. That he would take umbrage on my behalf raised a giddy swell of pleasure inside my breast that was girlish and quite unlike me.

"Come, we must not allow such a spiteful creature to ruin our dinner," I said. "She is hardly worth our notice." I indicated the long stone wall and the widemouthed hearth. "I have been meaning to ask you all evening if you know where Mrs. Danby's mother is tonight? She is conspicuously absent from her chair. Is she well?"

"Lord save us," Suddington grumbled. "If only we should find such good fortune as to find Old Madge barred from the room. Her mind is uncertain and she can go off on some, well, rather disturbing rants. But what a kind sort you are to care about her." He punctuated this remark with a regard of such warm appreciation that I felt myself blush. It was getting to be a common occurrence when I was with him—me blushing; me who never did such coquettish things.

"You do surprise me," he said, his voice lowering. "A person of your intelligence paired with compassion such as you possess is a rare thing."

I lifted my chin and raised my eyebrows, the picture—I hoped—of skepticism. "You are being quite flattering tonight, and I think it is a game with you."

He smiled thoughtfully. His tongue ran slowly across his upper lip in a journey I found fascinating. "Game? Mrs. Andrews, I assure you that while I adore gaming, I am sincere with you."

Janet appeared with our dessert, a cobbler for me and the single glass of claret for Suddington. We enjoyed our indulgence in companionable silence. I was filled with a contentment I knew I would not have again for a while. Meals at Blackbriar would no doubt be less fine, both from a culinary and a social standpoint.

Suddington seemed to be thinking the same. "I must not be deprived for long of our delightful dinners. Promise you will dine with me here at the inn again soon. Do not allow that wretched Sloane-Smith to bully you into giving all your time to the school. You must have your freedoms. And if she should prove disagreeable, you will let me know. My family is old here and I am not without influence."

"Miss Sloane-Smith is stern, it is true, but she is nothing as terrible as she is made out to be."

His smile slid wider, sultry and mesmerizing. "How charming you are, always so positive and hopeful. It is inspiring, such an attitude. But I do not wish you to be naïve." He leaned forward, and I felt a wave of lightheadedness come over me. I noticed the male scent coming off him, reaching out like a delicate finger to stroke my sense of smell. It made me shiver with pleasure. "There is cruelty up on the fells, make no mistake. And so have a care, Mrs. Andrews. I would not like it if anything happened to you. I am already anticipating our next encounter."

I smiled at the compliment, but it was a shaky smile. Was he warning me? I could not fathom his meaning, or if perhaps this was simply another way of flirting with me. If so, it was decidedly strange, and I did not see what sort of danger he was cautioning me against.

After he'd taken his leave, I was about to climb the stairs to my chamber—my last night at the inn, as I would be moving on to the staff quarters at the school in the morning—when my gaze espied the hearth blanket used yesterday evening by Mrs. Danby's mother, lying in a heap on the floor next to her empty chair. I took a moment to go and fold it neatly.

As I placed it carefully on the seat, my eye caught something irregular in the wall. The mortared stones were all of a size, more or less, except one to the right of the hearth opening. That particular stone was elongated, about as high as my ankle to my hip, and about as wide as my arm was long. It was flatter, its surface unnaturally smooth.

It nearly looked—and I was sure my imagination was running to the macabre these days—to be the exact size and shape of a gravestone, except the arched end was at the bottom and the straight end was at the top. Peering closer, I saw that there was something written on it.

I crouched so that I could study the runnels cut into the stone. I made out an N, an I, then something I could not read, then an inverted D. On the other side, a strangely wrought M and another I. I peered closer, puzzled, for the letters made no sense. Then, in a flash of insight, I realized the stone was upside down. The M was a W and the word, or name, rather, was *Winifred*.

"Are you needing anything before you retire, Mrs. Andrews?" Mrs. Danby said, coming up behind me.

I whirled, a bit startled. "Nothing, thank you. That was a lovely meal, Mrs. Danby. Is your mother well?"

"Oh, she is in a state. I am so sorry about last night. I kept her to her bed today."

I wanted to ask more, but could not find a way to do so without seeming to pry. Mrs. Danby was clearly embarrassed.

"I shall retire now. I am almost sad to leave tomorrow, although I am very excited to begin my new position," I said. "I have enjoyed your excellent cooking and felt quite at home here."

Mrs. Danby beamed. "Oh, my dear, I am so glad. We will miss you, but goodness, you aren't going far. Now, go on and get a good night's rest. I've turned down your bed. Oh, and I've had Janet repack your trunk. I told her to leave out the things you'll need tonight and in the morning, so you're all set."

"Thank you so much," I said. I had the urge to embrace her, but I refrained. It was a silly impulse; I was always touched when someone fussed over me. It always felt as if I could never get enough of it, having had so little of it in my life.

I went upstairs and found that Janet had done an excellent job tidying my trunk. I decided I would close it up now and leave the few belongings left over to be packed in a separate valise. I was buckling the straps to the compartments when I noticed a tear in the leather straps that bound the edge of the interior wood frame. I silently cursed. No doubt the handiwork of Mr. Danby's rough handling. That disagreeable old goat must have dropped it right on the corner, which I could see had been patched before.

I told myself not to worry over it; the tear could be repaired again. But this was my mother's portmanteau. My father had given it to her for their wedding trip to France. Her name was written in gold letters on the front, worn away now but with the impressions of the embossing still evident. I liked how large it was, how it opened like a double-hung wardrobe on two sets of hinges to best display all that was packed inside, how I could cram quite an astounding amount in it. The leather was cracked, the brass hinges green with age, but it was infinitely precious to me.

My fingers smoothed the tear, as if rubbing would mend it, and I noticed something written on the underside of the hide covering. Prying it up, I found words printed in faded India ink, written in a jagged, spidery scrawl.

Darkling I listen: And for many a time I have been half in love with easeful Death.

My heart did a queer flip and bump. My mother's hand? I did not know, for I had never seen anything written by her, not even her name on the inside cover of a book. But it had to be hers. My hand shook. It was as if she had reached across time, across space, to speak to me. I struggled for a moment against a surge of emotion, sadness warring with the thrill of hearing something from the woman I had longed to know all of my life.

But, oh God, what words these were. *Half in love with easeful Death . . .* I recognized the line. It was from Keats. His *Ode to a Nightingale* was one of his best-known works, a moody treatise to the night bird, a harbinger of death. He had written it while mortally stricken with tuberculosis. In a grim period in my early adolescence, I had reveled in the lines, finding a match for my pubescent suffering and my unfortunate preoccupation with death. Those had been the hardest years, with Judith at her most domineering. I had found kinship with the suffering poet, who longed for the release of eternal sleep.

I closed my eyes tight against my raging emotions. Laura, my mother, could not die, though she, too, longed for death—real death, that is. Deliverance from the fate which I only recently learned had been her misfortune to bear. I vowed again—this must have been the hundredth, perhaps thousandth time—to find her, release her, do what I was born to do. To kill her. No. I mustn't think of it that way. To bring her the gift of death.

Of easeful death.

The hour was late. I tucked the flap of hide back into place. Dashing the wetness from my eyes, I undressed and climbed into bed.

With her so much on my mind, I expected to dream of my mother. I was wrong.

My sleep was ravaged by something else, something unexpected and raw, even wicked. It reared into my dreams, dreams that whipped through my mind like a tempest. Erotic charges, like a heat storm playing over my flesh, darted and flashed through my nerve endings. Images of lust were cast in my mind in shades of gold and shadow, sequenced with shocking clarity: of me making love with a man.

I saw myself upon a bed with silken sheets and gauzy bed curtains tangling around me, their movements as sinewy and sensual as my own, touching my naked skin like a caress. Hands—a man's hands—touched me, trailing in the wake of the silk. I reached for him, my unseen lover, my limbs languid and heavy with desire. His naked torso emerged from the undulating fabric, gleaming in light cast from an unseen fire, and masculine arms reached for me, locked me in an embrace, and held me against warm flesh as hard as Italian marble. Living flame behind alabaster, bringing me both pain and pleasure.

I tossed restlessly, trying to fend off these images, these feelings. My vision leaned in, pressing heavily down upon me. I saw him more clearly, his dusky skin, smooth, hairless, molded by the muscle and sinew that lay underneath. I lifted my mouth for a kiss and in my dream, my eyes slitted open to see the fair head that bent to me, seducing my mouth with lips red and lush and dark eyes as soft as lakes of mist.

With a muffled cry, I ripped myself from his arms and came

awake. A thin sheen of perspiration dampened my night rail. For a moment, I thought someone had really been in bed with me. I crawled out of the bed like one heaving herself out of a sucking tide. The wooden floor was cold, my toes curling in protest, but the slight shock helped awaken me.

I held my arms tightly clasped about my chest. My head ached brutally and a burning lump lodged so tightly in my throat I could not swallow.

The man in my dream had been Suddington. This confused me, even sickened me a little, for I felt disgusted with myself. Was I so fickle that I had already forgotten the feelings Valerian Fox had evoked only months earlier? I had thought I loved him, even told myself I understood why he had abandoned me.

While I did not love Lord Suddington, I realized his effect on me was heady and exciting. I did not want his laughter nor his strength, did not want to know the depths of thought and feeling that hid deep in his heart. These were things I had once yearned for from Mr. Fox. But with Suddington, my attraction was physical. With a shock—for I had never before been subject to such carnal yearnings—I realized that I had a very disturbing desire for him to touch me.

I wanted, I admitted to myself, for my dream to come true.

Chapter Five

I arrived at the Blackbriar School for Young Ladies the following morning in time for breakfast. The meal proved informal, as the girls came and went from the dining room, which this morning was flooded with a moody purple light. There would be rain later; it was good I had set out as early as I had.

My belongings were being taken to the modest rooms I was to use, and though I was not hungry—Mrs. Danby having risen early to serve me a hearty breakfast of deviled kidneys, bacon, and eggs before I left the inn—I took a seat at the table by the corner with several members of the staff. I recognized the dance instructor, who beamed a welcoming smile as I headed her way.

"Are you not eating?" Mrs. Boniface asked as I sat next to

her. "You must try the shaved potatoes. They are excellent this morning. Very crisp." She speared one and placed it in her mouth, savoring it. Her round face beamed.

She was once again dressed in black. It somehow suited her, made her dignified, not somber. I saw she had once been quite fetching in her youth, and her face still wore the kind of prettiness that remained pink and fresh as she aged. "Did you meet the sketching teacher, Miss Grisholm?" she inquired as she ate more of the potatoes. She turned to the woman on her left. "Trudy, this is Emma Andrews, who is to teach literature."

The other teacher sniffed and twisted her mouth in a smile that did not reach her lips. "You mean try. Victoria had the worst time of it. These girls are ignorant."

"Oh, I do not know about that. The third-form girls are coming along beautifully with the Viennese waltz."

The deflection was agile, and made without so much as a blink from Mrs. Boniface. I had a sense it was a longtime habit of hers to contend with the sour-faced Trudy. The other woman sitting at the table with us was shy, nodding and smiling sweetly when Mrs. Boniface introduced her as Susannah Graves, the first and second form grammar instructor.

We were joined by Miss Thompson, who I saw at once was much changed from yesterday. Then, she had made the presentation of a most robust woman. Today, she seemed pale, tired, and subdued.

Mrs. Boniface must have agreed with my assessment. "What is wrong with you, Agatha?" she asked. "Did you not sleep well again?"

Miss Thompson frowned but did not reply. The uncomfortable moment was skillfully avoided by Mrs. Boniface, who turned to engage me in conversation. She insisted I address her as Eloise. "Mrs. Boniface makes me feel ancient! Really, Emma, we are to be friends."

"Thank you, Eloise." I paused, both getting used to the more casual form of address and wondering if it were too soon to ask her about what had been much on my mind since meeting her yesterday. Her friendliness emboldened me. "When you mentioned how long you have been teaching here at Blackbriar, I wondered if it were possible you remembered my mother. She attended the school . . . oh, twenty-five years ago or perhaps a little more; I do not know exactly. Her name was Laura Newly."

Hearing it put out there, I realized how thin the possibility existed that Eloise would remember one student over a span of so much time. I felt immediately sheepish, a condition not aided by the scathingly incredulous stare I received from Trudy Grisholm.

Bless Eloise Boniface, for after a moment's ponder she exclaimed, "Why I do remember her! Yes. Laura Newly. She was a lovely girl. I'd only been teaching a few years and she was one of those you tended to notice. Pretty enough, but very quiet. Nice girl, I recall. I also remember I had thought she'd be an excellent dancer because she had the figure to be light on her feet. But . . . oh, dear, she had no grace whatsoever."

I did not know firsthand if my mother was clumsy, but as I had no gift for gliding across a parquet floor in a ball gown, I assumed it was true. I was amazed Eloise would recollect such a thing, or anything at all about a single student from the past. "I am embarrassed to have asked you. It seems so absurd to expect you to remember her, and yet you do."

"Well, not much, I am afraid. I do seem to think she was more a poet than one who liked soirees and such. As I said, she had no gift for dance." Eloise nodded as she frowned in thought. "A dreamer. She had a book with her at all times. Perhaps that is why she did not take to dancing, it meant she had to put down her Tennyson, or Spenser, or some other poet. And always writing in her books. Yes, now I recall. Writing,

writing, always. But for all of her flighty ways, she was a good girl, bright and pleasant, as far as I can recall."

I breathed in slowly, deeply, filling myself with this rare connection. My father's best friend, Peter Ivanescu, whom I had known all my life as Uncle Peter, had given me the basics in understanding, at least from his vantage point, what had happened to Laura. Other than furtive whispers about her descent into "madness" I had managed to overhear from the house staff as I was growing up, I had no knowledge of my mother.

A dreamer. A writer, and always reading poetry—like me. This small tidbit from Eloise Boniface was a jewel, and I hugged it close.

"Thank you," I said. Trudy made a sound, a kind of a snort, but I did not so much as glance in her direction.

Eloise patted my hand, and her eyes crinkled warmly. But then her expression changed suddenly. A small furrow appeared between her eyebrows. I felt more than saw Agatha Thompson stiffen beside me, and I turned to find Margaret and Vanessa entering the dining room.

Eloise recovered first and picked up her fork. "Agatha? Your eggs are growing cold."

"I am afraid I have no appetite this morning," the other woman replied. Her voice was strained, and I saw her complexion had taken an ashen tone.

Trudy and Susannah had their backs to the door and seemed oblivious to the subtle tension that rippled around the table. Although Eloise and Agatha were clearly unsettled, I knew I was the only one who saw the oily darkness trailing in the girls' wake.

What was happening to these girls? Back in Avebury, Henrietta had been enthralled by a master vampire, a creature capable of a type of awful mesmerism. But she had demonstrated fear and secrecy. I myself had sampled the touch of that same master vampire; the infusion of an alien mind inside my own was as repulsive as live insects burrowing under the flesh. These girls looked pleased, even smug. They seemed to suffer not at all from their strange anointing. Nor did they appear to be suffering at all from the "wasting disease" a victim of a vampire displayed upon being bled. No, their only oddity was their cohesiveness as a group, their exclusivity, which Victoria Markam had noted.

Looking back to Agatha Thompson, I caught her staring at the girls. Could she see it, too—that oily smudge in the air? Or did she, like Miss Markam, mistrust the students' cliquish-ness? I was sure that she knew something.

She rose suddenly, sucking in a great gulp of air that conveyed a certain determination. "Excuse me, please."

Mrs. Boniface swung back toward her, away from the girls. "But you haven't eaten. Really, Agatha—"

But Miss Thompson had gone, moving swiftly across the room. Eloise Boniface sighed and addressed herself to her breakfast, but with noticeably less enthusiasm. To my right, the first fat raindrops pelted the window, sounding like an insistent finger tapping on the glass as if a ghoul were begging entrance.

Vanessa and Margaret brought the shadow with them to my class, as did two others, whose names I later learned were Lilliana Milford and Therese Beckwith. I felt as if a tiny storm had invaded the classroom, and the once-bright space seemed smoke-filled and gloomy.

I had given no thought to how I would begin my day. This was stupid. I had been caught up in dreams of Suddington, selfishly mulling about the latest revelations of my mother, and fretting over vampires, and, in doing so, I had completely forgotten that I had a class to teach.

I stood before them, having lined their desks in front of the windows in one long row, with them seated side by side. I belatedly realized this was a mistake, for it made me feel as if I were facing a panel of Inquisition judges.

"Dante," I said with a ringing air of authority I hoped would impress, "was inspired by love."

Their heads came up; nothing interested girls of fifteen or sixteen years of age more than talk of love. "He felt so strongly that it was the most important thing in the universe," I told them, heartily glad that my voice was not wavering although I had clasped my hands behind my back so no one would see them shaking, "that he wrote the poem—this entire epic masterpiece—on the balance of his belief in the healing power of love. Do any of you know the name of the object of Dante's love?"

No one replied. Then a girl who looked a bit younger than the rest tentatively raised her hand, braving the scowls from the others.

"Your name?" I asked.

"Eustacia Murray, ma'am," she replied politely. "Her name was Beatrice."

Margaret gave the girl a snide glance. Vanessa, wearing a stiff mien that was ill-seeming on her graceful form, pressed her lips together, and their friends exchanged glances. I knew at once what was afoot. The game was to freeze me out today, and Eustacia had broken ranks. Bless her.

I began to pace. The faces of the other seven or so students in the classroom were wary. They were not with the little coven, but they would wait and see who would prevail before choosing a side.

"Correct," I said. "She died when both she and the author were still young, and Dante never recovered from his grief. In *The Inferno*, he tells the story of himself as he descends into hell with his guide, the poet Virgil, who was sent to him through

Beatrice's intervention with God. So great was her love for him that she was able to persuade the Lord to grant him this extraordinary experience to save him from the despair and despondency he was feeling. Here—"

I unlocked my hands and picked up my copy of the poem, grateful that my shaking fingers were steady. "'Midway upon the journey of our life,'" I read, "'I found myself in a dark wilderness, for I had wandered from the straight and true.'"

I began to pace up and down in front of the long table. "So, then," I paused, picking out one of the girls not in Vanessa's group. "Is it possible to be saved by love?"

The girl went crimson, her eyes wide with panic. I sighed, smiling to let her know I forgave her for her silence, and moved on.

"If Beatrice loved Dante," I said, facing down the wary faces of my students, determined not to give up, "why did she want Virgil to show him the various levels of hell?"

I got no response. I had to be patient, I knew. The girls were still assessing me, and none, save Eustacia, seemed inclined to participate. Flipping the pages of my copy of *The Inferno*, I led with a different question. "Can anyone tell me what is written over the gates of Hell?"

Margaret surprised me, raising her hand but not waiting for me to call upon her before she spoke. "'Abandon hope all who enter here.'"

It was a small thing, but I corrected her. "Not exactly. 'Abandon every hope, ye who enter here' are the exact words in the final line. But what does the inscription say in its entirety?"

Another girl's hand went up, a pert little blonde named Sarah, who read with shy excitement: "'I am the way into the city of woe—'"

"The part about its creator," I urged her.

She paused, found the spot, and continued. "'Divine omnipotence created, the highest wisdom, and the . . .'" She looked up. "'. . . The primal love,'" she finished.

"Yes. Think of it. Hell was created from God's love," I explained.

Eustacia was clearly thunderstruck, her eyes as round as saucers, her mouth making a little O of surprise. "But I don't understand."

"If you look at the line above, Dante explains that hell is the place where the Lord delivers justice. Can you find that line?"

Eustacia did so quickly. "'Justice inspired my creator.'"

Margaret was becoming agitated, I noticed, but I ignored her as I forged ahead with the discussion. "He is saying that hell is part of God's love. After all, it is not very loving for the Holy Father to allow evil to go unpunished. A rather moral view, to be sure, but this was written at a time when the Catholic Church wielded much influence. Dante was a devout man, and as such—"

"This is outrageous!" Margaret exclaimed.

I blinked, probably too innocently to fool her, and said, "Did you have another opinion, Margaret?"

"No one believes in hell anymore. That was merely the way the Old Church controlled us, threatening us with damnation if we broke their rules. They wanted obedience so they could have power over the masses."

I was taken aback, both by this line of reasoning, which was quite sophisticated, and her vehemence. "That is a very modern view, Margaret."

Her eyes narrowed at me. "Sin is always in the world, it is normal. It is not evil. I do not even believe evil exists." She glanced at her friends, who watched her with rapt attention. "All sinning is, is not following the Church's rules. Dante uses pretty language, but he is a child reciting a child's catechism."

I might not have liked Margaret, but the intellectual in me recognized an equal. Too passionate and perhaps not fully developed, but interesting nonetheless. But these ideas were far too advanced for a teenager. I felt certain she was parroting someone else.

I wanted to coax more from her. "Many scholars who have studied the Scriptures would disagree with you. Dante himself based his writing on extensive study of the *Summa Theologica* of Saint Thomas Aquinas."

Margaret went absolutely purple. "This book is an utter waste of time," she said in a tone so dismissive it set my teeth on edge. "Such stories are for those who cannot think for themselves. I am not one of those. I am different. We all are." She looked to Vanessa, who smiled serenely back at her. I heard snickers from Lilliana and Therese. I knew exactly whom she meant by "we" and so did every other girl in the room.

That was when I noticed Eustacia. She alone appeared frightened. Not wary or excited like the others, but truly terrified. Perhaps I had gone too far, I suddenly thought. I ought to tread carefully. It was my first day, for goodness sake. "As much as I would like to pursue this line of debate, we must move on," I said breezily, seeming to dismiss the topic with a flick of my wrist. "I thought the best way for me to get to know you all would be to have you write me a theme on your favorite subject."

There were shocked faces, and then groans. From Margaret, a glare that made me grateful that looks could not indeed kill. But I ignored all of this, donning an expression of sublime equanimity I did not feel as I sat at my desk.

I had to collect myself, concentrate on processing the strange interchange with Margaret. While the class worked, I pretended to be writing, but kept glancing covertly at the five girls.

How likely was it that this vampire—whatever its dealing with these particular girls—was the same one that had taken my mother?

But this did not make any sense. Laura had not been made *strigoii vii* while a student at Blackbriar. It was years later, after she'd married my father, a year or so before I was born.

As I had learned in my long hours of research in Denmark, vampires favored certain hunting grounds, and lived a nomadic existence traveling among them. Most of the local people never realized what it was that had come to their quiet worlds. They believed in pestilence, or plague. Some blamed innocents in accusations of witchcraft. If awareness of the monsters did arise, it died out in subsequent generations, becoming scarce-believed legends and superstitions.

But the vampire would return, safe under the cloak of faded memory and rationality. Therefore, it was entirely possible that the vampire whose reeking presence I could sense on these girls had been here back when my mother was a student. I resolved to find some local histories to see if I could unearth an accounting of past tragedies.

Yet, I was bothered by my theory. I knew the timing was not right, none of it. Even if my mother had been touched somehow as these girls were, why would her symptoms not emerge until more than five years after she had left Blackbriar? And would a vampire return within living memory of the locals? I had thought that was never done.

After the girls had handed in their themes, I ate a quick lunch and went for a walk. It always helped me to stride briskly when I was working out a particular problem. It was cold, however, much more so than I'd thought, and I soon became chilled. I refused to go back inside. I am afraid I was in something of a state, confused, and a little lonely. I would have given anything to have had Sebastian with me.

And Valerian. I walked faster, my breath coming in puffs of clean, white steam. Was he hunting Marius across the continent, into the jungles of Africa, or the sweeping Persian desert? Or was he sitting in a London parlor, sipping tea and flipping the pages of a book? I longed for his friendship, and the particular feeling his companionship gave to me. My little infatuation with Lord Robert Suddington had not altered that.

But I was alone. That was the heart of it. I should have been used to it, for I had a long acquaintance with the solitary state. Alone, even as a child. Motherless, odd, suspicious lest I manifest the madness of my mother. I, Emma, seemed destined ever to be alone.

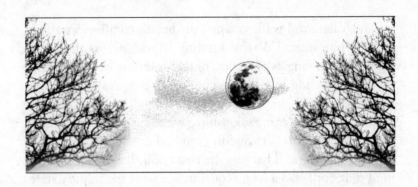

Chapter Six

guilty conscience is the heaviest burden to bear. My father used to say that, an admonition I did not need for it was my usual impulse to maintain scrupulous honesty—or at least it used to be, before all this business with vampires started. I used to speak frankly as a habit, and disliked deceit of any kind.

Thus when the headmistress called me to her office unexpectedly a few days later, all the lies I had told to get myself this position sprung instantly to mind, and I had but one, urgent thought: *Caught!*

She kept me waiting, and I used the time to contemplate the thorough humiliation I was sure awaited me. After a half hour, Miss Sloane-Smith glided in with an imperial air, and I stood, ready to take the storm on full force, for it was no less than I deserved.

However, what followed was not accusation and dismissal. She made her way to the desk and said: "You are faring well in your new post, Mrs. Andrews."

She spoke it as if this displeased her, although I could not imagine why it would. I murmured a modest thanks.

"And how do you find your students?" she asked.

"Interesting," I said. She said nothing more, so I filled the silence with, "I enjoy our discussions immensely."

"Really." Her tone was flat as she lifted her gaze to mine. "I am so glad you are enjoying yourself."

I smiled, pretending I missed her sarcasm. "I doubt *The Inferno* is any young girl's idea of pleasure reading, but they do engage in the discussion and practice their conversation skills. It is a good exercise."

She sniffed. "There is no indication of anyone with intellectual leanings, I trust."

I knew the correct answer was no. The girls were being trained to be appropriate foils for men to wax prosaic, an audience merely, never the orator. "We speak in terms of morality, at least how Dante envisioned it."

"Very good. And what of Miss Kingston? It is up to you to see she does not prove impertinent."

She meant Margaret. "Indeed, she is challenging each and every day. But I can manage her."

She sniffed, her eyebrows twitching to indicate a grudging approval. "The girl is incorrigible. Her family is new money, you know. Crude people, made their fortune in trade." Her look of distaste turned sly. "But they are very wealthy."

The conversation lapsed, and I assumed it was over. "Very well, then," I murmured and made to step past her to exit the room.

She held up her hand. "There is another matter," she said with a twitch of her pointed nose, and I knew that whatever it was, it was the true reason why she had summoned me. I also saw she was deeply displeased and doing a poor job of covering it. "I have received an invitation to a dinner party being given at Holt Manor. I was not aware you had made the acquaintance of Lord Suddington."

At the sound of his name, my heart gave an unexpected and slightly thrilling little leap. "We dined together at the Rood and Cup several times while I was staying there."

"Indeed." The single word could have frozen seawater. "It seems he regards you two to have struck up something of a friendship. He and I have known each other for some time, of course. We are distantly related, cousins, and our families have been involved with the Blackbriar School for generations. His father was a member of the board of trustees at the time I was appointed headmistress and Lord Suddington has been an en- thusiastic member of the board since he returned to the area."

"I did not realize."

She preened. "Did you not realize he is an important man in the county? Well, he most certainly is, and as such he is very attentive to his social duties as a leader of the community. His guest lists are unfailingly comprised of local luminaries. And yet, for some reason, he has seen fit to invite you to his upcom- ing dinner party."

My surprise was too great to hide. "How kind of him."

"Well, it is not done, you see, the staff socializing freely with the local gentry. Now we have quite a situation, as you have seen fit to flout convention. I do not wish to be rude, but it needs being said: he is quite above your station. But as Lord Suddington made this especial request, I am prepared to make an exception and give you permission to attend."

I could see that making this concession galled her. She could not hide it, nor did she much bother. I had to content myself with the secret knowledge that my fortune could buy and sell this school, and my family pedigree dwarf whatever accolades she could boast for hers. I smiled inwardly at the irony: when Alyssa spoke of such things, I thought her a snob. Yet here I was, doing the same thing to soothe my bruised pride.

Miss Sloane-Smith narrowed her eyes at me. "I trust you will dress appropriately. You no doubt have something suitable."

Consideration of my many fine gowns almost cracked a smile on my tightly controlled features, but I caught myself. "I am sure I can find something. May I know the date?"

"Thursday next. I will let you know what time to be ready." When her eyes flashed, I realized she was more than merely upset about keeping the social hierarchy of power here at the school intact. She was *jealous*. Was she in love with Suddington?

"That is all," she said, and I all but dashed through the doorway, pulling it closed behind me. Just before it latched, I paused. Perhaps I was making a mistake. Pride aside, I should not accept the invitation to Suddington's party. I was not at Blackbriar to engage in diversions such as dinner parties. My pleasure at Suddington's having remembered me in the invitation had clouded my better judgment. Yes, attending was definitely a poor move. I pushed the door I had almost closed and stepped inside, my mouth open to beg Miss Sloane-Smith's pardon.

But she was bent to pull a slender volume from beneath a large bookcase. I waited, suddenly unsure. She might be angry at my intrusion. I hesitated, then stepped quietly back so that I could knock on the door. But before I could fully retreat, she straightened and found me standing there.

I expected her to be angry. In fact, I did not blame her. But her startlement went far beyond the annoyance my intrusion deserved. She gasped and fell back, whipping the book she had just retrieved behind her back in a transparent, almost childish effort to conceal it.

"What are you still doing here?" she demanded. Her voice rang with indignation.

I opened my mouth. This was a terrible mess. "I think it best to decline the dinner invitation," I said. "I would not wish an exception to be made just for me."

"It is not important what you wish," she snapped sharply. "Lord Suddington has made his request and you will honor it. You will not disgrace this school or me." Narrowing her eyes, she said, "Make certain, however, that there is no cause for him to seek to include you in future gatherings."

I nodded and backed out, rather like a slave leaving the presence of a barbarian queen, grateful to have escaped with her head. Then I turned, and while my pride forbade me to rush unduly, I confess I did not tarry as I hurried to my room.

I was halfway up the stairs when the first, subtle brush whispered in my mind. My head came up sharply, and my first thought was: *Marius!* I had felt that lurid touch before, a disgusting blend of hateful pleasure and torment. A terrible dread filled me.

After a minute I realized that this, however, was not his presence. This was more subtle, the touch of a glance, the kind one feels when finding a stranger's gaze on you. Not quite the claxon alarm of true danger, although the discomfiture of unseen eyes was enough to rattle my nerves, but a sensation so deeply and thoroughly unsettling . . .

My flesh began to prick. My breathing was coming heavily, and I turned sharply down the hallway toward my room, arrowing into it without closing the door behind me. I reached out a trembling hand to open the window. My fingers fumbled, and a voice called my name. I spun to see a shadow in the hall.

"Emma." It was Ann Easterly coming toward me. Her room was next to mine. "Are you headed to luncheon?"

I closed my eyes briefly, gathering my strength. Whatever

had been present was gone. Clearing my throat, I said, "Yes. Of course. I just wanted to freshen up." I wanted just a little time to myself. After patting my face dry and smoothing my hair, I joined Ann, who was waiting for me in the hallway.

"Sunday is our day off," she said as we descended the stairs I had climbed only moments before. "Some of us teachers spend the afternoon in the village browsing the shops and taking tea at Mrs. Brixton's tea and coffee room. Do you think you would like to join us?"

"Thank you," I said, thinking that my preference would be to enjoy Mrs. Danby's cooking and perhaps catch a glimpse of Lord Suddington. But I knew I could not take the time for either indulgence when there was so much upon which to concentrate here at the school. "I will let you know by the end of the week," I assured her.

When we entered the dining hall, we were immediately met with confusion. The students were out of their tables, appearing agitated and talking too loudly. The teachers were not at their place at the large staff table by the French doors.

"What . . . ?" Ann murmured beside me.

But I was in motion, having noticed plump Mrs. Boniface standing among a group of girls. She was openly weeping as she comforted a young student in a similar state of distress.

"My God," I muttered. "Something terrible has happened."

Agatha Thompson was dead. Mrs. Brown had found her lying on the floor of the conservatory when she'd arrived to water her plants after morning classes. The doctor had been called to determine the cause of death.

The news tore through the school like a blast of fire, igniting a flurry of tears and fainting spells among the girls. Though I suspected the majority of these were histrionics, done with the flourish to which only an adolescent girl can do justice, the place was in chaos. We teachers were required to be a calming force and it fell to us to funnel pots of tea and barrelfuls of sympathy to the student population to keep them consoled.

Dorothea Brown was in shock. I pressed a cup of tea into her hands. "It must have been terrible for you, being the one to find her," I said with deep sympathy.

She looked at me searchingly. "It was her heart," she murmured. "I saw how pale she'd been of late. And she said she'd not been sleeping well. The other morning she was not herself. I should have insisted—"

She broke off, and I put a comforting hand on her arm. My gaze caught the group of coven girls watching us. There were five of them now: the four from my class—Margaret, Vanessa, Lilliana, and Therese—had been joined by another, Marion Tilman. They were standing apart from the others and they remained placid, unmoved. Their remarkable composure sent a chill through my veins.

I moved to the headmistress, who was poised in the center hallway in readiness for the arrival of the doctor. "I can wait here for the doctor if you like," I told her kindly. "You must be needed elsewhere." In truth, I was desperate to see Agatha's body and thought I might get a glimpse of the corpse if I were to be permitted to take the doctor to where it lay upstairs in Miss Thompson's bedchamber.

Miss Sloane-Smith shook her head in that definitive way of hers. "There is nothing any one of us can do."

When the ruddy-faced doctor arrived, Miss Sloane-Smith rushed him toward the stairs. "Thank you for coming, Dr. Kellum," I heard her say. "She has been laid in her bed."

He hesitated, his heavy-lidded eyes watery in the light spilling through the windows. "Have her brought down here," he said in a hard, gravelly voice. "My gout is bad enough. I cannot climb all those stairs."

The headmistress was caught off guard. "But we cannot move her out into the open, not with the girls . . ."

He sighed. "Very well." With his blue-veined face betraying his irritation, he mounted the steps with a ponderous gait, leaning heavily on the banister. I watched his laborious progress, taking silent exception to his coldness and weariness that seemed to border on boredom.

Kellum's pronouncement of Miss Thompson's death took only a few moments. I heard his heavy tread slowly proceeding back down the stairs and through the hall. He exited without making any formal farewell to anyone. I could observe him climbing into his carriage where, hardly settled in his seat, he produced a flask and tipped back his head to take a deep draught. The carriage lurched forward, taking him away and leaving us to the dead.

No, not "us." It was up to me alone to do what I must as only I was equipped to.

The knowledge sat heavily on me. That day was monstrously long. That night, as I waited for the great house to fall asleep, I sat on the edge of my bed and weighed my options. While I knew it was rare that a vampire would transform its victim—contrary to how the legends had every victim rising itself from the dead—I had been surprised before. It was my job to be sure—for Agatha Thompson's sake, for all our sakes.

From my mother's portmanteau, I retrieved the items I needed. The timing was wrong. The night was, of course, the vampire's time. But I could not wait until dawn and risk being seen. I gingerly drew out the rough stake hewn to a sharp point by my own hand, the flat-headed mallet, the cross, the vial of water blessed by a confessed saint, all of which I had used before. I inspected the tools of my craft, arranged them in my sack, and blew out the lamp. For this task, I required darkness.

The corpse had been properly cleaned and dressed, brought down from the staff dormitories, and laid out after the girls had had their supper. It lay arranged on a table draped in black crepe in the good parlor. The lamps had been left burning, and I could see that flowers had been brought in. No doubt Mrs. Brown's conservatory had been denuded for the purpose of honoring one of our own. No one else would do so. Miss Thompson was a woman alone in the world—very like myself—without husband or children to mourn her.

But she had me to shrive her, and that was an act of love.

"Hello, Agatha," I said softly. I needed to hear the sound of a voice, even my own. As I stood at the body, my nostrils flared, catching the sour tang of the revenant's blood. Yes. I sensed it now. This was what my blood knew and what I was made for.

My fingers caught the high, starched collar furling at her neck and bent it back on both sides. I found the marks, very neat and barely visible: two small punctures behind the ear piercing the skin to sever the carotid artery. The blood had been let neatly, so that not a trace of it had betrayed the violent end. A vampire who wants to hide his kill will refrain from draining the victim, so that the death will appear natural. Sometimes, the wounds could even be charmed and disappear, but this time the fiend hadn't bothered. He hadn't needed to expend the effort. His ploy had certainly fooled that ridiculous excuse for a doctor.

At least she had not suffered the slow agony of being bled over time. This was the usual way a vampire fed. This one had glutted himself, not wishing to waste any time in ending Agatha Thompson's life. He had wanted her dead and quickly. Knowing this reinforced my conviction that Agatha had known something—something about the coven girls.

I made the mistake of looking at her face. Her skin was cast bluish gray, her lips gunmetal, her eyes smudged circles of charcoal. I had not known her well, but I felt close to her in that moment, a slice of time so intimate it stung my eyes. If I were to be honest with myself, I saw my own fate before me. Dying alone. A person well liked, but not loved, not in the way that makes one really immortal, the kind of immortality that matters.

I had to turn away, suddenly overwhelmed with—as much as I detest admitting it—a wave of self-pity. My footsteps were sharp as I went to the window. The rich tasseled velvet felt like a barrier, keeping me trapped with the dead. I pushed aside the heavy draperies and opened the window, lifting my gaze to the fullness of the moon shining like a silver sun. Outside, the air was crisp. The bare landscape below was still.

My voice was barely a whisper. I spoke to the window, not ready to face the body. "I think you saw something, Agatha, didn't you? I think that is why you are dead. How it must have frightened you. Not only because it was unholy—for I wager it was—but also because you feared you'd lost your mind. That you'd be thought mad if you told anyone, as mad as Victoria Markam. I wish I had been given the chance to persuade you to tell me what happened. I would have believed you."

I turned back to the body and opened my sack. "I hope you will forgive me," I said. "I think you understand, though. I know your death was terrible, but there are worse things. I am here to keep you safe."

The stake I drew out was slender, made from the branch of an ordinary hawthorn. The tip was cut to a point as thin as a needle. It was my own handiwork; I'd gotten skilled with a carving knife.

I approached the body. Opening the buttons of her shirt-waist, I arranged the fabric carefully out of the way. "I've done this before," I said to reassure her—and also, if I were to be honest, myself—as I set the stake in position.

A chill crawled through me, and from outside the window I heard the high, mournful wail of a wild creature. A wolf?

Miss Thompson's eyes remained closed. I hesitated, suddenly imagining them flying open, her pale hands reaching for me and her mouth opening to reveal grotesque incisors, razor-sharp and hungry for my flesh. Around me, the smell of flowers was cloying. The wolf howled again, and I bared my teeth in a bracing grimace. I raised my hand to draw the mallet high into the air. My knuckles showed white on the stake, and I cried out a little as I swung the mallet down, using all my force to drive the stake into her heart.

It slipped into her chest bloodlessly, spearing her heart. The body jerked from my strike. I jumped back, startled, and let out a scream, then clamped my mouth shut to stifle it. I paused, squeezing my eyes shut for a moment before I drew in a bracing breath and forced myself back up to the table.

My hands shook and tears silently coursed down my cheeks as I finished my work. Snapping off the end of the stake, I covered her body carefully so that no one would know what I had done. Lovingly, I smoothed the lines of her skirt and touched her hand. "Rest in peace," I whispered.

The light shifted as if something had passed outside the window, blocking the silvery moon for a moment. I swung around to peer intently into the night. Nothing was there.

I went to the window and closed the drapes, letting the velvet fall back into place. And then suddenly I froze. It was as if the air had rushed out of the room, soundlessly vacating the space. A voice echoed in the vacuum that had been created, pronouncing crisp and rhythmic words that coiled around me like a constrictor suffocating its prey.

Who are you?

I struggled against the feeling of it crawling inside my

skull—the same feeling I'd had on the stairs earlier today. The feeling from my dream.

Emma? My name hissed around me. I spun, desperate to find the source of the voice. *Emma. You are Emma.*

I rushed to Agatha Thompson's corpse. It had not moved. I stood my ground, turning a full circle to peer into the tight shadows where the lamplight dared not venture.

Sister? Yes. Yes! I feel you, I feel the blood of my father . . .

"Marius?" I called softly.

I felt something twist, a hesitation, then: *You speak the name of our enemy.*

Before I could respond, the presence receded, pulling away from me like a fast-moving tide. I could breathe again. I sat for a long time, just Miss Agatha Thompson and I. Then I gathered up my implements and packed them away in my bag, sneaking through the shadowy halls to my room, dogged by the sinister implications that crawled over me, through me, in my mind—echoing in that single, terrible word.

Sister.

Chapter Seven

After a somber and uneasy week, Miss Sloane-Smith all but ordered the students out of the school, granting rare permission for them to go into the village. No doubt it was her plan that such a diversion would restore the equilibrium after the school's tragic loss. And I had to admit that the girls were excited at the prospect of the outing. Grief was a fleeting thing for the young, I observed, as they were packed off into carriages and traps for transport. Most of the teachers agreed to go as chaperones, but I elected to stay behind. I had some spying to do.

I felt uneasy in the empty hallways. A few times in recent days I had felt again that alien presence, that sense that something was reaching out to me, hovering just behind me, about to tap me on the shoulder. I was acutely aware of my disadvantage:

it knew something about me, although it was clearly unsure of what possible threat I might pose. I, however, was woefully without so much as a clue to its identity or whereabouts. Or intention.

As I made my way to the third floor, a prickle of apprehension raised gooseflesh along my arms as I became keenly aware of my solitude. The girls' dormitory room for the sixth form students was located in the back of the oldest part of the house. I entered the dormitory and began my examination without so much as a hiccough of conscience. All was fair, as they say, in love and war. I rather thought that when one was dealing with the cursed undead, it was always the latter.

I paused at each one of the bedsteads lined against the inside wall, then traversed to those positioned opposite, situated between tall windows. Each girl possessed a standing chest of drawers, the small flat surfaces on top the only opportunity for personalization in this severely regimented environment. Upon some of these were Bibles and miniature paintings, schoolbooks, papers, paste beads, pen nubs, hairpins, and the like. A few were neatly arranged. Most were a heaping mess.

At Vanessa's bed, flowers wilted in a chipped vase among the usual hodgepodge of items. I bent low so that my head almost touched her pillow and breathed in. I felt the tremor of my blood vibrating in my veins, a sign I had come to know meant the presence of the vampire was here in some detached form. That was nothing I did not already know, however. The oily smudge wrapped around her had told me that upon first meeting. I rifled through the jumbled contents of her belongings, in her drawers and under her bed, but learned nothing more.

Margaret's area, predictably directly next to Vanessa's, was extremely orderly. Her quilt was neatly folded at the foot of the bed, her sheets crisply tucked and her pillow fluffed and poised at the head. On the table a candle and a book were placed at precise angles.

Beginning at the bottom of her bed, I held out my hand, moving up. I felt the same slight tingle. It was unpleasant, almost painful, but I could bear it. Margaret's slyness made it easy to dislike her, and I suspected she was the most cunning of all the girls, so I took extra care with her things. This turned out to be fortuitous, for had I not been attuned to details, I would have missed the name of the book by her bed. I'd assumed it was a Bible; that was what most of the girls had on hand. But this was not a holy book. Or, at least, not *that* holy book.

There were no markings on the cover or spine, and the volume was cheaply bound in a thick paper covering. Opening it, I found a small square of brown paper folded over something bulky. On the paper were written these words:

> *Her breath's the breath of Love,*
> *Wherewith he lures the dove*
> *Of the fair Cyprian Queen.*

My hand tensed. It was Margaret's handwriting; the bold, impatient hand was identifiable. The citation was attributed to Sappho of Lesbos, which she signed with a flourish at the end of the verse. I knew little of the ancient Greek poetess and champion of woman, but as I pondered this excerpt, I recollected there was significant scholarly speculation on the nature of Sappho's and her female followers' love for one another. Most believed it had been what most would term "unnatural."

The Cyprian Queen—the same term Old Madge had used. She had said the girls thought she was love. I wondered briefly on the nature of the close friendship among the students. I could imagine such experimentation was not uncommon in schools. But how far did it go?

Inside the paper was a flower, crushed flat but carefully arranged in its delicate shape. The faded colors were still apparent in ghostly traces among the crisp petals.

I turned to the title page, and frowned to see the book was an old translation of the *Malleus Maleficarum*. The print was faded, the paper cheap. I did not need to read it; I was familiar with this work. Written in the fifteenth century by two German Inquisitors, it was the handbook of witch-hunters but later became, in a twist of ironic perverseness, a sort of witchcraft manual for those whose penchants for evil turned toward the heretical.

Witches.

A sound startled me. I turned quickly, dropping the book. The thud of it hitting the floor sounded like an explosion, and made me jump again.

Eustacia stood in the doorway. She must have been passing by and seen me in here, rooting about. She was too bright not to comprehend at once what I was doing.

"Oh, I am sorry," she said quickly and disappeared.

I replaced the book on Margaret's table and sprinted after her. "Eustacia, do not leave." I caught up with her at the doorway to her dormitory, a smaller chamber where the younger girls slept. "I have been meaning to talk to you. I know you are in possession of a quick mind, which is why you take classes with the older girls. Yet I notice you hesitate to answer my questions in the classroom, when you clearly know the answer."

She flushed. "Oh."

"I realize, of course, your predicament with the older girls. It must be difficult for you to be separated from your friends in the younger classes. But I have noticed Margaret and Vanessa, Lilliana and Therese and . . . who is the other girl? Ah, well, that group—you know them—they try to include you."

"Yes, ma'am," she said, casting a longing look inside the

dormitory. She wanted to escape me. I wondered why. Was it something the girls had said about me, to make her fear me? It distressed me to think she would not trust me, for I liked her. I wanted to help her.

I also had more mercenary reasons: she had information I needed. I was not about to allow her to slip away. "I was wondering if you've ever heard the older girls talking about . . . *witches*?"

She blinked, unsuccessfully attempting to appear surprised. "Witches, ma'am?"

"I saw Margaret has a book about witches."

"I don't know anything about that." She turned to go, but I moved quickly to cut her off. There was no mark of the vampire on her, so I knew she was not a part of the group. Not yet. But they had her in their sights. I had seen how Margaret tried to dominate her, draw her in. She might not be able to tell me much, but any detail could be of help to me. And I found I cared deeply about being of help to her, for clearly she was distressed. I even sensed she wanted to confide in me.

"Is there something wrong, Eustacia?" I asked, softening my voice. "I might be able to help, you know."

She shook her head. "No, really, Mrs. Andrews. I'm fine."

"I'm sorry, dear, but I find it difficult to believe that."

She stammered, "No, there's nothing wrong. I don't know anything about the book, really. Margaret . . . she gets strange ideas sometimes, that's all."

"She frightens you," I said.

She opened her mouth but said nothing, and I realized she was too afraid to speak. My chest tightened. I was determined to help her, but how could I get her to tell me what was wrong?

"Please, I have to go," she said and tried to duck past me again.

I put a restraining hand on her shoulder. "Just a minute." I felt cruel pressing her so, but I was doing it as much for her own good as my need to learn what she knew. "I can assure you, Eustacia, I will tell no one—not a soul—of anything you say to me. No matter what. You would not be tattling to tell me because I am not interested in disciplining them. I want to help them. I want to help you."

I struck the right chord, for uncertainty gathered in her gaze. The poor girl wanted desperately to confide in me.

Therefore, I pressed on. "They are sneaking out. I already know that and I have told no one. They have a group, a club of some sort, and it involves something very . . . very dark. Very dangerous."

"The wicked things they do!" she said in almost a moan, and reached out for me and wrapped her smaller hand in mine. I grasped that desperate hand, moved by her torment, and murmured encouragingly, "It's all right."

"They like it," she whispered, her mouth trembling. "They want me to be part . . . They say there must be seven. They say I must join them." She stepped back suddenly, pulling her hands free and burying them in her hair.

"Eustacia?" I reached out to comfort her and her eyes snapped up to hold my gaze.

"I shouldn't have told you!"

"No, it is quite all right, I promise—"

"If they find out, they will murder me."

I must say, the thrust of her terror was like a physical thing, and in the same manner that a blow to the wrist will numb the hand, so too did her fear transfix me for a moment. When she wheeled and fled out of sight, I remained frozen.

Murder her? Surely she was exaggerating, using the term to describe the social torture the girls would put her through, excluding her from their circle, bullying her with taunts and nasty pranks.

But I remembered the bodies Victoria Markam had seen

and was uneasy. No, that was absurd. The girls were not murderers, for they were not vampires.

However, they were clearly putting a crushing amount of pressure on her. Why—what did they want with her? They needed seven girls, Eustacia had said. I counted five students. Eustacia would make a sixth. There had to be one more I did not know to make up the septet.

As I exited the dormitory wing, I resolved to keep an eye on Eustacia, perhaps try again to gain her trust. She could be a valuable resource to understand what was happening with the . . . well, *the witches* was as accurate a term as any.

After luncheon, I thought I might venture out to the frozen garden, as a means to help myself think. I dressed warmly, bringing along a volume of Keats's poetry. I had found some interesting insights about vampires and other mystical creatures in the work of the Romantic poets. Coleridge's *Christabel* contained a line that had saved my life this past spring, once I realized its relevance to the strange happenings in Avebury. Other writers, too, had pondered the subject of the vampires. Polidori's *The Vampyr*, Lord Byron's *Manfred*—both written during a storm-ravaged summer the two men spent trapped indoors while they were vacationing with Percy Bysshe Shelley and Mary Shelley on the shores of Lake Geneva. The two writers' accounts were ominously acute in describing the vampire sensibility. I had often wondered what transpired that summer, for it was here Mary Shelley had begun her chilling *Frankenstein*, another story of the dead come to life.

But of all the Romantic poets, Keats, in his tragically short career, had written the most stunning works involving the undead. *La Belle Dame sans Merci* and *Lamia* were almost certainly about vampires. I thought I might find some inspiration in his poetry.

And it was Keats my mother had scribbled on the inside leather flap of her torn portmanteau. Thus, I thought he might have something to tell me.

It was colder outside than I'd thought, and the sun was blurry and thin. If I were less stubborn, I would have gone indoors posthaste, but I liked the privacy out here and I'd missed the crisp air of a chill winter's day. As I began *In a Drear-Nighted December*, a curiously cheerful poem completely out of character with the poet, a voice cut into the quiet.

"I should have known you would have your nose in a book. Lud, you are helpless, Emma, and freezing to boot. When the woman at the house directed me to find you out here, I thought she was daft." It was a droll tone, infused with humor and mockery, and I caught my breath, recognizing it at once.

Sebastian stood on the grass with his feet braced apart, arms akimbo, an apple-green cape artfully draped over slight shoulders. Upon his head was a jaunty hat that made him look like Robin Hood. He was laughing at me, his smile as mischievous as that of Eros.

I was up off the bench and in his arms before I drew another breath. "Sebastian!" I shouted.

"Heavens, gel, you'll muss my hair." But his arms were around me, and although he was a slightly built man, his embrace was tight and sure.

"How I missed you," I said. My voice was muffled against the extravagant knot of his cravat. I could not seem to let him go.

"Now, now, what is this?" he said, pulling back so he could look down into my face. I did not realize my cheeks were wet until he touched a finger of his forest-green velvet glove to my skin.

"Nothing. Nothing." My reassurances were hollow.

His smile stiffened and faded, and he appeared stricken. "I knew I should have come sooner."

I shook my head. "No. No, I am fine, really I am."

He did not believe me, and his frown of concern made me twist away. I forced a smile with some effort and he shook his head at me. "Good God, that is a ghastly excuse for a smile. There is no use for it, I have found you out. You are miserable."

"I am not miserable," I told him. "I just . . ." I sighed, looking out over the lawn to the school. The long row of mullioned windows stretched to my north, the sun glancing off the panes so that nothing could be seen inside. "I fear I have botched this entire thing," I said at last.

"There, there, what are you saying?" He pulled me to the bench and made me sit with him. The wind blew, but it did not trouble me now. Sebastian was here, and his warmth could not be dulled by the winter wind.

I told him the entire tale—Madge's cryptic warnings, Lord Suddington, the coven girls, Miss Thompson. "I had to shrive her," I said. I brushed the tendrils of hair from my eyes, where the wind had caught them in my eyelashes.

His gloved hands reached for mine. "I am sorry. It must have been dreadful."

I felt as if I was confessing a terrible deficiency, but made myself tell him: "I was afraid."

"Yes." He said it simply.

I shook my head. "It is difficult to see myself as a coward."

"But you are a woman, Emma. That is all."

"I am supposed to be Dhampir," I told him in a sudden rush of heat. "What good has that done me? I've accomplished nothing here."

He held up a staying finger. "You expect too much from yourself."

I sulked slightly, lulled into the comfort of having him at my side. "I felt something. Someone." My eyes slid tentatively to his face. "In my head. I could hear him speaking, like thoughts but they were not mine."

Sebastian cocked his head. "What do you mean—like when Marius spoke to you in your mind?"

"A little, yes. But this was different. It seemed to call to me. It was curious, questing. It said . . ." I lost courage. Sebastian showed the patience of one who knows silence is the best form of persuasion, and finally, I blurted it out. "It called me *sister*."

His head snapped back, his body went rigid. "That is hogwash. Do not even begin to credit anything meaningful to that phrase. You know Alyssa is in her confinement now. Her child is due to arrive in a few weeks time. She has nothing to do with this."

"Of course not. I know it holds nothing of merit. It is only that it frightened me. It was so . . . *intimate* and just wretched."

Sebastian twisted his lips into his most scathing grin. "Well, then, I have made it in time, for we cannot have you *wretched*. It does not suit you." He wagged a finger at me. "It makes you far too pale. And you've got shadows under your eyes. Why, look at your drab clothing. Gray is *not* for you, my dear. Promise me you will allow me to burn that dress."

I smiled, as he intended me to, and played my part. "Sebastian, I am a schoolteacher."

"Darling, these girls are going to return to wealthy families and shall attend the most prestigious parties in Town. They will know fashion. You must think of the advantages of giving them a proper model to view. And your hair is simply too plain. Ugh."

I laughed. "I do not know what is wrong with me, but here you are insulting me and it cheers me so."

He shrugged. "It is a talent, perhaps my only one. Oh, that and the ability to consume vast amounts of spirits." And then we were smiling at each other again. "Did you think I would not come?"

"You said you would not."

He angled his head in a silent admonition. "I did not mean it. Yes, I suppose I am a rogue, but I am not a cad. There is a difference. A rogue has principles."

I thought he was joking, although I wasn't certain. Sebastian was so unusual it sometimes seemed he was being ridiculous when he was quite serious. And yet, just when you thought him sincere, his wicked grin would appear and you knew you'd been caught.

"You do not know how happy I am to see you," I said suddenly.

Waving a hand, he pretended to dismiss me. "Oh, bother, that is enough sentiment. I may be an unconventional Englishman but I am an Englishman all the same, and you know how we dread these vulgar displays of sentiment. Decorum, please."

He made a production of straightening his clothing as if I'd mauled him. My spirits seemed to have taken flight, for I was so happy I could barely contain myself. I laughed.

"Are you not at all cross with me for not coming sooner?" he inquired amiably, finally taking a seat, or rather draping himself in it.

"I am beyond cross," I countered pleasantly. "But it seems rather irrelevant now."

"Curious, at least?" He regarded me indolently.

I narrowed my gaze on him, smiling. "You have something to tell me. Why do you not just say it?"

"In that you are mistaken." He surged to his feet and held out his hand to me. When I took it, he pulled me up beside him. "I have something I must show you. Come with me now. We must go into the village."

That was when I saw that behind his merry façade was a

vein of dead seriousness. Sebastian was fond of foolery, but he was no fool. Whatever he had to show me was of the utmost importance, I could tell.

I sobered immediately. "Let me just fetch my cape, and send word to my friend Mrs. Boniface that I am leaving, in case anyone looks for me."

Sebastian gave no hint on the ride down the Fell as to what surprise lay in store for me. I could see by the tension around his eyes that it was not a pleasant one, though he tried to divert me with the tale of how his latest light o' love groomsman had stolen a jeweled snuffbox from him and taken up with a wealthy widow. He cursed the fellow, but I could see he was not hurt. In fact, the man's ingenuity was a thing Sebastian most likely admired.

His demeanor altered sharply as the rented carriage drew up to the Rood and Cup. He paused just before opening the door for me. "Brace yourself, Emma."

Mrs. Danby nearly accosted me when I entered the common room. "Goodness, it is wonderful to see you. I have been wondering after you, Mrs. Andrews. How are you faring there in that school? Is that wretched Sloane-Smith woman—well, the less said of her the better. And that poor teacher. We barely saw her here in town, of course. She wasn't like Miss Easterly and Miss Grisholm. Those two come into the village every Sunday, regular. Oh, but listen to me go on, come inside, come inside."

My gaze went instantly to the hearth, but Old Madge was not at her seat today. "How is your mother?" I asked.

"You are kind to ask after her. But please don't you trouble yourself, Mrs. Andrews."

Actually, my reasons were far more selfish than kind. I wanted to press her on what she meant by her mention of the Cyprian Queen. Also, it had occurred to me that I might ask the ancient woman about the time period when my mother had been in these parts. She probably had not known my mother, and would not know specifically about happenings at the school, but there was a chance she could tell me if there'd been any unusual disturbance in the village then.

Sebastian said, "We shall have some wine in my rooms, Mrs. Danby." His almost curt tone was out of character, and I looked at him. "I trust all has been quiet," he added meaningfully.

"He has been sleeping," she assured him.

She walked with us up the stairs. The way was familiar, although we turned in the opposite direction from where my room had been located. When Mrs. Danby seemed ready to enter the first room on the left, Sebastian made a quick move to cut her off. With his hand on the knob, he said, "Thank you, now will you see to that wine, please? And some biscuits? I have a propensity for sweets."

She threw him a caustic look, one I would not have guessed the pleasant woman could manifest, then glanced at me. I suppose she was thinking of propriety. The dear woman was attempting to serve as chaperone.

"My cousin and I are quite thirsty," Sebastian insisted, stressing the relation.

"Very well," she muttered, and walked off in a huff.

"That got rid of her," Sebastian said under his breath.

"You were being beastly," I countered.

"Hush, now, Emma. When you see who is inside—"

I cut him off with a nervous laugh. "What do you have in there, a three-headed beast?"

I had never seen Sebastian as doleful as he was now. "No, darling. A ghost."

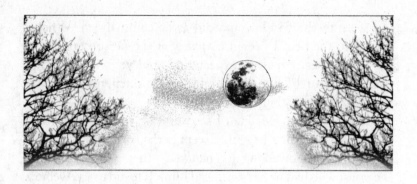

Chapter Eight

The interior of the room was dimmed, the heavy woolen draperies drawn against the afternoon light so that I felt like I was entering a cave. The air was pungent, smelling of an apothecary, and chilled with a cold that somehow seemed deeper, thicker, than the air outside.

The grate in the fireplace was dark, a sullen pile of barely smoking ash. Sebastian muttered a curse and hurried past me to fix the fire. I looked about, seeing nothing but shadows crowding the room, but I heard a rustle to my left and was shocked to see someone stirring on the bed.

"I told you not to close the curtains," Sebastian said as he stoked the embers to life and fed the fire from a supply of faggots piled on the hearth. "I've brought Emma." To me, he said, "Open the drape. Let some light in here."

I went to the window and did as he commanded. When I turned to the bed, I peered curiously at the person tangled in the bedclothes. I had no expectation, and yet when I recognized the figure, I actually stumbled back a step, my shock was so great. It was Father Luke.

He was so changed! Had I seen him on the street, I would have taken him for a beggar. Except perhaps for his eyes. How they blazed, hollowed out and haunted—there I saw my friend, the priest who had nearly sacrificed himself to aid us in Avebury.

When he spoke, the sound was that of sand against rusted metal. "Let in the light, Emma. Isn't that why you've come? Sebastian brought you to send me to the light, having dragged me like a screaming demon out of the dark."

He paused. I tried to say something, but I could not find words. Sebastian had been right; this was a ghost.

He nodded, as if he had expected as much, although I could see it pained him to see my reaction. "I am a wretch, I know. You should go. Suffer me no more humiliations."

"You would not be so much a fright if you would eat," Sebastian said simply, whipping off his green cape with a flourish. He might have been chiding a child for complaining of a stomachache after consuming too many sweets.

Father Luke smiled ever so slightly. "You see Sebastian here is my good friend, and my chief tormentor." Easing his head back among the crushed pillows, he allowed the smile to deepen. "Perhaps merely my just penance."

"Well, then, you should have behaved better," Sebastian said without rancor.

I found my voice. "What is the matter with him? It is clear he is suffering. Should we call in a doctor?"

Sebastian snorted but it was Father Luke who answered. "No doctor. Sebastian is doing the right thing. It is I who am the beast." He closed his eyes for a moment as if to gird himself. "Sebastian, you have overreached yourself this time. This is no place for Mrs. Andrews."

I glanced to Sebastian. "Should I go?"

Sebastian shrugged. "It is up to you. If you cannot bear it."

"It is not that."

"I want nothing from you," Father Luke bellowed, suddenly surging up off the pillows, "except that you leave now."

"It is not a question of what you want," Sebastian said, stepping forward to take the brunt of Father Luke's rage, "but what you need."

"You should have left me where I was!" Father Luke croaked, his hoarse voice rising to the level of fast-moving thunder. "Why did you bring me here at all—for this, to show me to this woman and complete my devastation?"

Sebastian hardly twitched an eyebrow. "You are feeling stronger, I see. Enough to bellow rudely at me. Ah, well, I suppose it is a good sign."

Father Luke's lips peeled back from his teeth. They were still strong, white, shining out from his ashen face like a bay of lights along a granite wall. He was about to reply when some kind of pain or convulsion gripped him, and he stopped, his voice choking in his throat.

I made a step to aid him only to be halted by Sebastian. "Leave him, Emma. It is the opium, or lack of it."

My God! I could have been tumbled by the strength of a kitten's breath. Opium? Frozen on the spot, I could only gape at the paleness of the man, the skeletal remains of the robust, imposing picture he'd once made.

Sebastian nodded. "I found him in an opium den in East London. Ah Sing was not too happy to lose his very good customer, and I nearly came to blows with the man." To Father Luke, he said, more loudly, "Do you know what trouble you caused me?"

"You should have left me there," Father Luke gasped, shaking harder now. "You fool. You silly, stupid fool." Another shudder wracked him and he tucked his chin in, rolling his back as if to brace for a great wave to break over him.

"Oh, bother, he is going into a seizure." Sebastian sprinted forward, grabbing the priest around the shoulders and holding tight.

"What should I do?" I cried.

"Just—see to the fire for me. There is nothing we can do to stave it off. It is the disease, it must run the course."

Father Luke struggled to speak. "Please, make her go. This is no place—"

"There is no time. Ah, damn, keep your back turned, Emma."

"I'll wait out in the hallway—"

"Just stay, damn it all, and get the fire going strong!" Sebastian bit out as he grappled with the priest. Under the grinding devastation of his opium hunger, and in the wake of the terrible things that drug had done to his body, Father Luke was much weakened, but still muscled and broad in the shoulders with legs like tree trunks and a neck the same. He had been a warrior priest once, trained both spiritually and physically to do battle. Sebastian was a wisp next to him, but he held on tightly to his patient. Father Luke's grip had to be crushing, his clammy body sour with the hours spent despondent on the bed, but Sebastian never flinched.

I backed into the corner, the fire forgotten. A knock at the door sent me jumping.

"The wine," Sebastian ground out roughly. "It's Mrs. Danby. Do not let her in."

I nodded jerkily and scrambled to the door before the innkeeper grew impatient. I opened it, only wide enough to peek out at Mrs. Danby.

"That room needs a good airing," she told me, trying to peer around me as I plucked the tray from her arms.

I positioned myself to block her view into the room. I had no doubt even her kind nature would be tried at the sight of the convulsing invalid on the bed in the arms of another man. "Indeed. But if you would be patient with my friends a while longer, it would be so helpful."

Her gaze was concerned. "There's sickness in there? I am used to tending the sick, you know dear."

"How kind of you to offer, but we are fine for now." I stepped back quickly and shut the door, hoping she would forgive my rudeness. My arms cramped under the heavy weight of the tray and I hurried to lay it down. She had brought us wine and a pile of biscuits, as requested, as well as an assortment of sandwiches.

"And you are going to eat," Sebastian said crossly to the now spiritless priest, all gentleness gone.

"Has it passed?" I asked anxiously.

He was grim as he straightened. "For now. Lud, look at me." He pulled his waistcoat smartly into place and began to smooth the expensive fabric.

I skirted around him, intent on the figure lying on the bed. Father Luke did not move. I took one of the sandwiches and tore off a piece. "Take it," I said to Father Luke. "Or Sebastian will have your hide."

His face was parchment-white, glistening with sweat. He only ignored me for a moment before relenting, taking the shred of food from my hands and putting it into his mouth.

While he chewed, I grabbed the basin of water and wet a cloth, then sat on the edge of the bed and began to sponge off the priest's face and neck.

"You do not have to show me compassion," he murmured. "I brought this upon myself."

"Hush." I paused to hand him another fragment of the sandwich. His great chin squared stubbornly in refusal.

"I lost faith," he whispered, still not meeting my eye.

"Yes. I remember."

He turned from me and shortly fell into a restless sleep. I remained beside him for a time, partially as an act of kindness and partially to give myself time to steady my emotions.

Sebastian handed me a cup of wine when I rose. We crept softly to the other end of the room where we might whisper without disturbing the sleeping priest.

"How did you find him?" I asked.

Sebastian frowned at his reflection in a pier glass on the wall. "He came to me in Town for money. Just came to the townhouse one night. I was carousing, as you might imagine, and rather indecorously. Imagine my surprise to find a priest in my hallway. I thought at first he'd come to save my soul. I offered him some brandy—as a jest, mind you—and he accepted. Then I saw how bad off he was, and I was sorry for the fellow. I thought him ill. Stupid of me, but how was I to suspect? I gave him some coins and sent him on his way, with promises to meet for tea or coffee or ale or something or other. Neither one of us meant it and I barely thought of afterward."

"He must have shown up again?"

He nodded. "And that time, I knew it was not ague that ailed him. His shaking hands, his sweating—he was nearly as bad as you see now. He begged money from me again, and when I suggested he go to a hospital instead, he grew agitated. I admit, it frightened me that he would become violent. You know, he is a formidably large man."

"He is indeed," I agreed.

"Quite right. So I gave him all the money I had and hoped he would leave me. He did, with such shame and remorse on his face that I knew—at once, I knew he was eating opium. That desperate look . . . there is no mistaking it. But he was gone, you see, and I was glad to be rid of him, glad he had not killed me."

Sebastian sighed, fussing with his cravat. Glancing at me, he appeared sheepish. "Then my conscience got me. Yes, indeed—a conscience. It appears I am actually in possession of one. Who knew? And it began to assert itself most inconveniently and so I set out to find him, which did not prove easy. The Ah Sings of this world like their customers without complications. They have men to deal with complications. Large men with disagreeable temperaments. Who can snap a delicate neck like mine with a flick of a wrist." He shuddered.

"So what did you do?"

Sebastian smirked. "I hired larger men," he said. "One of the advantages of frequenting the underworld, and being free with my coin as I am, is that you make the most unlikely of friends."

"Then you managed to take him safely away from the opium den?"

"Three times, in fact. He kept escaping. Terribly determined, he is. Terrorized my staff and I almost lost my housekeeper over the whole affair. But even that old tartar couldn't abandon the wretch." Sebastian jerked his head toward the bed. "It was she who made me go after him again that last time. She told me to go into that disgusting, vile place once more, this time *without* the brawny fellows. And thus the priest would be forced to come to my rescue. She insisted the man would never allow harm to come to me after all I'd done for him."

I nodded. "She knew his heart was still good and sound."

His head whipped round and he snorted. "Heavens, no. She was quite wrong, as it turned out. The cur lay there insensate while I was mauled."

I gasped. "What? Then tell me at last, Sebastian, how the devil you got that man all the way up here in Cumbria and lying on that bed."

He lifted a boyishly lean shoulder. "I barely made it out of there with my life, and when I stumbled into my townhouse, I was just about to take a stick to Mrs. Oxney when he arrived at my door. A deplorably sloppy scene ensued in which he actually berated me for endangering my life for him. Imagine! Well, I tried to cast him out, as I had had my fill of the entire matter, but he was insistent on getting me to agree never to return to Ah Sing's establishment, which of course I would not."

"Of course," I agreed mildly.

"He actually manhandled me! Tore my best surcoat, the ham-fisted oaf. You would think all of that opium would have made him weak. Then I informed him he would soon be quit of me, at least for a while, as I was leaving that very night to travel here to see you, and he suddenly changed at the mention of your name. He became calm and the next thing I knew, he had thrust himself in my carriage and would not budge when I ordered him out. He said nothing, only that he was determined to come along, and as I had no hope of moving him, I let him. The journey was grueling for him, as you might imagine."

I took a moment to digest this. "What do you plan to do with him?"

"Get him off the drug. After that, I have not given a thought." His head jerked toward me. "I do not expect you to help nurse him. That is not why I brought him with me. I simply did not have another place for him."

I glanced at the bed. The priest slept. Where was the proper place for a fallen priest? I wondered. And what could I do besides offer kindness and comfort?

"Have you heard from him?" Sebastian asked me. I did not need to ask to whom he referred. I knew he meant Valerian. I did not look at him when I shook my head.

He muttered something softly, perhaps not meant for my ears. I pretended I had not heard, but I silently agreed with him. For his long absence and incomprehensible silence these past months, Valerian Fox was a bloody bastard.

Darkness had fallen when I returned to Blackbriar. I was exhausted, my mind weighted with the day's revelation, and had thoughts only of finding my bed. The sixth form girls had returned, I noted as I passed the dining hall, seeing they were seated awaiting their supper. My stomach had been sated quite sublimely by Mrs. Danby's meat pies and dessert custard, so I did not join the others for supper but proceeded toward stairs, seeking the solitude of my room to mull over the day's disturbing events.

"Emma!" Eloise Boniface called to me. She must have seen me pass by the dining room and had rushed out to meet me in the hall. "I was looking for you all day. I hope it was all right to send that peculiar gentleman out to the garden to see you. He said he was a relative, but when I could not find you this afternoon, I grew worried."

"Oh, no, it was fine. Sebastian is my cousin by marriage, and a dear friend. I went into the village with him. I am just getting back right now."

She was obviously relieved. "I am so glad. Oh, and if you've a moment, I have been wanting to talk to you regarding what you asked me about the other day. I believe I have recollected something about your mother. Actually, once I remembered, I can't imagine how I could have forgotten."

It was as if an electrical charge went through me. "That is wonderful!" I exclaimed, surging forward in excitement. "Please tell me. I am so anxious to learn anything I can about her."

"Come in to dinner and sit with me while I finish my meal and I will tell you about it. It was a terrible accident, you see. It was something of a scandal at the time, with what eventually happened with Alistair."

She was leading me into the dining room when a shadow

passed, and I caught a vague movement out of the corner of my eye. I turned to look more closely at it and saw it was the floating smudge of soiled air I normally associated with the little witches. It darted across the ceiling, as a streamer might unfurl behind someone running. My nostrils flared, detecting an acrid, sulfurous smell that clenched my full stomach in a terrible cramp.

If I had not seen the dark mark, I would not have looked in the shadows at the end of the hallway. But I did and saw Vanessa there, stealing furtively and silently away from the dining room. She clearly did not want to be noticed.

Eloise had seen nothing, neither the smudge, of course, nor the fleeing student. I was in a dilemma. I wanted desperately to hear what Eloise had to tell me of my mother, but I had to follow Vanessa who was obviously up to something.

"I am so very sorry, but this is an inconvenient time. I am eager to hear your recollection, but perhaps another time?"

Blinking in surprise, Eloise stammered, "W-why . . . of course. I suppose you are tired."

I was sorry, for she seemed disappointed, and I was anxious to speak with her, but my muscles twitched to be underway lest Vanessa get too much of a head start. "Yes, very. Would you excuse me?"

I broke away and headed down the hallway as if to take the stairs that led up to the teachers' quarters. Once I saw Mrs. Boniface had returned to the dining hall, I reversed my direction, going back to where I had last seen Vanessa, and slipped into the opposite hallway.

I spied her at once. The long, willowy form threaded gracefully through light and shadow of the dimly lit corridor leading to the back of the house. When she reached the kitchens, she had no trouble stealing around a distracted cook to gain the back door. Without anyone else but me to notice, she opened it just enough to dart outside.

Cook looked up when I passed through her domain. She nodded grimly at my smile, saying nothing as I went out the door to the kitchen gardens. I paused, scanning the warren of walled gardens in which cook oversaw the vegetable rows and thatches of herbs.

Denuded apple trees stood in rows to my left. They appeared like ghastly regiments of the dead, I observed with a shiver. Against the starlit sky, their graceless branches were flung in wild, desperate angles. I heard nothing for a moment, then the faint sound of whispers beckoned me deeper into the orchard.

I moved as quickly and silently as I could. When I saw the pair of them—Vanessa unmistakable with her long, glorious waves streaming down her back, her head thrown back, and a tall male figure bent over her—I nearly screamed.

I had nothing with me with which to do battle, for my tools were secreted upstairs in my room. I did not think I had time to return for them. Vanessa writhed in the creature's arms, and a low, guttural moan rippled through the air, igniting pinpricks of horror across the back of my neck. I had to do something, I decided. Even unarmed, I had to try.

Prayers, I thought, my mind going to the opening vesper prayer used by those priests secretly anointed as vampire extirpators. I began to mutter, drawing on my strength.

"Deus, in adiutorium meum intende." God, come to my assistance.

I rose, stepping out of the shadows. *"Domine, ad adiuvandum me festina."* O Lord, make haste to help me.

I walked forward. *"Gloria Patri, et Filio, et Spiritui Sancto."*

I raised my voice, but the fiend was too enraptured; it did not raise its head. The prayer was having no effect. Fear constricted my throat, and my voice strained against it to be heard: *"Sicut erat in principio, et nunc et semper, et in saecula saeculorum."*

As it was in the beginning, both now and ever, and unto ages of ages.

Suddenly, the Latin died on my lips and shock froze me in my tracks. I blinked as comprehension dawned. My God, I saw suddenly that I'd completely misread what was happening.

Vanessa's hands grasped the man, pulling him close. She was not struggling at all. Her movements were not a result of fear . . . but of passion. Embarrassment flushed through me like a scalding rain. This was not a victim in the death throes of a ravenous vampire! I saw now that the man's hands cupped her breasts, which were nearly bared by her disarrayed clothing. His mouth was on her neck, but not to feed. Her moans were driven by ecstasy, not helplessness. Moreover, I saw, too, who the male figure was. Colin O'Hara. Vanessa and the Irish boy were lovers.

He must have driven the girls back from the village, then waited for her to sneak away. How many times had they arranged meetings like this? Did the other girls know about it?

Eustacia did. And Margaret was too keen not to.

Stepping out of my hiding place, I called out: "Vanessa!" I strode up to them purposefully, a sharp admonition in mind.

The Irish boy released her. Vanessa made a little purr of protest, and looked about. She turned lazily toward me, her expression petulant. It appeared she was utterly unconcerned with her gaping dress, nor was she showing any indication of shame at having been found in flagrante delicto.

"Do up your blouse at once," I told her. "Get into the house and wait for me in the students' parlor. I will deal with you in a moment."

She glanced back at the Irish boy and smiled sadly. "Sorry, love," she whispered with a coquettish little moue. She sighed. "I shall warn you not to bother running to tell Miss Sloane-Smith. She'll do nothing, you know. She did nothing when that whining Miss Markam told her all about us."

My hand flexed at my side. It was all I could do not to slap the supercilious expression from her face. "I think you are mistaken if you believe she would condone this."

"She understands something you should, too, Mrs. Andrews. She may not know all, but she knows enough to fear it, and she will protect the secret of the Cyprian Queen."

I tensed. "What is this Cyprian Queen?"

"She is beauty, and love." She smiled coyly. "She is the goddess."

Goddess. Now I understood! The goddess of beauty and love was, of course, Aphrodite. I knew my Greek mythology well. Aphrodite, or Venus to the Romans, was said to have been born from the sea, carried aloft on the foam to Greece from Cyprus. She was sometimes referred to by her country of origin, thus the Cyprian.

Yes, and now I recalled why the term had seemed familiar. Cyprian was also an old-fashioned name for a sophisticated prostitute. For Aphrodite was the goddess of love, beauty, and sexual appetites.

"What are you playing with, Vanessa?" I whispered, horrified. A terrible thought occurred to me, and I wondered if the girls were actually engaged in selling their bodies. Was this a cadre of prostitutes operating out of one of the most prestigious girls' academies in all of England?

"Miss Sloane-Smith will never wish anything to be revealed or all at the school would be ruined. Every last girl." She held a finger to her lips and giggled as she skipped past me.

My gaze shot to the boy. He was a young man, really, strapping and handsome with his Black Irish coloring. "I will tell the headmistress," I informed him, putting starch in my words, "and she will no doubt forbid your coming to the school ever again."

His bleak gaze did not move as Vanessa drifted through the

orchard, fading into the darkness. His mouth was twisted in a bitter line. "It doesn't matter, I'll not come back here again." Suddenly he swung his eyes at me. I saw the faint sheen of tears unshed. "I am not the one she loves," he spat, and he glanced over his shoulder, into the thickest part of the blackness around us. I followed his gaze but saw nothing.

He turned back to me, and it seemed he wanted to say more. His lips peeled back, suddenly grotesque in a grimace of unspoken suffering. Then, suddenly, he was gone.

A trickle of fear bled cold down my spine, but I did not call out to him, demand he come back and explain what he had meant. I looked to where he had glanced, his face full of impotent rage. What was out there?

In truth, I had no wish to find out, not unarmed and alone in the darkness as I was. I hurried inside.

I thought about what Vanessa had said about Miss Sloane-Smith, and had no doubt there was some merit to her confidence the headmistress would not take action even if I told her of Vanessa's transgression. I had seen firsthand the headmistress' priority to keep the name of the school pristine. I was not so naïve I did not recognize her motivations: not the welfare of the girls but the welfare of the school, an entity fed by the pounds charged to wealthy families each year, parents who wanted the prestige of a society education for their daughters.

If I brought a scandal like this to her attention, it would not be met with gratitude. And I was already on such shaky ground with her. I hated the decision I made, but I had more important things than the moral failure of a student to contend with. If I were dismissed, I would not be here to fight the vampire when I found him.

Or her. The Cyprian Queen, she'd said—just as Madge had done. Who was she? Was it a myth, a fiction? Did it mean anything at all?

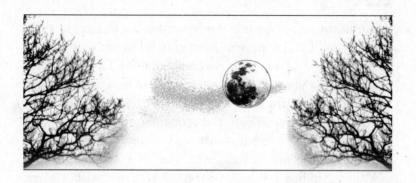

Chapter Nine

I chose unwisely when I selected my gown on the night of Suddington's dinner party. It was made of French silk in a shade of ivory so rich it swallowed the light, throwing it back to the eye in a soft, pearlescent gleam. The intricate folds around the bodice glowed like swirls of thick cream. In the full skirt, the delicate shimmer of mother-of-pearl rippled so that each footstep was a dizzying concert of fairy light combined with the crisp symphony of expensive silk.

My sister, Alyssa, had designed it, conspiring with a ridiculously expensive dressmaker one rainy afternoon a few summers ago when we were in Bath. She was good with fashion and always on me to dress better, never failing to stress that I could afford it. She was rather infatuated with the wealth my late husband had left to me, far more so than I ever was. I had to admit my wardrobe was the better for her interest in these matters, and I was at present most grateful to her.

As I pinned up my hair, I wondered at my foresight in including this elaborate gown among the more practical selections I'd had sent from my home after settling into Blackbriar. I'd done that after making the acquaintance of Lord Robert Suddington. Had I perhaps harbored a secret hope that I might have occasion to wear it for him?

When I joined my headmistress, I was met with a glare. This I took as a sort of reverse compliment, as I had known it would displease her to see me dressed so grandly. However, Miss Sloane-Smith herself made an impressive appearance. Her hair was perfectly in place, her dress made from swaths of gray lace, very artful and flattering to her figure. The color did her justice, and I glimpsed the beauty she'd once been.

She studied my appearance from head to toe, and I saw jealousy glitter in her eyes. "You have kept me waiting," she snapped.

"I beg your pardon," I murmured, not pointing out that I had presented myself at exactly the appointed time.

We did not speak as we traveled through the dark, chilly night across the great Fell, through forested lanes to Holt Manor. I was surprised to find it was smaller than my own home in Dartmoor—or, rather, Simon's home, which was now my possession—and less grand. The structure was a great deal older, a plain rectangle of lichen-covered stone with no embellishments, not even a single tower.

There was music coming from inside, a string quartet of some skill measuring out a dignified air. The light from the windows glowed and I hurried up the steps like a moth flitting heedlessly to bare flame.

A footman in smartly appointed livery opened the door with a solemn flourish, and in contrast to the drab gray exterior, the inner sanctum was lushly carpeted in crimson Aubusson rugs and draped richly with dense gold velvet. Mirrors and glass sparkled blindingly, set afire by countless tapers rising from candelabras on every gleaming wooden surface and standing in iron stands. Spectacular flowers were placed in pots all around, their thick scent perfuming the air, and it all went to my head as Miss Sloane-Smith and I proceeded into a grand parlor crowded with people.

"Do not disgrace the school," Miss Sloane-Smith said under her breath. When I glanced at her, I saw the warning had been forced through a stiff jaw frozen in a smile. No one looking at us would suspect it, but I knew the headmistress resented deeply my presence at her side. And then her expression changed, her youth returning in a flood as her eyes gleamed and her smile grew real. Robert Suddington had come up to greet us.

I was blessed by fate when he greeted Miss Sloane-Smith first, for I was temporarily overcome by his presence. He cut a magnificent figure, his coat and trousers black, his shirt white, his cravat a snowy froth at his neck, all of the finest cloth and tailoring. "My dear Glorianna," his warm voice intoned, folding her hands in both of his. I watched Miss Sloane-Smith's steel features quiver with barely repressed delight. "It is too long since we have seen one another, cousin. Being liberated from the walls of the school suits you. You are a vision. Thank you so much for coming tonight."

"It is my pleasure," Miss Sloane-Smith murmured, a hint of flirtation in her voice. She was a woman suddenly, no longer a headmistress, and I was rather awed by the transformation. I did not see how my host could fail to be charmed, and I experienced an unpleasant twinge of jealousy when Suddington lingered over her hand. Then he released her and turned to me, and my heart gave a small lurch.

"Ah, Mrs. Andrews. Thank you so much for joining us this evening."

My voice sounded breathy and too feminine when I answered. "Indeed. Thank you for the kind invitation."

He led us into the room, introducing us—or, rather, me, since Miss Sloane-Smith was well known to the other guests. I was too overwhelmed to remember any names, but I smiled pleasantly, if vacantly, while Miss Sloane-Smith engaged in conversation at once.

Standing to the side, I felt foolish and out of place. Worse, I was revisited by memories of my youth, when I had gone to soirees and balls with my sister. Alyssa had been and remained the uncontested beauty of the family. I, as my father affectionately remarked, was the odd duck. But as I grew, I realized the world did not regard us odd ducks kindly. I quickly learned that to be one was to be an outcast, invisible, even scorned, although I confess this latter only happened when I provoked it by being unpleasant. For several years of my adolescence, that was my game.

I went through an unfortunate period of rebellion, insolently insisting on conversing in topics I had known very well would be ill-received. But I liked discussing the new discoveries being made in the field of science. I adored debating the merits of Milton over Spenser and could make my opponent dizzy with my impassioned opinions. I could not sing, stitch a needlepoint sampler, or play the pianoforte worth a fig, but I could shoot better than most men, and I am ashamed to admit I boasted of it. There it was—I was an odd duck.

I'd thought these feelings were gone for good. Because Simon, my late husband, had found me like a diamond in the rough, and I had been loved and had loved in return, though it was not the romantic sort but practical, easy companionship and regard that was enough to make me happy, or at least content. How dear Simon had been, for he had cherished those things I'd been told to suppress about myself.

I had not felt like an odd duck for some time, but here I was again, self-conscious and unwieldy among these strangers.

And then a hand closed over my elbow, and a low, masculine voice murmured in my ear, "Now we can slip away. I wish to show you something."

I did not look back as Suddington led me out of the room. He laughed once we were out of earshot, having glanced at my face. "Dear Emma, do relax your guard. It is not my intention to abduct you."

He'd removed his glove so that his warm, bare skin touched mine when he grasped my hand, long fingers curling ever so slightly to take possession of my wrist. The contact sent a thrill up my arm.

"I wish to show you something of my house," he explained. "I am rather proud of the place. I wish I could be here more often."

"And here I thought you were the essence of the country squire," I countered, floating a little as he drew me along a hallway. On both sides, arched embrasures were cut into the wall. These housed Chinese pots containing more exotic flowers perched on long stalks. Their perfume was intoxicating, adding a dreamy quality to our little adventure.

"You are a botanist?" I inquired.

"Of sorts. It is a hobby, merely. I love beauty in all its forms, but most especially in flowers. You might say I am a devotee." His smile was secret, seductive. "At the risk of sounding boastful, I keep a rather impressive hothouse. You must come back and see it in the daylight. I promise it will dazzle you."

I thrilled a little at the invitation. "I would be very pleased to do so."

He consulted his pocket watch and frowned. "I would show

you now, even though it is not to full advantage, but there is not time before dinner." He moved to one of the potted plants.

"Instead let me show you an excellent specimen right here, which is new to my collection. My business interests take me all over the world, and I have taken to bringing back plants as a particular type of souvenir." He gazed lovingly at the flower, his voice hushed in tones of reverence. "This is the *Cattleya labiata*, which caused such a sensation several decades ago. Its introduction to England incited quite a scandal."

I moved closer, then froze. I could see why the plant has inspired controversy. Billowing white petals unfurled in an outer blossom to frame a more emphatic inner bloom that was disturbingly sensual. It emanated a strong perfume. "An orchid, isn't it?" I asked.

"Indeed." He gazed lovingly at the plant. "The forbidden orchid."

The vague sense of embarrassment I had felt upon viewing the plant blossomed into a full, hot flush when I realized what I was seeing. It was like looking at the most intimate parts of the female anatomy, the shameless petals approaching the vulgar in their blatant resemblance to nearly every detail.

"This mysterious plant has inspired unmatched devotion by collectors," Suddington explained. "Did you know there is an underground network of wealthy connoisseurs whose passion for the exotic flower has inspired intrigues the like of which has not been seen since Napoleon tried to sweep through Europe?"

I could not look at the flower any longer. "Of which you are one?"

"Not I, no. I keep myself to some of the more tame of the species." He smiled at me, frowning a bit while he did so. "You do not find the plant pleasing?"

I thought it lurid, but I did not say so. "I think it is marvelous, but then, your home is filled with so many wonders I can

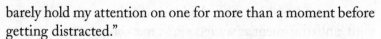

barely hold my attention on one for more than a moment before getting distracted."

He indicated a closed set of doors. "Here, then, this is what I wished to show you. You've often mentioned books you've read, and I thought you might appreciate this." Flinging open the doors dramatically, he stood back and ushered me in. I could feel his eyes on me, awaiting my reaction.

I stepped into a library unlike any I'd ever seen in a private home. It was two stories high and as large as a ballroom. I rushed in, a tiny gasp of excitement escaping me before I realized it.

He chuckled, coming to stand beside me. "I had my servants light the sconces, knowing I would show it off to you." Linking my arm in his, he drew me deeper into the room. "The sad truth is I know precious little about the collection. It was a pet project of my grandfather's, though I have never been in residence long enough to take the time to peruse it in depth. I do know, however, the basic layout. We have local histories over here. One of my ancestors was obsessed with archeology, so there is a grand collection on Egyptian history and such somewhere over there. I content myself with this section. The classics—Spenser, Milton, Shakespeare, Marlowe . . ." He grinned mischievously, pausing to gaze into my dazed eyes, and quoted: "'Is this the face that launched a thousand ships, and burnt the topless towers of Illium?'"

His light manner suddenly sobered, and he was no longer smiling. He gazed at me with an alarming intensity that drove my pulse up to a frantic flutter. For a moment, I could not breathe. He was quoting Marlowe to me, I thought in wonder. As if he knew beautiful literature was my passion, as if he knew *me*.

I should move away, an inner voice cautioned, and yet I stayed as securely as a pinned butterfly as he drew closer. If he were about to kiss me, I suddenly realized, I would not have the strength to deny him. That made me rear back, glancing away with embarrassment as we recovered our composure.

His low voice rumbled in the quiet. "My deepest apologies, Emma. I am afraid I got carried away."

"No matter," I said in an attempt to make light of it. I turned my attention to the wonders of the library, glad of the excuse to put some distance between us and the heady effect he had on me. "Are those your ancestors?" I inquired, pointing to the inner wall where a row of portraits hung in frames of ornate gold leaf.

"Ah, yes," he said, taking my cue, "the esteemed and illustrious Suddington men and women. My mother." He indicated a regal-looking woman whose strong presence and handsomeness put me to mind of Miss Sloane-Smith, which I mentioned.

"See, the nose, and the arch of the eyebrows," I observed.

He laughed, nodding. "I suppose. We are cousins, countless times removed. Not unusual for these parts, you know. The families hereabouts have been interbreeding for generations."

"And your father?" I inquired, looking about. "Is there a portrait of him as well?"

"Unfortunately, his portrait was destroyed. After his death, my mother had it hung in her rooms, where a small fire damaged it beyond repair. But do not look so bereaved; I do not miss it. We did not get on. In fact, my ancestors as a whole were an atrocious lot. It is a history I do not enjoy retelling."

I noticed the rather baleful glance he gave to the faces lined along the wall. I do not know what it is that fascinates about a portrait but I have always enjoyed examining them. In looking at the face, one imagines so much about the nature of the subject.

As I studied these paintings, I began to postulate about the subjects. "He was a womanizer," I said, pointing to a dark

Jacobean figure in a neck ruff sporting pointed mustache and beard. "You can see the glint in his eye."

"No doubt," he agreed. Warming to the game, he indicated a woman near the end of the row. "She is said to have been King Henry's mistress, for a time. But then, who wasn't? She was lucky not to become one of his many wives."

The woman in question wore a very ornate gown. "The poor painter probably spent months on the seed pearls alone," I commented, taking notice of how exquisitely they were depicted, each one so real I felt I could pluck it from the canvas. Two larger pearls dropped from her ears, complimented by a lone teardrop-shaped pearl dangling from a rather ugly snarled clasp of silver secured to a ribbon around her neck. "She was very wealthy," I commented.

"Money has never been a problem for Suddingtons. Is that conceit to say so?"

"Not if it is true."

"Not unlike yourself," he commented, and when I cast him a questioning look, he cocked his head playfully. "That dress cost a fortune."

I felt rather sheepish. He must have guessed I had dressed for him. I cast about for a diversion and noticed a tapestry on the wall behind a massive carved desk. "My, look at this! It is absolutely marvelous. The medieval Suddington ladies must have labored long and hard on it. It is quite intricate. Look at all of the figures . . ." I stopped. My heart gave a bump in my chest. One of the scenes was unmistakably of Saint George, seated upon a white horse, red cape billowing behind him dramatically as he bore his spear upon the dragon he was so famous for vanquishing.

England's patron saint was not an uncommon motif in English art, but I would never view the image without dread. The dragon, or serpent, was an icon of evil, but it was also a symbol of eternal life. It was sometimes used, I'd learned this past spring, as the sign of the vampire, invoking the memory of the Dragon Prince, Dracule, or the Dracula, as he was better known. But despite my dislike of the subject matter, this was, I had to admit, a magnificent depiction. Never had heroic Saint George battled a more ferocious foe, for the dragon on this was huge, monstrous, and regal.

"Rather more violent than you typically see," Suddington commented thoughtfully. "We were a despicably warlike clan, I am afraid." He took me by the arm. "Come away. It does me a disservice for you to see the worst of my lineage put so plainly on display."

As I turned, my eye was caught by one of the other battle scenes, and I recoiled. A number of men were impaled in rows, as the Romans used to do, in a grisly scene, like a forest of corpses. I shivered, thinking of Miss Markam making her horrific discovery of the mass grave. "It is a rather disturbing history."

"Indeed, it is a bloody one," he said, and his voice was colored heavily with an emotion I could not name. "Please, come away. I've never really looked at that horrid thing before. It hangs behind the desk where my back is to it. I've a mind to remove it now that I notice how monstrous it is."

"Please do not. It is no less than the kings and queens need to apologize for." What had made me move toward him, as if to comfort him? I found myself once again squarely in his sights, and the sensual energy that seemed just below the surface with us two began to rise.

"I suppose you are right," he murmured, his gaze fixed on my mouth.

My heart began to swell, sending blood rushing through my veins, making me dizzy. My eyelids lowered and I even swayed forward the slightest bit in an invitation for him to do what I knew he was thinking of doing. I wanted him to kiss me . . .

I realized the unseemliness of this in a sudden rush of common sense, and I pulled away. I do not think it was my vanity that made me think he was disappointed.

He adjusted his features into a mask of composure, suddenly very correct and cool. He was pleasant, however, and offered his arm. "Let us join the others. We've already been gone longer than I planned, and I would hate for our absence to be noticed. I would not wish to put you out of your employer's good graces."

"Yes," I agreed. As we traversed the hallways once again, I said, "Miss Sloane-Smith is good to tolerate my presence tonight. It cannot be typical for her to socialize with her staff. I am, after all, one of the teachers under her administration."

I was a bit flustered, and, realizing I was babbling, cut off the gush of words.

He did not seem to notice. "Oh, it is not that. She does not like women much. Glorianna never did. It has always struck me odd, as she lives with all women and is responsible for the instruction of young girls." He shrugged.

I cast a sideways glance at him. "She seems very fond of you," I observed, unable to resist.

He blushed, a gesture I found inordinately endearing. "Glorianna and I work closely with regards to Blackbriar when I am in the district. It is part of our heritage to be patrons of the school." And then he said, very quietly, very thoughtfully, "It is not easy to escape the obligations of the past."

I could not get Suddington out of my mind. *Why had I stopped him?* I wondered as I sat in my bed replaying the scene in the library over and over again in my mind. It was far past the hour I should have been asleep. I had been trying to read for the past half hour to no avail; my concentration would not cooperate.

I suspected the answer to why I had evaded Robert

Suddington's kiss lay in misplaced loyalty to Valerian Fox. Why would I, after his having ignored me these past five months, feel I owed him anything? I should have kissed Suddington. Should the opportunity present itself again, I would not draw away.

A soft sound broke into my thoughts, and I cocked an ear to listen, but heard nothing else. Turning to my book, I resolved to put away this ridiculous romantic pining (but for whom—Suddington or Fox?). Then I heard it again.

The fine hairs on my arms rose as I felt the coverlet tighten over my legs. It was as if something on the floor were pulling on it. The sound came again, and with a shock of horror, I realized it was the scuttling of tiny feet.

I felt the cold drenching of terror come over me, paralyzing me for one agonizing moment before I forced myself to move. I leaped up, standing on the bed, and saw a large, red-eyed rat staring at me from the foot.

I bit off the scream that tore from my throat as I struck out at it with a swift kick of my foot. My aim, as always, was true, connecting with the solid muscle of the quivering little beast and sending it flying. I leaped back, clinging to the bedstead for support as a number of plump rats swarmed over the bed-clothes and gathered at the foot of my bed.

I fought to fend off panic. I had to stay calm. And quiet. I had no doubt should I scream for help the vermin would flee, leaving me no better off than Victoria Markam had been, babbling about rats instead of corpses.

The small cabal of rats huddled together, eying me with greedy intelligence. Beyond these little leaders, others waited on the floor for their chance at me. They jumped and squirmed, fat flesh-colored tails whipping about like worms. There had to be at least a hundred of them.

My gaze darted desperately from the group on the bed to those on the floor. What was I to do if they all moved as one?

I could not keep on top of them, not if they came at me from different directions.

Just looking at the writhing mass—let alone imagining coming into contact with any of them—made my stomach clench. But I knew I had to ignore these feelings, to concentrate and bring to bear those instincts inside of me that had saved me before. I tried to focus . . .

I felt a sharp pain in my heel. Letting out a cry of pain, I whirled to find a rat had come up behind me and sunk his jaws into my foot. I kicked my leg furiously, but the rat clung tight. I felt hysteria rising, driven by the repulsion I felt for these vile little creatures. *Think!* I screamed inwardly, fighting it off. I deliberately slowed my breathing, but my heartbeat pounded like a fist in my chest.

Fighting the urge to tear off the disgusting creature, I reached down and grasped the wriggling body. A moan of revulsion escaped me, but I ruthlessly pried open its jaws, livid with my blood. The thing was vicious, lashing about in my hands, trying to sink its long incisors into my flesh. I lifted it over my head and flung the heaving body against the wall. It hit with a sickening thud, then slid to the floor, leaving a trail of gore in a red streak. I very much doubted an ordinary person would have been able to throw the rat with such force, but I had ceased to be surprised by what I could do. I did not always understand my Dhampir powers, but I was getting used to the habit of reaching deep inside myself for solutions, and finding myself capable.

I scanned the mass of wriggling rats. I could not fight the lot of them, not if they swarmed. They watched me, eyes gleaming like tiny red pinpricks. *What would they do?* I wondered, forcing myself to stare back at their glowing eyes. My body was tensed, waiting, just as they were. I was in that frame of functioning where instinct took over. It was nearly as if I had no thoughts, just impulses and quiet knowledge; this was how it had been before when I was in battle.

There was no doubt, of course, that these were the animal minions, or familiars, to use the term often cited to describe them, of a vampire lord. There was certainly a will at work, a vampire unseen—but close. Was it here in the room, hiding, watching? My eyes scanned the shadows. I did not *feel* it, but then I was preoccupied. *What are the rats waiting for?* I puzzled.

Then one of them broke away. A ripple of excitement twitched through the pack, riding over their sleek backs as the intrepid charger dug its way up the coverlet and onto the bed. Then it hurled itself straight at me. I jerked back—the damnable thing had surprised me!

It scrabbled up to my neck before I could get a hold of it and sunk its teeth into the artery below my ear. Horror reared inside me, but my Dhampir nature overrode it, bringing me back into control. With a well-aimed blow, I smacked the rat hard before it could latch on, sending it to the floor with a thump. It writhed for a moment, red eyes glaring malevolently at me as it died slowly. Painfully, I hoped.

I slapped my hand on the wound. I was bleeding, of course, but the bite had not penetrated to the artery. A gust of cool wind ruffled my hair. I snapped my head to the window to see the sash slide upward with no hand to guide it. My breath hitched, knowing it was here; the vampire was here. I saw it, barely—merely a shadow hovering outside in the night, although my chamber was three stories above the ground.

It began to climb inside and the rats went into a frenzy.

I glanced wildly around me, fighting a mounting feeling of being outmatched. I tried to remain calm, remain in control and obey the instincts in my blood that had served me well in the past. But I could not keep my eyes from the growing shape, a man's shape, impossibly tall with wide shoulders the breadth of the sash. The clatter of the rats' nails on the wood floor rose as they leaped over one another, snapping their powerful jaws in agitation and excitement. They were ready; they were coming for me.

I concentrated on the vampire in my room, and in a strange way that steadied me. This was a fiend I knew, one I had battled before. The disgust and repulsion at the sight, the feel, of the rats had undone me for a moment, but now I felt on familiar ground.

The vampire was inside now, towering above me in the little room, an enormous shadow in the shape of a giant, a monstrous male figure without a face—more terrible for its anonymity.

Then I realized suddenly that I could not reach my tools. What a fool I was to be caught unprepared! My confidence was once again shaken.

I realized how badly I had miscalculated. I had left myself unprepared.

Then, in the midst of my despairing bent of thought, I recollected something. I gasped as the idea took hold. I'd done something once with a pack of unearthly dogs Marius had sent to kill me. By the power of my will, I had turned their minds, warping the hold the vampire lord had on them, and set them to devour each other. Perhaps I could do a similar thing with these rats.

I reached out with my mind. However, I was instantly repelled by their primitive, bloodthirsty instincts. Bile rose in my throat. I was sick, no less than had I eaten their putrid flesh.

As I struggled to regain myself, I realized their sheer number was overwhelming me. Their leader was the one I should target. Did I dare? I'd once done mental battle with Marius. With this in mind, I flung out a dagger-like thought with my mind toward the creature hovering in the window. I sensed its hesitation. Its surprise?

Why would it be surprised? Unless—

It did not know I was Dhampir.

But then, why was I being attacked? What had I done to draw the attention of the vampire if not for the fact that I was its natural enemy?

Another rat bit me, sinking its teeth into my ankle, but it did not latch on, choosing instead to scuttle away quickly. I smiled, ignoring the blood it had drawn, for I saw the creature was not so brave now that I had killed a few of its comrades.

Leaping out of the bed, I landed square on the floor, sure-footed, and the rats scattered with a hail of high-pitched squeals, save one whose tail was pinned beneath my heel. I sidestepped, squeamish about the contact, and it scurried away, angrily hissing at me over its back. I thought fleetingly that I should have killed it instead of letting it escape, but I did not want to take the time.

I then turned to the window, and in a move I was certain shocked the creature hovering there, headed straight for the vampire. I made sure not to look at it directly, instead angling my sight to the left so our gazes did not connect. I had learned the hard way never to look a vampire in the eye.

On the chest of drawers lay my comb and my brush (why had I not unpacked my crucifix and hung it on the wall over my bed—I knew better!). I grabbed these, and a well-worn ribbon I'd tossed there when I'd taken down my hair. Quickly, I lashed the long silver handle of the brush with the comb, converting it quickly into a makeshift cross. In addition, the entire thing was of silver, which was repulsive to the undead. Still it was a puny weapon, but my brazenness, rather more than my weapon, brought the vampire up short.

The thing cringed, and as it did, it reversed through the window, flying backward without turning its back to me, as if the night itself had sucked it to its bosom. Then the rats swarmed over me, their tiny claws scrabbling up my legs.

I fought in horror as I whirled, swatting wildly at them. The vampire was escaping! I let out a cry of fury as it disappeared, with nothing but a rush of wind blasting me in my face to mark its departure. I reached out, trying to get to the window, but the solid muscular bodies of the rats weighed me down and their nails bit deep to secure a hold in my flesh. Their squealing was loud in my ears. I cried out, overcome by the repugnance and pain, and went down on one knee.

The comb and brush fell from my hand. I lunged for them, but a rat intercepted me and bit down hard on my hand, its teeth scraping bone. The pain was tremendous. I began to sob, drawing in wracking breaths as I struggled to think, to stand and fight! But I realized with dawning despair that I could not contend with this many, not even with a real weapon.

They began to bite me, sending me into twisting convulsions of pain as their ravenous mouths sank into my flesh over and over again. I rose and staggered against the wall and fought back as my consciousness wavered momentarily. My mind cast about desperately for what I might do to save myself. I had to think like a Dhampir, to use what I knew!

I thought of something. Losing no time, I battled against the pain and waded laboriously to the bed, kicking aside the rats that surged toward me. I fell to my knees and scrabbled desperately for my bag.

The vial of holy water was full, thank God. I wrenched it open with shaking hands and splashed the rats liberally. It set them immediately smoking, as if they'd been touched by fire, and they dropped with leaden thuds to the floor. Breathless and frantic, I spun, holding the vial out before me to show the others, threaten them with it. It was a bluff. I did not have enough to vanquish all of them, but I hoped they would not realize this.

The undulating mass flinched, shrinking back from my outstretched hand. Slowly, I stepped forward. I did not feel my bites, for I was intent on facing them down.

There was one moment when I did not know whether or not my ploy would succeed. They moved stubbornly, clustering against the far wall. I sensed they were loath to give up their advantage. *Go*, I prayed fervently. *Please go.*

Then they fled, moving as one mass, spilling over the windowsill and out into the blackness where I knew their master hovered unseen.

I waited in the silence left in the wake of their departure, garnering my wits and my strength before lifting myself up off the floor. When I could move, I threw the dead rats out the window, then I shut it tight. I pressed my forehead against the glass in relief, hearing nothing but the rasp of my own breathing, how it sawed rapidly, then slowed, quieted as my heartbeat slowly returned to normal. As it did, exhaustion filled me. My limbs felt heavy as lead, and I began to notice the pain from the bites. Heaving myself away from the window, I lit the lamp and inspected the wounds in the small pier glass.

They were not terribly serious; at least none appeared to require stitching. I washed each bite thoroughly, wincing at the sting when the cold water hit them. I would find some medicines in the apothecary tomorrow. For tonight, I did not think I could move, even to defend myself should the rats return.

I climbed into bed, but I did not feel safe. The vampire had gone for now. I had surprised him by fighting. He had not suspected I was a hunter.

But he would be back, in some manner, to get revenge. Neophyte though I was in the ways of the undead, I did know that much, and I vowed to myself that I must never allow myself to be caught unawares again.

Chapter Ten

I have no idea why I was the target of such an attack," I told Sebastian the following afternoon as we sat in his room at the inn. I'd come here as soon as I could get away. "I was able to drive it off only because I caught it off guard."

We were seated at the small table and chairs by the window. In the corner of the room, Father Luke lay fully dressed upon the bed. "It knows you are Dhampir now," he growled, his voice rough from his illness. "It is far more dangerous for you."

I smiled wanly. "It can kill me for one reason as well as the other."

Sebastian would not break his solemn look. "But what was the reason of the attack if not your being Dhampir?"

My smile faded. "I wish I knew. Then perhaps I'd have some clue to this entire mystery."

Sebastian sighed. His eyes flickered over me as he frowned. "Are you certain you do not wish me to look at those bites? You are certain you washed them thoroughly?"

I touched one of the bandages. I'd raided the apothecary closet that morning. "Yes, and salved each one before sealing them under a bandage. Do not worry, Sebastian. Our stillroom maid at home was talented at making medicines and instructed me well."

Father Luke rose up laboriously off the bed. "The vampire was afraid of you, you say."

"I said it was surprised," I clarified, then thought about this. "I suppose it was afraid. It ran off, didn't it? It was caught off its guard when it realized what I was."

"Hmm." He rubbed his chin. I saw his big, blunt-fingered hand still held a tremor, if only a slight one these days. "The Dhampir is rare, of course. No vampire makes the *strigoii vii* lightly, nor do they leave one of them unattended."

"Yes," I agreed, for I had read of this as well when I was at the archive. "The vampire world has great fear of us children. We are its only natural enemy."

Father Luke gripped the bedpost as he made his way toward us. "That is what I do not understand. If a Dhampir is identified, the news spreads quickly through revenant society so that all might beware."

I tensed, ready to rise to go to his aid, but Sebastian stopped me with a single raised finger and a quick shake of his head. I reluctantly remained in my seat.

Father Luke said, "Why was the news of you kept secret?"

"Wait," Sebastian said impatiently. "You forget I have not studied at a secret archive." He raised his eyebrows at me, then turned to Father Luke. "Nor am I member of a secret Vatican society of vampire extirpators. Please explain to me why those like Emma are rare."

"There is the belief," the priest said, his voice wheezing with the effort it took him to remain on his feet. Still, Sebastian made no move to help him. "There is the belief," Father Luke repeated, "that vampires prefer to kill their victims when they initiate them. This is not true, although it can happen. The *strigoii mort*, which we have told you about, is such a creature. It is to guard against this possibility why precautions are taken when a person dies under mysterious circumstances."

"Well, of course." Sebastian looked from me to Father Luke. "I recall the story you told of the gypsy that attacked you in Avebury, Emma. What was his name? Wadim?"

"Yes, he was one of Marius's minions. But he had been made *strigoii vii* first. That is the way the vampire prefers to do it, because to transform a person without giving it time to acclimate to its undead existence is very dangerous. The creatures that result are useful only as soldiers—they are vicious beyond imagining, although once trained they can be fiercely loyal."

"So it is not typical for a person to be killed by a vampire, then rise from the dead," Sebastian said. "I don't believe I understood that completely before. After all, it is how most of the legends have it, isn't it?"

"From the most primitive cultures, there has always been the knowledge of the vampire," Father Luke agreed. "Some of the particulars vary. In India, it is said *Kali* wears a necklace of skulls and has four arms. The Greek *vrykolakas* is believed to ape human behavior. In Scotland, *boabhan-sithe* are wild, uncivilized flesh-eaters." He nodded to me, adding, "You have studied all of this?"

"I have," I replied. "I have found, however, that when one looks closely, one sees commonalities."

Father Luke looked feverish as he grinned. "Of course, for their nature does not change any more than a human being is a different creature from another person with different customs and culture."

His eyes were bright, almost glazed. I grew concerned at this, then thought that perhaps it was not so much his illness (it was charitable to call what afflicted him an illness and I much preferred to think of it that way) but the intensity of his thoughts. His passions ran deep and hot on the subject of the vampire. Whatever loss he had experienced in his faltering faith, his dedication to eradicating the undead was not part of it.

"What are you thinking?" I inquired, suddenly aware that he had a theory he was in the process of sorting out.

"Among those traits all of the undead have in common is their propensity to fashion companions for themselves. The compulsion, even though it puts them at great risk, weakens them and makes them vulnerable while they recover their strength."

"Companions?" Sebastian said, his voice squeaking with alarm. "Do you mean like mates?" His powdered complexion grew paler, his eyes wide with horror. "My God, they mate?"

I patted his hand. "Not in the sense we think. They cannot reproduce, you know. They are dead, Sebastian."

"It is their great failing," Father Luke said. His eyes were hollow, his jaw too lean. The addiction had ravaged his once-powerful form, but had not blunted the sheer magnitude of the man. "Indeed, they need that nearly as much as they need blood. It makes them stupid and often careless, this great, burning need to not be alone."

"So they make . . . families?" Sebastian asked, incredulous. "Is that what you are saying? Families of undead?"

"Imagine the loneliness if you could never tell a single one of your thoughts to another," I said, attempting to explain. "Or laugh at a shared amusement, or be appreciated, or feel pride at the admiration of another for your intellect or accomplishment."

"I never thought those creatures felt anything," he groused.

"They do. The great lords do, certainly. That is why they take the great risk to make the *strigoii vii*. When a person becomes the living vampire, he retains his personality and all which made him unique. The *strigoii vii* are aware, thinking, even feeling beings. They are vampire, make no mistake, but in the aspect of their intellect and emotions they are human. Thus, when they die, their passage to the undead, the truly undead, is gentle, expected, anticipated, and they become sentient beings. They desire to form bonds, to connect and live with at least one comrade, usually their creator. After all, what creature, alive or undead, would wish to face eternity without the comforts of others like themselves?"

Sebastian seemed to be having a difficult time ingesting all of this. He shook his head as if confused. "If all this is so, and they yearn for the company of one another so badly, then why are there not whole cities of these fiends?"

Father Luke laughed, a low, vicious sound. "Ah, you forget their downfall, Sebastian: they are evil. You have only to consider what sort of person consents to the three bites. The weak, those without conscience, those who are already evil, the worst of humanity, by and large. And so they take their proclivities with them into their revenant life. Therefore, they are flawed, antisocial, unable to trust and be trusted, and so they are fated to create an unstable society filled with betrayal and strife, with constant feuding and chaos among their ranks."

"Well, that is a relief." Sebastian let out a breath. "It is good to know they have such a fatal weakness. Did you know all of this, Emma?"

"I knew some of these facts, but my time at the archive had not permitted me to delve into the matter to this much degree.

I admit, Father Luke, your conclusions about the inherently doomed world of the undead are illuminating, as well as heartening. But I have to wonder how it applies to our situation here at Blackbriar?"

He chuckled, the sound like a low rumble of thunder. "Ah, yes. I did digress, didn't I?" It was plain to see he was tiring. He even wavered, causing Sebastian to bolt to his feet and say, "You are going to exhaust yourself. Go on back to bed now. We will continue this discussion later."

"I am not returning to that bed," Father Luke said, and lowered himself into the seat Sebastian had vacated.

I was surprised Sebastian did not insist, for I could tell he was still concerned. "Very well. You may stay at the table *if* you do not exert yourself."

A snort from the priest preceded his very mildly spoken "Why, thank you."

Sebastian rolled his eyes.

"As we mentioned, the making of a new *strigoii vii* is of great impact in the vampire world for precisely the reasons you noted, Emma. Naturally, word of such a deed spreads quickly. There is, as noted, potential danger to all vampires from a future foe in the form of any child born to that living vampire. I need not go into great explanation on how the revenant world hates and fears the Dhampir. So all know of the *strigoii vii*. All know of any children from them."

Understanding dawned. I saw the same understanding come into Sebastian's eyes as he turned to stare at me in amazement. "But he did not know about you," he said.

That was right. Yes. I never realized the import of that fact before. "Neither did Marius, not until he and I met face to face," I added.

Sebastian looked from Father Luke back to me. "So that means . . . ? What? We could have assumed all along they didn't know about you, Emma, or else they would have killed you long ago."

I shook my head. "My understanding is that it is not easy to kill my kind. Even as children, the gifts we possess are formidable and arise instinctively in the presence of a vampire. That is what eventually happened to me in Avebury. But the important thing from this is to understand that if the vampire world is not aware of me, then that must mean . . ." I was suddenly overcome, my heart pounding as the words choked in my throat.

"What?" Sebastian demanded impatiently.

I swallowed, cleared the lump, and said, "It means my mother's existence is also unknown to them."

"She was made by a pariah," Father Luke stated, fatigue making his voice light and soft.

"A pariah," I repeated. "An outlaw vampire?"

Father Luke gave Sebastian and me a grave look, and said, "All pariahs are marked for destruction by the terrible Dragon Prince, the Dracula."

"After Marius discovered what I was," I said slowly, comprehension dawning, "the word would have spread—about me, and about my mother. Yet, this vampire knows nothing of Laura or me."

"More questions, and no more answers," Sebastian said soberly.

I sighed. "Very well, let us drop the subject for now. Sebastian, I will miss supper tonight when I return to school. Would you mind getting some cold meats for a quick meal here before I leave? I would do it myself, but I am attempting to avoid Mrs. Danby. You know how she disapproves of our meeting privately in your rooms."

Rolling his eyes, he sighed heavily in exasperation. "I am your cousin and he is a priest—what impropriety is there in that? Lud, that woman is a trial. Meddlesome baggage, she is." He headed for the door, still heated. "If it were not for her cooking, I would pitch a tent in the field behind the stable before I'd stay in this inn."

When the door closed, I angled an assessing look at Father Luke. "Your knowledge of vampires—of the entire revenant world—has grown considerably. I'll wager you did not study at one of the archives, so how did you learn so fast?"

His hands, set on the table, clenched into white-knuckled fists and his mouth contorted with shame. "I set out to find answers when I left you at Avebury. I was . . . Well, you and I spoke at the church, after it was over. You know what frame my mind was in at that time." His eyes narrowed, squinting into two fine lines. "I wanted answers. The Church refused to give them to me, so I decided to find my own.

"The lower-order fiends seek their society in the hells of great cities where the unfortunate and refuse of humanity mingle in unimaginable conditions. There they are free to feed off those who will never be missed. I found them easily enough."

"What do you know of the Dracula?"

"Ah, that. He is quite a mysterious figure." He shook his head. "I am afraid I must disappoint you for I know no more than what I have already said. Which is nothing but a name."

"I was not able to find out more than that in my research. Even the archive contains little. Marius undoubtedly had a connection to him, but I was never able to discover it." A thought dawned on me and I looked at him in amazement. "You said you talked to vampires? How in the world did you manage that?"

"Brutal methods, I am afraid." His tone was flat, unapologetic. "Remember, I was dealing with lower orders, not the more evolved. I simply tortured them until they told me what I wished to know."

"Tortured them?" I must have sounded shocked, for he laughed.

"You forget, I am still a priest," he told me. "I have powers, too."

I thought for a moment, then dared to ask, "Are you still a priest?"

The question caught him off guard. He took a moment to answer. "I love God. But the Church? I hate the ignorance and the power-mongering. I do not trust the part of it that is comprised of men—fallible, flawed men who are as subject to avarice and pride as the rest of us. But . . ." He paused, and seemed to realize something. "I cannot let it go. If you knew what it had meant to me, once . . ." He shook his head, as if ridding himself of this reflection as a dog might shed droplets of water. "It saved me. Not just my life, either, Emma. No, I am not leaving the priesthood. It is who I am. But I am not staying, not as I was. I am in my own little limbo, a purgatory of uncertainty."

He leaned in. His gaze was keen. "You said once that we were friends. I did not believe it then, but I came here because I knew you'd been right. After everything else failed me, you did not. We are friends. And friends should tell each other the truth." He smiled, and his smile was so warm and genuine, my heart wrenched. Here was the ghost of the man I'd known still alive inside the broken shell. "I can get my vestments if you like. I recall you found solace in the sacrament of Penance, though you are not Catholic."

I laughed, easier now. "No, no vestments, father. It is nothing to cause concern. It is just—about the *strigoii vii* being willing. I knew, of course, that this is the typical way a person is transformed, but what of others, who had not submitted willingly to the bite?"

"You speak of Mr. Fox."

I started, aghast at his knowledge of Valerian's condition. "You know?"

"It was not a difficult deduction to make. But never mind about him, this is not what is on your mind, I can tell by your reaction. What was it you came to know?"

I took a moment to compose myself. "My mother had to agree, did she not? She became *strigoii vii* and that means she had to give her consent."

"Oh, Emma," he said, his face contorting into a wince. "I am sorry. I did not realize."

"I think she changed her mind later, but when I spoke to my father's friend who was there during that period of her supposed 'madness,' he told me of a woman who wanted my father and sought to make my mother jealous. This happened at the onset of her illness. In a weak moment, she could have been seduced and said yes to the vampire in her desolation. I had not thought of it before, you see, about her being willing. But now I . . ." The words dammed up in my throat.

His hand, still strong, closed over mine. Its heat was as comforting as a blazing fire on winter's coldest day. "You must believe you will find your answers. In time."

"But what if . . ." What if they are horrible truths that I must face? What if my mother was not tragic, not reluctant, but one of the weak, evil ones Father Luke had spoken of? What if she had gladly traded her humanity for the chance to live forever?

Sebastian stomped into the room just then, muttering a tirade of epithets against the innkeeper. "I nearly had to wrestle the tray out of her hand! Stubborn woman," he raged.

The tirade was the perfect cure for my sadness. I made a fuss over the assorted meats, a fine loaf of crusty bread, and a carafe of Mrs. Danby's homemade wine. Father Luke rose, intent on retuning to the bed, but I scolded him soundly and he stayed, eating under my supervision while Sebastian gloated. "We shall gang up against you, you brute," he said with satisfaction. "You will be snapping tree trunks like twigs in no time."

It was a moment of such pleasantness—the three of us together sharing a modest repast—and it meant much to restore my spirit. When we finished eating, Sebastian took me down to the courtyard, intent on following me back to Blackbriar on horseback alongside the trap I'd borrowed to ensure my safety.

"That is ridiculous," I told him. "I have my bag with me. Should I come under attack, I would be worried about you. I can handle myself, Sebastian, as long as I am prepared."

These were courageous words. I did not mean them. I wished I did, and so hoped by putting on a brave face I might fool him. Maybe myself, as well.

"I will take you halfway, then. I want to take this chance to speak with you away from Father Luke. I do not wish him to know this—God knows what he will get into that thick skull of his to do—but there is another family gone missing in the village. A woman and her young child. The man is under suspicion, of course."

"You think that he has harmed them?"

"No, I think the vampire had them for its supper," he quipped sharply. "And that poor man will swing for it unless we intervene."

I shook my head. "No, Sebastian. I can take on nothing else. I am doing my best as it is, and it is not enough. It is not—"

"Emma, Emma—I did not mean for you to worry about this. I will see to it, as much can be done. I wanted you to know, that is all. You are, after all, our de facto leader."

I swallowed at that. It was a daunting title, and yet I knew it was true. "I am a wreck. Forgive my snapping at you."

He took me all the way to the edge of Blackbriar lands and I rode the rest of the way by myself. Upon arriving at the school stables, I made quick work of getting the horse brushed and safely into its stall without disturbing the groom. That done, I slipped unseen into the building. I met up with no one as I crept upstairs, but just as I was about to enter my bedchamber, a small shadow lurking in the hallway startled me.

"My God, Eustacia!" I exclaimed as I recognized her. My hand withdrew from the bag I had slung over my shoulder, where it had already closed about a sharpened stake.

The girl was wide-eyed and wan as she stepped into the light cast by the wall sconces. Her appearance alarmed me. "What is it?" I demanded. "Is something wrong? Is someone hurt?"

"I was afraid you had been . . . The girls said she would come to you. Mrs. Andrews, you are in danger!"

I took a step toward her, but that was the wrong move. She shied away, and I realized she was here on a thread of courage that might snap at any moment. "Do you mean Margaret? Vanessa? Did they threaten me?"

"She did," Eustacia said.

"Who, darling?" I urged. I almost reached out my arms to give her comfort, but constrained myself.

She began to cry silently, fast-moving tears streaming down her cheeks. I could see the struggle within her. She wanted so badly to tell me, but her terror would not let her. "We are all alone," I promised in a whisper. "And I will never speak of what you tell me to anyone. I vow it. Who said they would harm me, Eustacia?"

She shook her head, backing away. I did move then, suddenly so as to surprise her. I grasped her by the shoulders, my voice steady. "Who is this *she*?"

"I do not know!" she wailed. She struggled in my hands, but I clamped down, gripping her cruelly.

"Tell me," I commanded. But I knew, even before she hissed the name through trembling lips.

"They call her the Cyprian Queen!"

My hands went numb. Eustacia slipped away as I stood stunned in the dimly lit hall.

That night, I dreamed of my mother. She was pale as snow, her lips livid crimson, her eyes black and flat and devoid of expression or intelligence. She leaned over me, her mouth gaping into a lurid smile. I wanted to scream, but in the dream, the sound choked me, closing, tightening in my throat until I could not breathe.

I saw the elongated teeth, gleaming like Diana's moon on a velvet midnight sky. Light glinted off them, as it does on fine steel, and a small scarlet tongue darted out in anticipation.

"No. Stop."

My words came out slowly, painfully. I was unable to call out, even to beg for my life.

Then she changed. Her face became the one I knew, the image of the portrait I'd studied as a child. It was a soft face, pretty in repose. Uncle Peter had told me she could dazzle an entire room. I had no memories of her, save one sad one of her weeping that had come to me only recently, so I had had to imagine those features animated. Here, in my dream, I saw the rosebud mouth curve into a soft smile. The eyes, no longer dead, shined down at me with love.

I reached for her. But she began to fade away, as if pulled by some unseen force. The farther away she got, the more she struggled to return to me. A shadow fell between us, and I looked up at a towering figure, large, muscular, broad, with something of a bully's face and a pugilist's physique.

He smiled at me, as if we shared a secret. I saw, then, two men behind him, wearing metal-plated armor fashioned into breastplates and short skirts. Sandals bound their feet. One carried a spear, the other a sword. There were chains in one's hand, and they led to the large man's wrists and ankles.

With two fingers, he traced the shape of a cross in the air, first one long down stroke, then the cross stroke, but this latter he did at the lower end: it was the inverted cross, the sign of the devil, of black magic. Of witchcraft.

I awoke, breathless and drenched in sweat. Leaping out of bed, I checked the windows and my door. The fine line of salt I'd drizzled on the sill to seal it was unbroken. I lit the candle and inspected the room, listening intently for the scuttling sound of rats. When I was certain I was safe, that it had been nothing but a dream, I crawled back into my bed. I was exhausted. I needed sleep. I curled up tight under the coverlet, clutching my crucifix in one hand and a vial of holy water in the other.

Chapter Eleven

I was no longer going to be denied or thwarted; I would have the story of my mother today. This was my resolve when I awoke, and I hurried to breakfast, found Eloise Boniface and told her in no uncertain terms that I must speak with her without delay. I led her, rather mystified, away from her toast and coffee and pulled her into the salon.

"I know you remembered something about my mother," I said without preamble. "I would like not to wait any longer for you to tell me what it is."

"Dear Emma, please do not be so disconcerted. The event I recollected was of no import, really. I simply thought you might find it interesting."

There was trepidation in her tone and on her face and I realized how I must have come off. Given my state of mind—after yesterday's discussion and my restless night—my lack of tact was not surprising. I tempered myself. "I am having dreams, you see. I thought if we talked, it might help put to rest some of the wild imaginings that have come over me."

It was not exactly a lie. Not the truth, either—not completely. But it worked. Eloise's expression changed from one of mild alarm to compassion. "Poor dear. I should never have said anything in the first place."

"You mentioned an accident. What happened?"

"Laura had a bad fall, you see. Your mother was a dreadful horsewoman, did you know?"

Unexpectedly, I laughed. "No, I did not, but as it happens, so am I."

Eloise smiled. "Yes, well, despite Laura's lack of skill, she liked to be alone, so she would ride during her free time, to get away, you know. Alistair was the son of the hired man here and he worked with his father. He was infatuated with your mother, though no one knew it, not even Laura, I'll wager. But it turned out to be fortuitous one day when she was out alone, for she was thrown from her horse and seriously injured. She probably would have died, but Alistair had followed her, you see, and seen the fall. He took her to his mother, who was a local woman, good with herbs. And though people called her a witch and other dreadful names—you know how they whisper about odd folk—Winifred was kindness itself—"

"Winifred?" I exclaimed, remembering at once the upside-down tombstone in the wall of the Rood and Cup. But no, I corrected myself. Surely that had to have been placed long before this Winifred lived, and died, for the events being spoken of had taken place a mere score and ten years ago and the hearth wall at the inn was far older than that.

"Yes, that was her name. She was well known for being a healer. If you had the headache or an attack of bile, she was the one who would mix you something and make you feel right. So that was why Alistair took her there, and the headmistress at the time allowed it, as it was sensible to have her tend Laura."

"Did my mother fall in love with him as well?" I asked.

"Heavens, no, dear, for all he tried, and his mother, too, when she saw how her son doted on Laura. I cannot fault your mother. Forgive me for putting it this crudely, but he was unsightly. He was so tall, and wretchedly thin, and he forever had this very dour expression. Now, I believe Laura was fond of Alistair, but not in the same fashion as he was of her. He was something of a self-taught man, and they shared a passion for the classical literatures. I believe she thought of him as a friend but nothing more."

"But she regarded him well?"

"Oh, yes. I recollect she was quite enthused about him when she returned to school. She spoke of how well-read he was, how he had educated himself in the library of the Suddington residence, for his father and he maintained the property when the family was away, as they often were for long periods of time. Oh, your mother was very impressed with Alistair's knowledge of mythology, history, and literature. She liked him quite well and for a time after she returned to the school, they spent a great deal of time together due to their shared interest in these subjects. Then it all came to a head when he gave her that necklace. It was a wretched, ugly thing, not the sort of thing any Christian woman would wear. Imagine, a thing like that with that terrifying dragon on it—"

I started. "A dragon?"

"He had stolen it, and we all knew it, and where he had gotten it."

"Holt Manor," I said, remembering the necklace from the portrait Lord Suddington had shown me.

"Exactly. He was always lurking about that place, as if he belonged there! He thought better of himself than he was. Young Alistair was somewhat obsessed with that house."

"What happened to the necklace?"

"It was returned, and there was no real harm done. After that, Laura began to grow uncomfortable and she put an end to all of it."

I leaned forward anxiously. "What do you mean? That was the end of the friendship?"

"That was the end of Alistair." Eloise waved her hand as if to demonstrate the justifiable dismissal of the thief. "He was disgraced. After all, he had stolen an heirloom from the most prominent family in the neighborhood. Laura was right to turn in the necklace, and cut him off without a word afterward."

"What happened to him?" I felt myself tense. Somehow, this sign of the Dracula had to be significant.

I was disappointed, however, when Eloise shrugged and told me, "His mother sent him away and we never saw him again." She studied me, and frowned. "Oh, do not look so, dear Emma. Yes, I know it is not much of a story, not for a daughter seeking to learn of her mother when she was a young lady. You see this is why I wish you had not made so much of my small recollection. It was nothing so important, not even of much interest, I'll wager."

"That is not true," I replied honestly. "I have always been eager for any information about my mother. No matter how small or insignificant this memory might be to you, it means a great deal to me." I hesitated. "Let me ask you a question of a completely different sort. I am trying to find out information about something known as the Cyprian Queen. Have you heard any mention of such a thing?"

Eloise blinked and seemed bemused by my question. "No. What is that, dear?"

"I am not sure." I sighed. "It seems some of the girls are

talking about it. From what I have gathered, I am not certain it is wholesome."

She raised her eyebrow. "The . . . Cyprian Queen? As in the queen of Cyprus?"

"Mrs. Boniface! Mrs. Andrews!" a sharp voice cut in. Miss Sloane-Smith had come up behind us, and by the look of her, with her high color and sternly set jaw, she was in a temper. "What is this nonsense? Should you not be with your classes?"

I rose. "As a matter of fact, we were just finishing our conversation."

Eloise seemed oblivious to the headmistress's state as she gathered her knitting and headed for the door. "I must be getting my classroom in order myself."

I followed her out, but Miss Sloane-Smith waited at the door and grabbed my arm, silently staying me. I stared at her, but she did not meet my gaze until we were alone. The glare she gave me then took me aback. "I will not have nonsense spread about my school. We have had a difficult year, and I want all to go smoothly from here on out."

"I am sure I agree," I told her.

"Why were you asking about the Cyprian Queen?"

I froze for a moment, then answered carefully. "I was curious. I heard some things—"

"When I retained you, you assured me you did not listen to gossip!"

I glanced meaningfully to where her hand gripped my arm, and after a moment, she released me. I thought I saw the blaze of hatred flare in her eyes before just as quickly subsiding. It clearly galled her that she could not terrorize me as she did Miss Easterly and the others.

Drawing in a steadying breath, she said, "I do not know what you meant, bringing up this thing, this Cyprian Queen, but I do not want it mentioned again. Am I making myself clear?"

"Why?" I snapped, my pride stealing my good sense. I could not help myself; she reminded me so much of Judith.

"Because it is nonsense, that is why. Dangerous nonsense far beneath the attention of a teacher of this school." She leveled a finger at me and began to point. "We do not deal with superstition, Mrs. Andrews. It is bad for the school."

I was stunned by her fervor. She knows, I thought suddenly. She knew about the Cyprian Queen!

I could hardly demand she tell me. Lord, how I wanted to shake her, to rail at her to open her eyes to what was going on. People had died, and she wanted only to bury the happenings as deeply as possible. That was deadly, I was convinced.

Ironically, it was to Judith's credit I maintained my composure. All of those critical lectures on my overly "warm" nature had left their mark, and I held my tongue, nodding to show I understood.

She left me then, and I closed my eyes, taking in deep breaths to steady me. But I was shaken. Deeply shaken, and equally determined Miss Sloane-Smith would give up her secrets one way or another.

A few days later, there was great rejoicing in the village of Blackbriar. The woman, Rose, who had gone missing a week ago along with her child had returned. She offered no explanation for her absence, but it was generally acknowledged that some nefarious man had seen her, wanted her, and taken her but that she'd managed to escape with her child, although she could not bring herself to speak of her ordeal. So many had gone missing in recent months, never to be seen again, it was considered a veritable miracle by all that she and her child had come home safely.

Sebastian and I knew better. When the rumors of her sickness—nerves, it was said—reached us, we paid special heed. It appeared she had developed a severe depression. She abhorred light. She was found wandering in the night. She had no appetite and suffered severe moodiness.

We digested this news soberly. We understood clearly what had happened to Rose, and perhaps her child. And what we had to do.

I arrived at the inn just before dawn, once again sneaking out of the school and into Sebastian's rooms without detection. "My bag is down in the trap, behind the inn."

"Excellent. The timing should be good. James, her husband, will be gone before the sun comes up. And she will be weak. But we must hurry. We don't want it to get too late and risk being seen by anyone else."

Father Luke stepped forward. "I am coming with you," he said, shouldering the bag Sebastian had prepared.

I balked at the idea. "Absolutely not," I insisted. "You are not strong enough."

Sebastian was not so kind. "You will be a hindrance."

"If I drop dead on the spot, let me lie there, then," the priest growled as he pulled on a woolen coat. "I am not allowing the two of you to go out there alone."

"It is my job," I said with an effort at patience.

He leaned in close to me, frightening me a little. "It is my job to save souls."

"Ah, here is the righteous avenger for God!" Sebastian exclaimed, throwing up his hands. "You were not so devout wallowing in the opium hell I found you in."

"Sebastian!"

"He needs to be made to see sense."

"I need to cease being treated as a child!" Father Luke thundered.

"You are an invalid," Sebastian yelled back, completely undaunted by the priest's towering rage.

The priest's lips peeled back as he surveyed Sebastian. "Now enough discussion," he said at last with soft menace. "Neither of you have the physical means to stop me, despite my weakened state, and we are wasting time."

There was no more arguing after that.

The cottage was a humble but neatly kept dwelling on the edge of the south woods, a few miles from the cobbled streets of the village. We pulled the trap I'd brought from the school behind a thick tangle of brambles set a little way off. Father Luke took up a position nearby to keep guard while Sebastian and I crept close.

"The husband is gone," I whispered, pointing to a row of boots by the back door. A pair made for slender feet—woman's feet—and a tiny pair for a child. I paused, staring at those boots. They were very small indeed. Dear God.

"I wonder if he has noticed anything," Sebastian said.

I unpacked my crucifix, tucking it under my arm, and I handed two stakes to Sebastian. "We could be wrong, you know. Perhaps she was merely abducted." I kept looking at those little boots. "We must be certain. Here, hide these. Where is the vial . . . ? All right. We must be very quiet."

"Will she not be asleep? I thought vampires sleep during the day."

"If she is *strigoii vii* then she can endure sunlight, though it will weaken her." I paused. "I think."

He braced a hand on my shoulder. "You will do well. Have confidence."

That was easier said than done. I did not feel at all confident. I never did, not until the moment I had to do these unspeakable things to survive.

The door was not locked. We entered the house, Sebastian surprisingly stealthy by my side. The dwelling was simple: a hearth with a table and chairs at one end of a long room, a window and several chairs at another. I saw a basket with a modest selection of well-used toys by a chair with sewing draped over it, as if the mother and child had just left but a moment ago.

"The bedroom," I said, barely audible, and we advanced.

The room was in disorder, and as dark as a cave. We could barely make out the two figures on the pallet. The mother lay on her side, curled like a question mark around the child, a cherubic-faced boy with a cap of straw hair.

My equilibrium dipped, and I had to blink rapidly to gain my head. The child was beautiful. Grabbing Sebastian, I repeated, "We must be very, very sure."

He nodded, squeezing my hand back, and I silently unsealed the vial of holy water. I readied my cross, and averted my gaze from that beautiful child. Then I nodded to Sebastian.

Let me be wrong.

My hopes were dashed once the first droplets of holy water hit the sleeping woman. The pain of their contact with her skin brought her awake with a deafening shout. The child beside her woke as well, eyes at once alert and malignant, all beauty gone.

I immediately wielded the crucifix, and the pair cringed in unison against their pallet, the woman hissing like a cornered asp as she closed her hands protectively about her child.

My own words came back to me, of how the *strigoii vii* retain their identities, still think and feel. She still loved her child, although she was no longer human. My stomach lurched sickeningly, but my hand was steady when I held it out for the stake. Sebastian thrust it into my hand, and my fingers closed on it, strong and sure as I brought it up, aiming it like a spear with the point trained on the woman's undead heart.

"Please," she pleaded.

I could not allow myself to think of her as a mother. She was not even a person, not any longer.

But the child . . .

"Emma," Sebastian said, and his voice snapped me back into focus.

"My name is Rose," the thing mewled. "Do not kill me. I am helpless, see? We are helpless. Please. *Please.* Do not kill my baby. My little Jamie."

"You are already dead," I replied, and lunged.

It was not artful, or done with particular finesse. But it was effective. She surged up, one hand grasping the pole as I drove the tip in deeply. There was no blood, for that source of life did not run in her veins as she had not fed recently, it appeared. The heart I skewered did not pump. For all her presentation of vitality, she was nothing but a corpse.

I stood over my work, taking a moment to study the thing that had once been a young wife and mother. I was not un-feeling, but neither did I have any remorse, and my thoughts strayed to my mother and whether or not I would one day stand over her dead body, just like this, and how I would bear it.

The sound of the door being flung open behind me startled me out of these disturbing thoughts. I spun around, my mallet raised in defense. A man stood in the doorway. By the look of horror on his face, I knew he must be the woman's husband. I braced myself, ready should he show himself to be a vampire. But his eyes were filled with anguish as they stared at his dead wife.

"What have you done?" he wailed, then rushed toward me. I threw up my hands in defense, but he shoved me aside and made directly for the baby, who was wailing plaintively and holding its hands out for its father.

"No!" I screamed, realizing what would happen.

But it was too late. The child was a vampire; it craved blood and the guidance of its mother was gone. As soon as its father had it in his arms, the tiny mouth opened. I think the man saw this, for he froze, horror-stricken as his son surged up at his neck, jaws working.

The father yelled, this time a terrible keening sound of a heart in agony, as he flung the child from him. The little vampire rolled, landing on all fours and remaining crouched, its rabid little eyes fastened hungrily on the man. A thunder of footsteps brought me around and I saw Father Luke burst into the room, his face as pale as snow.

"It's the father. Get him out of here," I directed sharply. "He should not see this."

The thing's father shouted again, this time in fear. I turned to find him backwheeling rapidly as the boy scrabbled toward him, mouth red from the blood he'd drawn, thirsting for more. The air was redolent with the sickening, raw smell of blood.

Father Luke, powerful even weakened as he'd been from his illness, effortlessly grabbed the father by the scruff of his neck and pulled him back, then out of the room. The child screamed in protest, a sound far beyond human. It turned to me, then, and I braced myself.

I closed my eyes—even I could not watch what needed to be done—and then I planted my foot on the child's back and drove the second stake in a downward arc. The thing—I refused to think of it as a baby any longer—wriggled like a mighty sturgeon on a harpoon, its strength astounding me. The sounds . . . I discovered I was screaming myself to drown out the noise and then . . . then it was still. Still and, at last, silent.

I sucked in a great gasp of air, as if coming out of the depths of the ocean. I found that I was unable to open my eyes.

"Emma." Sebastian's arms came around me, drawing me up from where I knelt over the body.

I threw off his hands and ran.

In the outer room, I confronted Father Luke and the man. Poor fellow. He was a husband and father no more. His eyes met mine, and I saw he'd known, or at least suspected, for though there was horror, grief, shock in his face, there was relief as well. He must have suspected something was terribly wrong when his wife and child had returned to him different in a way that had to have frightened him.

I felt like I was suffocating. I ran outside, past him, my chest heaving as I tried to draw in clean air. I could smell the blood even out here, and so I stumbled away from the cottage, trampling the dried stalks of herbs Rose had planted. The crushed plants filled the air with sweetness. I felt my gorge rise in my throat, my stomach not being too steady to begin with.

I made it to the edge of the copse before going down on my knees. I fought nausea, determined not to give in. As I sucked in great gulps of air, I heard Father Luke's voice behind me, explaining to the poor man what had happened, and assuring him that he and Sebastian would dispose of the bodies. I knew I should get up, help them, but I could not. I was spent.

A sound, a movement, brought my attention up. My eyes were filmed with unshed tears but I could see through my blurred sight a wolf, standing still as a statue up near the tree line. It was huge, with thick fur, staring at me with eyes as gray as the sky before a snowstorm.

I was not afraid. The creature appeared calm, even intelligent as our gazes met and held. My physical discomforts faded. I slowly came to my feet.

It turned slowly, and walked toward the trees. Without thinking, without question, I followed, walking at first, then breaking into a run to keep up with the wolf as it led me deep into the forest.

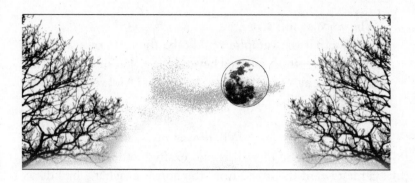

Chapter Twelve

The morning mists that had burned off in the clearing still clung to the ground, twisting over the grass like the ghosts of serpents. I wanted to escape the scene at the cottage, what I'd done. And the wolf was so beautiful. I had no sense of danger, even when a low growl penetrated my thoughts. I pulled up fast, breathless and exhilarated from my run. The wolf was standing in front of me, facing me now. Then, slowly, it came toward me.

Words floated from nowhere into my consciousness: *I set the trap for you, and you came. You did not disappoint me. I know you now. How pleased I am to find you, sister.*

A small part of my mind beat frantically against the actions of my body, called out for me to run away, run as fast as I could back to the carnage, to my friends. To that terrible, dead child.

The voice again: *Come.*

I knew that the vampire could take the form of a wolf. All vampires can—those evolved beyond the stages of the slavering newly born, anyway. Of course I knew this. And yet I remained transfixed, even jubilant, as it advanced.

Sister . . .

Where was my fear? Where was my skill? Ah, but I was filled with a sense of well-being, exalted and immobilized at it came toward me, freed from the horror of what I had done. The cautious voice I'd heard in my head a moment ago was but a faraway whisper now.

Let me show you something beautiful.

The first touch was a lance of pleasure, taking me to my knees. I sucked in sharply as a second shard of sensation bit into my body. My bones had no substance, and I melted into a heap on the ground.

There was no one around me, just the wolf still two dozen or so paces off. I stood, panting in reaction. What had I just felt?

Then again, an invisible hand traced a light pattern up my back, riding the ridges of my spine. I cried out, spinning about—but no one was there! I felt it again. Underneath my clothes, my skin rippled as though my naked flesh had been lightly brushed with the gentlest fingertip.

Even as my body responded, my mind recoiled. I hissed in a breath as it—whatever *it* was—cupped my breast, then pinched me. I tried to cover myself but nothing I did stopped the feeling of being touched so intimately. I moaned loudly in desperation to be free as greedy unseen fingers slid up my thigh. This *thing's* insidious touch was everywhere, yet there was no one here with me, nothing around save the wolf who calmly watched me with its translucent eyes, solemn, mysterious.

This was the vampire, it had to be—but why did I not see it?

The Dhampir was supposed to be able to see vampires in their invisible form and yet I saw nothing. I was alone, as wave after wave of the unwelcome pleasure stole over me. Stole into me.

Give yourself to me. To the pleasure I can bring.

I thought I heard my name, shouted from far away. I could not tell if it were spoken by friend or foe, but I could not answer in either case.

Here is my servant.

Out of the woods strode a figure. Confident, smiling, tall and lean. I blinked, and recognized the Irish boy. His face was blank, hardened so I barely recognized him. What was he doing here?

"Help me," I said.

He seemed shocked. "What?" He took a step forward, confused. "Don't you want it?"

I shook my head violently, wheeling away from him when he extended his hands to me. I scratched hard at my body, nails digging in to where my flesh tingled. Tears spilled onto my cheeks, but my voice was locked in my throat. I remembered the feel of the rats. This touch was a thousand times more repulsive than their devouring mouths.

When I looked up again, the Irish boy was gone.

I heard shouts nearby and I opened my mouth to call back, but only gasped as a terribly invasive feeling breached my thighs. My voice gone, I folded into a protective coil onto the ground.

Let the coward flee.

The wolf began to pace in agitation. I reached out to it with my mind, hoping to make contact with it, which was what I'd done before in Avebury when confronted by vampire minion wolves, but I could not concentrate.

"Emma."

Was that someone calling to me? Or merely my imagination? I could not tell. I mewled in desperation, twisting feebly, ineffectively, to escape the sensations of a lover's hand.

The seductive voice cooed to me: *Do not resist.*

I began to pray, muttering fragments of prayers I'd memorized in Latin. Immediately, I felt a reaction ripple through the air, and for a moment I was free.

I heard him: *No!*

"Get away," I managed.

A low chuckle was my only response, and I felt a touch so intimate I split the air with a wail of rage and disgust. My hands went to where I felt him—it—and clawed to get it away.

"Emma!" I heard my name called out again, louder now. The grip that held me trapped let up slightly, only to renew when I strained against it.

"Emma!"

That voice! I was delirious. I had to be. In my desperation, my mind had gone to *him*. But he was not here. He'd abandoned me long ago.

The wolf snarled, his haunches bunching as voices grew closer behind me. A form darted past me, and as I lay on the ground, I knew I was hallucinating. The man I saw was neither of the slight, boyish build of Sebastian, nor of the large-framed Father Luke. Slender, athletic, he sprinted past more swiftly than any mortal man. I only got a glimpse of dark hair, and a face set in grim lines.

The world spun, and I felt as if I'd been tossed down a towering cliff. This new cruelty far surpassed anything I'd endured so far. My heart broke, finally, completely, and I began to cry, openly, loudly, in great convulsions.

Then someone cradled me in capable hands and lifted me into the air as if I were but a doll. I beat against the form, finding solid flesh this time, a human masculine breast.

It was by his scent I knew. It is strange how memory works. Had I been asked a day ago if Valerian Fox's skin held a particular smell, I would not have remembered. But the moment it hit my senses, I knew who held me. My disorientation was banished.

Was I incoherent, to think he was here, bearing me away from that unspeakable violation? This was a dream, a wish. He could not really be here now.

But I could feel him. A man's coat felt crisp and thick under my palm. When I turned my head, there was masculine roughness against my cheek. I felt the soft press of a kiss at my temple.

"She is insensate," he said. Again, his voice, floating over me like a soft rain. He twisted me in his arms, and I knew he wanted to look at me. I was afraid to meet his gaze. I was afraid this was nothing but a dream, and if I awakened, he would disappear.

I swallowed hard, braced myself, and raised my eyes.

The swarthy, saturnine face of Valerian Fox hovered for a moment in my vision, faintly out of focus, then suddenly clear. The strong, finely wrought nose, the elegantly turned mouth that could be cruel or sensitive according to his mood, the angular jaw, the heavy-lidded eyes—all these features that were so familiar, so utterly *known*. I was suddenly aware of relief, as if I'd been holding my breath for a long, long time and I could at last breathe.

"Emma," he murmured, touching my face. "Are you in pain?"

Pain? Memory returned, and I cringed. It had been worse than pain. It had been a foul perversion of pleasure. I shook my head, and he stared at me, confused. "You are bleeding," he stated.

"Where have you been?" I asked.

His features were softened with concern and tenderness. He

spoke comfortingly. "Time later for that. There is blood all over you. Is it yours? Are you injured?"

I had little patience for talking about blood or injuries. I had a hundred questions that demanded answers. "I . . . I don't know."

"We shall get you to a doctor," he pronounced, and turned to Sebastian with me still snugly in his arms.

Sebastian replied, "The doctor is a sod. I would not trust him with her, but there is a woman not far away, Serena Black. I purchased some draughts from her, to help the priest."

"Is she a healer?"

"The draughts did what she promised, that is all I can say."

I heard the grimness in Valerian's tone. "Then lead the way."

"Father Luke," I said. "Where is he?"

Sebastian explained, "He will bring the trap back to the school and wait for me to fetch him. Do not worry, I told him to have a care not to be seen."

I shook my head. Father Luke must be weakened—how could he be expected to perform such a task in his present state?

The matter was taken out of my hands as Valerian strode back through the woods with me in his arms. He was not *strigoii vii*, nor, in fact, any kind of vampire, but he had the blood of the vampire in him. It made him not immortal but possessed of incredibly long life and slowed aging, with abnormally sharp senses and superior strength.

Thus it was that he swung astride his great stallion while holding me, all with very little effort. We sped across the wide moorlands, Sebastian following.

I was numb, withdrawn. I did not want to feel and so I remained wooden in Valerian's arms when he bore me to the ground once we reached our destination.

"What is wrong with her?" Sebastian's voice inquired anxiously.

"She is in shock." There was a short pause, and the strain

in his voice increased. "The blood is hers. She is covered with wounds."

I heard rapping at the door, voices speaking. From my well of paralysis, I heard a woman stridently order me to be brought inside. She told the men to leave, and Valerian argued. Then we were alone, she and I. I was in the hands of a stranger.

"I am Serena Black," she told me in a gentle Slavic accent. I tried to focus on her face, but my eyes were drawn by the glint of metal. She held a knife, the edge gleaming in the light. She brought it toward me and, with a flick of her wrist, she cut into the sturdy wool of my bodice and peeled away a blood-soaked strip. I cried out, clutching the shred to me. My hands, slick with my own blood, closed around her wrist. I could not be naked. I *could not*.

Her palm came down hard on my cheek, snapping my head back. The shock of the slap jolted me out of my hysteria. I lay unmoving under her ministrations, wanting Valerian. I wanted to feel him, hear his low, rumbling voice soothing me. But he had abandoned me again.

My consciousness bobbed like a cork breaking the surface of reality, in and out. When I was awake, everything was faded, far away. When I was not, there was peace.

"The wolf did that to her?" Was that Valerian speaking? I had not dreamt him? "The gashes are many, but not terribly deep."

The woman's voice answered. "Her nails were clotted with blood. She did it to herself."

A beat of silence. "Why would she do such a thing?" When the woman did not answer, he continued, "Is there risk of fever?"

"But little. I will make her a draught to ward off infection."

"You are a healer then?"

There was a low laugh. The woman's reply, however, bore no amusement. "Have you not heard? They call me witch."

I heard breathing even before I opened my eyes.

She was there, in a chair drawn up close to my side of the bed. A lamp on the table between us cast shadows on her lap where she'd laid her sewing. She was watching me, and when my gaze lifted to hers, she leaned forward. "I am Serena Black," she said.

"I remember. The witch."

She smiled. Her mouth was full-lipped and her eyes, the same coal-black as her hair, were perfectly almond-shaped. Her look was very Slavic, with flat, high cheekbones and a small, sultry mouth. She was breathtakingly lovely. "Some say."

"Are you the Cyprian Queen?"

Her smile froze into a rictus. "No. I am not that."

I settled back. "I do not feel any pain."

She nodded. "It is best."

"Do you know . . . ? Do you know what happened to me?"

She stared at me, and fatigue pulled me back into the void before I got my answer.

When I woke again, she was still there. I sat up and asked for water, which she gave me from a pitcher and glass she had ready at my bedside.

"Your man will be back for you in the morning. I sent him away. He was underfoot, and I had no patience for it."

"He is not my man," I said in a rough voice. "How long have I been sleeping?"

"A day, perhaps." She lowered her gaze to where her hands were working swiftly with her needle. "What were you doing at the Woodcock cottage?"

I blinked, confused. "Where?"

"Rose, and her baby. James said that the man who abducted

his wife and child came back for them and now they are gone."
She gave an expressive shrug, and did not seem overly sympathetic. Her gaze was sharp on me. "But I know what you did. I
saw you. You and the other man, the one who came to me for
the draughts to help his friend."

Cold dread flowered in my chest as I digested this. "You
mean . . . you saw us?"

"Do not worry, for I know what you are. I am familiar with
the Dhampir. In my country, such things need not be secret.
But here . . ." Another shrug, and her needle began to move
again.

"Your country. Where are you from?"

"The Ukraine. I am from the city of Odessa." She leaned
forward. "Do you know what happened to you?"

I tried to think about the forest, but my head hurt too much.
"I could see nothing. I can always see vampires when they are
invisible to others, but there was nothing there."

"But you did see it. The wolf—you kept talking about the
wolf in your sleep."

"The . . . attack . . . was different. It was like . . . it was as if
an incubus were . . . Could it be some demon—?" I cut off, rec-
ollecting the book on witchcraft I'd found in Margaret's room.

"I did not see much. I did not get close. I cannot afford to be
caught there. There is already too much superstition about me,
because I am foreign."

"Why were you at the cottage?"

"The same reason as you. No, I am not Dhampir. I would
not have killed it—what she had become. I thought perhaps the
baby had not been made over, so I went with some protections
for it, in case it was still living—garlic, salt, these things."

I winced as a clear image of the child came into my mind.
"He had been."

"Yes. I know now."

I sighed, my thoughts slowing. I thought suddenly of Miss Sloane-Smith, who would be angry wondering where I was. "Did anyone send word to the school?"

"That other man, the little one with the fussy curls who knew to bring you to me. He came to me before, for tonics to help the opium sickness. He said to tell you that you are not to worry and that he will take care of everything. You are only to rest. Your man will be back for you soon."

I relaxed, but I said again, "He is not my man."

Her lush mouth pulled into a wry, knowing smile, but she said nothing. Picking up her sewing, she began to hum a lullaby. Despite my efforts not to, I slept again.

Chapter Thirteen

Valerian was there when I woke again. It was a new day, and the sun was just clearing the eastern horizon.

He did not smile at me. The sun fell on his face, casting the angular chin and pointed cheekbones in crude shapes of light and shadow. He slowly leaned forward and took my limp hand in his, then stayed there, head bowed over it as he stroked it gently.

I looked down and saw the scratches on my arms. My nails had been cleaned, but I could still see traces of blood. I remembered Serena saying I had done this damage to myself.

Valerian did not speak, and neither did I, not for a long while. Finally, he said, "You were to study in Denmark for the winter."

"My plans changed."

"I . . ."

I what? What would he say? I am sorry. I should have written you. I should have given you a place to contact me so that you would not be here alone without me?

I should have never left you?

"I thought you safe," he said at last. "But apparently you have not been, not at all. Sebastian has caught me up on what brought you here, and all that has been happening since."

"Good. I've not the energy to explain."

There was a long silence again. He wanted me to look at him, but I would not.

"If anything had happened to you," he said, his voice like gravel, harsh and strained with emotion, "I would never have forgiven myself for leaving you."

I clenched my teeth together and slipped my hand out of his grasp.

He bowed his head. "I owe you an explanation."

"No."

He cut a dark, blazing glare at me as emotion played on his sharp features. "Too much stands between us for it to be as I would have it."

"I do not care," I said, trying to appear convincing. "Your life is your own to command."

"But my will is not."

"You think that is enough?"

"You speak as if I am free."

I said, "You are speaking in riddles," although I knew what he meant.

"It is no riddle. You know my condition. I am in constant danger of the transformation. While the stain of Marius's blood lies in my veins, I am not free, not to choose what I would if I were to live as my own man."

"But you have chosen. You've been hunting Marius."

He was incredulous at my lack of understanding. I was surprised myself at how hard my heart was against him. Up until now I had not realized the depth of the betrayal I felt.

"No, that is not what I have been doing. If you will let me, I will tell you what was so important to take me to the other side of the world. I would have gotten word sooner, but there was no way to send a message to you."

"There is always a way," I said, and heard the sullenness in my own voice.

He gave a humorless laugh. "Yes, I suppose that is true. I confess I feared you might follow me."

"Your conceit is astonishing," I countered, although it was not such a far-fetched idea. "Nevertheless, I can see you are itching to tell me where you went, so do so."

"To Anatolia. I went to Naimah."

I gasped in shock and disbelief, and not a little jealousy. "But Naimah cannot still be alive!"

Hundreds of years ago, when Valerian had first been bitten, it was Naimah who had taken him under her wing and taught him the ways of the vampire. She'd been his nurse, his mentor. His lover. She'd been Dhampir, like myself.

"She lives no longer, but she did live for hundreds of years, Emma. How she did so was her great secret. I never knew it, until now. She would never tell me, not in all these years."

I tried to assimilate this, but my mind was sluggish. It could have been Serena's draught, for my body felt light and still blissfully free of pain. Bless the woman, I silently prayed. If only she had something in her medicines to take away the anger that simmered in my veins. It numbed my hand that would reach for him, caress his skin. It kept me motionless when I wished so much to fold myself into his arms, lie there just as I had when he'd brought me out of the woods. I could see earnestness in his face and yet I was unmoved.

"This is precisely why I had to go," he continued. "Just after that business at Avebury, I tracked Marius, as you knew I would. All that business with the Dragon took me East, to the old kingdom of Wallachia."

I narrowed my eyes. "To the Dracula?"

"That was where I was headed, but I never arrived. I got as far as Buda-Pest, then began to follow Marius's trail south when I received word that Naimah was dying." He reached for me, touching my shoulder. "Surely you understand that I had to go to her."

As resentful as I had been for his absence, I was not in so unreasonable a state that I could not understand the importance of her death to him. I spoke tightly, hating to admit my sympathy. "I understand Naimah needed you."

"She was dying, Emma. All these many, many years she has been with me. Now she is gone."

"It is always difficult to lose someone you love."

His eyes flashed for an instant before he lowered his lids, covering the surge of emotion. "Yes. My love for her was at times the one and only good thing in many years of solitude. I did love her, Emma, but not in the way you think." He ran a hand through his hair. "It is true we were lovers, but that was long ago. We became friends. More than that, we were family. It might seem strange to you."

Not really. When I thought of the loneliness of living two hundred and sixty years, I could not hold his bond with Naimah against him.

"There are things about her you do not understand," he said. "Things I never knew until the end. I hope to discover much more in her writings. You see, over the centuries, Naimah put her accumulated wisdom and experiences into journals, which she bequeathed to me."

I found myself somewhat unwillingly intrigued. "So how was it she existed as a true human for so long?"

He made a vague gesture. "I know only a little of that story. It turned out to be a curse as well as a gift. Long life such as she had is unnatural and it comes with a price. A terrible price. Let me explain it this way: do you know of the Sibyls?"

"Vaguely," I said. "They were wise women—even prophets, correct? I only know about them from the frequent references in literature . . . Are you telling me Naimah was one of these? A Sibyl?"

"No, I am merely trying to explain by example, knowing how well versed you are in literature and mythological references. You may remember a particular tale of a Sibyl out of the city of Cumae." I shook my head and he went on: "She was a priestess for Apollo. The story has it she asked the god to grant her as many years of life as there were grains of sand in her hour glass. Apollo granted her wish, but she neglected to ask also for eternal youth. And so, as the years passed, she aged and shrunk so that she became very, very small, so small that she was kept in a jar, and eventually all that remained was her voice, which continued to prophesize. In Petronius's *Satyricon*, he writes that when she was asked what she wished for most of all, the Cumean Sibyl replied, 'I would die.' And that, you see, is the story of Naimah."

"And so Naimah first got what she wished for—to live. But in the end what she wanted most was to simply die?"

He nodded. "I was happy for her that she at last got her wish."

He was sad, though. I knew that despite his acceptance, even rejoicing, in her passing, he was still experiencing a profound loss. "What reason did she give you for never divulging the source of her longevity?"

"She didn't. It was the only time she was unreasonable, even irrational. At the end, she told me a little, of an alchemist living on the island of Santorini, in Greece. Have you read in your studies of this place?"

"I know it, yes of course. It is said to have the greatest population of vampires, although I have never found a decent explanation as to why."

He nodded. "Nor have I. In any event, this man is a devoutly religious Jew who has dedicated his life to the study of vampires. Naturally, he would conduct his studies in Santorini. It was from him that Naimah was able to obtain that which gave her long life."

"But I do not see why she would not tell you about this before."

He swallowed with difficulty. "I think she feared to do so, knowing I would want to find the man. Indeed, that is exactly what I want to do as soon as I am able. I suspect there is more to Naimah's story, and that the part which she kept hidden is . . . unsavory, something very dark. It would have to be for her to have kept this secret all of her life. You did not know Naimah. She was clever, instinctive, and ruthless when she wished. I suspect her method of gaining the elixir of extended life was not something she was proud of."

Sebastian interrupted us with a soft knock as he entered the room. "There you are. Let me see you. My God, Emma, you look wretched."

I gave him a huff of a laugh in response. "You are too honest, Sebastian."

"There is no such thing," he countered, and cast a malevolent look in Valerian's direction. If I was angry at Valerian, then Sebastian was twice so.

"Father Luke is all right?" I asked.

"Oh, he had to spend some time in bed, roaring like a bear

the whole time as if I were responsible. I nearly brained him with the fire iron to shut him up. But just in case there really is a God, I thought He might not look with favor on my abusing one of His priests. So I restrained myself."

I smiled. "Good for you."

"Indeed, I am swollen with pride at my accomplishment. But to answer your question, he is fine and in a foul temper, so let us say all is normal."

Serena entered. I glanced from her to Sebastian. "When can I go home . . . well, back to the school?"

"Serena says you will be strong enough by tomorrow. Oh, by the by, I told them you were out walking and got caught in a bog. The only means of dragging yourself out was some thorny bracken, and you were scratched. It will explain the . . . ah . . ."

He indicated my appearance in a swirl of his finger. I had not yet seen my face, but I guessed it was scored with scratches similar to what I'd done to my arms.

"That sounds preposterous," I said mildly. "Especially after I supposedly fell into a gorse bush not long ago. That was the story I put out to explain the rat bites."

"Well, we cannot by rights tell the truth, can we?" He pursed his lips. "On which, as it happens, I am not completely clear."

"She was attacked by the vampire," Valerian stated impatiently.

"I am not certain of that," I corrected. "I did not see it."

"It was the vampire," Serena said with a definitive nod, "but some spell kept you from seeing him."

Sebastian was visibly upset by this. "Fabulous. Just what we need—a vampire who does not follow the rules."

"There is always a rule," Valerian countered. "That is not to say we always understand them."

I cut off the conversation. As valuable as our typical debating sessions proved to be in sorting out the mysteries we frequently faced, I could not bear to have one right now. "I feel a bit fatigued," I told them. "Serena's medicines are wonders, but they make me sleepy."

They left without delay, Sebastian first. Valerian lingered at the door, and I thought he wanted to say something, but I closed my eyes, wishing fervently for him to leave me alone.

At last I heard the door click shut, and I let out a breath of relief. Outside my door, voices drifted to me in muffled tones. Valerian and Sebastian were arguing. I could make out enough of what they said for me to understand it was about me.

I sighed. I wondered if Valerian regretted coming back. And I wondered again what had brought him to me.

The memory of my assault manifested in my dreams. First, the sweet smell, like a harlot's perfume, tickled my nose. Then the memory of those relentless hands, and the most horrible of all—the helplessness—rose up until I was sweating and thrashing in futile efforts to get free.

I was blind. All around me was black. I could not see to fight my attacker.

I awoke with a gasp in the night. After lighting a candle, I slowly lay back down. Serena was beside me moments later.

"It was just a dream," I told her. "Go back to sleep."

"Your man is here, sleeping outside. Should I wake him?"

"No," I said, easing back onto the downy pallet. I was going to add that he was not my man, but I did not bother.

The vividness of the memories worsened as I prepared to return to Blackbriar. She sent me back with a vial full of powder and explicit instructions—along with a warning on carefully watching the size of the dose—and I did not argue with her although I had no intention of drugging myself. I could not afford to chance being caught off guard.

I had been receiving letters from my sister all during my stay at Blackbriar. Alyssa was entering the end of her confinement; her baby was due in a month. Upon arriving back at school, I found awaiting me a particularly nasty missive accusing me of abandoning her, for she had been after me for some time to attend her as she prepared to give birth. Although Alyssa had plenty of people around her, including her doting husband, none but me would do, it seemed, to be by her side for the big event.

I sighed, feeling disturbed as I folded the letter and put it away. I could not, of course, tell her the truth of what I was doing in Blackbriar, so my replies had until now been vague. Now, with her temper rising beyond tolerance, I had to think of something to placate her. Our relationship was not an easy one, but it was precious to me. I drew out a fresh piece of expensive parchment I used for correspondence and wrote her back immediately, positing a date during my term break when I might, if all complications subsided, travel to Derbyshire. I hoped this half-promise would be enough to hold her until I could spare some time for the maintenance of our sisterly affections.

The morning following my return, I was summoned down to Miss Sloane-Smith's office. She kept me waiting in the straight-backed chair opposite the grand throne behind her desk for a quarter of an hour. At last she came in, sat down, put her glasses on the tip of her nose, and peered at me with unbridled displeasure.

"How are you feeling?" she asked without a trace of concern.

"I am much better. I take up my classes again tomorrow," I told her.

"I questioned your returning to the classroom, looking as you do. But as long as the students do not seem disturbed, I suppose it will be all right." I noticed her jaw working in irritation. "This arrived for you," she said, and she rose and extracted a potted plant from behind a screen near the window.

"It is from Lord Suddington. He is, of course, very concerned about the school, especially after the rash of misfortunes we have had. It is good of him to take such an interest in the staff."

The plant was extraordinarily lovely, a cascade of snowy-white star flowers veined with vivid pink. It had to be one of Suddington's precious orchids.

I was greatly moved by his sacrifice. There was a card addressed to me stuffed among the tendril-like leaves and I opened it.

> *Dearest Emma, I was so very grieved to learn of your accident. Please accept one of my pets. May its beauty bring you comfort as you recover.*

I folded the note. "Thank you, Miss Sloane-Smith. Is there anything else?"

Her mouth twisted, lines of age showing as she shook her head. I left her, taking my gift up to my room and positioning it by the window. As it was a plant that thrived under tropical conditions, I assumed it needed a great deal of light and would die if not kept warm, so I stuffed the cracks around the window with several of my undergarments to keep the draft out. Suddington could not think I would be able to do much to keep the thing alive without benefit of the hothouses he employed but I supposed he thought it would at least bring me a small measure of joy before it succumbed to the less than ideal conditions here.

I made certain my "pet" was as comfortable as I could make it before sneaking down the back stairs in my usual way, hitching up the trap, and escaping down to the village. I had been giving my next move a great deal of thought, and there was something I wanted very much to do before proceeding.

Chapter Fourteen

This time, I did not sneak into the Rood and Cup, but entered the inn by the front door and sought out Mrs. Danby. She was happy to see me, enough to make me feel guilty for having avoided her on past occasions, no matter how necessary it had been. I had come at an hour too late for luncheon and too early for dinner, and not the hour for tea. Therefore, the dining room was empty, just as I'd planned.

I endured her fussing and proclamations over my recent "accident," but after my assurances that I was mending just fine, she offered me some of her cider. "And I have the most delicious spice cakes," she added.

"That would be lovely," I replied, smiling.

In the corner, her old mother sat wrapped in her rug next to a high-burning fire. Mrs. Danby had no sooner disappeared into the kitchens than I was over by Madge's side.

"Hello," I said gently.

The rheumy eyes gazed at me for a moment but remained vague. "Do I know you?"

"We were not introduced, actually. I was a guest here a while ago, and we spoke."

"I do not remember," she said in a plaintive way that moved my heart.

"That is all right. I was curious, however . . . ah . . . just a moment."

I had heard the noises of Mrs. Danby's return, and, worried she would bustle her mother off again as she'd done before, I hurried back to my table. As expected, she appeared with the tray of cider and cake, which she laid before me.

"Please excuse me, but there's work to do for the dinner. Janet has decided to go off, fickle girl." She threw her hands up in the air as she rolled her eyes. "They do, you know, run off with their romantic dreams and leave me far behind. I'd thought I'd have longer with Janet, she's only sixteen, but it's old enough, I suppose."

I started at this news. "Janet is gone? To where?"

"I wish I knew," she said with a shrug. "But you know how girls that age are."

I had been made acutely aware of how impulsive and misguided they could be, and perhaps that explained the sense of disquiet that rippled through me.

"Well, then, enjoy your cider while it's hot, missus," Mrs. Danby said. "I'd love to sit and have a cup myself, but the custard is boiling and I've got a bushel of peas to shell."

"By all means, Mrs. Danby, go about your business. You do not have to entertain me. I am quite content."

She smiled. "We are having roasted chickens and parsnips and peas if you wish to stay."

"Ah, you tempt me, but it is frowned upon for us to miss meals at the school, and I've stretched Miss Sloane-Smith's patience to the limit as it is, I am afraid."

She made a face to let me know what she thought of the headmistress and disappeared. I took my cup and plate and hurried back to Madge's side. "Do you want something to eat?" I offered.

Her eyes seemed clearer. She remembered me from a moment ago. "My daughter feeds me well."

I pulled up a chair quickly. "When I was here before, you told me something. You appeared to be very worried, and you spoke about the Cyprian Queen."

Her face transformed at once. "Hush, child. Do not speak her name."

"What is it? Is it a person?"

"It is a curse," she said vehemently.

"You said, 'They think it is beauty, but it is death.' Do you remember?"

Her expression wrenched with grief. "Yes. Those were words I will never forget. They were my sister's words. Beautiful Dora."

My heart began to pound with excitement. "Your sister knew of the Cyprian Queen?"

"It killed her. Oh, it was long ago, but I've never made my peace with it." Her bony hands emerged, knotted with rheumatism, and clasped one another restlessly. "Dora was so beautiful. When it all began, she was a happy girl. It was like she'd fallen in love. I could see the difference in her right away, but she would tell me nothing. I begged her to confide in me. But she kept her secret, and it killed her."

"What? What did she do?" I leaned forward. "You can tell me. I will believe you."

She stared at me. She wanted to, I could see. But no doubt her daughter, and others, had hushed her for so long she didn't speak easily. "She and the others had conjured a demon."

"The Cyprian Queen? She is a demon, then? Are you saying the girls practiced witchcraft, and summoned her?"

She nodded. "I suppose. I do not know how it began."

The door to the outside opened, and I looked up, alarmed that Mrs. Danby had come to check on me and would discover—and put an end to—my interview with her mother. But it was just a man, someone I did not know, coming into the inn. Still, I would only have a few moments before Mrs. Danby arrived to serve him.

"I spied on her," Madge confessed with an impish smile. "I saw—saw what she did, she and the others. It was sinful, lustful. Evil."

"A coven?" I said. "Are you saying they practiced witchcraft?" I thought of my attack. Was this Cyprian Queen something else, then, not a vampire at all but a demonic force that preyed sexually on young girls? But that made no sense; Miss Markam had seen bodies drained of blood. And I had the evidence of my own eyes that there was a vampire at work here—I'd staked a mother and child. Even now, the recollection brought a surge of disgust. I would not recover from that day for a long time.

"I do not know," Madge replied. "I never knew what the Cyprian Queen was. All I could see was what she did to them." Her old hands locked onto my wrist. I grasped her back tightly. "She excited their blood. They had no modesty. They were caught in a most dreadful fever until they wasted away and expired."

Several words set off triggers in my brain. "How do you mean, they wasted away?"

"She became but a wisp of a thing, a shade walking among the living, dead long before she ended her own life. And all the other girls, too—girls from the school who had been good girls before it all began to happen. It was as if it was some kind of plague, but I knew it was not. It was the evil of the game they called the Cyprian Queen."

I frowned. This sounded too much like the working of a vampire. But a vampire was incapable of the carnal act. It made no sense that it would gather a coven of girls to itself to instigate promiscuity. What interest would this hold for one undead?

"I remember at the end, Dora was so bereft." Old Madge shook her head. She was growing weary, and her grief was getting the better of her. I knew I should stop her, but I did not.

"What happened?" I prompted.

The old woman's eyes glazed over with tears. Her voice quavered. "Those words, the last I ever heard from her. She told me the Cyprian Queen was death because she needs the blood."

I nearly came up out of my chair. "Blood? What did she say about blood?"

"There was so much I did not understand. But the girls all died. They wasted away, most of them. Ann flung herself into a bog. Dora hung herself in my mother's house. Mama told me she would come back."

"Dora?" My God, had her mother suspected her child had become a vampire and expect her to rise from the dead?

"No. No." Madge was nearly slurring her words. I could see the bleariness in her eyes, and knew my time with her was over. "The Cyprian Queen, child." She nodded, wetting her lips fretfully. "She said the Cyprian Queen would return."

As I well and bitterly knew, the Cyprian Queen had indeed returned to Blackbriar.

I could not in good conscience push her any further. Patting her hand gently, I wrapped her tight in her blanket again. Then I took my plate and cup and returned to my table.

As it happened, I was in the nick of time. Mrs. Danby bustled in, drawing a pint for the new arrival from the bar in the corner, and I paid my bill while I had her in the room. I gathered up my cloak and reticule. As I was doing so, the man stood and came up to me.

"That old woman is mad," he said sharply.

"Excuse me?"

He was holding his cup, already half-drunk. And it was not the first of the day, I could see by the red veins in his eyes. The broken blood vessels in his face attested to the fact that this was no doubt a habit.

"She spreads lies to get attention. She is daft and so are you if you give her disgusting fantasies any credence."

"I do not think, sir, that it is any of your business."

"It is my business when poison is spread for the amusement of others, when it hurts me and mine." He glared at me haughtily. "You do not remember me, do you?"

"Should I?"

"You are a teacher at the school." His lips curved smugly. "You would do well to curb your insolence. I shall have to speak to my cousin."

"If you feel so inclined, then I cannot stop you, and as for your cousin—" I was saved from sending both of them to perdition when footsteps on the stairs leading to the guest rooms upstairs cut me off and Valerian stepped into view.

"Emma!" he said, surprised.

The man glared back and forth between the two of us before tossing back the rest of his ale and slamming the cup on a nearby table. He stormed off, banging the door behind him. I glanced over at Madge, but she was already dozing and this disturbance had not wakened her.

Valerian took in the little scene, and looked questioningly at me. "Are you here to speak to me?"

"No," I said, and, clutching my belongings, I headed for the door.

He caught up to me in time to cover my hand as I was lifting the latch. "When are you going to forgive me?"

"I was not aware you had asked my forgiveness," I said.

"I told you I was sorry."

"That is a comfort to me," I replied with a studied politeness I knew drove him mad.

His sharp features took on a hard cast. "You have to talk to me sooner or later. There is too much at stake."

"Then it will have to be later. I must get back to school before I am missed," I said, pushing aside his hand and lifting the latch. When I was outside, however, he fell into step with me as I headed for the stable where I'd left the trap.

"At least tell me what you were doing here," he said. "You may not like to admit it, but I can help you."

He was right on both counts. I did not like admitting it, but he could help me, and I was not too proud to reach for that help. My steps slowed. "I spoke to the old woman." I told him about my short conversation with Madge.

"So the girls are involved in a cult that revels in promiscuity?" This clearly puzzled him as much as it did me. "And this sort of thing happened before?"

"It appears so."

"But it makes no sense," he said. "A vampire cannot have sexual relations with a human. Quite possibly, you are better versed in the revenant world than I at this point, so you know their lust is purely for blood. The pleasures of the flesh hold no allure for the undead."

"And yet these girls are engaged in some kind of . . . orgiastic cult. And it all happened exactly this way all those years ago—perhaps fifty years or more. That cannot be coincidence."

"Maybe it is. Maybe there's something here, just as there was something in Avebury that had been there since ancient times. Something that draws this sort of phenomenon."

"Is it a vampire, though? Or something else? There is quite a tradition of witchcraft in these parts. Perhaps we are not dealing with a vampire at all, but some other form of being."

He frowned. "Who is the witch? Serena Black? She's the only one they call *witch* around here."

I thought about this. "And before that there was Winifred. But they are merely women who know of herbs and act as local healers. Even if it is often the case that superstition has caused them to be called the devil's handmaidens or witches."

He nodded with a sigh. "It is too medieval to be believed, but in these rural regions, the old traditions die hard. Still, I cannot believe the girls really conjured up a demon. Why would that explain how the same thing happened twice, separated by so many years?"

What, then, had attacked me? My flesh began to crawl at the thought of it. "I do not know if witchcraft can be real," I said, untying the reins of the piebald roan that pulled the trap. "But I cannot be too quick to dismiss the existence of real witches. There are those who would staunchly deny the reality of vampires, after all. In fact—most rational people would."

Valerian took the reins from me and led the horse and wagon out to the street. "You would think the secret archives would mention such a thing," he said.

"Each place has an area of specialty," I told him. "The archive in which I studied might just have been the wrong place for learning about witches." I turned away abruptly and said, "I cannot stay away from school any longer. Lately, I have been taking too many risks. It wouldn't do to lose my post."

He helped me into the driver's box. The pressure of his warm fingers where he gripped my glove sent a sharp reaction through me, sweet and soothing like cool water poured over feverish skin. I pulled away and snapped the reins, and the trap lurched away.

It was not that I reviled his touch. I did not. In fact, I craved it and that terrified me nearly as much as any vampire. I had to take care not to get too attached to Valerian Fox. There was a time I thought I might fall in love with him. Now I saw that that would be disastrous.

Back in my room, I felt safe. Secure. The faint trace of the orchid's perfume eased me.

The Cyprian Queen, the incubus . . . these things were dark, twisted perversions of love. On the other hand, there existed around me bonds of friendship strong enough to bring us together: myself, Father Luke, Sebastian, and Valerian. That was a form of love, was it not? The best kind, the kind that was no stranger to sacrifice, and did not shrink from the ugliness of the dark world surrounding us.

What tied any of them here? For the first time, I realized it was me. I was the anchor that kept each and every one of them in this place when all three wanted desperately to be about very important business elsewhere. That included Sebastian, I mentally noted with a smile. To him, carousing was serious business.

Valerian had Marius to find. Father Luke had a reckoning with life, with his church, and with himself. And yet they were here.

My devotion to my mother, to learn all I could about her, to perhaps help her, had brought me here. Perhaps she was a vampire, perhaps (God forbid it!) no better than the fiend that stalked the Cumbrian fells and lakes. But I was her daughter, and love bound me to her. To find her, to save her.

Love. Both pure and foul.

Sister?

I lay on my back, staring at the square of gray light framed in my window, disoriented. Lassitude held me fast to the bed. I moaned, and uttered a denial. "No."

Yes, it is I, your brother, Ruthven.

I was shocked. A name. He'd given me his name!

It is our father's blood that makes us kin. Did you know? You are made from Lliam, as am I. His blood is diluted in you, and somehow changed, but it is there. I felt it from the first.

I was somehow enchanted by this voice. Tendrils of sleep—or some spell—lashed me to a half-dozing state. I saw him there, a coil of shadow just by the window, but I could not bring myself to rise. My heart thumped in terror. I was paralyzed.

Pride rang out as he spoke again.

You are from noble lineage, not like the other, the half-made brat of Marius's.

He meant Valerian, I thought with a start.

Marius knows the war is coming, and he thinks to seed himself in many so that when the time comes, he will call upon his army.

An army? A war? Fighting my instinctive repulsion, I opened my mind and welcomed the voice. I knew—some part of me knew—this was the thing that had violated me, that sent the rats against me.

"What do you want with me?" I quailed, my voice not quite as brave as I would have had it.

I did not understand you at first. When you called to my enemy, I thought I'd been wrong and that you were Marius-made. I thought you had come to destroy me. But now I see, and I forgive you. Oh, sister, the possibilities for us! Do not be afraid. I am not angry with you for resisting me. I am glad I did not give you to the Irish boy. You battled bravely, the blood of our father—our great, noble blood—

gave you surprising strength. How it thrills me to know you are my equal!

"Tell me more," I begged, inspired by the knowledge that he was eager to talk.

Pleasure quickened his voice. *Ah, sister, if you only knew how desperately I want to talk with you, to share all that I am. My father Lliam—our father—is one of the sons of the great Dragon. If you but knew how he has favored our clan over that Cain who would usurp our favor. How proud you will be when you know of how the Dragon Prince has fostered our line, exalted us.*

Yes, I will tell you of our lineage, but there is something else, something so much greater that I am longing to show you. For it is now, when I am in my prime, that all my beauty is here for you to see.

The air around me seemed to pulse as his voice grew in intensity.

My blood calls to yours, and I think you will see as none of them ever could. You will understand. How wonderful it is not to be alone! Oh, at last! In time, you will know everything of me, and my works. I am giddy, as I have not been in ages. And you . . . you want me to tell you. Yes?

I sensed his uncertainty in a slight pause. I whispered as fervently as I could manage, "Yes!"

I felt the joy in him as he exclaimed: *Blood calls to blood. Lliam's line is strong. Oh, Emma, it is magnificent, what I will show you! And you already understand so much about the Cyprian Queen.*

My mistake was how I pounced on that—born of my frustration and fear, I strained forward, overreaching. "Are you the Cyprian Queen?"

I felt it recede a little. Before it could respond, I realized something else, something deeper and of far more consequence, which my sluggish mind had been slow to grasp, and

I demanded, "What does the Dragon Prince have to do with any of this?"

The vampire's anger gathered around me. I had been too harsh, and I had trespassed where I was not welcome.

Patience.

The warning bit cold into the air around me, and the presence began to withdraw.

"Do not go!" I cried. There was so much at stake. I steeled myself and reached, ignoring the way my flesh crawled as I sought him.

You do not demand!

"Ruthven? Please." I choked, and made myself say it: "Brother?"

Silence stretched out for a long time. I sat up, pulling my knees to my chest, and wrapped myself into a tight ball. The scratches I'd inflicted on myself throbbed anew.

I wanted Valerian so badly then, I thought seriously of dressing and flying to the village, casting all my resentments aside and burrowing into his embrace, letting him take care of me. Then I spied the orchid, which was not faring well under my inexpert care. But it reminded me of Lord Suddington, and I thought perhaps I should bring the dying orchid to him. The idea of seeing him again was calming.

But I could never confide in him, not the way I could in Valerian. And there was much to discuss. My thoughts spun with what I had learned tonight.

Through my mother, through some vampire named Lliam— was I truly tied in blood to the Dragon Prince? Was I somehow of the line of the great and terrible Dracula?

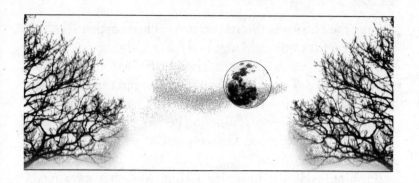

Chapter Fifteen

I went into my first class with the heavy, leaden feeling that I remembered from my nineteenth year, when I had, in a supreme act of rebellion, snuck into my father's study and consumed a large amount of the quality gin he kept in a cut-crystal decanter. I had paid a dear price the next day, after a night spent over a chamber pot, sporting an abused head and two pits of fire where my eyes had been.

I could not let my physical state slow me down, however, and I had set a mental agenda for the things I needed to accomplish. I had so many questions: How much were the girls aware of what they were dealing with? Had they been promised eternal life? Were they, even now, made by Ruthven into a harem of companions? Yet, if the vampire created them as *stri-*

goii vii, then how was this related to what had happened before, to Dora and the others Madge had told me about?

If I could get to Eustacia, I might be able to find some answers—if I could get her to trust me. Margaret and the others knew she was their weak link, however. They surrounded her as soon as my class ended, ushering her out with a tight escort. Margaret lagged behind and smirked at me. "Is something wrong, Mrs. Andrews?"

Pushing aside the unsettled feeling Margaret gave me, I strode up to her. "I met your Cyprian Queen," I told her with quiet confidence. "His name is Ruthven and he likes me quite well." I allowed my smile to grow sly even as hers went slack. "*Very* well indeed."

Rage gathered on her features. Lilliana, who stood behind Margaret and had heard me, grabbed at Margaret's arm as if she were afraid of what she might do.

"You best go," I said pleasantly.

Margaret allowed herself to be pulled back. Lilliana was talking to her, trying to calm the anger that was noticeably boiling behind her shock.

"Oh, Margaret," I called. "By any chance do you know what happened to Janet, who works down at the Rood and Cup? She's gone missing."

I immediately saw I had hit my mark. Apprehensiveness sprang to her wide eyes.

"I thought so," I intoned mysteriously. "Go on now, get out," I commanded, not bothering to glance to see if they obeyed.

My triumph, sweet as it was, was shallow and short-lived. No sooner had I quit the girls than I spied from my window a familiar and disturbing face that doused my momentary triumph. Outside, a man I recognized as the fellow who had berated me yesterday at the Rood and Cup was walking purposefully toward the front entrance of the school. My immediate—and panicked—thought was that he was here to make good on his threat to complain to the headmistress about me.

I had not long to wait to find out. Miss Sloane-Smith walked through the door of my classroom not an hour later, her face pinched with irritation. "A word, please, Mrs. Andrews," she said.

I waved her to a seat. She remained standing.

"Sir Charles Morton paid me a visit today, bearing a story that was quite unbecoming to a representative of Blackbriar School. I received a complaint that you were seen engaging in an unbecoming display of gossip."

"That is not true."

She narrowed her eyes at me. "That is not what Charles told me."

I cocked my head, a rush of temper making me rather reckless. "And I object to having my behavior characterized as unbecoming."

She was clearly shocked by my change in tactic. "Pardon me?"

My reply was sharp. "I am not in the habit of having to defend the quality of my behavior, and I will not do so now, and certainly not on the basis of a cowardly tale told by someone who is a stranger to me. I have conducted myself at all times in a manner that not only befits a teacher at Blackbriar but exemplifies it."

"The stranger you refer to," Miss Sloane-Smith said tightly, "is my cousin, and I trust his word."

"That does not change the fact that he mistook the situation," I replied defensively. "Old Madge and I were having a private conversation, which is hardly subject to the approval of anyone who might decide to eavesdrop."

Her shock was so great—and her anger as well—that she could not speak for a moment. "I was told you were easily overheard conversing on the topic of the Cyprian Queen, which is a dangerous and unpleasant subject in these parts. And I know you were talking to Mrs. Boniface about it the other day. What is the reason for this obsession?"

"It has to do with the students. I have observed their interest in this thing, this Cyprian Queen. They are somehow involved in something unsavory and I think the two are connected."

A contemptuous look came over her features. "You are beginning to sound like Victoria Markam."

That was a low blow. I notched my chin up mutely as she took a step toward me.

"I hope you are not getting ridiculous ideas in the same manner as she did," she said. "It is true there is a certain hysteria in these parts about an old, rather lurid legend. It is tempting to the baser interests of girls of this age, and very dangerous for their reputations, as well as the reputation of this school. Be warned: people in these parts dislike such talk. It is incalculably harmful. It opens old wounds that respectable families would rather not have subjected to lascivious consumption."

"Then explain it to me, this legend." My heart was beating rapidly.

"I certainly will not." She folded her arms across her chest. "I have to wonder, Mrs. Andrews, if you even belong here. Term break is coming up. Many of the students will return to their families and the staff is allowed a holiday as well. At that time, I will assess your performance here. I admit you are an excellent instructor, but these other matters make me question whether you are a good match for the school overall."

"If that is a threat, then perhaps I can save you the bother. I might have to withdraw my employment." The words spilled out of me—foolish words, but my temper was so riled I could not stop them. If I had to leave Blackbriar, I would find another way to battle Ruthven and Cyprian Queen, whether or not they were one and the same. "I cannot tolerate employment where the administration is preoccupied with preserving the reputation of the school at the expense of the girls' safety. I wonder what the trustees would think of your neglect of these matters."

She was taken aback by my thinly veiled threat, and I was surprised to realize that she appeared nervous. Then I remembered how Lord Robert Suddington had shown me favor, and I thought he might be the source of my empowerment.

I had no wish to humiliate her, so I said, "Of course, the best interests of the school are uppermost in my mind, as they are yours. But I will not ignore something I think might pose danger, not even on your orders."

Her jaw worked, but she could see I would give no other quarter. "Then do me the courtesy of informing me before you go about the neighborhood stirring up nasty and possibly slanderous untruths about the good families in these parts."

"But I did nothing of the kind," I objected.

She did not answer, just gave me a glare. Then she left me.

Though I was more confused than ever, I had a pressing meeting to get to. I had snuck out a message to Valerian and Sebastian to meet me during the luncheon hour, and I was going to be late. I hurried through the woods, my senses on heightened alert, but I encountered nothing as I made my way to Serena's cottage.

It was a crisp, sunny day with a temperature that was far lower than I'd supposed. Winter was locked down, and I wished I'd worn something warmer. The men were waiting for me outside, I was surprised to see. Father Luke had made the journey as well, seated on a mounting block, hunched over with his troubled face staring into space.

Sebastian waved when he saw me come into view. "Here she is. We can now call this meeting to order. These fools refused to wait inside, and I am freezing."

Valerian, all sinew and masculine grace as he paced the small yard like a caged panther, cast a dark look of irritation at Sebastian. "The priest needs the outdoors if he is to recover."

Sebastian snapped his head to Valerian. "And I suppose you trained with Nurse Nightingale in the last war, did you? Really, you have to stick your hand in every matter. I have taken perfectly good care of him since I—I!—fished him out of the sewers." He did not see Father Luke wince as he tossed his head pointedly to signal he was done with Valerian, and looked instead at me. "I wish to go inside, now. I am not dressed for the cold."

The men were grating on each other's nerves, it was plain to see. It must be hell on them being cooped up like chickens in their rooms at the inn, Mrs. Danby's fine cuisine notwithstanding.

Valerian said, "Perhaps it will be more . . . discreet if we remain out here where we are sure not to be overheard."

"Serena can be trusted," I said. "She already knows much, and I do believe we would be more comfortable indoors. I, too, am not prepared to be out in these temperatures for too long."

As I guessed, each man's chivalry overrode their present disagreement, and we filed into the cottage, where Serena was waiting with steaming mugs of cider.

I embraced her affectionately and, in reply to her inquiries, assured her my health was improving quickly. "You should be resting," she scolded.

Smiling at her, I said, "The matter is not one that can wait."

She frowned and nodded, and I appreciated how easily she accepted all of this. In the cultures of Eastern Europe, the dark superstitions were not ridiculed as they were in England but rather respected. On impulse, I gave her another hug. "Thank you for what you did for me and for what you do for us now. You do not even know us, yet you have helped us so much."

Pulling away, I saw she was blushing. "I made *tortul casei*," she said. "It is a kind of chocolate cake. It is very good. You will like."

Sebastian called to me, and I quickly thanked our hostess before joining my friends. "I have much to tell you," I said, and related the encounter I'd had with the vampire the night before.

It was Valerian who pounced on me when I mentioned the name it had given me. "Did you say Ruthven?" He shook his head, incredulous. "But do you not remember?"

"I know it is familiar, but I haven't been able to place it. Do you know this vampire?"

He laughed. "The vampire does not exist. It is the name of the main character in the story 'The Vampyre,' written by a Doctor Polidori."

"Of course!" I cried, making the connection now.

"Who is Polidori?" Sebastian demanded.

"He was a friend of Lord Byron's," I explained. "They summered together in Geneva, with Percy Bysshe Shelley and his wife, Mary Shelley. You will recognize her as the author of *Frankenstein*."

"I told you I do not read," Sebastian groused.

"Well, it is not necessary, to understand the significance of this story. You see, it was a rainy summer—a 'wet, uncongenial summer' Mary called it—and they were confined indoors, so they challenged each other to write a supernatural story of some kind. That was when she got the inspiration for her great novel. And Polidori, who was not a writer of any merit, wrote 'The Vampyre.'"

"So the vampire has taken the name Ruthven," Valerian mused. "Unless this vampire is, in fact, Ruthven—that is, he actually exists—and was there that summer of 1816. Perhaps they came to know him in some manner."

I raised my index finger. "An interesting way to say it—to know him. I could tell he was obsessed with being known, with sharing his greatness. He is very proud, and was positively ecstatic that he had found someone to whom he could reveal himself."

Sebastian shook his head in consternation. "He wants recognition?"

Raising my eyebrows, I emphasized, "He craves it."

"So," Valerian said, "perhaps he was Polidori's inspiration."

"It is possible. You know, of course, how nomadic the vampire is. Perhaps one of his hunting grounds is there, near the Swiss lake. And, if I recall correctly, Polidori committed suicide."

"Suicide," Valerian reflected. "Vampire legends in almost every culture contain the idea that a suicide rises as the undead. This might be attributable to the fact that often those who have been made *strigoii vii* wish to immediately transition to *strigoii mort* and elect to speed that process along by taking their own life."

Sebastian said, "So Polidori . . . ?"

Valerian shrugged. "Who knows. But it is suspicious."

"And relevant for us because this Ruthven wishes to be associated with a rather famous story." I looked from man to man. "This is very different than normal. Consider Marius, who always seeks anonymity. He has even used many names to avoid being tracked." I nodded toward Valerian. "You met him when he was known as Emil."

I thought for a moment, then said, "It claims kinship to me, through this Lliam, which he says is Marius's enemy. Have you ever heard of him?"

Thinking for a moment, Valerian slowly shook his head. "I have not, and I agree we must learn as much as we can about Lliam, and about this feud. It may give us some clue to Ruth-

ven, understand what he wants and how he may be related to
the Cyprian Queen. Emma, did he give you any hints?"

"Only in how he . . . it . . . talked. Sometimes, when he
speaks to me, he feels like a person. I think of him as 'he,' not
'it,' so I can imagine how well he wheedles his spells into the
minds of the girls. He speaks of love, and he is so . . . seductive.
Those girls cannot hope to resist him, even if they wanted to.
But I believe things are beginning to turn for the worse. Janet,
the maid at the Rood and Cup, is still missing. She has to be
part of this—perhaps she is one of them. Eustacia said they
needed her for the seventh, but when one counts the students
involved, her joining them would only make her the sixth."

Sebastian raised his eyebrows. "A local girl as part of the
group? We hadn't thought of that, but I suppose it is possible.
It happened before. Remember Old Madge's sister Dora?"

"Of course. We also know from Madge that the visit from
the Cyprian Queen will turn violent. It is only a matter of time."
I felt a sudden chill and wrapped my arms around myself. "The
danger is mounting, and to compound matters, my position at
the school is precarious. What shall I do if I am asked to resign
my post?"

No one seemed to have a proper answer for that. Valerian
ended the heavy silence with a question. "I am intrigued with
Ruthven's reference to the Dracula."

I sighed, massaging the bridge of my nose to relieve my
tension. "I don't know about that. I know so little about the
Dracula, mainly that his very name summons terror and awe in
whomever speaks of him, and I'm afraid that is becoming con-
tagious, for I tremble every time I hear that name, especially
with what Ruthven said of war . . ." The specter of large-scale
violence sent a ripple of apprehension down my spine. "What
could he have meant?"

Valerian thought on this, rubbing his fingers over his chin as he did so. "At least I now know why Marius bit me that night and never returned. I never understood before why he would waste himself on the first bite, which is the most taxing on him, and not come back for me. I see at last that it was merely to prime me, set the stage for an easy transformation when he needs me. I am to be conscripted to fight for Marius in this war of the undead, but we have no idea against whom."

Sebastian leaned forward. "Could it be the Dracula? Is Marius planning a coup, rising up against the great Dragon Prince?"

The sound of shattering china split the air, and we all jumped, Valerian in front of me, shoving me behind him protectively. His speed and strength surprised me, as it ever did. It was so easy to forget that about him, that he had the blood of the vampire in him.

The noise had been Serena, who was standing stone-still over a shattered plate. At her feet, her cake lay in a heap on the floor.

"I—I am sorry," she muttered. "Look what I did."

I scooted out from behind Valerian and went to her as she bent to pick up the debris. I put my hand on her wrist, putting a stop to her nervous movement. "Leave it for now."

Valerian's eyes met mine meaningfully. He said to Serena, "Perhaps you might join our discussion."

She had recovered herself. Her eyes were again wise, slightly cunning. "You mean, this talk of the Dracula?" She pronounced the name in her native tongue, with guttural inflection that added a chilling menace. "I can tell you only what everyone in my part of the world knows."

"And what is that?"

She laughed mirthlessly. "That if you have any dealings with him, you and everyone you love will die a most unpleasant death. And not only will you die, but then you will live again, undead, yes? And then, you are damned. Your curse is that you will kill everyone you loved in life, and the only thing you will crave is to drink their blood." She paused. "This is why it is dangerous to speak of him. He wishes to remain a mystery, a secret. He is more powerful that way."

A pall had come over us, and we sat in silence for a long time. Finally, I rose and said to Serena, "Come. Let me help you clean up this mess."

She tried to refuse, but I needed to be in motion. I concentrated on sweeping up the shards of the shattered plate while she shoveled the cake into the dust bin. While we were busy in the small kitchen, she sidled close to me. "The priest," she said in a low voice, "tell me about him. I know about his sickness. What happened to him to make him do such a thing?"

I glanced over my shoulder to Father Luke. "He is—well, he was—a member of a very secret order who served as guardians over a place where evil had been imprisoned long ago. It was his duty to protect the world from those, living or undead, who would come to unleash that evil for their own means. When the seal of the prison was broken this last spring, Father Luke's duty was to sacrifice everything and everyone to ensure that the evil was destroyed once and for all."

"Which he did?" she inquired.

"Yes. Well, we all did together. But there was loss of life, and he took it very hard. Very personal. I think he believed that he should have been able to save everyone. But what happened was not his fault. Now he feels betrayed by the Church that trained him."

She nodded. Her gaze lingered on Father Luke as she murmured, "Then I will pray for him."

I came away from our discussion with the urgent need to delve deeper into the mystery of the Dracula. I sent a letter to Uncle

Peter. As a diplomat for his native country of Romania, he traveled all around England and the European continent, but he was often in London. I would be on term break soon and hoped I would be lucky enough to find him in England. The Austro-Hungarian Empire recognized the existence of the undead openly, and accounts of vampirism ranging from the simplest villager to the viceroy of Serbia, the duke of Wirtemberg, were kept on record in the Vatican archive. It stood to reason the people of this region would be long acquainted with the undead, seeing as how the Dragon Prince was reported to rule from his mist-shrouded castle in the Carpathian Mountains of Transylvania.

Uncle Peter might be able to shed some light on our understanding of how the Dracula might be at work here in England, either directly or through one of his agents.

Over the following days, I stayed very busy. I felt it imperative I keep a close eye on the coven girls. Their attitude toward me had altered; they treated me with a mingling of respect and fear. That I was knowledgeable about Ruthven had removed their contempt. They were wary, and took care to stay out of my way. I was content with this, and now that I believed the Cyprian Queen was in truth some manner of vampire, I set about to put protections in place. The school was a large building with many windows, and it took much of my free time, made more burdensome by the need to operate in secret, to seal the windows with a thin line of salt. I put holy water and secreted garlic in strategic positions to guard the dormitories.

I knew much of this was in vain. Any one of the handful of girls—the witches—could undo all of my stealthy work any time they wished. Or they could simply sneak outside in the night, as was their custom. Still, I could not do nothing to help them. In addition, Valerian and Sebastian took up shifts in an attempt to prevent the girls from sneaking out after hours.

I had to decrease my visits to the village after Trudy Grisholm cornered me one day. I had a feeling she'd been lying in wait for me. "You visit the inn frequently where you often are seen in the company of three men, I heard. Are they relations?"

"One is," I said, trying to appear unperturbed. I did not clarify the connection. Sebastian's brother was my cousin's husband, hardly a close enough sanguinity to preclude scandal. Not to mention the smoldering presence of Valerian, nor Father Luke, who no longer wore any vestments to make it known he was a priest. The time I spent with them no doubt appeared odd, even scandalous.

"What are they doing here so long?"

"They have business here," I explained curtly.

"How fortunate for you," she said slyly. "Three men of your acquaintance happen to have business in a remote place like this, and for such a protracted length of time." She simpered at me. "It must be so comforting to have familiar faces around."

After that, I was much more careful not to be seen in the village.

Lord Suddington appeared at the school one day when the weather broke. I was summoned outside to find him holding the reins of a sleek open carriage. "It is one of those teasingly mild days that make me impatient for spring," he announced. "Come for a ride with me. I have been longing to be out in the open air."

I was delighted, despite knowing full well that should Miss Sloane-Smith learn of the outing, she would be angry. I always felt a bit giddy when I saw Suddington, however, and I allowed him to hand me up into the seat beside him. He was flirtatious, as always, and utterly charming as we toured the school grounds. He returned me to the school an hour later, just as evening was sealing shut over the land. "That was wonderful," I told him as we drew to a stop.

"There will not be many days like this until March," he said. "I will come for you again then, and we'll venture out farther along some paths I know that give breathtaking views of the fells and tarns."

My pulse quickened with the excitement of such a promise. "I shall look forward to it."

He paused, his gloved fingers grasping mine. "It is already growing chilly, and your hands are cold."

But I was warm, something I kept to myself lest he guess the reason for the internal glow. My luck held, and no one at school seemed the wiser for my absence. I curled into bed that night, smiling secretly when my eye caught the orchid sitting in its pot. I had not been able to keep it alive very long.

With the end of term approaching, I had much work to do with my teaching, and had to put aside all matters vampiric and romantic the following day. I felt the headmistress's gaze on me, as I often did, filled with dark speculation. I knew she was thinking of whether to retain me for another term.

Why *did* she dislike me so much, anyway, I wondered. I had really done nothing to merit it. I had always put it down to jealousy over Lord Suddington, but I suddenly considered if there was something more to the animosity she so obviously felt toward me. Now that I pondered her behavior, it seemed to me she had approached the entire matter of Margaret, Vanessa, and the other girls in a singularly odd manner. And Vanessa had gloated to me, gleeful in her certainty that Miss Sloane-Smith would not condemn the coven.

Why had I never thought to question her role in all of this? I remembered that secret book I'd caught her hiding and grew excited. Was it a journal? Would there be some hint of her strange motivations?

It was as if providence wanted me to find out, for not more than a quarter hour after these doubts assailed me, I was passing by her office when she came out with Mrs. Brown, who seemed to be making some complaint about cracked windows and a leaking problem. As the conservatory was on the other side of the school, I saw I had enough time to duck into Miss Sloane-Smith's office while she was off inspecting the damage.

The journal was where I'd seen it before. I flipped the pages, and my hopes sank. From what I read quickly, it was a catalogue of her accomplishments and the accolades (real or imagined?) she received from parents and the trustees. I did find mention of me in later entries. I had to chuckle at the curt assessments of my character flaws, my inadequacies, my inappropriate demeanor, and even an unkind reference to my "ungainly height." I was vaguely insulted but not alarmed, and I realized there was nothing in here that was of any import.

I replaced the journal, and gauged the time. I had already stayed longer than was safe. But I could not resist a quick look through her desk drawers. Knowing I was pressing my luck, I gave them a cursory inspection. They revealed nothing.

I knew my time was running out. But then I remembered the little hiding place she had—the screen behind the desk where she had put the plant Lord Suddington had sent to me. I peered into the little alcove and found a group of objects, none of which appeared interesting save an old wooden box inlaid with mother-of-pearl flowers. I lifted the lid to find something inside. Drawing it out, I saw it was a teardrop pearl necklace. The precious gem dangled from a clasp wrought of silver shaped into a dragon rampant, its coiled tail extending so that the chain was attached to the tip. It was a ghastly representation of menace, its talons clutching the precious stone cruelly.

Recognition dawned—double recognition. This was the necklace I'd seen in the portrait in Suddington's library. It was also the same necklace Alistair had stolen to give to my mother.

The sound of someone entering the office startled me. I

dropped the necklace into the box, placed the lid very carefully on top so as to not make a sound, and stepped deeply into the crevice behind the screen.

I was certain my breathing, which sounded like a gale-force wind to my own panicked ear, would be audible to Miss Sloane-Smith as she sat at her desk. But heaven, it seemed, was inclined to be generous to me that day, for no sooner had the headmistress sat down than there was a knock at the door.

I recognized Ann Easterly's twittering voice. "There is a problem in the kitchens. Cook says luncheon will be delayed."

Sloane-Smith stood. "What? Again?" She stalked out, slamming the door behind her. I counted to thirty and slipped out of my hiding place, carefully peeking into the hallway to find it all clear. I clicked the door shut behind me as quietly as I could, then fled to my room as if the devil himself were in pursuit.

Valerian wanted to see me.

He sent a messenger with a sealed note the next day, asking me to meet him at Serena Black's cottage as early as possible. I sent back a time I was free, which was late afternoon that day.

As I handed back the message, I realized the youthful messenger was none other than the Irish boy. My God, how the handsome youth had changed! His face was drawn into lines of unhappiness, and his pale Celtic complexion was waxy. I was thinking of what I might say to him when he spun away and was gone, as if he could not get away from the school fast enough.

There was no time to wonder about his strange behavior, for I had a class waiting, and a busy day giving examinations. When the appointed time arrived, I made my way to the cottage in a cold, wet downpour, arriving drenched and in a foul temperament on Serena's doorstep.

"Your man said he would be here at five," she said as she took my coat and shook it out for me. "You still have half an hour to wait."

"I told you before, he is not my man."

Serena looked at me. "I do not know why you always say that. Of course he is."

I did not have the energy to argue with her—and besides, what in the world would I say to try to explain the complicated relationship Valerian and I shared?—so I silently followed her into the kitchen, where she prepared a pot of tea for us.

"You steep tea as expertly as any Englishwoman," I complimented, taking a bracing sip from my steaming cup.

"I have been here long enough to learn."

"When did you come to England?"

"After the war. My man was an English officer. He brought me back with him as his wife."

Her face, beautiful as a Roman statue, was perfectly still. "Sometimes that seems like another lifetime ago."

I asked, "Do you miss your country?"

She smiled. "My country? Yes. It is very different there, of course. My house is here, my medicines and my plants, so I stay here. But sometimes, I long to see the gentle hills, and hear again the songs that we all sang at every celebration." She carefully touched the rim of her cup to her lips and sipped in genteel silence.

"You must miss your family," I said sympathetically.

Her expression changed, eyebrows forking down into a deep V. "No. That I do not miss."

"I am sorry," I said. "I do know something of strained relations with one's relatives."

"It is not strain," she said sharply, and I could see in her fathomless, liquid-brown eyes nothing but defiance. "They are dead to me. And I to them."

I was taken aback, naturally. "Did they object to your marrying an Englishman?"

"They objected to my being a whore," she said without apology.

That gave me pause. "Oh."

"You are shocked?"

I was, most certainly. This gentle, intelligent woman was the farthest thing from what I thought a prostitute was like—not that I had ever known any. But one hears of coarse women, and I would have never guessed Serena Black to be associated with them.

"It is none of my business, after all," I said diplomatically. "All I know of you is how kind you have been to me. We were strangers when you took me in your home and cared for me. You never judged me then, when surely the situation had to appear scandalous."

She stared at me for a moment, then shrugged. "My family did not mind the food I provided. They enjoyed the bread, the cheese, the occasional joint of meat for their table. My mother and sisters and brother had food to eat during the war when so many starved. The fact that it was gotten in payment for nights when I warmed a certain officer's bed . . . Well, that they could not accept. Though they ate the bounty my sins bought them, the guilt of it was all mine." She spoke woodenly, as if she'd frozen out all feeling on the matter a long time ago.

"Oh, Serena, I am so sorry."

She shrugged. "I am not ashamed of what I did. I am proud." Her chin jutted out as if to show me how untroubled she was about her confession. "I *survived*, yes? And they survived. I loved them, and so I did what I did. There is no shame. Not my shame, anyway."

"No. I can see no shame." I meant it. I thought her heroic.

"I met a soldier later, after the English were leaving, and he brought me to England. He married me, even knowing what I was. So, I am here now, where I am a mystery, being a foreigner, and people are a little afraid of me. They stay away. I like it that way."

I understood completely. When you were alone, no one could hurt you.

The sound of Valerian's horse outside drew Serena to the window. "He is here," she said. "I will leave you alone."

The cottage atmosphere changed the instant Valerian swept in the door, tall and dark-visaged. He was scowling.

Serena took his rain-sodden cloak and ducked out of the room.

"There is tea in the pot," I said, making no move to rise to get it for him.

He managed quite well on his own, and joined me at the scrubbed oak table. "I spent the last few days going through church records. I wanted to check out what the old woman told you about the Cyprian Queen coming when she was young."

"Was she telling the truth? Were there any reported deaths of young girls back then?"

He nodded. "In the early years of this century, five girls died, two of them local, the other three students at the school. Their parents buried them here. I went back further, and it happened again, roughly seventy years before. Four deaths were recorded near the beginning of the eighteenth century, all girls around the age of fourteen."

Though I had expected this, the news was still weighty. "How far back does it go?"

"Although the records date back only to the Anglican reform, the first documented case of large numbers of girls dying in a few-months span—outside of a general sort of illness—was in 1587. It seems it began then, under circumstances much worse than what has occurred since. That year more than twenty girls were found dead, and I would surmise not all who went missing were found. A nobleman, a Sir Reginald Smyth, was tried for these crimes by the assizes. He was found guilty and hung at the crossroads. After the execution, the murders ceased."

"But how? They would have killed an innocent man." I took a sip of my tea. "The murders would have been committed by a vampire who poses as the Cyprian Queen, would they not?"

"I would think so . . ." He shook his head. "It must be so."

"I wonder how many others fell under suspicion through the years."

Valerian nodded. "I've found a few people in town who vaguely recall talk of the Cyprian Queen, but it is not a flourishing legend. There is not much interest in it, except one fellow. Ah . . . Charles . . ."

I perked up. "Charles Morton?"

Valerian raised his eyebrows. "He nearly took my head off when he heard me asking around about it."

"He is Miss Sloane-Smith's cousin. He reacted the same way to me, as if I were spreading slander against him personally."

Valerian was thoughtful. "That is interesting."

"Perhaps Ruthven has merely borrowed from a local tragedy. This Smythe attacked young girls, so the vampire uses this affectation of the Cyprian Queen to ensnare and seduce girls in his hunting ritual, returning to do it again and again through the years."

"But that makes no sense. Ruthven cannot achieve carnal gratification, so why the elaborate ruse?"

"Just indulge the idea for a moment. Blackbriar must be one of this vampire's hunting grounds. Just as local memory fades, he comes again, repeating the process over the years as he cycles through his nomadic existence." I paused, thinking.

"But why would both Sloane-Smith and Morton be so sensitive about the subject of the Cyprian Queen? What could their connection be? I cannot believe they are minions, or *strigoii vii*. There is not a shred of evidence for that."

Valerian frowned. "It is possible she is merely protecting the reputation of the school, as she claims. And Morton is a trustee, by the way. The branches of that family are all tied to the school going back generations." He shrugged. "I have seen people attach themselves to far more trivial things to achieve a sense of self-importance."

"Sloane-Smith lives and breathes Blackbriar. It is her whole world," I agreed. "She is very proud of the fact that her entire family is dedicated to the school."

"She is not the only one. Morton clearly takes being a trustee very seriously. He would want to protect the prestige of the school at all costs."

I sighed. "Yes, I see how this all makes sense." But I could not dismiss the possibility that there was some other, darker reason for their secrecy on the topic of the Cyprian Queen.

Valerian stood for a moment, deep in thought. "Something has been troubling me, something Naimah told me."

My spine stiffened, as it did every time Naimah's name was mentioned.

He regarded me carefully, and I wondered if he knew how sensitive I was on the topic of his mentor and former lover. "Naimah guarded many secrets. I mentioned to you the alchemist who gave her the gift of long life. She writes in her journals of him, how he devoted his life—his many lifetimes, I should note—to studying vampirism."

"He is not a vampire," I said, stating what seemed obvious. My heart kicked with excitement. "How does he know how to cheat death, then?"

"Not cheat, not completely, but evade." Valerian nodded

slowly. "He has made it possible for mortal man to evade death for a long, long time. He has done this in the hopes of finding a cure one day, a cure for vampirism." His eyes were dark and intense as they watched me.

"But . . . is it possible?" I asked, incredulous.

"He has not succeeded yet, not completely. But during his quest, he has discovered something scarce to be believed."

"A way to give a human long life?"

"Exactly that, but there is more. Naimah writes in her journals of hearing a tale many years ago of a German man whose young daughter had been transformed into a vampire a very long time ago. This young girl was purported to still live as *strigoii vii*, imprisoned by her father on the island of Santorini, where he has studied and conducted extensive research to cure her. There is something about that place that has made it possible to develop this elixir for long life. Through this elixir, he has been able to sustain her in her state of *strigoii vii*."

"Of course," I offered, "so that if he can cure her, she will still be alive."

He nodded. "How Naimah learned of this, or got him to give her the elixir, I do not yet know. Perhaps it will be revealed in one of the other journals. I know only that she was sworn to secrecy, a vow she honored until the hour of her death. That was why she made me promise a long time ago that I would come to her, no matter what, when she neared death."

"She wanted to give you her journals," I said, understanding now why it was Valerian had been gone so long, unable to communicate with me. "She must have thought there was a chance that this information might save you."

His jaw worked. I found I was not jealous at this sign of emotion. I realized, suddenly, that petty state no longer bothered me. "In death, she is no longer bound to her vow of silence."

"You want to find the alchemist, don't you?" I inquired. "You must. He might have the cure by now, and it will release you. Why did you not go directly to Santorini to search for him? Why did you come here?"

He looked at me as if I were daft to not know already. "I came for you. What if you needed me? And you did—you do, don't you?"

A lump pressed painfully in my throat. "But what of you? Now that we know the reason you were bitten, now more than ever it is imperative you find a way to be released. You cannot become part of this war Ruthven warned about . . ."

"But I will be. What was it Ruthven called me? Ah, yes: Marius's 'half-made brat.' Seeded with the blood of the vampire so that I will become a soldier one day as a vampire newly born, vicious and hungry, ready to fight for my maker." His voice grew reedy and thin, filled with disgust. "I would be *strigoii mort*, a monster robbed of all personality or . . ." He choked off, his brave exterior deserting him. I reached out my hand and grasped his arm. Cutting a self-conscious glance my way, he cleared his throat. "What point is it to wonder?"

My heart broke at the dispassionate way he spoke, as if he were trying desperately not to care. "We shall not let that happen to you," I vowed. "You came to me because you knew I would be stronger with you. And you also know that you are stronger with me. I will help you. When this is done, we will search for the alchemist of Santorini."

He smiled at me, kindness and gentleness in his eyes. "So then, dare I hope that you have forgiven me?"

"Forgiven you?"

"For deserting you."

I cast my gaze away from his. "There is nothing to forgive. You have explained it all. And I feel rather foolish, so perhaps you should be the one to forgive me."

He stepped forward, frowning. "Whatever for?"

"I could have trusted there was a good reason for your leaving. And after all, we owed each other nothing after Avebury. What more could I ask from you? You saved my life several times over, and gave up Marius—and your freedom—in order to keep me from harm . . ." To my utter shame, I felt tears welling up. "That is why I did not understand after you left, why there was no word month after month. I knew why you had to go—I accepted that. You had to hunt Marius, of course. But it was as if—"

"Emma." He gently but firmly pulled me about so that I had to look at him.

I dashed away the tears splashing onto my cheeks. "Pay me no mind. I . . . I am overset these days. Ever since the cottage. Shriving that child took a terrible toll on me and then the business with Ruthven after . . . I . . . I am not myself."

He shook his head. "You have been angry with me, I know. I am sorry."

I was trying desperately to gather my composure, to distance myself from the upsetting emotion of this conversation. "You have nothing to regret. You've come here to help me when you have urgent business elsewhere. It is very nice of you, and—"

"I am not nice," he murmured. "And I did not come here just for you."

My tongue failed me, and I stared blankly at him, my heart hammering wildly. I was afraid to speak, and yet somehow the words in my head escaped in a whisper. "What did you come for, then?"

His gaze swept my face. And then he kissed me.

His hand came to cradle the back of my head, holding me fast, and I felt overcome. If the earth had opened up right then and we had fallen together through space, I do not think I would have known it. This was what I had been wanting. My entire body wanted to melt, but my pride bit deep and I remained rigid in his arms.

He pulled back after a moment, staring at me. Dark questions lingered unspoken between us. My bravado was failing me, but I did not relent. He released me at last and turned toward the window.

"Do you want me to go?" he asked. His face in profile was sad, reflective. "From Blackbriar, I mean?"

"No!" The word exploded from me.

He smiled bitterly, casting me a sidelong glance over his shoulder. "But can you say you want me to stay?"

I threw my head back, closing my eyes as emotion swept over me. "What I want, Valerian, you cannot give me. *I want to not want you.* You do not know how much I pray to be free of this ache to have something I can never possess. I must be too weak, for I cannot seem to achieve it."

He opened his mouth, and I cut him off with a sharp movement of my hand. "Do not dare tell me a thing—I know all of it already. Yes, I know, I must understand—your situation, and therefore *our* situation. And I do. I do understand, more than anyone else, perhaps, for I have my own demons to torment me, do I not? But I have noticed that being understanding has no reward. What has it brought to me, what favor, what advantage? Why must I always *understand*? Do you know how tired I am of it?"

There was an interval of silence, during which I glared at him until the realization of what I'd just blurted so furiously settled on me, bringing a flood of shame. I cut my head sharply to the right. I could not look at him.

But I could feel him staring at me. "My God, I never saw it."

I finally forced my gaze to his. He appeared bemused. He gave me that smile, the secret, tender one that always made me want to weep.

"You've always dazzled me," he said. "You are so brave—always, without fail. Oh, do not scowl at me, you are brave, you know—braver than anyone I've ever known in my life, and it has been a long, long life, Emma. And you are good. Such goodness I've scarce dared imagine. And then, as if that weren't enough, you are—we all forget, all of us who've come to depend on you. Except maybe Sebastian, he knows. Yes, Sebastian knows, but he is the only one."

"Knows what?" I whispered. It is a truth of human nature that we both fear and crave being known, and although I was not sure I could bear to hear more of this, I wanted more than anything for this man to know me. As I waited for him to answer, I felt my heartbeat throb against my ribs like a trapped bird.

"How vulnerable you are." He reached out, then thought better of it and his hand dropped to his side. "Strong, brilliant Emma. In some ways—Lord, curse me for a dolt for not seeing it before this—but in some ways, you are so vulnerable."

My entire body began to shake. I thought I would scream. A feeling welled up inside me, something like joy and terror mixed together in a blend that made the world tilt on its axis. I struggled to remain calm. Strong.

His arms were on me, suddenly, hands cupping my shoulders, giving me something steady. But he did not embrace me. We were not lovers, no matter what our hearts wished, for we were still separated by the blood of Marius, by the part of himself he despised. If it came to it, he wanted to die rather than be made over. And he had made me promise that if he could not see it through himself, then I would kill him. Of all of the sacrifices anyone could have asked of me, this was too much.

He had bound me by solemn vow to kill the man I loved.

How I hated him for that.

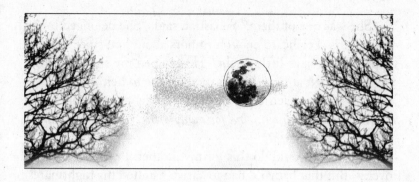

Chapter Sixteen

Sebastian brought me the news of Janet's death. She was found hanged from a tree in the woods, an apparent suicide in precisely the same location where Victoria Markam had claimed to have found all the dead bodies that had subsequently disappeared.

That spot had to be significant to the girls, and I suspected I knew why. Miss Markam had found the cache of corpses by following the girls when they snuck out of the dorm. I could only surmise this was the place where they had conducted their lurid revels.

I do not know why, but the loss of the young girl with whom I'd only had a glancing acquaintance affected me deeply. She had been beautiful, and she'd been so young, with all of her life ahead of her.

"She was one of them," Sebastian said. "She belonged to the coven girls. I've heard enough rumors about her, since she disappeared, to have little doubt." He grasped my shoulder, forcing me to look at him. "Then we must see to her," he said.

I felt my stomach twist in on itself, clenching itself into a knot. *Darkling I listen: And for many a time I have been half in love with easeful Death.*

One day, I would do this for my mother. I could not grieve over it. But that baby I'd had to shrive haunted my nightmares, and I was still tender.

Sebastian had more news when he, Valerian, and Father Luke came to fetch me the following dawn. "This might not be necessary," he told me before I climbed into the carriage with the two men. "I heard in the village that Janet was pregnant. She'd been to see the doctor and he confirmed it."

With so clear a reason for her despair, perhaps her death was not linked to the business with the vampire. I was so eager to avoid this duty, I almost turned around right then and returned to my warm bed. I was also of a mind to avoid Valerian, who sat in broody silence in the dark interior.

"We should be certain," I said instead, and climbed in.

Sebastian sighed, and nodded in reluctant agreement. He'd been affected by the child vampire, too. He would not have argued had I called off our sojourn this day.

But the shriving was uneventful. Janet, pale and strangely beautiful in death, had not awakened, and I felt a sense of peace as I did my duty to protect her soul.

Father Luke stood beside me, wearing his vestments, and I made no comment as he raised his hand, the first two fingers extended, and traced a sign of the cross, first in the air, then over the corpse. This was the first time since last spring that he'd taken his proper role in the shriving of the dead.

He began his prayers, and I bowed my head, finding myself

silently reciting the Latin along with him: *Absolve, we beseech Thee, O Lord, the soul of thy servant, Janet, from every bond of sin, that being raised in the glory of the resurrection . . .*

When he faltered, I glanced at him. His pale skin shimmered with a sheen of fine sweat. He swallowed with difficulty, as if emotion dammed in his throat.

He began the prayer again, and once more he stumbled over the blessings.

I exchanged a worried look with Valerian. Sebastian, too, was staring hard at the priest. Finally, he managed to finish his prayers, picking up the edge of his embroidered stole draped around his neck and kissing it in conclusion of the rite. No sooner had he done so than he spun on his heel and quit the cottage.

"Perhaps it is what happened, that last time with the woman and the child in the cottage," Sebastian said, quietly coming up beside me. "God knows it was horrible."

I nodded. I was sure that was it. The carnage of that dawn was very much with us all on this day. "Thank God we've been spared another scene like it," I murmured.

As the sun broke over the horizon, we set about packing our belongings back into the carriage. We were anxious to be away before we were discovered. That was when we noticed Father Luke was no longer with us.

He was not in his room at the inn, either. I waited by the trap, eager to get underway lest I be late returning to school. Sebastian brought out the troublesome news. "He's gone," he told Valerian and me with something akin to panic. "He's gone to find opium. I was afraid of this. The melancholy still weighs on him."

Valerian was quick to reply. "I will search for him. He can't have gotten far. He's got to be up in the woods where we just were."

"I am coming with you," I said.

"Do you think that wise?" Valerian said. "They will miss you."

My position was precarious with Miss Sloane-Smith, and the gossiping Trudy Grisholm was watching me closely. That, in addition to Sebastian's rightful assertion that I would slow them down—"You are a dreadful horsewoman," he reminded me—convinced me to leave the two of them to it. I hurried back to the school and managed to stable the trap and the horse, get inside, freshen my appearance, and change my clothes just in time for my first class.

I waited the entire day for word, which came in the form of a sealed note late that afternoon. Eloise Boniface brought it into the dining room when we gathered for supper.

"The innkeeper sent this up from the village for you," she whispered, and I noticed gratefully she made certain Trudy was nowhere in sight.

I hastened out of the dining hall to a private spot and tore open the note with clumsy fingers. "We have him," it read in Valerian's spidery hand. "He is safe. He is asking for you. Come when you are able."

It was not until Sunday that I was able to get free and go down to the village. As painfully impatient as I was to have to wait until then, I realized my position at Blackbriar was on thinner ice than I would have thought. I could tell by the manner among the teachers I counted as my friends, Eloise and Ann Easterly particularly, for they tried to give me gentle advice.

"Why don't you come and sit with me this evening?" Eloise had prodded soon after we returned. "You are alone far too much."

And Ann always was there to fetch me for every meal, during which she made special effort to draw me into conversations.

I suppose her intention was to make me seem friendlier, less aloof, and I was touched by her loyalty.

I became aware that there was a line being drawn, with me on one side and the sly Trudy Grisholm on the other. So I was present at every meal, sat with the teachers in the parlor in the evening, joined in their discussions, and in every way tried to appear dependable, sensible, scholarly, and untroubled. But all the while I was biding my time, and after services on Sunday I slipped away to the inn at last.

Valerian was in the common room when I arrived. He knew better than to approach me in a public place. Mrs. Danby greeted me in between her rounds seeing to the tables. While she was occupied, I wandered over to the empty hearth. Madge was not in her chair, but I wanted to get another look at the headstone.

I found it a curiosity, more so since the name Winifred had come up in the story about my mother that Eloise Boniface had told me.

"Are you that chilled?" Mrs. Danby said as she found me by the hearth.

"No. I was looking at this," I said, pointing to the headstone.

She frowned. "It's depressing, isn't it? Well, at least they put it in upside down so it's not so obvious there's a gravestone there."

"Why was it put in the wall?"

"Well, now, we aren't ones here in the fells to waste." She clasped her hands together under her ample bosom. "When that wall was built—hundreds of years ago it was—they used all the stone they could scavenge. That's how it's always been around here, make use of what's at hand. So, they put the headstone in there."

"So it was removed from the grave?"

"Well," she said, giving a sigh, "that's an ugly tale. That

Winifred's grave got opened up after she was gone and her remains burned. They said it was because she was a witch, but women like that—known to have the sight, and maybe know a thing or two about herbs—were always regarded with suspicion. It was how it was with all the women in that family, through the generations."

I wondered if that suspicion was due to her healing gifts, or the close association with Holt Manor. I was still unsettled by the connection of that dragon necklace I'd seen; I didn't know what to make of it.

"I heard of a Winifred whose son, Alistair, was a groundskeeper up at the school," I said. "They also took care of Lord Suddington's house. Was this her relative?"

"Oh, yes, indeed, that's right. The husband and son did the school, took care of Holt Manor before Lord Suddington came back. She was the last of the Winifreds around these parts."

This made sense. I felt anger at the prejudice against women whose only crime was a desire to help others with their healing talents. I felt it for this Winifred whose grave had been defiled and her headstone stolen and placed in the inn's wall, and for the Winifred who had tended my mother. And I felt it for me, for the tale of this poor woman's persecution was a cautionary one. Women with powers were thought to be dangerous, even if those powers saved your life. You could be thought a witch, or insane, or worse . . . evil.

I shook off this dark thought. "Well, thank you for telling me," I said. "I had wondered. I notice your mother is not in her usual place in her chair. Is she well?"

"Oh, bless you for asking, Mrs. Andrews, but she's having her rheumatism today. I keep her in bed through the worst of it."

"Oh, I am sorry to hear she is suffering," I said sincerely. "Please send my regards."

"Kindness itself you are, and understanding of the old. The mind goes, you know. Some complain about her. She can ramble on so. I'm glad it didn't upset you."

"Not at all." I hesitated, and then said, "Although when I was in here last, Sir Charles Morton had a fit of pique over it."

"Oh, him," Mrs. Danby said with a sneer. "What was he on about?"

"Your mother mentioned something called the Cyprian Queen. It upset him a great deal."

She made a snorting sound, a kind of derisive laugh. "Oh, well, he wouldn't care to have his high and mighty self associated with that old legend, would he? He's complained about her before—my mother, I mean. But I can't keep her locked in her bed day and night, and her talk is harmless. It's just an old scary story nobody else puts any stock in."

"I suppose he believes that kind of talk casts a bad light on the school somehow."

"He's a popinjay," she agreed. "Thinks better of himself than he is, that one. But I can't say that I blame him. Rumors of girls going missing from time to time would hardly benefit any institution educating female students."

I had noticed Valerian watching me the entire time I conversed with Mrs. Danby. He said nothing, wisely keeping his distance so as not to draw attention to our frequent meetings. He followed me with his obsidian gaze as I crossed to Sebastian, who was waiting for me at the bottom of the stairs. "He just returned," he said, referring to Valerian as we climbed the stairs. "He went into Penwith to see about several deaths that appeared to be the work of our vampire."

"Ruthven is feeding far away now, so he will not stir suspicions," I surmised.

"Exactly. Valerian thinks he favors the larger city, where the more dense population makes it less likely the strange deaths will be noticed."

We were at the top of the stairs. The door to Father Luke's room was to our left. "How is he?" I asked.

Sebastian's face puckered into a dark scowl. "You will see for yourself. He will not speak to either Valerian or myself, the ungrateful cur. I have a mind to leave him to this business of destroying himself, to which he seems so devoted." The cloud of grief in his eyes bespoke his deep feeling in contrast to his brash words.

I braced myself and entered the room. It was darkened again and it stank of unwashed body, and of despair.

"Do not open the drapes," Father Luke said. I had expected him to be abed, as he had been in the early days of his recovery, but he was seated at the table. "I will light a lamp if you want."

I approached slowly and sat down. "Please," I said.

He took the flint box and used it to light an oil lamp among the refuse strewn on the table surface. We sat in silence.

"Do you recall the time you came to me, and asked me to hear your confession?" he said finally.

"I do, yes."

"I have no one to hear mine," he said.

I blinked in astonishment, not certain I was getting the correct inference. "Do you want to make a confession to me? But I am obviously no priest."

He closed his eyes. "I want to say it. Say it all. If I do not, Emma, I will go mad. It keeps spinning inside my head, and I need to get it out." He shook his head violently. "Even if the bishop himself were here, I could not speak. I took vows—not just the ordinary ones of ordination. Vows of secrecy that bind me . . ."

He took a moment, frowning in thought. Then he said, "I have broken them already, so many times. But I cannot go to the

Church for this. The truth is, I do not trust it anymore. That is part of my suffering. I want to tell you. I trust you, Emma."

My throat constricted, but I found my voice. "Then I am here, father."

"Do not call me that," he snapped. "Call me Luke if you must, although that is not even my name. I am a man of lies, Emma. That is the first thing you must know. Luke is the man who lived a good life, but I am only part him. The other parts . . . I have done terrible things."

"We all have," I told him.

"No. I do not want comfort. I do not want compassion or understanding. Just . . ."

"All right," I assured him. "I will only listen."

He paused, then nodded slowly. "Very good, then. Very good." His mouth twisted very slightly. "Do you still have the crucifix you stole from my church?"

"It hangs over my bed. I learned my lesson after the incident with the rats."

"I stole a crucifix from a church once," he said. "That was why I never minded you took it. I thought if it were important enough for you to remove it without asking permission, then you must have it. I know that was the case for me." Then he settled in. His voice was steady, emotionless. He told me this story:

My family was not religious, although I was raised Calvinist. I envied the Catholics, with their cheerful priest and their statues and paintings and colored light from the stained glass. I used to sneak into the village church and stare at those things, imagining the Bible stories they depicted. It was an escape from my home. My home was a terrible place.

We were poor. My two brothers, older than me,

were brutes. It was nothing for me, the youngest, to be pummeled into submission over the most trivial matter—a scrap of bread or the use of a threadbare sweater—and come away sporting a welt or a bloody lip. My father was unsympathetic. All he cared about was drink. My mother was too busy working to put food on the table to bother with us boys, and she caught her share of cuffs and kicks as well from my da's fists. It was a miserable house, a miserable life, and it made me mean.

We used to steal, my brothers and I. Those were the good times, when I was with them as opposed to being the brunt of their aimless rage. One day, they put me up to taking the money from the poor box at St. Alfonse's. I had no compunctions about doing so. We were poor, weren't we? And I had no morality back then. I liked the crucifix hanging near to the box, and I took that as well. But the priest, Father Lawrence, caught me in the act. I thought I was done for, but instead of getting the lash, as expected, I was taken inside and given a meal. Later, Father Lawrence told me he'd been ready to beat me, as I deserved, but when he'd grabbed my collar he'd seen the bruises along my neck.

So, I kept the crucifix and got away without a scratch. Except I could not live with what the priest had done. It was like something foreign, and it haunted me. For the first time in my life, I felt pangs of guilt. I kept the gold crucifix secret, knowing it would have been nearly my life if I was discovered keeping such a valuable trinket from my greedy family. But I would take it out when I was alone and gaze at it for long periods of time. The look of agony on the Savior's face mesmerized me. I knew enough Christian doctrine to realize Christ had died for sinners. And I knew that I was a sinner.

I began to do things to pay the priest back for his kindness. They were of dubious virtue, but they were the only way I knew to try to make reparations in order to put a stop to the disturbing rumblings of my conscience. I stole apples from a neighbor's orchard and left them on the back stoop of the rectory. I even dared encroach on the squire's land and left a brace of rabbits for the priest's dinner. Given these offerings, I felt entitled to sneak inside the church and gaze at the beautiful pictures of the saints. I continued to raid and pillage, leaving my spoils like a well-trained hound at the priest's doorstep.

Then one time, the father was lying in wait, having camped out in the cold all night to catch me. He gave me a proposition. He would teach me, for he had noticed my fascination with the church, in exchange for my doing legitimate chores for him. I wanted to leap at this chance, but you cannot imagine how terrified I was, for I knew if my brothers learned what I was doing, they would beat me senseless. I accepted anyway.

But they caught on eventually, and did what I knew they would. When Father Lawrence saw the results, he was appalled. I was in a bad state, you understand, so much so that Father Lawrence insisted I move into the rectory.

That was when I was able to study in earnest. Father was also teaching another student, George

Wentworth. George possessed an intellect far beyond mine. His mother baked and cleaned for Father Lawrence in exchange for her son's education. I discovered, not long after moving to the rectory, that she and Father Lawrence were lovers. I was shocked to learn this, of course, but I was also happy for the father. I had always sensed a sadness in him, and I hoped love could cure it. And George's mother was a pretty woman. It was easy to see she was neglected by her husband and she was kind to me. She would bring me clothing, and food treats from time to time, although they could ill afford it. George's sister, Bethany, often came with her mother when Mrs. Wentworth was at the church. She would practice reading with us while they were gone. I was besotted with her.

One day, when I was fifteen years of age, a bishop visited the parish. Father Lawrence presented young George to him. I was so jealous I could not keep away, and hid myself to spy on the meeting. The bishop spotted me hovering, and I felt he picked up instantly on the resentment I could not keep from my face. I had been told I had heavy, unpleasant features, and tended to glower. I fled, thinking I'd been exposed as the ungrateful sinner I was.

Bethany found me sulking behind the barn. While she consoled me, something magical happened: she kissed me and, to my utter shock, she told me she loved me. I was incredulous. I had never before had anyone's love. We began seeing each other every chance we could get and soon we decided to marry. I abandoned my education to find work. I saved every ha'penny I earned so Bethany and I could be wed as soon as possible. It soon became urgent, for she gave me the news that she was carrying my child.

Now, my brothers had come around through the years to bully me. I had found if I gave them money, they left quickly. But when they came to me during this time, I refused to give them any of my hard-earned wages. I had grown taller and stronger than them. I gave notice that they were never to come around again, that I was marrying Bethany and soon would have a family to provide for. Intimidating them felt good. I thought I had won, that I had broken free of the dark, shameful past they represented. But I did not understand, not yet, that evil will never be denied.

A week later, Bethany went missing. I was a madman, searching all day and all night. I finally found her, out on the moors, soaking wet and nearly dead from exposure. She'd been beaten and obviously badly abused. Raped. I brought her to her parents' house. Her mother took her from me to clean her up and put her to bed. But after Bethany was recovered, she would not see me. Her mother told me it was because Bethany feared I would despise her, sullied as she felt. I wanted so badly to assure her nothing was further from the truth. I loved her; nothing would change that. But before I could reassure her, she succumbed to despair. She tore open her delicate wrists in great, shredding gashes and let the life's blood drain from her . . .

I never loved drink as the other men in my family did, but I sought the tavern that night. I would have inhaled fire if I thought it would dull the pain. I found my brothers already well into their cups. They were of good cheer and welcomed me, and I emptied my purse buying round after round. When my money was exhausted, one of my brothers fished a trinket out of his pocket and slapped it down on the table in lieu of coin. I recognized Bethany's necklace immediately and I knew then it had been these two who had killed her, and my child. The stupid brutes were too drunk to realize they'd just given themselves away.

I said nothing. I was somehow stone-sober. And cold. I remember being very cold.

When my brothers had consumed the last of the gin their money would buy, I stumbled out of the pub with them, pretending to be as drunk as they were. Then, when there was no one around to see, I knocked them unconscious. Then I placed my hands around their necks—first one, then the other—and snuffed the life from each one in turn.

I did not fight when the magistrates came for me. I was imprisoned to await the trial. I was sure to be found guilty and hung. That was fine with me; I was ready to die. But I did not wish to go to hell. Bethany and our baby would be in heaven and I wished desperately to be with them. I asked for Father Lawrence to hear my confession. I told him my entire tale.

A few days later, I received a surprise in the form of the bishop. He told me he had noticed me when he'd come to the village to inspect George for the order. He said he liked the hungry look in my eye and my recent actions showed I had certain desirable qualities. That was when he told me of the Order of the Knights of Saint Michael's Wing.

I recall him asking me, with a keen eye to watch

my every reaction, "You know what it is to hate. I need someone whom I can teach to hate the right things, evil things. That strength—your strength—can save the world."

That was how he made me believe I could achieve redemption for what I had done. I entered my training in the Order while at the same time studying to take my vows as a priest. I learned to listen, to submit, to suspend all thought of self. The authority of the Church was a solace, and I, its servant, was redeemed. I did not have to think for myself. They taught me all the answers, what to do, what to believe. They gave me purpose, one so great, so vital, it eclipsed all I had ever been or hoped to be, and I embraced it.

I was sent to Saint Michael in the Fields, one of the most important outposts that guarded the fragile line where the worlds of the living and the dead come together. They gave me all the tools I would need should I be the one called to battle. Life was suddenly simple, clean. I was good again. A priest of God. A protector of the world. I had found redemption. For a time, at least. Until I lost it all over again.

Father Luke lapsed into silence. He had not looked at me the entire time he'd spoken. I did not know what to say. What came to my mind was inadequate, trivial. As if I could make an impact with mere words.

"My mother is a vampire," I said suddenly. "I am made from the very fact that she is undead, that she drinks the blood of human beings to subsist. I know nothing about her, save this. And I do not know how much of that blood, which flows in my veins, lays claim to my soul.

"Valerian Fox is a partially made vampire. He is caught between two worlds. Not human, not completely. Not yet undead. If Marius bites him once more, Valerian will become stricken with the thirst and crave nothing more than that final bite, that transformation into evil.

"Sebastian cannot be accepted by society. He clowns to cover his pain, but the man's heart is nothing but love although he can never have love, not openly. He pretends it does not matter. But he feels; he *feels* it all, and deeply.

"We are all broken, father. We are all lost, and frightened. That is why we need each other."

He shook his head. "You do not understand. I am not just broken. I am shattered. I am beyond redemption. I want the opium. I want oblivion."

"I love you," I whispered fervently. "I cannot imagine what I would have done these past weeks without you here with me. I need you."

He shook his head, refusing the consolation I offered. "The others—"

"They are not enough. None of us are enough without each other."

He finally looked at me. "Emma. You forgive too easily."

"Forgive? I cannot afford to forgive. I am merely being selfish. You tell me of your suffering, of your desire for your drug, and I say the one thing I know will trap you here with me. I tell you I love you and that I need you, and I know I have just bound you as surely as with iron chains anchoring you to that chair. You can no more leave me than you could take my life."

He blinked, his hard features blank. I could believe that face had taken blows, I could believe those hands had killed. I could believe he had both loved and hated. He was no saint. He was just a man.

"We will talk again," I told him. "I will pray for you, father. I will pray this telling will unburden you."

He bowed his head, his jaw working with emotion. I left swiftly, knowing that if he were close to tears he would not wish me to see it.

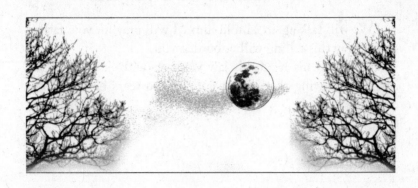

Chapter Seventeen

Suddington was in the dining room when I descended the stairs. I paused to say hello, acutely aware of Valerian's stare. Suddington immediately came to his feet.

"Ah, here is that face which launched a thousand ships. Not to mention those poor topless towers!" He laughed and held out his hands to me. "Mrs. Andrews, I am cruel to tease you so, but you blush so prettily. This is an unexpected pleasure. Will you join me for supper?"

I would have welcomed his hearty charm any other time, but I was not up to it after my talk with Father Luke. And there was Valerian's presence, keenly felt, glaring from the other side of the room.

"I have to decline, I am afraid. I have student reports to prepare. We are finishing up the term this week, you know."

"Then I shall look forward to your having some free time during the break," he replied amiably.

I might have more than a term break's free time if I did not redeem myself with Miss Sloane-Smith, I thought.

Valerian caught up with me in the stable. "I am taking you back," he announced.

"Do not be foolish. I travel the road all the time."

"You do not have to fight me at *every* turn, Emma," he countered wryly.

"I am merely being sensible. It would not do for me to be seen in the company of a man when my status at the school is fragile. We cannot afford for me to be dismissed."

He bowed, yielding. But as he retraced his steps back into the inn, I noticed his jaw grinding in frustration.

I almost called him back. I was equally as frustrated. If truth be told and I were honest, I thought as I pointed the trap toward the road that led up to Blackbriar, I would see that I was afraid. But that fear was not something I was willing to explore.

My breath came in puffs of smoke but I barely noticed the cold as my mind turned from the subject of Valerian Fox to Father Luke. I was much affected by his story, and my empathy for his terrible loss put me in a somber mood.

Then, just when I was about to climb the series of switchbacks and inclines that paved the way from village up the fell to the school, the voice of Ruthven rose like a snake from the gathering darkness and hissed into my ear. *I have missed you, Sister.*

I pulled the conveyance to a halt. All around me was still, and I realized how silent and still the woods had been all the while I'd been passing through. "Ruthven? Is that you?"

Have you yearned for me?

"I want to know more of you," I replied. "Are you what they

call the Cyprian Queen?" I peered into the woods, where shadows gathered into knots of secret darkness. Where was he?

I do use that name, for it embodies beauty and romance, and erotic love. I shall show you all the wonders of these things.

I felt the touch of a finger trip lightly down my spine and jumped, crying out softly. He was before me all of a sudden, seeming to materialize from nowhere. In the darkness, I felt his power emanating across space to me, affecting each nerve. I struggled to make out his features, for I could see no more than a suggestion of golden hair, of a wide, inviting smile in a shadow-hidden face, of a lithe male figure clad in black. He was affecting an appearance, merely. Well did I know the vampire's true form was hideous; this was merely an illusion.

Yes, I am indeed a god, my love. He reached toward me. I cringed from him, even as a part of me wanted to take that hand stretched out . . .

You will marvel at me, at my beauty and my power. You will know me as none other ever has. My long wait will end. We shall roam my kingdoms, and find our pleasures together.

I forced myself to concentrate. "Is this what you offered my mother? Laura Newly. It was many years ago, but you have been here before, haven't you?"

The timbre of a chuckle floated around me. *She was never one of mine.*

I was shocked. My mind railed against this—it couldn't be! "But . . . You made her. It had to be you."

Enough with your questions. What does any of it matter? You will care for no one else from your old life when you have me. You are destined for me and only me. I understand at last why I failed with all the others. You are whom I've waited for all these ages.

Something touched the back of my hand. I started, crying out softly and swatting furiously at the spot. I could not stand to have this *thing* violate me again. "Stop that!" I shouted.

*I will show you what I am. I will show you the Cyprian Queen—
and all I can give to you.*

And then it was happening again—that vile touch was on
me, everywhere. All my courage, all my independence drained
from me. "Please! Please, no!" Panic made me beg. I could not
bear it again.

I tore at my clothes, needing desperately to reach those
unseen hands. I could feel them all over me, invading, grasping, pinching, pulling me apart. I heard him whispering, cajol-
ing, wheedling.

Then I heard a different voice, a new one, speaking my
name. And hands, different hands, feeling wonderfully substantial and secure, holding me.

"Emma! Emma! It's Valerian."

The horrid touch was gone. The beautiful shadow figure was
gone. Valerian has chased him off. I surged upward, clutching,
climbing, writhing into the safety of Valerian's arms.

"He was here!" I cried.

"Hush. I know. I followed you from the village. I saw you
talking to someone."

"Did you see him? He wants to . . . He tried to take me,
Valerian." I was sobbing, unable to calm my racing heart, my
stomach sick with revulsion and fear.

"He cannot now," he said, yanking off his crucifix and placing it over my neck. "I am here." He dragged me down from
the trap, the exertion nothing to his extreme strength, and he
bore me away. I did not know where he was taking me, and I
did not care. I buried my head in the curve of his shoulder and
inhaled his scent, ridding my lungs of the sickening stench of
Ruthven's perfumed presence. I pressed my cheek, my lips, and
my temple against his skin, wanting to fill my senses with as
much of Valerian as I could get.

When he laid me down, I was amazed to find I was in his

rooms. He had carried me all the way to the inn, I realized. "I will get Serena," he whispered.

I pulled at him, preventing him from leaving. "Do not leave me!"

He grasped my hands, freeing himself, and folded them in his warm, strong palms. "I have protections here. You will be safe while I am gone."

"No. I need you," I gasped. "He tried to do to me what he did before. Eustacia said they liked it, but she was horrified by it as I was. He is the Cyprian Queen, do you not understand? This is what he does to them!"

"To whom, Emma?"

"The girls. He uses . . . desire. He makes them want him. He fools them into thinking he is their demon lover, but he is a vampire, Valerian. He makes them think it is all some kind of a wonderful adventure when it is simple lust, and he controls them with it."

"We have discussed this," he told me calmly. "No manner of vampire craves sensual pleasure."

"It's not that. He used the Irish boy. That was why he sent him . . . before. It's . . . It was power. It is all about power. He talks of being a god. It is a game to him, to move these girls this way and that, manipulate them and twist them. They are mere amusements."

He bowed his head and brought my fingers to his lips, squeezing his eyes shut as he kissed them. "Your hands are cold."

He was trying to distract me, calm me. I was touched, and I realized that my faith in him, which had been so sorely strained, was restored. I suddenly had the impulse to trust him with the deepest horror. "He speaks of me as the one."

"The one?"

"His mate," I choked.

Valerian's dark gaze glittered. His fingers stroked my skin. The fluttering pulse in my wrist lay under his fingertips, and I had an acute sense of connection to him. It was like a balm, this small caress. "Why is he doing this to me?" I whispered.

I do not know why I asked him, when I knew the answer. The blood of my mother, the vampire who had made her, bound me to Ruthven. He thought me a sister, and as the gods of Olympus had lain with each other, sanguinity notwithstanding, he believed that blood connection would satisfy something he'd been searching for all of his existence. Something his sadistic games only soothed for a little while but never fully satisfied.

He expected me to revel in the pleasure he inflicted on me. To him, he was offering a great gift . . . "I am going to retch!" I exclaimed, mortified that I was so weak.

"I am here."

"No, you . . ." Valerian gathered me into his arms and the swell of nausea subsided. I clung to him desperately, taking everything I needed to breathe, to exist, from him.

"Is it possible for a vampire to be mad?" I whispered.

"There is much that is possible," he murmured soothingly, stroking my hair.

My breathing eventually slowed under his calming touch. My thoughts unlocked, and I realized something. "The sick game, it is all a puppet play for his vanity. There is more than the evil of the vampire in him, Valerian. There is something else, something twisted and . . . wrong. He craves being all-powerful, toying with these girls as gods play idly with the fates of mortals."

Valerian sat back, but he still held my hands. My thoughts were falling into place quickly. I could scarcely speak fast enough to keep pace with them. "Yes, a god. That is how he sees himself. And so he seduces the girls. But it is not sex that he craves. He wants for them to admire him, adore him, make him their everything. If you could sense what I did, the sickness in him to be acknowledged as superior, even supreme."

Our bodies were pressed intimately against one another. I knew it was improper, but I could not bear to break contact, wanting every inch of myself entwined with his lean strength.

"He did not make my mother. I thought perhaps . . ." He squeezed my hand. I said, "Yet we are made both from Lliam. And I do not even know who that is."

"Enough for now. You have been through an ordeal." Valerian reached for my face, gently molding his palm to the contour of my cheek. "You will find the answers in time. We will search together."

"I cannot go through another attack," I said. I noticed then how my fingers were biting into his flesh. The ghost of Ruthven's putrid touch still shivered along my skin. I felt better here with Valerian. More than better. I felt safe.

"Then I will protect you," he said tenderly. "You have only to let me, Emma."

Could he do so? I believed that he would. He had always given me courage. That was why I had felt his absence so keenly. I had not wanted to accept how vulnerable I was where he was concerned. But I could not fight it any longer. I no longer even wanted to.

He was a part of me in some way, a stranger in many others. But our connection was real, tangible almost—elemental, essential. And as I lay with him, shivering as my flesh twitched in the aftermath of Ruthven's invasion, I turned my face to his, my hands pulling him toward me. I sealed my lips against his.

This was nothing like the kisses we'd shared before. This kiss flared instantly, filled with passionate need that was unapologetically carnal. Everything the abhorrent Ruthven had tried to stir in me now flowered, flowed, flooded. I could do nothing to control it, to stop myself. My fingers dug into the silk of his hair and my mouth opened to invite the sensual kiss of lovers.

He did not indulge me for long. When my hands went to untie his cravat, he locked his grip over my wrists. "Emma," he warned, pulling away.

My fingers wheedled into the knot and deftly undid it.

"No," he said more firmly. He kept his body rigid, and I opened the neck cloth, exposing his secret. Bending my head, I kissed him there, overlaying the old puncture wounds with my own kiss.

Nothing magical happened. They did not disappear. He did not even seem to register what I had done. But I sensed a war within him. Looking into his face, my gaze touched those piercing, sharp cheekbones, then slid down the shadows that stretched like gouges underneath. It was a lean face, a bleak face.

"This is not right," he murmured, but I knew he was weakening. I placed my hands flat on the smooth skin of his chest where his shirt gaped. He was pale, warm, unblemished, devoid of the roughness of a man. I thought him exotic, unspeakably beautiful, graceful, masculine. For all his leanness, power shifted under my questing hands, strength of far more consequence than the most heavily muscled of men.

I reveled in his realness, his pureness. The infliction of Ruthven's touch had been a mere impostor, thin and feeble now that I had the truth in my grasp.

"Emma," he whispered, as if begging me to allow him to stop. He could have extricated himself any time he wished. "Not now, not like this."

I was suddenly afraid his better judgment would defeat me. I could not bear that. I kissed him again.

"I am not strong enough to keep refusing," he murmured against my cheek. "If you knew . . . I've thought of this, of us together. Of making love to you. But not like this. You are not yourself."

"I am at last myself, and it is because of you."

"This is because of *him*. Of Ruthven."

Coldness gripped me, and such a panic as to make me cruel. "What if it is? Would you condemn me to enduring his filthy touch, to the memory of it alive on my flesh like a thousand devouring spiders?"

His face froze, sealed in a rigor mortis of horror. I pressed forward, my hands frantic, snaking around his neck. "Valerian, do not leave me alone with this . . . thing inside me."

He could not hide his reaction. I was using him, and he knew it. What feeling we shared that might have led us to become lovers was not what made my body burn for him. He was right; I was not myself. But I was in pain, and I needed him nonetheless.

He moved suddenly toward me, surprising me, for I had expected him to turn me away. His hands gripped my waist firmly, locking us together as he pushed me back onto the bed. He made to undress me, but I could not tolerate his patience. Our clothing was discarded in a flurry, without gentleness. What feeling he tried to bring to it, I would not abide. In the end, our lovemaking was swift, fed by my desperation and lust. The pleasure of it shattered me, breaking apart the grip of the vampire, restoring me, giving me what I sought.

Afterward, however, as I lay in his arms, I felt hollow.

I'd paid a terrible price for my healing. It became suddenly clear to me in the silence, and the cold distance that seemed to seal us apart, that I had bargained away a most precious thing.

"I am leaving when the week is out," I told him. "The term is over. I promised Alyssa I would go see her."

"She has had her child?"

"It will come any day."

"I will come with you."

I wished he had not said that. I selfishly wanted him with me, of course, but I was feeling particularly ashamed of myself right now. I'd cheated us both of something I'd had no right to.

"I think Sebastian and Father Luke should stay here," I said.

"It will be up to them. We are all our own masters."

How untrue. None of us had the least bit of freedom, or so it felt to me at that moment.

"I suppose." I rose to dress. Valerian said nothing. I thought perhaps he was angry with me, or perhaps he felt sorry for me. I did not know which was worse.

He took me back to Blackbriar, this time uneventfully. I said good-bye and thanked him, then winced, for it might seem to him that I was thanking him for taking me to his bed. I had not meant that, but it was true I did owe him. What I had taken from him—from both of us—was a debt that might be forever impossible to repay.

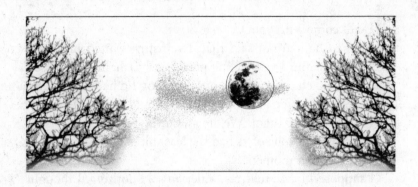

Chapter Eighteen

Father Luke wanted to go to Rome. He would tell no one what it was he wished to do there. I had great fears on this account, but I could not take the time to question him about it.

The students left the school for the term break, a surprisingly rapid procedure whereupon they piled into the trap in turns, to be taken down into the vale, and on to holiday spots and reunions with their families from there. I had a train out of Penwith to catch, for I was headed to the Peak District, where Alyssa was. Without discussion, it was somehow decided Valerian would travel with me. Sebastian rather reluctantly accompanied a very grouchy Father Luke on his journey, but I could not tell if he was truly put out or merely making a show of it. I suspected the latter.

Father Luke, however, was not pleased with his travel companion. "I will not have you pester me," the priest had warned as they readied to leave. "I will be about my own business. I will have none of your hovering."

"Good God, man, I plan to be inebriated the entire time." Sebastian snapped his gloves into alignment. "I hate traveling, you know. I do not suppose Rome is known for its parties. All those priests."

I had come to accept their unusual relationship, but even I had to wonder at times how they tolerated the barbs that were so freely flung between them. It seemed, however, they rather enjoyed it.

It was a very different atmosphere with Valerian and me. During our travel, he was dour. I was too shamed by what I'd done to breach the long stretches of silence with anything more than the absolutely most necessary conversation. There was no repeat of our surrender to passion, if that was what it had been. In fact, there was more distance between us than had ever existed before. In those long silences, as we rumbled across lengths of rutted country roads, I often found Valerian looking pensive, a dark frown on his face. And I wished I could do over again that which I'd done wrong.

But fate blessed me with a reprieve when I arrived at Castleton, the estate where I had grown up and where my sister and her husband now resided. Alyssa, having just been delivered of a healthy, beautiful son, was too overjoyed to pout very long at my having neglected her. I saw at once that motherhood had changed her. My sister glowed with pride and happiness, and was in such good spirits that she satisfied herself with only a mild rebuke before presenting the most majestic Roderick Alan for my inspection.

I must confess: it was love at first sight. "He is gorgeous," I breathed, taken aback by the feeling that came over me as

I held the tiny infant. I adored my cousin's child, Henrietta, but that was an affection that had grown over time, and so my almost violent response to little Roderick took me by surprise. "Absolutely perfect."

"He is handsome," she corrected. "He is a boy, Emma. Boys are handsome."

"He is lovely," I insisted with a smile, "like his mother."

She giggled. Alyssa was partial to compliments. "And his father."

"Indeed," I agreed. "Alan is quite pretty as well."

We laughed, and I marveled how we had at last moved beyond the ill will that had followed her accepting Alan's proposal of marriage. I had been wrong on that account, and had learned a valuable lesson. Though Alan still wouldn't have been my choice of husband, unpossessed as he was of intelligence or personality, it was true he was devoted to her, and that she was mostly happy with her life as his wife.

He was not in the mood for our usual sniping at one another, however, being of good humor in the aftermath of the birth of so perfect a son. When I saw him later, I felt my gushing over the baby made him forget his dislike of me. And so the visit was surprisingly fine, going along with unanticipated pleasantness. Valerian and I spent little time together, for I was helping with Roderick as much as Alyssa would allow me. We were all of us getting along immensely well—that is, until the subject of my whereabouts for the last several months was at last broached.

"I think it best," I replied carefully, having rehearsed what I would say, "that you not know too much about why, but I am in Cumbria in a town near Penwith."

"But what could be so important there?" she demanded.

I paused. It would have been so easy to slip into my old role. When faced with my pouting sister, long habit had taught me that apologies and platitudes were the quickest way to appease her. I did not think I could bring myself to do that now, however. I certainly could not tell her she had no right to question my whereabouts. That would be going too far.

I found a neutral compromise. "Will it help to know I am doing good there?"

Was I? I wondered suddenly. It did not seem like I had accomplished much. Alyssa watched me carefully. "I still do not understand that business at Dulwich Manor," she said, a hint of accusation in her tone.

"It was my impression you were comfortable not knowing."

Her sullenness increased. "It seemed very unpleasant and I thought it best nothing upset me when I was in my condition."

"A very sound choice," I concurred.

She sighed. "Oh, Emma, why can you not be the normal sort who stays put and takes up gardening or some such hobby? Why do you have to be so . . . unusual?"

It seemed that for all of my life, someone or other was asking that question of me.

"And that Mr. Fox," she added disapprovingly. "What is going on with the two of you? Why have you brought him here with you? I hope you are not intending to marry him. He is very unsuitable, to say the least. Does he ever smile?"

I bit my lip. "On occasion. But it takes a great deal of provocation."

She seemed puzzled, missing my joke. "He is so dark. Much too complicated for my taste."

I secretly agreed and, further, I feared I would lose control of my emotions if we continued discussing Valerian. Forcing a smile, I said, "That is why Alan is such a perfect husband for you. He is simple."

She beamed, missing my unintentional insult. "And we've made a fine son."

Later that day, Valerian found me in the library. It was one of the places, besides my sister's bedside or cooing over Roderick, I was almost always sure to be found.

I had that morning recollected the peculiar habits of the vampires of Greece that I'd been studying at the archive when Sebastian's letter had arrived, and this had inspired me to do some research in my family's library. We had an extensive collection of the classical writings from that country's golden age and I had previously discovered a great deal of information was to be gained in literary references of varying kinds.

I'd been at it all morning. When Valerian entered, I was ecstatic to see him, for I had found something. I'd been poring over a work by Philostratus, *The Life of Apollonius of Tyana*, in which I had found several mentions of vampires.

"These beings fall in love and they are devoted to the delights of Aphrodite . . . and they decoy with such delights those whom they mean to devour in their feasts."

I saw that Valerian was ill at ease as he settled into a chair near mine, but I was too excited to inquire as to why. "I believe I have found something very relevant to our Cyprian Queen," I told him anxiously. I reread the lines for him.

He nodded, deep in thought, but he did not take up the topic as I thought he would.

I put the book aside. "What is it?" I asked, seeing I did not have his full attention.

"I have gotten word through my sources that Marius may be in London," he began, "so I am preparing to leave. If I can pick up his trail again, I—"

"You do not need to explain yourself," I said.

He drew in a deep breath. "I know you think I am abandoning you."

"No," I rushed to assure him. He should not be begging my pardon this time; it was I who had done wrong to him. "Oh, Valerian, I know you have to go. I know why."

"Do you?" he challenged, suddenly infused with fervent disbelief. "I do not know what you think, Emma, but my motivations are simple."

"Yes. I know. You must find Marius."

"Emma, listen to me. You deserve so much more than I can give you right now," he continued.

I cut him off curtly. "What a ridiculous thing to say, Valerian."

I could see he was taken aback. I tilted my head, my tone sharpening. "Why do I deserve so much? What makes me so special that I must be denied what I want because it is not as much as I should have? What nonsense, that I must be miserable in payment for being so utterly *deserving* of more than you can give."

I was not cowed by the storm gathering on his features. I stood, and peered down at him with my temper at full force. "I am so very sick of your obsession. I understand it, I even share it—but I am tired of it defining everything about you, and every moment between us. Your fears are yours, and you are welcome to them; I begrudge you nothing on that account. No one would argue your fate is unimaginably terrible. But what Marius did to you is only part of this lonely existence you have made. It is you yourself who decided you are unworthy of a real human life, with real human emotions. It is you who has banished yourself into isolation, stripped yourself of all else so that you are merely Marius's half-made minion and nothing more. You became his nemesis, his hunter, but to make that happen you gave all of yourself away. Yes, Marius took what he did, and it was a terrible thing. But it was you who fashioned the rest."

He studied me for a moment, then lowered his gaze. "Well. I have wanted to know what was in your mind, creating such a distance between us. I thought it was Naimah. Now I see it is more." He shrugged. "You are justified in what you say. I have made this life. The odd thing was, I was content with it before." His eyebrows twitched as a spasm of grief gripped him. "Now, it is like a prison."

I sank back in the chair. "Oh, Valerian, I am sorry. I do understand, it is just . . . Of course you must track Marius if you have a lead. Whenever there is a chance for your freedom, you must never hesitate to take it."

He was thoughtful, looking gently at me for a moment. "Emma. About what happened at the inn—"

"I would rather not speak of it," I said quickly.

But he was not of a mind to allow me my pride. "We will make this right," he vowed darkly.

I shivered. I wished I could believe him, but the gulf seemed insurmountable.

Valerian departed the following morning. Christmas came and went, and for once it was a merry atmosphere, until a letter arrived from Blackbriar on Boxing Day.

My hands trembled as I opened it; I feared it was my notice. It was not quite that, but still it did not bear good news. A meeting would be convened in the midst of January to determine my continued employment.

Suddington was on the board. There was hope yet that I would still retain my position. If not, I would have to think of something else to keep me in the village, at least, if not the school. I could not abandon the girls. As much as I disliked Vanessa, Margaret, and the others, they were but children playing at women's games, seduced and flattered into sin. Their callous and scandalous behavior was reprehensible, but they should not have to die for it.

It was Eustacia who was most in my thoughts. I fervently vowed to myself that I would allow nothing to happen to her. But how to protect her? I had to be clever, for I could not risk confiding in her. I could be exposed, banished, thought of in the same disgusted whispers as poor Victoria Markam.

One day not long after the letter from Sloane-Smith arrived, I was on my way into my sister's bedroom in the master suite. I came and went so frequently, as Alyssa kept the baby with her there, that I did not bother to knock. As I was about to enter, the mention of my name stopped me in my tracks.

"If your mother wanted Emma to have them, she would have given them to her." That was Alan. "What good will it do now?"

"My mother was not always fair when it came to Emma," Alyssa said. The petulance in her voice told me they were having a disagreement. "Or Laura."

I flattened myself against the wall as quietly as I could manage, and strained my ears.

"She was mad. Everyone knew it." Alan was dismissive, bored. "Why would you wish to hurt your sister by exposing her to that? Why have you suddenly grown concerned over those old letters? Really, Alyssa, just because she's fawned over Roderick a bit does not make up for how scandalously she neglected you all these months. I only hope she now sees the error of her past and makes amends to you."

"You sound like Mother used to sound," Alyssa said.

"I believe your mother and I would have been in perfect harmony in our opinions about Emma."

I realized that was exactly true, and probably the entirety of my dislike of the man. He and Judith would have adored each other.

"I still think she should have them, Alan. They are hers. I am feeling much differently about Emma since I've grown up. I am a mother now. It has made me see things differently. I do not understand Emma, I never will, but I do know she is not what Mother made her out to be."

"I am not so certain about that. Her mother was mad, and her sanity is questionable. Why, recall that ugly business in Avebury—"

"I do not want to know!" Alyssa exclaimed, then continued in an altered tone. "Yet, Alan, somehow I think she did something very important. Very . . . special. I just do not feel right keeping her mother's letters from her any longer."

I nearly dropped to the floor as my legs went suddenly and completely nerveless. The words shook through me, turning into quicksilver in my veins. Letters. From my mother?

My hands fisted at my side. I was overwhelmed by two thoughts. The first was that my mother had written to me! She had not forgotten me, after all.

The second was that they'd kept them from me—Judith and Alyssa. Judith I could not blame, for she was a small-hearted woman, consumed with jealousy and rivalry. She knew my father would never love another as he had my mother. That she could hurt me—Laura's child—like this I could well believe.

But Alyssa . . . Even now, I made an excuse, thinking that perhaps she could not help the heavy influence of her mother. But no—Judith was long dead, and I had been a faithful sister. Her conscience on this matter should have prodded her long before now.

I had to find a way to get the letters. I knew it would not do to stalk into the room and demand them. Therefore, I plastered a false smile in place as I entered. Nothing in my manner betrayed me; at least, I thought not.

I began the search for Laura's letters that afternoon.

Valerian returned on Twelfth Night, and brought a surprise with him—Peter Ivanescu, my beloved Uncle Peter.

"I do love surprising you," Uncle Peter said happily as I

rushed to embrace him. The foreign cadence of his words was like falling down a well to my youth. He had been a frequent visitor here at Castleton as one of my father's closest friends, and I had been hopelessly infatuated with him. Just his presence still brought a rush of warmth, of comfort and happiness.

"I received your letter, my dear," he intoned seriously. "I only just returned to England. I had gotten back but two days when Mr. Fox called upon me." He tsked. "There is still unrest in the Baltic, you know. It has kept me quite occupied, and I am sorry to say I have not been able to make much advance in what we discussed before."

He had vowed to help me find my mother. Now that his suspicions were confirmed—for he had long suspected she had become a vampire—he was committed to my quest of learning what had become of her, for he cared deeply about her fate, almost as much as I did.

"You are good to make a journey so soon after getting home," I told him.

"As a matter of fact, I am off again back to Latvia in less than a fortnight on another diplomatic mission."

I turned to Valerian and offered an uncharacteristically shy hello. He smiled, and I could see he was amused. I sensed it was because he knew well my awkwardness.

Naturally, Alyssa assumed Uncle Peter had come to pay homage to her son, and my very clever friend did not disabuse her of this notion. Thus we spent an agreeable afternoon and evening. But when it was time to retire, Uncle Peter cast me a meaningful look, and I nodded.

I returned to the parlor after the midnight bells had tolled through the house, and found him waiting for me, seated in a large leather chair with a tumbler of whiskey in his hand. He raised his glass as I joined him. "Your father always stocked the best. It is comforting to be here again at Castleton." His large eyebrows dipped. "But it makes me realize how much I miss him."

"You were more brothers than friends," I said. "I know he thought so."

He nodded, smiling warmly at me. "Mr. Fox is waiting to join us, but I wished to talk alone with you first. Your letter disturbed me, Emma, on two accounts. The more important is this foolishness concerning the Dracula. This we will wait to speak of with Mr. Fox. But first, I was terribly disturbed to hear you were investigating your mother's past. I promised you I would dedicate myself to finding her. My services have been needed over the Russian matter, but I am still determined to help. Have you found anything yet?"

"No. But I have many theories, although none of them very substantial. Did she ever mention the name 'Ruthven' to you?"

He rolled the name on his tongue as he frowned in thought. "No, child. That name is not familiar to me."

"What of the Cyprian Queen, did she ever speak of this during her madness? Or of Aphrodite, Venus, anything such as this?"

He seemed surprised. "Indeed, I do not recollect anything of this nature, and I have been laboring since we parted to remember as much as possible about Laura. Alas, those days are long gone and filled with regret. It is hard to look back." He sighed. "I should have saved her."

"We can save her now," I told him.

His eyes softened and he smiled. "There. That spirit always surprises me, coming from one so young. Stephen would have taken such pride in your strength. You are a great credit to my dear friend."

I lowered my eyes, emotion choking off any kind of reply. The idea of my father taking pride in me nearly overwhelmed me. I cleared my throat with difficulty, then said, "I share all information with Mr. Fox. It is not necessary for us to speak privately, even about this."

He nodded. "I am glad you have such a confidant as him. He impressed me much on our journey."

Valerian was waiting in the billiard room. He abandoned his game and followed me back into the drawing room. "I am eager to hear what you have to tell us. You know of the Dracula?" He waved off Uncle Peter's offer of whiskey as he sat.

"Where I am from, all know of the Dragon Prince."

"That is what Serena Black told me," I interjected. "She was raised in Eastern Europe. She told me no one dares speak openly of him."

"Indeed, there is great danger in doing so. Information about the Dragon Prince is tightly controlled. But I do know some things about him. I grew up not far from where he is rumored to have lived when alive, for as is true of all vampires, the Dragon Prince was once a man. But this vampire was not just any man. He was a prince of Wallachia, Prince Vlad— known to many by the appellation of Vlad the Impaler."

At the grotesque name, I swallowed with difficulty.

Uncle Peter continued, "Prince Vlad was a knight of the great Order of the Dragon, as his father had been. This was a holy society committed to defending Christiandom from invading Turks. Thus, his father was known as Vlad Dracule— the Dragon—and he came to power as the Dracula. Son of the Dragon."

"He was a holy man?" I said with a gasp. This seemed incredible.

"Indeed, he was a hero of his time. He was especially beloved, for he had achieved the throne by showing great prowess and cunning. The old prince pitted his sons in mortal combat against each other, for he wished to see which was the most worthy, the fiercest, the most ruthless, and thus the most fitting ruler of the princedom. The others had no chance, for in all of these things, the young Vlad was unsurpassed. He inflicted the most barbaric of torments on his adversaries, his brothers among them. But he ruled his country well and protected it from the Muslim hordes seeking to invade."

Peter's smile was humorless as he paused to give weight to his words. "He was feared by his own people, as well as his enemies. His cruelty, his bloodlust, his absolute absence of mercy or human pity knew no boundaries, nor loyalties. Thus, he was transformed by his wickedness into the undead."

"Is that simply legend or do you have proof?"

"What proof can there be? I tell you, I am convinced, as are legions of others, that despite his heroic defense of the Church in life, he searched and found the means for immortality. And so now he rules in secret from the shadows of mystery and fear. It is not wise to speak of him. Many who are familiar with the revenant world know of at least one instance when a loose tongue on the subject of the Dracula cost the speaker his life. And in a most . . ." His features blanched. "It is a horrible punishment."

I shivered. "Serena said as much," I said soberly as I recalled my friend's words. "He makes you over, and sends you back to kill all those you loved."

Uncle Peter nodded.

Valerian leaned forward to prop his elbows on his knees. His eyebrows knit together in concentration. "I have traveled far and wide in this world, to many exotic lands. I have been hunting for a long time, and I have only heard the Dracula spoken of in the vaguest of terms. That was why, when I saw his mark in Avebury, I was not certain what it meant."

Uncle Peter touched a hand thoughtfully to his lips. "Of

course, the legends of the Dracula have not been fully suppressed, at least not among those who know and see his power. That is why, in my country, we know of him." He laughed. "When I was a boy, we would dare each other to whisper of the Dragon Prince, the Dracula, as a test of manhood. You know how it is among youthful men; foolishness is often a badge of honor. We survived. Yet the fear is there, and very effective."

I asked, "Is there anyone to whom I can go who would be willing to speak to me of him?"

"Oh, there are fools who profess to know of the Dracula, or at least some part of the tale."

"But you said those who speak of him are destroyed."

"Only some. He allows some of self-proclaimed 'experts' to tout their theories, for it only advances the great Dracula's cause. You see, he is most clever. Consider: if he is spoken of only by those already discredited by society, if he remains merely a myth, a legend, a figment. What better way to maintain the anonymity of his true power? You see? What greater protection than the idle and unsubstantiated rumor to cast even the most ironclad proof of his existence into doubt?"

"He manipulates masterfully," I said, impressed.

Uncle Peter nodded gravely. "It grows worse with the dawn of our modern conceits. The progress of the world is his protection, the vanity of science, of philosophy that moves us away from the wisdom of the simple, basic ways that served humankind for thousands of years." He spread his hands. "People hardly need God anymore. Why on earth should they require monsters? As if either was their choosing. They put too much faith in intellect, but even the smartest of men does not know everything."

Father Luke came to my mind, for this sentiment seemed to echo his disillusionment. Had he found his answers in Rome?

"Who among the discredited fools is the most informed?" Valerian asked.

Uncle Peter laughed at this cleverness. "I know of only one man who ever dared investigate the legend of the Dracula openly. An Irishman named David Stoker, but he disappeared years ago."

I let out a pent-up breath. Disappointment weighed on my shoulders. "Then we are at a dead end."

When I glanced at Valerian, he appeared lost in thought. I wanted to mention the letters my mother had sent, but I did not think either one of the men would have any idea to help me. I had to be the one to find them, and I would read them first before bringing them to the others. They were, after all, written to me.

Valerian asked, "Do you know of the Dracula's connection to someone named Lliam?" He glanced at me. "Ruthven spoke of kinship to Emma through Lliam."

Uncle Peter shook his head. "I have not heard the name. But this Ruthven is a bold one indeed if he openly claims kinship with the Dracula. It is not only the living who fear the Dragon Prince. All of the undead are under his rule, across Europe and even into some parts of Asia. He can and indeed has destroyed many of his own kind in his quest for absolute power. I cannot see why this Ruthven would take so great a risk."

"Nor I," I admitted. "Perhaps it is simply that he is mad with power, and boasting foolishly because of it."

"That could be," Uncle Peter agreed.

"I think I understand how and what he is doing in Blackbriar, what he has been doing for centuries. But what has he to do with the Dragon Prince—or me?"

I did not expect answers, but that did not mean my spirits were immune to the gaping silence in the aftermath of my questions. I felt demoralized as we adjourned.

But the following morning, I rose from bed with a new reso-lution. I was going to find my mother's letters. I had not done so yet, because of the difficulty of the task. I was with Alyssa nearly all the time, and even though I'd grown up in the house, it was no longer my home; I could hardly wander about where I would.

It was a big house, however, and progress was slow. Alyssa's bedroom alone took over an hour. But by that night, I'd not had a hint of the letters' whereabouts. I lay in my bed and tried to think of more places I could search on the morrow.

By the second day, Valerian noticed my strange behavior—I was ever amazed at his powers of observation—and I told him what I'd overheard between my sister and her husband. He later suggested to Alan that he take his wife on a small outing, to get her out for a little while down to the village for a coffee and a bit of shopping. Alyssa pounced on the idea.

"I shall be happy to look after Roderick," I rushed to put in when I saw a shadow of doubt cross her features. She really was a devoted mother. "Or rather, look after nurse while she looks after Roderick."

With Uncle Peter busy at work on his mountain of corre-spondence, I had the entire day to do a search. In the end, I found nothing. And then, a terrible thought occurred to me, one I refused to allow myself to entertain, for it was too awful . . .

I did not know how I could manage to maintain my spirits if I found Alyssa had destroyed them.

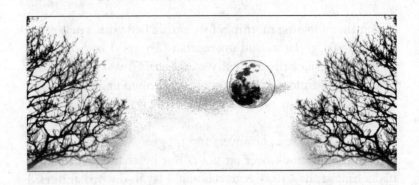

Chapter Nineteen

Judith had many sayings, always self-serving ones that drove her point home with the punctuation of ageless wisdoms. The one I remember her telling Alyssa all the time was: "It is always darkest before the dawn," which was meant to bolster Alyssa when she became dispirited, such as when her cheek sported a "ghastly" spot, or her courses came on just when she was looking forward to a particular outing. Judith's platitudes for me were of a different nature, designed to admonish me. When she thought I was being selfish, she would tell me that "good deeds bring their own reward."

It was ironic that I recalled this when I found the letters at last, for I was in the middle of doing a good deed when it happened. One particularly cold day, when Alyssa was fretting that Roderick would catch a chill, I offered to fetch a blanket for her from a trunk in a rarely used bedroom. This was the room where Judith had stashed my mother's portrait—barely waiting until my father was buried before she had it taken down from the drawing room where it always had hung. In the trunk, I searched through the pile of old quilts and knit blankets to find the softest, thickest one, for only the best would do for young Roddy.

And so, that was where I found them, nestled among the woolens scented with sachets of lavender. There were not very many, tied in a packet by a ribbon, but they were as pristine as the day they were delivered; I assumed most of them were unread. I recognized her hand, the one I'd seen only once before, when I'd found those terrible words written on the flap of her portmanteau. Emotion reared up in me, stinging my eyes with unshed tears, and my heart began to thunk heavily in my chest. This was the first real, tangible connection to my mother I'd ever had.

I gently thumbed through the pack. Those on top were addressed to my father. I took one out, opening it with shaking hands. The date was 1842, three years after my birth. The place was Inishmore, Ireland.

Ireland? How curious—my father had known, then, where she was. Why had he not brought her home?

My Beloved Stephen,

How can I express how sorry I am for the pain I caused you? I am wicked, and have no right to contact you, but I am weak. I am so alone, so lost and ashamed for what I've done. You cannot imagine how I torment myself with regret. Foolishness, vanity, spite—they are sins that carry their own penance, for in living mine I know the burn of true repentance. Perhaps this is what hell is, after all—the natural consequences of what we ourselves choose.

I skimmed through the entreaties for forgiveness, looking for a particular thing. I at last found it: my name.

> *How I miss my baby, my darling Emma. I think of*
> *her all the time. Tell her, Stephen. Tell her that I love her.*
> *Do not let her forget me, and tell her I would be with her*
> *if only that were possible.*

I closed the letter, too excited to read it all the way through. I gathered the pack, tying it back up into a ribbon, then thought better of taking them with me. I did not have time to get to my room with them without arousing suspicion. I had been gone too long already; Alyssa was impatient and would probably send someone after me if she did not come herself any second. Besides, what if I met someone in the hall? I had no way of hiding them. I decided my impatience notwithstanding, I would have to wait and come back for the letters later that night.

I summoned Valerian and Uncle Peter, arranging a rendezvous in the conservatory, where I told them about the letters.

"It does not surprise me your father did not go to her," Uncle Peter explained. "He knew there was another man. He did not, of course, imagine a vampire. Nor would he have thought for one moment, despite her paroxysms of conscience, that she was not with her lover willingly. No, dear Emma, remember your father's pride. He would believe she knew the way home if she had chosen to return."

"Could she still be there?" I asked.

"I very much doubt it. It was a long time ago," Uncle Peter replied sadly.

"But there could be traces of her there, or clues to where she traveled next," Valerian interjected. He leaned forward to address Uncle Peter. "Forgive me, for I know I am coming in late on this. Most assuredly, the two of you have already thoroughly discussed this matter. While I do not mean to make you go through it all again, I have some questions."

"Go right ahead," Uncle Peter agreed.

"When Laura began to change, what was different in the house, or even in the area? Can you remember any major alterations in normal life?"

"As I told Emma, there was the business of Astrid, who was a diabolically clever girl who set her sights on Stephen. It was through her manipulations that the seeds of mistrust and betrayal were sown. Stephen's pride made it worse."

"I've explained most of this to him," I clarified, to save time.

"Other than the business with Astrid, was there anything else unusual or out of the ordinary?" Valerian asked. "Was there anyone new in the neighborhood, anyone spotted lurking about the house?"

"There was a stranger in Weybourne. You know how it is in these country towns, a new arrival is the talk of the neighborhood. But as far as I know, they never met." Uncle Peter caught himself, his eyes glowing as realization dawned. "Oh, I see. You think he might have been the one who . . . But I am afraid there is nothing else I can tell you, not about him. I never even saw the man. If he was a man." His head jerked. "Wait. One more thing. When it first began, when Laura first began to show signs of secretiveness, she and Stephen had a terrible row. It was over a necklace he found her wearing. She refused to say where she had bought it. When Stephen tried to take it, she went wild. I never saw it again after that."

My blood went to ice. "Was this necklace a silver dragon with a teardrop pearl?" I asked desperately.

His eyes widened. "My God. How did you . . . ?"

I closed my eyes. My voice trembled. "Did she ever mention anyone by the name of Alistair?"

He frowned, about to deny it, then stopped. His swarthy complexion paled. "That was the name she called out when she was feverish. Well, we thought it was fever then. But she called out to him, begging him . . . You see why your father believed so soundly she had taken a lover. He told me once he feared the guilt was what had driven her mad."

Fighting back my rising state of emotion, I related the story Eloise Boniface had told me. Peter listened, frowning, nodding, and when I was finished, he gave a great sigh. "Well, then, we can assume at last this is the connection. This Alistair must be the one who made her over."

Valerian spread his hands. "But does this have any connection to the Cyprian Queen, to Ruthven and what he is doing now?"

"It has to," I replied. "There cannot be so much coincidence in all the world as this—two vampires in the same remote area, preying in different ways on students at a small girls' school like Blackbriar."

"But it did not happen at the same time," Valerian clarified. "You mother was never part of the Cyprian Queen business. You friend, the Boniface woman, would have told you if she had been acting strangely. What happened to her happened years later." He puzzled over this. "I agree it has to be related, but I don't see how."

"Perhaps when I have had an opportunity to read the rest of the letters, I will know more."

But I never got to see those letters. Alyssa must have belatedly realized her error in sending me to fetch the blankets. That evening, when I went back to the bedroom chest, I discovered every last one of them was gone.

The scene was ugly. Beyond ugly. I was . . . well, I would like to say I was not myself, but the harsh truth was I was myself.

I spoke truly from my heart—a very bruised heart—for the

first time in all my life with my sister, venting my full wrath and hurt when Alyssa told me that she had burned them. Alan was with her, and he stood behind her with his hands on her shoulders, looking stone-faced and unmoved as I shouted at the two of them.

"Those letters belonged to me! How could you have destroyed my property, something you have no right to do? How could you have been so selfish?"

"I was only thinking of you!" Alyssa insisted tearfully.

"No you most certainly were not," I countered. "You cannot bear to think of my attachment to my mother. You hate her, and you hate me."

"But, Emma, that is not true!"

"It is!" I thundered, pointing an accusing finger at her. "Your only use for me is when I dance attendance on you. You are a spoiled child—your mother's child through and through. You think every part of our relationship should serve your interest, and you are afraid of what makes me different from you. You had to destroy those letters to keep me to yourself."

"No! You must understand why I did it."

"I do, you see. You are weak and small. You think only of yourself, and you do not care whom you hurt to get what you want."

Alan's face gathered into a glower. "Shut up, Emma. You are upsetting Alyssa."

"No, we cannot have Alyssa upset!" I shot, incensed at his interference. I was fairly shrieking now, so hysterical was I. "It must not be allowed. My stepmother set that standard, and no matter how much grief it cost me, Alyssa's fair brow must never be marred by the pucker of a frown. This entitles her, I suppose, to destroy my life, to treat me no better than a servant whose duty it is to bow to her every whim—do not upset Alyssa at any cost! Well, that cost, it seems, is too often mine to pay.

This time, what you two took from me was irreplaceable, but it was the last thing I will ever sacrifice to this insipid brat again!"

"You sniping bitch!" Alan shouted, lunging for me. He moved quickly, rounding the chairs. It happened so quickly, I did not even have time to react, but suddenly Valerian was in between us. He had forgotten to move normally and his pre-ternatural speed put him between Alan and me in the blink of an eye. It was an unforgivable lapse, especially for a man who never lowered his guard.

But I doubted Alan would believe the evidence of his eyes; the stupid were ever easy to confound. Valerian stood in front of me, protective and threatening in that quiet, still way of his that so effectively diminished Alan's bluster.

"Move away." Valerian spoke in a velvet-smooth tone, yet there was no mistaking the steely threat. I watched Alan's face go red. By contrast, Valerian's paleness was unmarred by emotion. He seemed made of marble.

"Get out of here, Fox. This is a family matter. It does not concern you."

Meaning to brush past Valerian to get to me, Alan took one step. Only one. Then Valerian's hand shot out, grasping Alan's shoulder. Alan stopped cold, as if he'd come up against a stone wall. He pushed against Valerian. In response, Valerian flicked his wrist and Alan crumpled to the ground.

The rest was a blur. Alyssa began screaming. I felt Valerian's hand on my arm, his voice at my ear. "Let us go," he said commandingly. "Now."

I obeyed without thinking, turning my back on my sister prostrate over her groaning husband. Valerian took me upstairs. "Be ready to leave in an hour," he told me. "I am taking you away from this place."

* * *

Only a fool would set sail for Ireland on winter seas. I was one such fool, an angry, embittered one when I left Castleton. Valerian had found an Irish vessel sailing from Seaforth Dock in Merseyside, called *The Angel Gabriel*. I was a notoriously bad sailor, but with a name such as this, I thought it a good sign.

The cabin assigned to me was close and airless, and I was ill on the short voyage over the rough seas to Dublin. However, my mood was undaunted. I had a place, now, where I could look for my mother: Inishmoor, which lay on the other side of the island, just out from Galway.

Valerian went to work immediately upon our arrival to put the word out to his contacts. After five days, he informed me that so far his sources had unearthed no information about my mother in the area of Inishmoor.

"Perhaps I should go myself to the Inishmaan," I suggested. "This was where she was when she sent the letters."

"And look where?" he posited. "An island it might be, but it is hardly small enough for you to go knocking on every door. And who knows how long she was there? She might have spent only a night before moving someplace else. No, we should wait for more information. Give my agents time to work."

"Agents?" I asked, intrigued.

He gave me an apologetic grin. "They are not the usual sort, as you might well imagine. Not pretty, not principled. But they are dedicated, and are deeply entrenched in the sort of world we are interested in. How do you think I have managed to maintain close contact with a vampire of Marius's magnitude all these years?"

I had not thought of it, but I now realized his ability to track and find the undead was certainly formidable. "It sounds quite a sophisticated network."

"Let us just say it is effective. In any event, I wanted to tell you they've found out something I had them investigate—not about your mother, but another matter. Do you recall Peter mentioning a man by the name of David Stoker?"

"Yes. He was the one who was known to have information on the Dracula."

"Exactly. Obsessed with the Dracula legend is more to the point. Stoker's an Irishman, and a Dubliner to boot. He has family here. It is a tenuous connection, for they say his brother, Abraham, detests any mention of David. But as we are here, I thought I might pay them a visit and see what I can ascertain about the man."

"I am coming with you!"

Any other man would have informed me that such an errand was not the proper place for a woman. Valerian did not. Instead, he bobbed his head in agreement. "We have to come up with a ruse. Do you have any ideas?"

Our story was this: Valerian would pose as a Cambridge historian who was researching the expansion of the Ottoman Empire into Eastern Europe. I would be his dutiful wife, a bit of a bluestocking, who acted as his secretary. We contacted the family under this guise, requesting information on the legend associated with Vlad III, known as Vlad the Impaler.

"We are particularly interested in the supernatural aspects of the legends surrounding him," I said as we brainstormed our approach, "as we believe there are actual events of importance that have been misinterpreted, and are thus of substantial historical value."

"That is good," Valerian said. "I think it wise to apply to his vanity. He will not wish to expose his brother's obsession if he thinks we take it literally. Therefore, let us say David contacted us when he learned of our research, to offer his theories on how these 'preposterous' stories grew out of actual events."

"I am a terrible liar," I warned.

He gave me a mysterious smile. "Leave that to me."

And sure enough, we gained entrance into the very active Dublin home of Abraham Stoker and his wife, Charlotte, who I learned was something of a feminist—which was an unexpected blessing, assurance that Stoker would accept my presence as my "husband's" assistant. Getting the couple to talk about David's obsession, however, was nearly impossible.

"My brother's illness has brought our family great grief," the very austere Abraham Stoker told us. The couple had invited us into the formal parlor, but did not extend their hospitality to an offer of refreshment. I had the feeling the husband was receiving us at his wife's insistence. He was certainly making no secret of his reluctance.

Mrs. Stoker was patient with us. "David was not all bad. He had his problems, as most men of great mind do. Yes, it was true, he was too warm on the subject of certain . . . legends. But he was a scholar and a fine man. He was an exhaustive researcher, and dedicated beyond imagining. I for one am thrilled to learn his research might be of some service to the academic community."

A shadow passed by the door, the movement catching the corner of my eye. I glanced over but saw no one. Were we being watched?

"If you only knew how important he is to our needs," Valerian said, very carefully picking his way through the truth.

"Surely you know my brother disappeared two years ago. I have not seen or heard from him since."

Charlotte Stoker looked to her husband. "Perhaps they might wish to have a look through his papers."

Stoker colored, turning an alarming shade of vermillion only an Irishman could achieve. Mrs. Stoker said, "Oh, Abraham, you did not destroy them, did you?"

"Of course not, although why you prohibit that course of action, I cannot see. They are no use to anyone."

I would have interjected if Valerian had not. "If you please, Mr. Stoker, to allow us—my wife and me—to be the judge of that."

The couple ignored us. I had the impression they were well used to lively debate. "I insisted you keep his belongings for precisely this purpose, naturally. David was a brilliant man."

"There is a fine line between genius and madness," Abraham warned.

Something prickled the hairs on the back of my neck. I glanced over my shoulder, searching the hall. I had the uncanny impression once again that I was being watched. Yet I saw no one.

Valerian was speaking. "That may well be, but your brother's emotional well-being, or lack of it, does not diminish the fact that he may have made a very important contribution to our research."

Abraham Stoker harrumphed, but he rose and disappeared, his wife trailing after him. The sounds of their quarrel drifted back to Valerian and me, still seated in their parlor.

"What do you think?" I whispered.

He chuckled. "She is formidable. I'll wager we have the papers in our hands in moments."

He was correct. The Stokers returned quickly, Abraham with a sheaf of papers.

His stern expression bore testimony to his dislike of losing this particular battle. "I will not allow these out of this house. If you find something of value, excellent. You have one hour."

"Abraham," Mrs. Stoker murmured.

"Two hours," he corrected crankily.

"Thank you," I said sincerely, taking the packet as if I were receiving the Holy Grail. Mrs. Stoker pulled her husband out of the room, their quibbling resuming once the door was shut behind them.

Valerian and I exchanged an amused glance, then set to work.

Opening the file, we found nothing more than a collection of notes filled with handwriting, drawn figures, and snippets of newspaper. These were arranged in haphazard fashion, jottings and lengthy entries jumbled onto a page. Portions were circled, underlined, scored through. The whole effect was chaotic, nearly indecipherable.

I gave Valerian a helpless glance. "Two hours?"

He divided the file in half, slid a packet to me and settled in to peruse the other himself. I attended the first few pages of my assignment, making a discovery right off. "He mentions something known as 'Spring-heeled Jack' very often. Listen to this—an account from the *Times* in London. Let's see . . . this was some time ago, about twenty years ago. A woman named Mary Stevens was accosted by a strange figure who leaped at her from a dark alley. Hmm. It says the hysterical girl reported the strange creature ripped at her clothing and tore at her flesh with claws that were 'cold and clammy as those of a corpse.'"

"A vampire attack?" Valerian said.

"A very unusual one. Look at the rest of this."

The material described something quite different from the stealthy, fatally efficient killer we knew vampires to be. This thing was a gibbering miscreant bent on cruel mischief. Its sobriquet came from the ability to disappear by leaping great heights, a terrifying stunt it used to taunt its prey.

Several accounts throughout England and Ireland had been remarkably similar in describing the thing's appearance, which was reported as "devil-like." Many echoed the description given in public testimony in London of an eighteen-year-old victim named Jane Alsop. I read it aloud for Valerian.

"She says: 'He was wearing a kind of helmet, and a tight-fitting white costume like an oilskin. His face was hideous; his eyes were like balls of fire. His hands had claws of some metallic substance, and he vomited blue and white flames.'"

I stopped, my eyes fixed at the next word.

"Go on," Valerian urged.

"Here Stoker writes over the article. A name." I pointed to the circled word. "Lliam."

"Lliam?" Valerian's gaze held mine. "Stoker believed Lliam is this Spring-heeled Jack?"

But I had read ahead and could not answer him. "My God, Valerian!" I exclaimed, and I slid the pages so that we both might read the tale that unfolded in Stoker's own hand. "He has a theory that the Spring-heeled Jack phantom was one aspect of the vampire known as Lliam. He describes him here. See." I perused the notes, reading snippets aloud. "A capricious harlequin . . . With a boundless energy and an insatiable appetite for cruel amusements."

Pages of writing explored this hypothesis, supporting it with sightings and reports of mass killings where all the victims were found bloodless. I pointed to one report. "See how their bodies were left heaped in a pile? That is like what Miss Markam described."

Valerian nodded, his attention captivated by another entry. "This is interesting. Look at this account of a haunted field. It is not too far from here. Hmm." He paused to read on. "The locals regard the land as unholy. Stoker says nothing can grow on it."

I perused the notes myself. Stoker claimed in an extensive explanation that he had investigated this phenomenon and concluded that this was the site where Lliam had executed one of his followers.

"Stoker thinks he discovered some betrayal." Valerian paused as he read on. "It looks as if it happened only ten years ago or thereabouts. He says that Lliam killed one of his own kind, burned the pieces, then sowed the charred remains into the ground. To this day, the ground is known to be cursed. It serves as a warning to any who might think of going up against his power. A priest died trying to bless it and the farmer who owns the plot has long since abandoned it. The locals say—"

"Oh God!" I exclaimed. I felt my world tilt as excitement rushed through me. Alistair. I trembled as I locked my gaze with Valerian's. "Could my mother be what they fought over?"

"It is possible."

"I know," I said eagerly. "She wrote letters to Father and me from here in Ireland. Her maker—if indeed Alistair is the vampire who made her over, and he has to be, doesn't he?—was killed here. By Lliam, and he is this mercurial monster; he is the link to Ruthven."

Valerian was silent. I knew he was wary of getting my hopes up too high. Even if we were correct, there was no telling where this new knowledge would lead. My mother had been here in this country, living her earliest days as a vampire. Where had she gone when Alistair was killed? Where was she now?

Longing for death, I knew. I knew it as surely as I knew my name. *Darkling I listen . . .*

In the final moments of our time with David Stoker's research, we finally uncovered some of the information he had managed to find of the Dracula. This was somewhat disappointing, however, as most of his knowledge matched what we had learned from Uncle Peter. But a few things were new, although it felt to me that what we learned posed more questions about the mysterious Dark Prince than it answered.

Stoker wrote reams about the Wallachian prince's mortal life, his rise to power after triumphing in his father's brutally orchestrated rivalry designed to ensure the strongest of his sons would ascend to the throne. There were extensive listings of a dragon symbol, where it had been found and what it had foretold, and a smattering of legends that collected around the presence of evil nestled safely in the mysterious Carpathian Mountains . . .

"Your two hours are over," a voice from the doorway announced, and Abraham Stoker swept into the room.

It was like the drop of the guillotine's blade, severing us from this font of information. There was so much more we had not yet read, but the deal had been struck and we had gotten our two hours. I might have greedily wheedled for more but Valerian gave my hand a reassuring squeeze as we were ushered into the hall and given our cloaks.

Stoker brushed aside our expressions of gratitude. He did not even ask if our search had been fruitful. He wanted us gone as soon as possible.

It was Charlotte Stoker, coming in at the last moment to bid us good-bye, who restored a measure of decorum to our ejection from the house. She folded her hands as she smiled kindly at us. "I am afraid this is all the access my husband will allow, and I must agree with him that we cannot be drawn into the controversies of my brother-in-law's world. We have our children to consider, and we like to protect them from this as much as possible."

A movement behind her, no more than a shifting shadow, alerted me to the presence I had sensed earlier. When a face poked around a corner, I saw it was a boy, perhaps fourteen or fifteen years of age.

Charlotte Stoker frowned, shaking her head. "Our son is fascinated by the subject, I am afraid."

I smiled at the lad, who was good-looking, with bright, intelligent eyes.

"Bram! Off with you, now!" his mother admonished. But when she returned her attention to me, her smile was indulgent.

"A good-looking boy," I said.

"Thank you. That is our son, Abraham, after his father. He

is off to school in a year or two, which is a miracle. He was bed-ridden until he was seven years old, and so to see him venturing out into the world is particularly gratifying. I am afraid, however, his years of infirmity made him fanciful, and he's rather desperate when it comes to trying to find out about his uncle. We—well, *I*—find it difficult to be harsh with him."

"Completely understandable," I murmured. "Thank you so much for your help."

"Oh, was it? A help, I mean?"

"Extremely so," I said with emphasis. This pleased her, and although we left Abraham glowering, I thought perhaps we had done a bit of good, perhaps planted a seed that might grow to something useful to that family in the future.

I truly did.

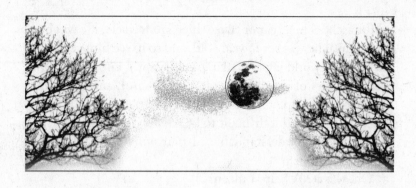

Chapter Twenty

The fells were locked in winter white when I returned to Cumbria, the deep cold freezing everything in a glittering case of ice. It was something out of a fairytale, and would have been a lovely sight if I had not felt unsettled by the stillness around me.

"What is it?" Valerian asked as we approached the village. He studied me. "Do you feel a change?"

I thought about this for a moment, then nodded. "Yes. Changes are coming. It will be the killing time soon."

I immediately saw a drastic difference in the girls. Margaret, Lilliana, and Therese moved like three who had lost their way and Vanessa's sparkle was diminished into wan lassitude. Eustacia was in a state of near paralysis, so terrified was she. Not once did her eager hand rise during the first lesson back.

I grabbed Eustacia on her way out of the classroom. "I wish to talk to you. Meet me here after your classes are done for the day."

She did not want to, that was plain to see, but she would not disobey a teacher's direct order. When she arrived that afternoon, she stood stiff, eyes downcast, in front of my desk.

I rose, coming to stand before her. "He is different, isn't he? Ruthven. Or the Cyprian Queen, as he styles himself."

Her eyes jerked to mine, but she said nothing.

"I know what is happening. I know about the things the girls do. I know they think they are handmaidens to a god. They think themselves glorious and exalted. They are not. Which you already know. But it is difficult, for they do not listen to you."

Her eyes were wide, round, desperate. Tears brimmed, then overflowed onto her cheeks, but she remained silent, not even shaking her head. She did not flee, however. I took this as a good sign.

"I know you are frightened," I said. I spoke calmly, hoping to ease her obvious fears. "But you must listen to me, Eustacia. I am going to trust you with something. Actually, I am going to show you something, and trust that you will tell no one of what you are about to see."

I picked up paperweight some previous teacher had left behind. It was half of a rock split open, showing a bristling array of amethyst crystals inside. I pointed to a basket across the room where the girls placed their assignments on their way out at the end of class.

"Do you think I can throw this in that basket?"

She blinked in surprise. "Pardon me?" she said.

I repeated the question. She eyes me suspiciously, clearly thinking I was playing some trick. "Of course not," she finally replied.

I smiled at her, and then I took a moment to eye the target, before tossing the rock. It landed with a smack in the basket, shaking it but staying put.

"Do you think I can do it ten times?"

Her eyes bulged.

I laughed. "Bring it back to me, please," I instructed. "You will see."

She did and I threw it again. Once more, my aim was perfect.

"Again."

By the seventh time, she was looking at me as if I were some supernatural being myself. "I have seen him," I told her as she gaped at me. I tossed the rock, barely looking now, for I had the feel of it. "I know what he is. I have done battle with his kind before, and won."

"I . . . what . . . how?"

I smiled at her, holding up the rock. "I could take out a spider at the other end of the room. I could toss this out the window and pinch a twig off one of the trees in the stand over near the stables. That is not my only talent, but I hope it will be enough to prove to you that I am capable. I can deal with this thing that is happening to you, to all the girls. You have but to trust me. I want you to tell me—promise me—if anything, *anything* happens that makes you feel in danger. Come to my room at any time of the night, find me in the school at any time of the day. Now, I am going to give you something, and you must promise me you will wear it."

I took the cross from around my neck. I would replace it as soon as possible, but for now I wanted Eustacia protected. She gazed at the tiny figure of the crucified Christ, frowning.

"There are strange things happening here at the school," I said to her. "Put that on, wear it always. It is made of silver, which is important. And its power is not only in the carved figure but in the blessing over it."

She placed it over her head solemnly, then looked at me with such a forlorn expression my heart wrenched. "What about the others?"

"I will attempt to do the same for them. But I do not trust them with what I just showed you, about my . . . abilities."

"Why do you trust me, then?"

"Because, darling," I said gently, reaching out to take her hand, "you see things differently. And I know something of what it is to be the one who does not quite belong but longs so desperately to be part of a world you admire. Take my word for it, Eustacia, there are worse things than being clever. It might mean some will not like you for it, but then, you will find their regard never quite makes up for giving yourself away."

Eustacia smiled tremulously. "Thank you, Mrs. Andrews."

"Remember your promise. Any time, you must let me know if there is a change, any change."

So we struck our bargain, and I retired to my room. I had not even had a moment to unpack. I cannot say I was eager to do so. I was half-afraid that at any moment, I would hear the haunting tremor of Ruthven's voice, feel his disgusting touch. But somehow, I did not think he would trouble me. I had repelled him successfully on his previous attempts. And he was distracted now by his coven of worshipers. It was they who were in danger.

Or maybe he was simply biding his time.

When I saw the dead orchid, I was even more depressed. I had never even thought of its care when I'd left it behind. But the reminder of Suddington sparked a new idea that reenergized me. I scratched off a message and placed it in the post on my way to dinner that night, asking him if I might make use of his library this Sunday. I had in mind to do some research into the local history.

I meant to uncover the true identity of the vampire, Ruthven.

Being in Suddington's library was like coming home. I could have languished the day away with Shakespeare and Marlowe. I smiled, recalling how Suddington had flattered me with words from Marlowe's *Doctor Faustus*: "Is this the face that launched a thousand ships . . ." It was meant as a compliment, although it was a bit ghoulish, for it was a line spoken by Faustus regarding Helen of Troy when Mephistopheles had summoned her to tempt the poor doctor into agreeing to bargain away his soul.

I went to the section Suddington had indicated held the local history, and was immediately absorbed in research. As I pulled book after book off the shelves, I saw a fascinating pattern begin to unfold. When the sound of Suddington's arrival broke me out of my reverie, I was astonished to find that four hours had gone by. Standing, I winced at the protest from my stiff joints. He, however, swept into the room with his usual grace.

"Hah! I knew I would find you thus. You are hopelessly predictable, Mrs. Andrews, as are all those who love books." He looked at one of the volumes I'd collected about me and frowned. "Local history? I thought you would be nose-deep in Spencer, or Dryden, or Pope. Or Marlowe. You know I think of Marlowe every time I see you."

"You have made that quite apparent," I replied, laughing.

He grinned playfully. "Ah, so I have. Well, then, are you searching for something particular?"

"Actually, I found a few interesting things," I said.

"Excellent. Are you ready for tea?" Before I could reply, he was already on his way to summon the servants. "I know it is late, but I have a sweet tooth and my cook makes the most delicious cakes. Oh, and have you noticed something different in the room?"

"You removed the tapestry," I replied, following his line of sight.

"That I did. The thing disgusted me once I realized what it was. And I did not want it to frighten you."

"I hope that was not the reason. If so, it was quite unnecessary. That tapestry was your family history; you should not feel compelled to hide it away."

He smiled at me, as if indulging a child. "Don't you know, Mrs. Andrews, that history can prove dangerous?"

It was a strange thing to say and I had no response as I mulled over its meaning. Tea arrived shortly, and we sat together. I was hungrier than I had thought, and we ate a hearty meal.

"So tell me what it is you have found," he inquired.

I hesitated, instinctively secretive, then thought, *Why not?* I had no reason not to speak openly with him. "I was looking for information on a gentleman who might have lived in the sixteenth century, and I did find someone."

"Really? Was he an ancestor of mine?"

"I do not know. His name was George Smythe. He lived at Kingsvale Grange."

"Ah, that is Glorianna's line. The Smythe became Smith at some point, and I suppose they ran out of male heirs and bargained for a hyphenated name. Although with a name like Smith you would not think they would have bothered."

The news of the relation between Miss Sloane-Smith and George Smythe stunned me. In light of the information I'd uncovered in Suddington's library, I thought it likely that George Smythe was the origin of the Cyprian Queen, at least the legend. I suspected it could be Smythe, or someone connected to him—perhaps a relative—that later became the vampire whom I now knew as Ruthven and who masqueraded under the hypnotic guise of the Cyprian Queen. It struck me as a suspiciously close association, but one I did not know what to make of.

Suddington was still speaking of the family. ". . . Plenty enough of them around. Well, I do know Kingsvale used to belong to her people, before the Commonwealth."

I could barely contain myself. I knew from my archive research that vampires often surfaced in their own families through subsequent generations, posing as one of them whenever they wanted to disguise themselves as human. All they had to do was feed from a suitable member of the family. That person's blood gave them the ability to take on their appearance.

"He must have been quite a horrible fellow," Suddington was saying, "if he was tried for murder. That was a time when nobles were a law unto themselves. They were rarely brought to justice, and almost never if the victims were commoners. What did he do?"

"I found a journal written by a mother whose daughter went missing. It appears she was found to have been one of the many who were . . ." I flushed with discomfort. It was not easy to speak about how the young women of the area had been violated sexually. "Harmed," I said significantly, "and then murdered. Many, many young girls were lost."

The weight of this tightened a knot in my chest. We were silent for a moment.

"What a terrible monster," he said with fervor. "However did they catch him?"

"In the beginning, no one had any idea who could be perpetrating the crimes, but over time he grew careless, almost taunting the authorities with his bold kidnapping and placing the bodies out in the open to be discovered in a ghastly manner."

Suddington soberly contemplated the scope of these atrocities. "The haughty devil probably thought he would be held above reproach."

I did not concur. "It actually seemed he grew more frenetic, and his judgment failed him. I suspect with each murder, he felt the thing he was seeking, this . . . compulsion that drove him to do such horrible things—perhaps this kept eluding him and he began to come undone."

A look came into Suddington's eye. "Really? That is an odd theory." He half-smiled, and I feared my bloodthirsty interest in so sordid a tale must have taken him by surprise. "So what happened to the fellow? How did they catch him in the end?"

"His guilt became apparent when he left the area and the murders ceased, only to resume upon his return. Once the townsfolk suspected him, they found ample evidence. As I said, he was quite demented at that time." I consulted my notes. "He was hung at the crossroads leading out of the village to the south." This suddenly struck me as odd. Crossroads had strong significance in the legends surrounding conjuring demons. Had there been suspicion of witchcraft?

"Fascinating. But what, Mrs. Andrews, has captured your interest in this macabre tale?"

I was on thin ground here, for it was impossible to tell him that I was searching for the origins of a sexually predatory vampire. I sought to change the subject. "You once promised me you would show me your orchid house. Is there enough daylight to do so now?"

My diversion achieved its aim, and he leaped to his feet enthusiastically. "Of course. In the dramatic light of late afternoon, the colors of the plants seem to glow. It will be a spectacular presentation."

He fairly pulled me through the conservatory to a smaller greenhouse filled with tables upon which were placed pots of flowers. The sultry air heated my skin as I moved among the weird, elongated stalks. Atop each of these were unique blooms, so widely varied in texture, shape, and hue that it was amazing they were of the same species.

Suddington paused at a cluster of white blossoms, strangely wrought among narrow leaves, each with a scooping bottom and narrower splayed petals of a most delicate construction.

"*Phragmipedium reticulatum*," he said, his voice filled with reverence. "Breathtaking. And here is the cheeky *Phalaenopsis schilleriana*." He indicated a more conventional flower in shades of pink and rose. The leaves were flat, broad, and white-veined. "Pretty little thing, isn't she?" he mused, and then moved on.

I found myself overwhelmed as I viewed the collection. From the lovely to the grotesque, the orchid petals boldly displayed suggestive shapes. There were delicately feminine unfurling petals, unabashedly displaying a nub of hooded stamens that made my skin so red and hot I felt scalded. Others were masculine, bulbous shapes appearing shockingly fertile among conceits of brightly colored plumage.

"You of course see the vein of sensuality in the plant." He glanced at me apologetically. "Pardon my frankness, but it is difficult to ignore."

"Yes," I agreed nervously.

"The orchid's name is from the Greek legend of Orchis, who was the son of a nymph and a satyr. He proved to be an alarming combination of beauty and sexual aggression. There is a great deal of mythology that attributes the ability of the plant to inspire some rather unsavory acts."

I tried to laugh, but I was too uncomfortable. It was too hot in here. Suddington had explained earlier that the heat and humidity were maintained by large furnaces underground, which kept a steady supply of steam coming up through ornate vents laid into the floor. Right now, however, it felt as if we were sitting on top of a volcano about to erupt.

"An interesting defense," I said, trying to shed some of my discomfort with humor. "Blame it on the flowers?"

"Ah, but not just flowers. Orchids. Mystical and noble flora. They embody not only life—which you see represented by its shocking appearance—but death as well. In Bohemia, certain orchids are known as the 'hand of death.'"

I stopped. "What is this one?" I asked, unable to keep the disbelief from my voice. The flower in question was quite horrible. Spotted petals folded around the core so that it resembled an angry face topped with spiny leaves. From its maw extended long, black spindles so that it looked like some insect of prey with grasping tentacles, crouched and ready to strike.

"Ah. That is the *dracula chimaera*. Very exotic, and rare. Its beauty is not always appreciated."

I could not reply for a moment, for the combination of the sight of the thing and the name struck me dumb. Foreboding throbbed, dull and distant in the back of my mind.

"I see it speaks to you," Suddington said, mistaking my silence for appreciating. "It usually repulses most. But it is a very special orchid. Some would say a lord among the rest."

I struggled for the right words. All I could come up with was to murmur, "It is quite unusual."

"You are a skilled diplomat. You know, it is one of my particular favorites, perhaps because it is often so misunderstood." He suddenly grabbed the pot and held it out to me. "You must take it. Yes, go ahead. Take it as a companion to the other I gave you."

"I cannot," I protested, recoiling from the thing.

"Indeed, I insist. What is beauty, if not shared?"

I stared dubiously at the orchid. Beauty? This looked like

something out of a nightmare. If I put it in my bedchamber I was certain to get no sleep.

"I absolutely refuse," I said firmly, and placed the pot back in its spot on the table. "I have no talent nor am I equipped to care for such a delicate plant."

Suddington's gaze flickered over me coldly. He was sorely disappointed, but I was beyond caring. The cloying air, the lascivious plants, the frightening *dracula chimaera* all combined to make me feel ill, and I wanted to get out of there as quickly as possible. "I must be getting back to school," I said, and turned to lead us out of the orchid house.

He did not follow immediately. I had to await him in the conservatory. Glancing over my shoulder, I saw him straightening the pots, taking care to make certain all was in order before coming to join me.

"Thank you for indulging me," he said, and again, his tone was stiff. Clearly, I had offended him. But the urge to flee had overcome me and I had no choice but to exit the orchid house as fast as I dared.

Chapter Twenty-one

In this new school term, Valerian appointed himself my guardian. He insisted on a daily meeting. Most times, we used Serena's cottage. She was always willing to give us our privacy for these summits. Sometimes, when my time was short, Valerian came to Blackbriar. Like clandestine lovers, we slipped into secret spots to exchange words. But there were no kisses, no embraces, not even a lingering touch.

Things between us were in careful balance. Neither one of us was satisfied with the unresolved nature of what had happened, but a solution evaded us both and so we never spoke of it.

On this day, I was eager to tell him what I had learned. As we drank tea and nibbled on poppy-seed cakes Serena had prepared for us, I told him of George Smythe, and of his connection to Miss Sloane-Smith. I described the extensive orchid collection. However, Valerian showed little interest, and I cut short my report.

After he left, I stayed to help Serena with the dishes. "Your man is jealous," she said sagely.

"It is foolish of him."

She gave me a curious look. "Is it?"

I was so shocked, I could not reply. The comment stuck in my thoughts like a bur under a blanket, and when the orchid arrived for me the following morning, I felt a sharp pang of guilt, remembering Serena's words.

The messenger sent a footman for me, and when I arrived in the hall, I found a pot tied up with a great ribbon, the elegant blossom seeming to radiate its exotic beauty in the dull surroundings rather like a beacon among shadows. There was no denying the rush of excitement as I held his gift. I was attracted to Suddington—the evidence of my own racing pulse was undeniable—but how could I have this visceral reaction to him when Valerian was so near? Was I so fickle?

A hot, unpleasant tide of shame rose up in me. My mother, I recalled, had betrayed my father. Was I that same, inconsistent sort?

The note from Suddington read: "*Grammatophyllum scriptum* is used for the making of love potions. Guard it carefully. Fondly, S."

I started when a chirpy voice rang out. "Oh, Emma, what is that you have?" I groaned softly, recognizing Trudy Grisholm's insincere tones. I turned to face her.

She eyed the extravagant flower with raised eyebrows and a secret smile. "What a lovely gift."

And one the entire school would know about by luncheon, I mentally wagered.

Trudy peeked at the card, her heavy eyebrows crawling up to

her hairline. "Lord Suddington? Why, I had no idea you two were such close . . . friends."

"Nor did I," I said with false lightness, attempting to step past her. I did not want to speak with her now, not when I was feeling a bit flustered.

She allowed me, but her smirk assured me she would have the last word, and most probably removed from my hearing. My guess proved correct when a few hours later Miss Sloane-Smith glowered at me from across the dining hall during lunch. If blood could boil, then surely she was being poached in her skin. I half-expected her to sack me on the spot.

As I tried to eat, I recalled she had the necklace, the same one Alistair had given my mother two separate times, the same one I'd seen in the portrait in Suddington's house. How had it come to be in her possession? Then something else occurred to me.

Smythe, who had begun the cycle of the Cyprian Queen, was *her* ancestor—after all, it was the Cyprian *Queen*. Why had I never considered that this vampire could be a woman?

My thoughts spun from there, a web of connections that drove me nearly dizzy. By the time I met with Valerian later that day, I had my reasoning ready.

"Do you recall your directive to read Coleridge's *Christabel* when we were in Avebury?" I began without preamble when he walked into Serena's cottage.

He cocked his head with a curious smile. "Ah . . . Certainly. What—?"

"Christabel was the victim, but her tormentor was a *female* revenant. Geraldine."

His eyes narrowed. "Yes, I know the work."

"What if Ruthven—which we know to be a false name, a conceit—is, in fact, a woman? What if she is the headmistress?

Glorianna Sloane-Smith." I held up a hand at his doubtful reaction. "Listen to what I have reasoned so far. I have been absolutely astonished by Miss Sloane-Smith's reluctance to address the girls' wicked behavior. She was completely dedicated to blaming Miss Markam, branding her as mad rather than confront what was really going on. She turns a blind eye to the antics of the coven girls—I've seen it again and again."

"But that is easily explained, if you are familiar with how administrators of these types of institutions think. It is all about appearance; the perception of a good school, and an education well worth the tuitions, is essential to survival."

"Correct, but what if that was not her motivation at all but simply her guise? What if she were in a uniquely powerful position to prey among these girls, and then repress and control the reaction so that she keeps them here, under her thrall, without interference from the outside world?"

Valerian's eyebrows forked down skeptically.

"When I was in Denmark, I read a novel by an Irishman, Sheridan Le Fanu. His *Carmilla* is a female vampire who preys on other women. Two mentions of such a phenomenon cannot be coincidence."

Valerian stroked his chin with his long fingers. "But the intensity, the violence, the sexual preoccupations of the vampire indicate to me that it is male."

In one of those leaps of memory, something else completely unanticipated sprung into my mind. "There is much to suggest the kind of sisterly affection that ventures into the sensual. I found quotes about the Cyprian Queen in a poem by Sappho, with Margaret's things. I wondered then if it was a sign of certain intimacies associated with the philosophy of womanly love found on the island of Lesbos, where Sappho lived and wrote."

Serena, who had come into the room to check on the tea she always insisted on serving us, paused. We had gotten used to having her around and had long ago stopped caring what she overheard; we were all convinced she was more than trustworthy, and she had occasional insights that were helpful, as on this occasion.

"Such women in my country are burned as witches," she volunteered, then shook her head angrily. "Terrible."

My head snapped up. "The girls themselves play with the idea of witchcraft. In fact, they revel in it."

Valerian peered at me with fresh interest. "What put you on to suspect Sloane-Smith?"

"I have felt tension between us since the beginning. I fear, now that I see it all in retrospect, that I attributed much of what I felt about her to the fact that she reminds me of my stepmother, Judith."

He rubbed a finger against his chin. "Do you know why she has disliked you?"

I was hesitant to mention Lord Suddington's attentions, but I could not afford to hold anything back. "She does not like my friendship with Suddington. I thought it was this, anyway. She becomes irate when he . . . well, he has been kind to me."

"Yes," Valerian said. His mouth was tight. "I know."

"This morning, he sent me one of his orchids, and her reaction was positively seething, and that is what got me to think of her again. It has occurred to me before that she is part of this, but I was unable to put together any evidence."

"And now?"

"Now I know about George Smythe—her ancestor." I leaned forward animatedly. "It could very well be she was at work back then and the wrong person was hanged. In my studies, I learned that vampires have frequently been discovered to weave into the fabric of their own families over generations. Sloane-Smith has such a family as would be perfect for this strategy, with long branches and many far-flung cousins. It would be a simple thing for the vampire to kill a victim and assume both its aspect and personality, able to live under that identity."

Valerian threw up his hands. "But this is no good. I myself have seen her out and about in broad daylight, Emma, as have you. She is at the school every day. She can be no vampire if she braves the sun."

Nonplussed at my obvious oversight, I flushed. "Yes," I agreed after a moment. "There is no way around that, for she is not by any means nocturnal."

By this necessity, my suspicions of the headmistress were brought to a halt. Still, it was a shame to abandon this line of thinking, for in every other aspect, it made perfect sense that she was behind the Cyprian Queen. It could have been merely personal, but I felt a deep malevolence from her. Was it only due to her perceived rivalry concerning Lord Suddington?

Demoralization hit me as I left Serena's cottage to return to Blackbriar. I'd had such hopes it was Sloane-Smith. What increased my despair was the fact that I had no one else in contention—not a single direction to go in to solve this thing before the killing began. And time—I was well aware—was quickly running out.

In my exhausting dreams that night, I saw the *dracula chimaera*. It seemed to loom large and predatory over me, its grotesque tentacles alive and quivering as they reached to me . . .

I awoke disoriented and confused. Nausea curdled my stomach as I fought my way out of bed to stand shivering barefoot on the wood floor of my room. What was this—the ague? I felt ill, almost to the point of delirium.

Lighting the lamp, I stared about me, thinking again of the rats. The memory of how they had swarmed me still made me tremble. I looked about. The room was empty. On a thought, I went to the window. It took nearly all of my courage to pull back the curtain to see if Ruthven was lurking outside. There was nothing there, and for a moment I was relieved.

Then I saw that the line of salt I'd used to seal the window was missing. Panic flooded into me as I circled the room wildly, finding it all gone—the small crucifixes, the garlic, everything!

I stumbled to the bag where I kept all of my talismans, my stakes made of holy hawthorn, and other tools of my kind. A quick inspection revealed most of its contents intact, but my vial of holy water and the large silver crucifix I'd once stolen from Saint Michael in the Fields were missing.

My head felt stuffed with cotton, my brain and limbs equally sluggish. What could this mean? It had to have happened recently. I would have noticed . . .

Would I? I did not check my supplies regularly.

What was wrong with me? I felt as if I had caught a fever, but what were the chances I would fall ill coincidentally when someone had tampered with my protections? It had to be some doing of the vampire. Or its little witches . . .

The sound of pounding footsteps penetrated my befuddled state and I heard Eustacia's voice calling my name. There was a pounding at my door.

"Mrs. Andrews!" she screamed. "Mrs. Andrews, please come! It is Vanessa—she is being murdered!"

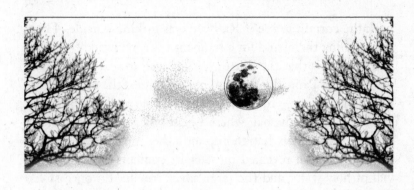

Chapter Twenty-two

My limbs were leaden, my vision blurred, my breathing shallow and quick. I felt as if I were swimming in a black sea, fighting against powerful currents to get to the door.

Eustacia stared at me, horror written on her young face. Her reaction sobered me somewhat, and I drew myself upright with supreme effort. "What is happening?" I managed, my voice a croak as air scratched against my parched throat. I could hear my words were slurred.

I must be drugged, I thought. I knew I was not right, and this could not be simple illness. I had not felt like this ever in my life.

The girl was before me, and I knew she was speaking, but

for some reason I was having a great deal of difficulty absorbing her words.

At last the sound of screams rising from the girls' dormitory penetrated my fog. I pushed Eustacia aside and launched myself down the corridor.

Where were the other teachers? Their rooms were near to mine. They were close enough to hear Eustacia pounding on my door, close enough to make out the cries of the girls in the quiet of the night. And how were the other students able to sleep through this? The sound of crying was a cacophony in the darkened halls.

I burst into the room where the sixth form girls slept, then stopped in my tracks at the terrifying sight before me. My strength seemed to run out of me, leaving me numb. I gasped for air, unable to get anything into my lungs.

In front of my eyes, bathed brilliantly in the light from an ample moon, the hideous form of a creature hovered in midair. The thing was part man, part . . . demon. It was naked, its flesh an inhumanly leathery texture tightly stretched over grotesque sinews and musculature that flexed like machine pulleys as it wavered, leering at me with its maw open, razor-sharp incisors gleaming in the light like diamonds. Its head was bald and whitish, its eyes fiery red. Plumes of smoke blew from enlarged nostrils, as though it were some great dragon, misting the glistening red blood that dripped wetly from its mouth.

I was taken aback only a moment; the blood of my mother asserted itself even as I hesitated. I knew the sensation, welcomed it as my focus tightened, my muscles tensed, ready to strike if need be. This was when I was at my best—in the fight, in the moment. All feeling of being drugged temporarily vanished. In moments like this, my Dhampir nature took over.

Valerian had told me long ago that the sight of a vampire feeding, in its unguarded state, stripped of all its ability to charm and deceive, was unspeakably revolting. He was correct. I knew that the thing before me was Ruthven—the vampire in its true form. But even more horrifying, Vanessa Braithwait languished in ecstasy in his arms, her mouth open and smiling, her blood black in the dim light of the dark room. Around her, crying loudly as they gazed up in mesmerized horror, were the other girls of the dorm, clinging to one another desperately in their state of terror. All except the other coven girls—Lilliana, Therese, Marion, and Margaret—who stood silent, watching the beast and Vanessa with something akin to rapture on their faces.

"Get out!" I cried. Again, my speech was sluggish, but it was strong enough to command the students. They broke out of their paralysis and began to scramble toward the door. "Go. Hurry!"

They ran out of the rooms, but the four silent girls stayed firm. I did not waste any time trying to convince them, but turned to the vampire. I put out my hand, but the Dhampir strength in me, which usually flowed in and out of me at such times when I called it, did not surge. The drugs, I thought. They were impairing me.

I could not give in to fear. It meant death for everyone in the room. With determination, I summoned my strength and shouted, "Stop!"—and to my surprise, this startled it. It blinked at me, and the tiniest of my preternatural resources bubbled just enough to reach the thing. Although my touch was more like a brushing-off than the punch I'd intended, the vampire's reaction was astonishing. It reared at the sight of me, mouth gaped in horror as it bellowed a single word: "No!"

The vampire dropped Vanessa to fling its hands up over its face, covering its hideous appearance. At this unexpected display of vanity, I instinctively stepped forward to catch Vanessa before she struck the floor, but I was not quick enough. She fell with a sickening thud and lay there in a state of semiconsciousness. A glimpse of blood under her head indicated a head wound. The pool spread quickly.

I stood frozen in fear that he'd killed her, but her head rolled slightly as she let out a small moan. Her arms reached up, as if begging for her tormentor to take her up into his arms again.

I lifted my gaze back to the hovering revenant still cowering from me. My momentary advantage would not last, and the effects of the drug were taking their toll. I belatedly realized I'd made a grave error by coming here without any protections, any weapons. I had been so groggy and disoriented I had not realized what I was doing when I left the room without them. Cold dread seeped into me, like a bloodstain spreading fast across linen.

Then Ruthven did a strange thing. Instead of pressing its obvious advantage, it withdrew, recoiling away from me. To my amazement, it retreated several steps to the corner. Its twisted body was hunkered over, its arms held as if to shield its face from view. I watched this, amazed and puzzled. Then, as it threw an agonized glance at me, I realized it was ashamed! The proud Ruthven did not want me—its sister, its equal, its mate—to see it like this.

It whimpered, betraying its desperate state. Oh, yes, I knew this creature, for it had revealed itself to me in trying to seduce me. It longed to be admired, loved even, worshiped as a god and goddess in one. But this vicious, loathsome beast before me was its true form, one it had to assume when it fed. All guise was gone, all pretense of the charming lover, revealed for what it was in truth—not glorious at all, but ugly and base, greedy, sniveling, insecure, childish.

"It always comes to this," I whispered. "It always ends in death. That was what Madge told me on the first day. These poor girls. They think you are beauty. But you are in reality this: A hideous monster. Death. Evil. Repulsive."

I stressed the last word, testing it. Ruthven twitched, as if touched by fire.

I turned to the girls he'd cast under his thrall. "See, all of you, see what your Cyprian Queen truly is. Not beautiful, but ugly. A monster, not a god."

They looked confused at first, then dawning terror claimed each one of them in turn. As it did, they scuttled away from the hulking creature in the corner, sobbing loudly and clinging to one another.

Ruthven's mournful wail came from a reptilian throat. "My lovesick beauties . . ." He reached a taloned hand toward them, and they screamed, clamoring to get away from him. The razor-sharp claws closed into a fist. An unearthly shriek shook the room, and the creature curled venomously as it turned back to me.

I reached out my hand toward it, clamping down my mind in fierce concentration. Sweat broke out on my brow as I searched for its mind, its essence. My skill was weak, but I clung to the knowledge that this was what I was made for. It would come to me. It had to.

"I once thought you worthy," it hissed. "You viper!"

It pushed back, and my connection snapped off. The girls' screaming pitched anew. The sound seemed to annoy Ruthven, and it swept its hand in an arc toward where they huddled together. "Sleep," it murmured, and silence fell as all in the room, save me, swooned into unconsciousness.

"No!" Margaret called, stepping forward with her hands held out beseechingly. "Not me! I want to see!"

I thought the demon smiled at her. It curled its talons in the air, a sickening gesture of affection, and as the other girls subsided, she remained standing.

"Eustacia," I called behind me, afraid the young girl, too,

would fall under the spell. But the vampire had not bothered to quiet her; she stood transfixed and silent. I urged her: "Fetch my bag from my room. It is under the bed—bring it to me immediately. Go!"

Out of the corner of my eye, I saw Margaret step toward Eustacia as the younger girl turned to flee. Margaret snagged Eustacia by her nightdress and yanked her so hard Eustacia flew onto her back and yelped in pain. She lay there, stunned and unmoving.

"Eustacia!" I called out in alarm.

Margaret whirled to me, her eyes gleaming with a wicked fever. "Vanessa wants this. You must not stop it!"

"It is not true," I shouted at her.

"He will make her eternal!"

"You ignorant fool! The transformation takes three times bitten. I assure you it is not giving you the transformation. It is feeding! Vanessa will die. You all will."

She sneered, as if I knew nothing. "She will be his immortal love. He promised."

"A cursed immortality," I said. "Look at your god now. Did he promise to take you as well?"

"She will." Margaret's gaze fell to her friend, writhing on the floor. Her gaze softened and I saw her love for Vanessa written on her features, so plaintive and lost it hurt to look at. Her breath hitched as she drew in a shaking breath laden with the full burden of her emotions, and murmured, "Sweet Helen, make me immortal with a kiss!"

I lost no time exploiting this moment of weakness. With a well-placed kick aimed squarely to her knee, I brought Margaret down.

With a groan, Eustacia struggled to her feet. "Run!" I urged her. To my great relief, she staggered out of the room. Neither Ruthven nor Margaret attempted to stop her.

A rush of air behind me brought me back around to see Ruthven had taken flight and was almost upon me.

As with so many times when I faced my supernatural foes, I let instinct bid me. This time, I let myself fall back, reaching my hand out as I hit the ground. My palm slapped into a puddle of Vanessa's blood. I felt its wet warmth on my skin.

I brought my hand up and held it in front of me. The creature's attack halted immediately, nearly a hair's breadth from my face. The blood of its victim seemed to have a deleterious effect.

My mind was working furiously, hampered by the drug. How long would it take Eustacia to get back with my bag? How long could I hold off the vampire like this?

"I would have made you a goddess," Ruthven murmured bitterly. "My greatness . . . My art . . . I thought you would be honored, but you . . . you were jealous all along! You hate me because you see my greatness. You want what I have gained, you ungrateful traitor."

"Her?" shrieked Margaret. "No! You promised Vanessa will be your goddess, and I her handmaiden!"

Ruthven swept its hand out with a cry of rage, and Margaret was flung away, up against a mirror standing in the corner. It shattered around her, and she fell among the shards, unconscious and bleeding.

The sound of running footsteps came from the hallway behind me, and I knew Eustacia was back. Ruthven knew it, too. It chuckled, and before my eyes, as it swiped the back of its long-fingered hand across its mouth, erasing the last trace of blood, it transformed into a beautiful youth. The face beyond lovely, with a serene smile and penetrating blue eyes, all capped with a halo of perfect gold curls.

Stretching out its arms, it flew up toward the ceiling, a vision of beauty neither male nor female, as transcendently awesome as Michelangelo Buonarroti's finest painted masterpiece.

It held its hands out, a smile shining from its face. "I am the Cyprian Queen, god and goddess of love beyond imagining, and ecstasy beyond any human touch."

A movement on the ground caught my attention, and I saw Vanessa had risen. Holding her hands out to the vision of youth, her blood-soaked hair clinging wetly to her body. She cried, "Her lips suck forth my soul!"

With a tinkling laughter, the angel came to stand before her. I moved quickly to intercept them, ready to fight for Vanessa. But she caught me off guard with a strength I didn't expect. Her shove sent me back wheeling, giving her time to fling herself at Ruthven.

The beautiful vampire's eyes shifted to me as it gathered her into its arms. "You will be very sorry," it promised, and then it soared into the air, Vanessa in its arms.

The sash of the window flew open, and a frigid gust of wind blasted into the room. Then the fiend dashed out into the night.

"Vanessa!" I called, rushing to the sill. But it was too late. She was gone.

"Mrs. Andrews!" Eustacia cried from behind me. I felt her press my bag into my hand. But I could not tear my gaze from the window. The wind blew into my face, leaving me gulping desperately for air, but I barely felt the cold as it bit through my nightdress. The night was brilliant with moonlight, alive with the movement of the wind as it thrashed the treetops.

I watched helplessly as Ruthven hovered outside the window, chuckling as it clutched its euphoric prize. The maniacal look of its evil intent, somehow incalculably worse when written on such heavenly loveliness, was horrible to behold.

I fumbled in the bag, my fingers closing around the shaft of the stake. Even as I extracted it, I knew it would do no good.

"Eustacia, do not look," I mumbled.

"But—"

"Do as I say. Close your eyes!"

I did not close mine. I watched Ruthven's victorious glee as it dropped Vanessa Braithwait. The sound of her scream as she fell four stories, the sound of her body hitting the ground below, the immediate silence after, was beyond dreadful.

I cried out, my wail of frustration and rage echoing in the night. The vampire whirled to leer at me, cackling an evil laugh as it did so. Its golden head caught the moonlight for an instant before it flew off into the night, and was gone.

I held Eustacia in my arms, rocking her back and forth as she screamed and cried in horror. I wished I could do the same, but all of my emotions were choked by the bitter knowledge that I had failed and a beautiful child was now dead.

I found myself staring at the puddle of Vanessa's blood seeping into the floorboards. It was on me, on my hand, on all I touched. I felt a wave of sickness and regret, making me sway on my feet.

"Mrs. Andrews," Eustacia pleaded. "We must go."

I knew she was right, but as she led me from the room, I stopped her. "No. Wait."

Margaret still lay on the floor, surrounded by shards of broken glass. I bent over her to see if I could find a pulse. I did, and it was strong enough, but she was still unconscious. "She needs tending," I said to Eustacia.

But she pulled at my shoulder. Her voice was filled with panic. "Come away. If they find you here they will suspect the worst. They already do not like you."

"I . . ." She was right. I had no way to explain the carnage all around us. As we left, I wondered why no one had come yet. Then I thought of my own foggy head and realized everyone must have been drugged. I wondered how this was achieved, and thought of Margaret. "Eustacia, could Margaret have done this?"

"Margaret can do anything," she whispered fearfully. "You do not know her. She is obsessed with the Cyprian Queen."

"She has been learning about witchcraft," I mused aloud.

Eustacia peered curiously at me. "You think she cast a spell?"

"No, of course not. I was thinking more that she might have used herbs to make everyone sleep." We made our way out into the hallway. "Do you know what you saw tonight?"

"No," she answered quickly, "and I do not want to. I am writing to my father and telling him that if he does not take me out of this school I will run away. Perhaps now that Vanessa is dead, he will believe what I have been telling him, that something terrible is happening here." She looked at me fiercely. "But I swear I will run away if he makes me stay."

"I do not think you will have trouble convincing him. Now that Vanessa . . . Well, it cannot be hidden or covered up any longer."

"You knew all along there was danger. You knew about that . . . that monster."

I sighed. There was little purpose in hiding anything now. "I did know. But I did not know enough. I should have done more." The words were empty, fed by emotion rather than rational thought. I knew I could not have saved Vanessa. The knowledge was bitter.

Eustacia shook her head, her face haunted by fear. "I cannot imagine what would have happened tonight if you had not come. I could have been killed, too." She swallowed, her fingers touching quivering lips. "I am sorry for Vanessa, but it was her own choice. Margaret and the monster poisoned her, but she *wanted* it."

"She didn't know," I said quietly. "It deals in lies and deceit.

It changes itself to what its prey desires. An angel, a demon, a god. It is some kind of evil chimera."

What I'd just said hit me. Chimera—that was the name of the grotesque orchid Suddington had shown to me. *Dracula chimaera.*

The plan Eustacia and I laid out went flawlessly. She raised the alarm at dawn, and told the story that Vanessa had thrown Margaret into the mirror when Margaret tried to stop her from leaping to her death. Once Margaret was subdued, Vanessa had carried out her plan to kill herself, presumably due to being distraught over an unrequited love. It was inevitable the Irish boy would be named as the reason. My presence was never mentioned and the other girls who had been sent out by Ruthven had succumbed to the sleeping potion with which Margaret had doused the rest of the school. They awoke disoriented and confused, remembering nothing to contradict our story.

I impressed upon the headmistress to summon Serena to see to Margaret's injuries. Sloane-Smith was dazed with the aftereffects of having been drugged and so she granted my request and my friend was called, bringing with her an urgent message for me that Valerian wanted to see me as soon as possible. There was much that required my attention at the school, however, both in my official capacity of teacher and in my unofficial one. I had to put the protections back in place, a task which proved a significant challenge as regular classes were suspended and the girls had free access to their dormitories. At last, during dinner, I was able to get inside and do what was needed.

I found something very curious in the execution of this duty. Small bags of seeds and some dried leaves or herbs were tucked into the coven girls' beds. Uncertain what they were, and taking no chances, I burned them.

Fire purifies—that was why witches were burned. But the

smoke from evil burning is toxic. As the tiny fire I had made with the bags in the brazier in my bedroom ignited, I nearly choked, recoiling from the potent aroma. And I saw in the flames tiny figures writhing—as if something malevolent was dying an agonizing death.

I felt a sense of deep satisfaction as the spell on each bag was broken.

In the quiet of Serena Black's cottage, I sat wrapped in a blanket, hunched over a cup of coffee made strong and sweet (in the Turkish manner, Serena informed me, learned from her grandfather, the son of an Ottoman sheik).

"Rather an exotic past," I had commented weakly when she'd handed me the brew.

"No more so than yours," she'd replied. "Now drink. It will soothe your nerves, and you need it."

After taking a sip, I gave her a questioning look, for I could taste the alcohol strongly. She merely shrugged and went about her kitchen works.

"We cannot stop him," I said without emotion. The addition of spirits to my coffee had been a good idea; I wanted to dull the feelings of despair inside me. "Ruthven has crossed over into the phase of his game where he is compelled to destroy each and every one of them. And I cannot do a thing about it."

"But he had a connection with you," she reminded me. "He called you sister."

"Where I was once his most desired object, he now reviles me for my betrayal. He will come for me as well. He drugged me. I did not anticipate that. And I suspect he has been doing something to me for a while. I have not been feeling well. I can't sleep. I have the most awful dreams, and I feel . . . weak in a way I can't describe."

Serena's soft hand closed over my shoulder. "Your man will be here soon. He will have some ideas, and a plan. Oh, and the priest has come back, you know. He and Sebastian are anxious to speak with you, I am told."

"Did they learn something in Rome?" I inquired anxiously.

She shook her head. "I do not know. But I know your man wants you to leave the school. He told Sebastian, and I believe they are preparing to speak to you together on this."

"It is out of the question," I said quickly, then stopped to consider it. If I did not find a remedy for my recent malaise, there was not much point to my being there. "What do you think?"

"You cannot stay to fight the vampire if your powers are weak." She brought her cup of coffee to join me at the table. "I made Sebastian tell me the story of what happened, how you all met, what you did to save that little girl. You who have never been trained killed an ancient vampire. That is no small thing." Sliding a plate of sandwiches toward me, she gestured for me to take one. "There. You eat."

They looked like an assortment of traditional finger sandwiches, but when I nibbled one, my mouth was treated to an interesting and exotic spice. She smiled at my obvious pleasure.

I realized how hungry I was, and she laughed when I immediately took another. "Why do you take such good care of us?" I asked.

She had been smiling, but the expression faded. Then she shrugged and turned away. I felt as if I had unwittingly broached a forbidden topic.

It was not a full minute later that Valerian slammed open the door and swept into the cottage amidst a whirl of cold wind. He did not even remove his cloak or shake the mud from his boots before coming directly to me. "What the devil happened last night?" he demanded.

He made me repeat every word the vampire had spoken, made me describe in exhausting detail every thought I had, every sensation I felt. The intense interrogation was both irritating and endearing. I did not take offense as his peremptory manner. I knew it was out of concern. Had the situation been reversed, I would have been just as impatient.

"I want you to stay here with Serena," he announced when I was finished. "Or with me, in the village. You cannot go back to the school."

I prepared for an argument. "I have to go back. I will only eat and drink here, at Serena's cottage, or at the inn, to prevent being drugged again."

He shook his head. "It was not something you ate or drank. I daresay that had a deleterious effect on your ability to exert your will, but a drug would not dilute in any way the strength of your talents."

I stared at him. "Of course it did. I felt like I was reaching inside myself for something I knew to be strong and sure, only to find dust in my hands."

"I believe what you felt. I only tell you, it was not Margaret's sleeping drug."

"Then what?" I snapped, my nerves frayed by the frightening possibility of something else at work here that I did not understand.

"I believe I have a theory," he said soothingly, seeing my consternation. "It has to do with what I told about the alchemist of Santorini."

My head snapped up in shock. "What? But how?"

"Consider that the alchemist's quest was—is—to restore the *strigoii vii* to humanness. A cure, in effect."

His eyes were hot, and I knew he was thinking of himself, of being fully human again. My heart wrenched, for I had no doubt there was no such thing as a cure for the poison in his blood, and there never would be.

"In Naimah's journal, she posited a theory that the basis of the alchemist's cure was in the exchange between humans and vampires. The vampire would regain some of its human nature once again and in return a human would acquire some of the qualities of a vampire, namely immortality." He paused to thank Serena as she handed him coffee.

I didn't trust Naimah. After all, we still did not know what she had bartered in order to live an unnatural lifespan. What had persuaded the secretive and reclusive alchemist to give her the power of long life?

But Valerian was animated as he continued. "Imagine if this should be the case, that it is possible for vampires and humans to trade in kind."

"This is interesting, yes," Serena broke in, "but what has any of it to do with Emma?"

Folding his hands in front of him, he bowed his head. "Whatever effects the alchemist might have discovered to extinguish the vampire living in his daughter, these might extend, to a lesser degree, of course, to having an effect on the Dhampir." His eyes cut to me. "The source of your capabilities come from the blood of the vampire in the *strigoii vii*. It is, at its essence, vampire blood."

I saw his meaning, and had to admit it seemed to have merit as a hypothesis. "Therefore, if there is such a thing as an elixir to lessen the powers of a vampire, it would dilute those powers in me as well."

"Why not?" His eyes were intense. "If there is such a thing as an elixir, that is."

I knew Valerian wanted to believe in this elixir desperately. A cure for him. And for my mother—if she still lived, if she had not passed on to the true undead, the powerful and terrible *strigoii mort*. I shook off the implausibility of it as questions arose in my mind. "Why would this alchemist give such a tool to a vampire? He's dedicated his life to curing his daughter, saving her from their number. Why would he ever lend aid to one?"

This, I saw, deflated Valerian's theory. He nodded, agreeing with my logic. "That I do not know."

Serena leaned forward, hands braced on the table between us. "Still, let us focus on our problem. Ruthven had some way to weaken Emma's powers. Where else, but from this alchemist, could he get such a means?"

"And more importantly, if he weakened you last night he can do it again," Valerian said with a meaningful look at me.

"I cannot simply retreat," I protested. "He is starting his rampage—he will kill all the girls and then he will disappear. You know he will go elsewhere, to another of his hunting grounds, and pick up the same game again. We have to fight." I knotted my hands together in frustration. "If we can figure out how he is weakening me, we can stop it. It must have some source, something I know somehow, something out of the ordinary. What is out of place, uncommon, even odd in the school?"

The cottage door opened and in walked Sebastian. He looked miserably windblown and exhausted. "Thank heavens, you are all still here. If I have to spend one more moment in the company of this priest I swear I'll—"

Father Luke stepped inside, filling the interior of the cottage with his bulk. He seemed larger, stood taller, shoulders thrown out wider. I noticed he was once again wearing his Roman collar. Something unfurled in my chest, a pride and love of the man I had known him once to be—strong, a leader, a man of conviction and purpose.

"Uncommon indeed," he said. He had apparently overheard our conversation as he was about to enter. He removed his cloak with a flourish, his movements fluid, almost graceful, as if a ponderous weight had been thrown off.

"I believe the power comes from the Dracula himself," he said as he sat at the table. "Let us put our heads together. The hand of the Great Dragon Prince is at work here." He grinned. "I have something to show you."

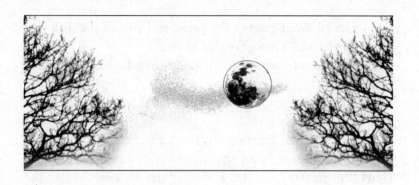

Chapter Twenty-three

Aripple of excitement went through the room as we watched Father Luke lay a cloth-wrapped package on the table. He motioned for me to take it. When I picked it up, I was surprised at its weight, which might have been as much as a full stone.

"From the Vatican archive in a Carmelite convent outside of Pompeii," he said. "A secret one, not official. Go on, open it." He waved his hand. "It is a gift."

Inside was a gold disk, large enough to cover my entire palm if I held it in my hand. It was very thick, and pierced in a pattern on the top. I could make out carvings on it, words in a different language—Latin, I would guess, but the light was too dim to see it clearly. I detected only one thing clearly—a single bold, deeply inscribed word: *Drăculea*.

I lifted an awed gaze to the priest as I passed the disk into Valerian's hand. "They gave this to you?"

One corner of Father Luke's mouth lifted. "No," he replied blandly.

Valerian and I exchanged a look. "Perhaps you should explain," I said gently.

He seemed well satisfied with the effect of his pronouncement. "You already know the men in the Order of Saint Michael kept secrets from me. I have always maintained that the Church of God is not bad in itself, but men can be, perhaps without knowing it. Even men who mean well can make terrible mistakes."

"So this is why you went to Rome?" Valerian asked as he examined the disk. "Revenge?"

"Perhaps not so much revenge as atonement. My church broke trust with me. I felt, very simply, that they owed me."

Sebastian threw his hands up and rolled his eyes. "So this is what all of the mystery was about, rushing off to meetings you would tell me nothing about, disappearing for days on end—all that to even the score? What in the name of heaven do you imagine they owed you?" He jabbed a finger at the disk. "That thing must be worth a fortune. It was a hefty debt."

"More than money," Father Luke replied. "The truth."

"Oh, I see. You merely swept into the Vatican and demanded the truth," Sebastian cried sarcastically, "and of course they said, 'Oh, certainly! Here are all the secrets we hid from you, so sorry for the inconvenience.' Honestly, I . . ." Sebastian paused, his eyebrows gathering on his smooth forehead. "Truth about what?"

Father Luke paused, and I could see he was savoring the moment. "About the Dracula." He tapped the gold disk. "And this."

"What is it?" Sebastian demanded.

"It is the seal of the Dragon Prince," Father Luke said. "You recognize it?"

I looked closely. Indeed, I had seen it written into the flesh of a vampire who had tried to kill me, in the form of a tattoo. Other places, too . . . I tried to remember where. A curl of apprehension tightened in the pit of my stomach.

"This was taken from his mightiest general, one who was vanquished long ago by a skilled and powerful vampire hunter," Father Luke explained. "The general's fate was to be imprisoned in the holy confines of a tree blessed for the thorns which once made up the cruel crown Our Savior's tormentors forced on his brow. A special tree of that kind, one situated in a sacred and mystical place where the living and the dead meet." He lifted his eyebrows to me expectantly.

Yes, I knew what he meant. Avebury. I felt my heart lurch. "The hawthorn. That vampire . . . this is him, then . . . The one . . . ?"

He nodded. "This seal belonged to one who called himself Oriax. The name comes from that demon who serves as Lucifer's general. That was not the vampire's real name in life, most certainly. However, it was an apt title, for he was the greatest of the Dracula's followers, and under his many campaigns spreading terror through Europe and western Asia, the Dracula's power was expanded far and wide, even here in England. But it was here he was vanquished." Father Luke took the disk back from Sebastian, who seemed suddenly uncertain what to do with it. "This was taken from him by the vampire extirpator who banished him in that tree long ago."

"This was the creature we destroyed last spring?" Serena asked.

"Yes," I replied. "I suppose it was. We did not know its identity, though. We knew only that Marius had come to release it so that he could consume it, take that ancient and great power into himself. His plan was to become the mightiest of all vampires."

"Indeed, that is exactly what his plan had been. He was sent by the Great Dragon Prince himself," Father Luke said. He stared meaningfully at Valerian and me in turn. "Anointed by him in a sense, to succeed Oriax, who had proved himself unworthy by being bested."

Valerian scrubbed a hand over his chin as his thoughts turned. "So the Dracula is grooming Marius to take Oriax's place at his side."

"Marius. And another." Father Luke paused, pausing as he let us digest this. "There will only be one in the end, but I suppose the Dracula learned from Oriax's defeat. It must have been crushing when his general, the only one that terrible prince had pinned all his hopes upon, was defeated in battle. The Dracula has learned from this disappointment. He has devised a different plan to ensure it does not happen again. This time, he has chosen two sons to vie for his favor. Brothers in strength and equal in their possession of their father's love. They despise each other, of course, for they are locked in a lethal rivalry, in which only one will survive. The Dracula pits them against each other to see which emerges the strongest, the most ruthless, the most clever and resourceful. It is this one who will be made his general, and sit at his right hand."

I said, "It is exactly what his father did to him and his brothers. Uncle Peter told me of the stories of Prince Vlad II, the Dracula's father, who set his sons in conflict against each other to see which one deserved to be prince of Wallachia."

"Marius is one of these sons?" Valerian asked.

"Marius is the wise one, patient, stealthy, and cunning beyond compare. He is capable of great strategy. He understands humans, knows how to use them as resources. While he is crafty, his brother—his enemy in this war to come—is much different. Impetuous, unpredictable, capricious and temperamental, he is just as dangerous and just as dedicated to winning the feud."

"Lliam," I said.

At Father Luke's expression of surprise, Valerian quickly explained what he and I had learned both through Ruthven and on our trip to Ireland.

"Well, then," he said, satisfied. "It all comes together. Ruthven is from Lliam's line. He must have made this Alistair, who in turn made your mother. He was right to call you sister."

"Don't say that!" I snapped heatedly.

"I apologize. I meant only that the source of the vampire was through the line of Lliam." He turned thoughtfully to Valerian. "And you are from Marius." He paused.

"Why does the Dracula wish to have a general?" Serena inquired. It was strange to hear her voice so timid.

Father Luke took a long inhalation of breath. "Ah."

Sebastian sank into a nearby chair. "That does not sound good."

"Serena asks a crucial question. There is indeed a reason why the Dracula requires such a powerful and ruthless general." Father Luke's eyebrows gathered as his face took on a troubled look. "It is, and always has been, his most fervent wish to vanquish the other Dark Princes of the Undead to rule all the world unchallenged."

Several beats of silence pulsed around us, filling the room. My mind spun, for I had never thought beyond the Dracula. It seemed incalculably horrible to imagine more of his kind, but it also made sense. The vampire had existed throughout time in all corners of the world; like humans, would they not be subjected to different lords, rulers, even governments, if anything in the revenant world could be so organized?

It had never occurred to me, and yet I had known of their

propensity for society. A natural outgrowth of society was governance, at the top of which was the one who held power. And where there was power, there was war.

"Y-you are saying there are others like him, like the Dracula?" Sebastian stammered.

Father Luke held up a cautionary finger. "Understand, there is no other like the Dracula. The Church believes there are seven princes of distinct domains, each ruling realms of varying sizes and of very different types."

Serena made a sound halfway between a moan and a gasp. I understood exactly how she felt.

"The greatest, the most powerful and dangerous, is, of course, the Dragon Prince," Father Luke continued. "The others are mere dukedoms to his great empire. The Dracula desires them all."

"Who are these other princes?" I asked.

"They are all very different—that is why legends surrounding vampires are so varied, in keeping with the cultures of the domain they rule. And they are kept very secret. I was able to learn only a very little bit about them. The Tiger Prince of the Dark Continent of Africa. The Serpent Prince of India."

I was aware of Serena making the sign of the cross, then kissing her fingers three times in an old-fashioned charm. Sebastian saw her, too, and he looked down at his hands as if he might follow suit.

"In the north, the undead carry on in the fashion of ancient Viking raiders," Father Luke continued. "I read accounts of how they waylay unfortunate ships, letting the captives loose in a savage hunt across the ice fields in a parody of sport. In contrast, the Greek have a very civilized, very small, elite clan. These vampires exist in mystery and isolation, remnants of their country's Golden Age of philosophy, science, and art. They are elevated thinkers, and are considered mystics."

"That must be why the Greek vampire is so difficult to figure," I ventured. "And why the alchemist has his research laboratory there."

"The Ruby Prince," Father Luke continued, "has dominion over all of Asia and Asia Minor. His minions are many, organized into armies with powerful generals to expand power and influence within the revenant and human worlds. Next to the Dracula, he is most feared."

Valerian jerked to attention. "So this is why the Dracula must have a general of unsurpassed quality."

Father Luke flexed his hand, a powerful hand that might, in another century past, have wielded a sword as deftly as a feather. "Will it be Marius or Lliam? Only one will rise. Who it will be is yet undetermined."

"That is six," Sebastian said. "Only six princes."

The priest nodded. "The last one is known only as the Spirit Prince. Its realm is far away, some believe in the Americas. I know nothing of its nature or what manner of vampires serve that realm."

Sebastian met my gaze. He seemed in shock. I, too, was in something of a daze, as if my head had gotten knocked one too many times. I rose on numb limbs and began to walk toward the door. I had had enough for tonight. I thought, perhaps, I'd had enough for a lifetime.

"It becomes deeper and deeper," I murmured bleakly. "And I can do nothing. I am defenseless, weaponless—"

Valerian caught me by the arm. "Emma, wait for me."

I stared at him blankly. "I have to go back. The girls are still in danger."

"There is nothing for you to do. Stay with me. I can protect you."

I do not know where it came from, but a great and terrible laughter welled up inside of me, and exploded from my throat. I backed away, shaking my head. "You would protect me from all the world? From the Great Dragon Prince, and all the princes of the undead? You would—"

He was never unkind to me, not even in the smallest way. Yet, his hand on my arm was firm—strong even, and his face as harsh as a knot. "Come with me," he said, and he took me from Serena's cottage. I pulled away, from pride, not fear, and once we were clear of the little house, he released me. "You are not going back to that school."

"He will kill them, Valerian."

"He will kill you."

"And am I to walk away, do nothing? Count myself lucky to live? Is that what you will do? And when the news comes of their deaths, shall we bow our heads in sadness and tell ourselves there was nothing else for us to do?"

He gazed at me helplessly. In the moonlight, his face was shadows, sharp with angles. His cheekbones stuck out like blades, his eyes hollow, his mouth obscured.

Then he did something very odd. He held his arms out to me, and whispered my name. Just once, but he said it with feeling, and I moved without thinking, obeying my heart and my broken courage, and fell into his embrace.

I did return to Blackbriar that night. Valerian came with me.

It had been decided quite simply. He had said, "You need me." After a beat of hesitation, he added, "And I need you."

I let him in by the pantry door and we snuck undetected into my bedchamber. On our way, he helped me check that the windows in the dormitories were secure and the salt lines were intact.

"Is there anyone you suspect will let him in if he calls to them?" Valerian asked as we were finishing our preparations.

"Possibly Margaret. I do not know her state of mind since Vanessa's death."

"Ruthven will eventually find his way in, if he wants to have at them."

I nodded in agreement, wrapping my arms about myself to ward off the chill. "He considers them to belong to him. Now that he is angry, and it is all falling apart once again, he will not rest until he has killed them or driven them to take their own lives."

Valerian paused. "And you?"

I answered him honestly. "I do not plan to die."

He grinned at me, shaking his head as if I had said something to amaze him. "Brave Emma."

"You mean foolish Emma," I said sadly.

He suddenly grew serious. "I mean beloved Emma."

That stopped me cold. My breath caught in my throat. He held his hand out to me, and I took it as we walked back to my room. In the moonlight, we did not need to bother with the light once the door was shut behind us.

He took out a shiny silver crucifix and hung it on the naked nail over my bed. That done, we looked at one another.

He touched my shoulders lightly. "I would like a chance to set something aright between us."

"It is I who should," I told him. "I owe you a . . . such a great apology."

He bent to kiss me. I hesitated, waiting to see what he did next. Pulling back to look at me, he seemed puzzled. "And I am sorry, also, Emma."

"Why?"

Deep lines folded over his brow. He seemed to struggle for words for a moment, then whispered, "You have had such darkness in your life."

I felt my heartbeat quicken. "Darkness has touched us both," I reminded him.

He appeared weighted down by emotion. "That is true. But I did not want *this* touched by darkness. I wanted to be whole before . . ."

"It is too long to wait for perfection. We are imperfect, and, yes, touched by this darkness we despise. But perhaps this is when we need each other the most."

"Ah," he smiled. "Wise Emma, too."

I lowered my gaze, suddenly shy. "I prefer the other one, what you said before."

He cupped my face in his hands. They were strong, vibrating with warmth and vitality. I fancied I felt the rush of blood where his palms lay against my cheek. "As do I. Beloved," he said softly, and kissed me again.

That night he erased what damage I had done, what Ruthven had driven me to do. That night we did not think about Ruthven at all. Both of us were flawed, burdened, and tragically imperfect, it was true, but for that short time that didn't matter.

He slipped out when the sun came up, and I lay awake as the daylight grew strong. I used to feel safe in the sunlight, but for some reason no reassurances calmed me as I thought about the day ahead. Would this be the last one for Lilliana or Margaret, or any of the other girls whose paths had fatally crossed that of the Cyprian Queen? What, if anything, could I do to stop it?

As I lay there, even after the peace and beauty of the night I had passed before, I felt my anxiety grow. By the time I rose, my head was heavy and my limbs sluggish. I was not drugged, I knew. It was despair creeping up upon me.

I noticed again the drooping orchid, Suddington's latest gift I had neglected to keep alive. I was feeling overset. So much so that the sight of the dying plant pricked tears of hopelessness into the backs of my eyes. I had had enough of death.

I fought the heavy cloud of dread the following morning when I crept up to the dormitories to check on the safety of the girls. Three of them—Lilliana, Marion, and Therese—were fast asleep in the dormitory. Eustacia was awake to greet me, having not slept a wink.

"He was at the window. All night," she told me, jumping from her bed. She pulled me aside, speaking in a frantic whisper. "Lilliana wanted to let him in, but we wouldn't let her. Therese and I had to hold her back." She shivered. I saw how pale she was, ashen gray with smudges of coal under her eyes. "I could see him, imploring us to open the window. He was beautiful, like he was with Vanessa . . . at the end."

"He cannot get to you," I reassured her. I heard the hollowness in my own ears. I wanted to convince her, but the memories of the horrible occurrences the night Vanessa died were fresh in my mind. "I sealed you in, protected you. And you have the cross?"

She shook her head, her eyes wide with terror. "He will find a way, I fear. They cannot withstand his will. He will make them invite him inside. Vampires can only come inside when invited, isn't that right?" She paused, realizing she'd said it out loud: *vampire.*

"Yes. Yes, you are right," I replied.

"He will make them do it. I was to be one of the seven. He will come for me. I must leave, Mrs. Andrews, or I will die! Please do not make me stay here another night," Eustacia pleaded. "Help me or I will go on my own."

I knew what it would cost me should it be discovered I'd helped her flee. Yet, how could I not help this terrified child?

At last I nodded. "You are right; you cannot stay here. Go

pack your things. I will take you to those who will keep you safe."

I brought Eustacia to the stables and hitched the trap to a sturdy mount. Strangely, our flight down the fell was anticlimactic, for we did so without interruption or trouble. I would have to answer for this when I returned, I knew. I would have to be brilliant to find some manner of plausibility for Eustacia's absence. But no matter what lies or patent groveling I had to do to appease Miss Sloane-Smith, I must make certain I remained at Blackbriar School, for the sake of the other girls. Just how I would manage to do this, I had no idea.

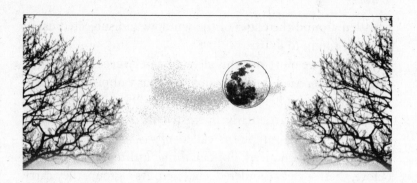

Chapter Twenty-four

It is so very odd how the mind works. One can labor for a solution—as I had done on this crisis of the Cyprian Queen—in intense concentration and acrobatics of thought and merely find one's self going round and round the same unanswered questions. And then, something happens—a stray word or a chance association—and it breaks open what all of that mental exercise could not. Such was the case when it all came together for me the very next day during a casual conversation with Father Luke.

He was saying, "Valerian and I have been discussing a possible plan," as he stirred his coffee at the table in his small room at the Rood and Cup. The day was bitter outside, a grayish overcast quality to the sky paired with a biting wind that whistled around the edges of the window and subjected us, in the cozy room, to drafts.

"I believe we must visit this alchemist in Greece. Valerian, of course, is interested in the possible cure for vampirism."

"It is always on his mind," I concurred. "His . . . condition."

"What I am particularly interested in is this unique situation. The Greek vampire is called *vrykolakas*, a very unique being among the undead. For one thing, as I mentioned to you before, their society is ordered, civilized. As a group, they carry on their country's classical traditions in philosophy, arts, and sciences. This is no doubt what attracted the alchemist to the island of Santorini."

"Do you think so? I assumed it was simply because the island is known to be heavily populated with vampires."

"Ah," he said. "But it begs the question: why does the vampire flock to the island?"

I gathered the corners of the rug I'd thrown over my shoulders a bit more closely as a chill snaked around my neck. "Well, then, why?"

Father Luke sighed. "It must be something on that island. In Greece, as I said, the vampires are different. Still vampires, do not mistake me. But less bloodthirsty. It is even possible the vampires cooperate with and facilitate this research. There is not much information in the Church archives on this, for as you know, the Greek Orthodox Church is separate from Rome, and their records were not at my disposal."

I leaned forward, my cold fingers clasping each other for warmth. "You mean to tell me you believe it possible that the alchemist conducts his research into vampirism with the permission of the local vampire establishment?"

He smiled at me slyly. "Think, Emma. How could he exist for all these many years, even in secret, if not for the tacit approval of the Orchid Prince? Athanas knows of the alchemist's

work—he must. And if so, that indicates he is complicit. Therefore, perhaps he can be approached, reasoned with, warned of
the Dragon Prince's plans for domination. Those of his clan are
the most highly evolved, and very invested in retaining their
freedoms. They might agree to help us."

My entire body went rigid as his words hit me, sparking a
sudden association that set me to shaking. "What did you say?"
I managed after a moment, my tone urgent and sharp.

Father Luke paused, puzzled. "I beg your pardon?"

"You called him the Orchid Prince," I clarified.

"Yes. Athanas—that is his name. His title is the Orchid
Prince, just as—"

"You did not say that before."

He peered at me. "Emma? What is wrong?"

My thoughts were moving quickly. I stepped toward the
window with a shake of my head, and as I did, I noticed the
disk, which lay uncovered, the sunlight making it glow like a
sun.

Like the sun . . .

"Call in Valerian," I said, burying my face in my hands as my
thoughts turned in surges. "Sebastian, too. We need to meet,
all of us."

By the time Valerian and Sebastian arrived, my ideas had
begun to knit together. Valerian could see my state, and sat
across from me with an anxious expression.

Sebastian went down on his knee to my right, drawing my
hands in his so I was forced to look at him. "You know something," he said. "You know who Ruthven is."

Valerian laid a hand on his wrist to ease Sebastian's grip.
"Leave her. She needs to think." He met my gaze, and I saw a
fervent light in his eye, his lip curled in cautious hopefulness.
"Emma?" he asked.

I inhaled a long breath, my eyes fastened onto the middle

distance. "You said the alchemist wanted to cure vampirism, and that the gift of long life Naimah got from him was a by-product of that quest."

"She wrote of it as a kind of limited exchange of vampire power to human," Valerian said.

"Then if it follows that it is possible that a similar exchange exists for vampires to attain some of the advantages of humans, a vampire might consume food, wine . . . might walk in sunlight. Not direct sunlight, perhaps, but on overcast days or when nightfall is due. It might, with the proper charm in place—this elixir—venture out of its lair, among the living." I paused as a thought struck me. "It might fool even me, or any Dhampir."

"What is it?" Sebastian inquired.

I shook my head and reached for the disk. Its carvings, revealed in daylight, were depicted in exquisite detail. My world tilted, keening first to one side, then the other, as a sick, scalding feeling began to crawl up from the marrow of my bones to light each and every nerve on fire. "My God," I murmured. I suddenly knew where I'd seen the sign of the Dracula, the dragon rampant, before.

"The seal of the Dragon Prince," Father Luke said, pointing to the figures carved on the surface.

"Yes," I said, nodding numbly. I traced my finger along the flow of the cape. Now that I spied the clever reversal, it seemed obvious that the great dragon was drinking the fountain of blood flowing forth from its adversary, which—I could now make out—lay skewered on one sinister talon.

"This . . . this is not a cape," I explained. "It is a gushing of blood." I pointed to the dragon figure. "This is the Dracula." Raising my eyes, I said, "I have seen this before. More than once, and most recently right here in Blackbriar."

The men waited expectantly, but my thoughts took an unexpected turn. I looked at Father Luke. "The vampire prince of Greece—you just referred to him as the Orchid Prince. Why did you call him that?"

Father Luke was a bit taken aback, but responded readily. "I don't really know. But you must know the legends associated with that particular flower. It has figured prominently in mystical lore . . . well, forever. The Church has banned it for its . . . er, sensual aspect. It was once outlawed—the forbidden flower. But in Greece, as in all very warm, moist climates, it grows in profusion, and . . ."

He trailed off. It must have been my expression.

Valerian leaned in. "Naimah mentions the orchids on Santorini in her journals. When she went to the island, she became enamored of their charm. She says they are magical, but I dismissed this as merely a romantic notion."

"No. She is right. They must have magic in them." I slammed the disk down on the table with a resounding ring. "Suddington keeps an orchid house." I pointed to the golden disk. "I saw a tapestry in his study one evening, but it was gone when I came in next. I suppose now he did not mean for me to see it, or to see what I saw in it. The figures—exactly like these—were embedded in the overall design."

Valerian held up his hands. "You are saying Lord Suddington—"

"He is Ruthven, and the Cyprian Queen. He is George Smythe."

There were several beats of silence, and I used them to gather my thoughts before I continued. "He wears the orchid at all times, on his coat. He surrounds himself with them. That is how he walks in daylight. Not full daylight, but in dusk and on rainy days, he can move among humans."

Valerian, I could see, was becoming convinced. "Go on," he said to me, his eyes blazing in rapt attention.

"On the night of his dinner party, he placed orchids all through his house. He gave me two of them."

Valerian muttered an expletive under his breath as a deep frown furrowed his face. I said, "Why would he do that when he must know I could not keep them alive for long? If he loves his plants so, why would he sacrifice any of them? Unless it was for some purpose. I've been sleepless, restless, fatigued. And my dreams have been so vivid and tormented. Now that I think of it, they have been worse when the orchids were fresh and strong, before my lack of proper care took effect."

Another thought occurred to me and I held up a finger. "I found little packets of dried flowers under the girls' pillows when I cleaned out their room and set in place new protections. I saw figures like tiny demons dancing in the flames when I burned them. They had been enchanted in some way."

"Magical flowers?" Sebastian asked skeptically.

"Orchids, somehow able to be imbued with magical properties. What a fool I've been not to see it!" I laughed, pinning him with a fervent gaze. "Why would a great prince of the undead name himself for a *flower* unless it represented power?"

I stopped, pausing as another thought occurred to me. "Wait. I don't understand something. The orchid he gave me is dead, yet I know the reason I was rendered nearly powerless the night Ruthven killed Vanessa was not merely the effects of being drugged. The weakening of my powers had to be due to some charm."

"An orchid?" Sebastian queried.

"Yes. It had to be. But not the one I was given . . ." I shot to my feet.

"Emma!" Sebastian exclaimed.

But I was already in motion. "I will be back. I cannot take you all. Just Valerian—you come with me."

* * *

It was here, in my small bedroom in the staff wing of Black-briar—it had to be. I tore the place apart, ripping open every drawer, pulling out the sparse furnishings and turning out the bedclothes.

I had not exercised stealth coming in with Valerian. In the midst of everyone's shock and outrage, I had marched him through the school, up the stairs to this room, and then locked them out.

Outside the closed door, I could hear shouts of alarm spread. They would be coming in soon, Trudy Grisholm in the lead, no doubt. The last I'd seen of her, she had been marching determinedly in the direction of the headmistress's office.

Valerian inspected the near-dead orchid sitting on top of the dresser. "You are right, this cannot be responsible for the charm. It is almost gone."

"Help me," I said, wanting to pull the frame of my bed away from the wall.

He put his back into it as the voices of discontent grew in volume on the other side of the door. And there we found it, tucked into a corner in the safety of the darkness under my bed. Its leaves were a bit blackened, its flower somewhat wilted, but it was still alive, as if it, like its owner, were immune to natural death.

Valerian recoiled at the grisly sight of the thing. "My God, it is hideous. What is it?"

I swallowed against a rise of nausea. "It is the *dracula chimaera*. Suddington showed it to me in his orchid house."

"But it cannot be the culprit here. It appears to be dead."

As soon as the answer came to me, I knew I was correct. "It does appear so, but it is not dead, Valerian. It is, in actuality, *undead*."

Valerian's head snapped around and he stared hard at me. "Good God."

"*The Blood is the Life*," I muttered, prodding the thing with my toe. That simple phrase had guided me from the earliest days of my awakening as Dhampir. It always came back to blood. This thing was as good as a vampire plant, sustained on blood. Undead. How else could it have survived without the light, heat, and humidity its species required?

Valerian drew it out with careful hands. The *dracula chimaera* looked like an insect, some kind of predatory thing that might animate at any moment and strike out, drawing blood, or worse. The smell of it was foul. I recoiled, feeling a dizzy falling sensation twist in my gut. This was how I had felt when I awoke to find Ruthven in the girls' dormitory, when my powers had deserted me.

"He gave the other to you in order to cover the perfume." Valerian cut a sharp look at me. "Are you feeling any effects now?"

I blinked rapidly to clear my thoughts. I could hardly concentrate, with the wretched plant at such a close distance.

My obvious struggle was answer enough. Valerian took the orchid to the other end of the room. I could hear people gathered outside my door.

Someone pounded. "Emma, dear, open up," Eloise pleaded.

Sharper voices, angry voices, and then an impatient tone I recognized as belonging to Trudy Grisholm: "Just break it down!"

My stomach tightened with tension. "What are you going to do with it?" I asked Valerian urgently.

"Destroy it," he replied. He nodded to the orchid nearest me. "Both of them. You start."

I pulled the orchid from its pot. Dirt scattered over the floor. Crushing it in my hands, I let it drop, stepping on it for good measure. The task was messy, but easily done.

Valerian gripped the thick, almost muscled, stalks of the

dracula chimaera. Even with his excessive strength, he had to exert himself so that the tendons on his neck popped out as he finally extricated the roots.

Once it was in his hands, he twisted the stalks, grunting with the effort. Then he muttered an exclamation and dropped it on the floor. We both stepped back, for the thing was still whole. The tendrils lay like snakes against the dirt-strewn floor.

"Are you all right?" I asked.

He nodded. "I think it bit me." He inspected his hands. "No blood. Not that I think it could harm me. But we really don't know what this thing is capable of, do we?"

I looked at the wound. The bite had not penetrated Valerian's flesh. I blew out a breath of relief.

"There," he indicated. The vile orchid was twisting on the floor.

Stepping forward, I angled my heel just under the head of the blossom. It gaped at me, dragon's jaws ready to snap into the flesh of my ankle. A wave of nausea came over me, and I realized this creature—or plant, which was it?—was doing this at will. With a cry of determination, I summoned my strength and brought my heel down sharply onto the stalk, where the base of the head of the flower lay. The sound of the flower's flesh being compressed was like the snap of bones. Valerian grabbed me, snatching me out of the way as the thing began to bleed.

An incredible stench rose up into the air, permeating the room. I choked and stumbled back, feeling like I had been struck in the chest by a hammer. As I doubled over, I heard Valerian mutter a curse and saw him throw himself between the writhing orchid and me.

The pounding at my door resumed, accompanied by Miss Sloane-Smith's commanding voice: "Emma Andrews, open up this door at once."

"Keep them out!" Valerian directed. He rummaged through my bag until he found an empty vial, one of those which I used to carry holy water. The water had been poured out a while ago—by one of the coven girls, I had little doubt. Valerian took the vial, dried it thoroughly with a corner of his shirttail, and blew in it to make certain it was completely dry.

"Hurry," I said. The pounding was like thunder in the small space.

He wagged his head, either to hush me or tell me he was hurrying as fast as he could, and stooped to the spreading pool of blood. The plant was still gushing in rhythmic spurts, as if a beating heart pushed the blood through human veins. Carefully, Valerian laid the vial on the floor, taking great care not to allow the blood to touch his skin as he collected as much as he could.

"What are you doing?"

He looked at me askance. "It is vampire blood, or something like it. We should not just throw it away." Carefully, he pushed the stopper in, sealed the vial, and stuffed it in his pocket. Then he turned back to me. "Get your things."

This I did swiftly, for I knew I would not be returning. It did not take me long to throw my belongings into a pelisse. I would send for the portmanteau later.

When I opened the door to my bedchamber and exited it for the last time, Glorianna Sloane-Smith was red-faced with indignation. If I had ever suspected her of being the Cyprian Queen, I would not believe it after seeing her now. Never was a member of the undead so ruddy-faced with impotent rage. If she could have struck me, I had no doubt she would have done so. I suspected Valerian's presence was the only thing that spared me that indignity.

"I am resigning my position" was all I offered as explanation for my extraordinary behavior as I swept past her. "I will send someone for the rest of my things."

My fellow teachers were crowded into the hall. Facing them felt like running a gauntlet. I felt the burn of shame, although I'd done nothing wrong; far to the contrary, I'd saved lives. But they did not know that. I would disappear into their memories as a madwoman, and a whore to boot as I'd openly brought a man into my bedchamber.

Catching the eye of Eloise Boniface, I saw she was confused and sympathetic. I wished I could explain, although I doubted she would believe me.

Valerian touched my arm gently. "Come, Emma. We must hurry."

His presence beside me was comforting and I shot him a grateful look. I had been the subject of scorn for nearly my whole life, but I had never had anyone with me, protecting me.

I turned and walked beside him with purpose, down the steps, through the hallway, and out the front doors of Black-briar School for Young Ladies for the last time.

By the time we arrived at the Rood and Cup, conferred with Sebastian and Father Luke, and laid out a simple but lethal plan, the hour had grown late. I felt nervousness grip my stomach as we discussed whether we dare wait until the morrow. It was decided we should not. This night might well be the last for the girls, and others.

Although I agreed that we must act quickly, I was filled with disquiet as we made our battle preparations. For the task we had before us, darkness was not our friend.

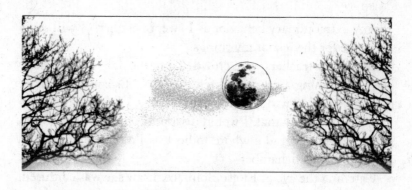

Chapter Twenty-five

When I entered Suddington's home with Valerian, I was struck by how empty it seemed. It was as if all of a sudden I could plainly see this was not the home of a living man.

"It appears deserted," I said, and listened to how my voice fell dead into the air. "When I was here at a party, it was enchanting."

Valerian nodded. "An excellent choice of words. The aura of charm a vampire can cast can beguile very thoroughly."

"I thought I would see through that . . . Oh. That is right— he had potted orchids all about."

"Well, that is your explanation."

"I also felt . . . beguiled when I saw him away from here,"

I said softly, and wondered at my desire for confession. I had been attracted to Suddington and I felt guilty on that account.

"He wore a flower on his coat, you said."

"Most times," I admitted, somewhat mollified.

"If it was not in sight, you can be certain he had it on his person somewhere."

He spoke as if that excused me for my unfaithful infatuation. I knew differently. I had felt betrayed by Valerian when I'd first come here, and I had welcomed the feelings toward Suddington. Knowing that now twisted my stomach with disgust.

Valerian pulled me into a corner. He hunkered down to open his sack, drawing out a long, curved sword I had never seen before. Meeting my gaze, he explained, "It was Naimah's." He unsheathed the slender scimitar from its scabbard, pausing for a moment as it winked in the light as if impishly acknowledging its handler. "We should get everything in place now. Sebastian has assured us there are no servants about."

Sebastian had braved his dislike of Mrs. Danby, deftly targeting her pride in knowing all that was to be known in the neighborhood, to learn that none of the Holt Manor staff lived in.

I fished in my own bag, taking out what I needed for my work. "All right, then. Where should we look for his bower? In the bedrooms?"

Valerian gave me a strange look. "I would wager the cellars are a more likely place."

Of course. "Right," I agreed.

We started toward the back of the house but I was suddenly overcome by an attack of anxiety and I stopped, pulling on Valerian's arm. "Hold on one moment. Should we wait for the signal from Father Luke?"

"No. They will go ahead." He peered at me, concerned. "Do you not remember, they need not wait for us. We discussed this, Emma."

Yes. I remembered now. I shook my head, wondering why I had gotten confused.

Valerian leaned in to speak softly. "The orchids. You are already feeling the effects, as am I."

I suddenly felt as if all my strength, my clarity, my focus were flowing out of me, leaving me weak and disoriented.

But Valerian was beside me. His strong grip on my shoulder reassured me. "We will feel better in a moment," he said, giving me a bracing look. "Wait for Father Luke and Sebastian."

I smiled and nodded. Once the orchids were destroyed, we could conduct our search for Ruthven's resting place in these waning hours of daylight.

But our hopes were in vain.

A voice cut into the air, filling the room, making us jump as it rose up and rebounded around us. "Ah. . . . Here she is. My sister has come to me at last."

Suddington stood before us, having materialized out of the gathering darkness in the space of a few heartbeats. I cringed, feeling unnaturally nervous. I should have seen him coming. That was one of my gifts. The damnable orchids were confounding me!

He reached for me imploringly, smiling a lascivious welcome. "Yes, my sweet Emma. She with the face that launched a thousand ships." He laughed, clapping his hands together in delight. "Did you never guess my little jest? *Is this the face that launched a thousand ships?*"

Valerian shouldered me aside, inserting himself between us as Suddington's voice rang out. *"And burnt the topless towers of Illium? Sweet Helen,* make me immortal with a kiss." Here he grinned, and the cracks of his guise showed in a terrible leer.

"Ah, Marlowe, he understood things. Did you never wonder at that phrase, and the next, *Her lips suck forth my soul . . .*"

Without preamble or reply, Valerian raised his scimitar.

Suddington appeared unperturbed. "Are you not a fan of Mister Christopher Marlowe? I knew him, you know." He grinned triumphantly. "I admired him so. I would follow him about, see every one of his plays as they were staged. Ah, but *Doctor Faustus* . . . that was a work of genius. To sell one's soul for the promise of immortality. You see what I mean, that he knew things?" He smiled almost dreamily. "At any rate, I like to think so."

He mused pleasantly, as if we were seated in a parlor leisurely sipping tea, "Those days, you cannot imagine such greatness as those among whom I walked. When I was changed, I wanted to take that capacity for beautiful language and make it mine. And so I did."

"You are saying you fed from him." There was disbelief in Valerian's tone.

Suddington lifted his chin. "I have elevated myself through the centuries, through him and many others. Oh, such stories I could tell."

"Save your stories," I interjected. The truth was, I could not bear to hear his voice. It was causing me to remember the attacks he perpetrated on me, and I felt my flesh cringe and crawl.

Suddington peered at me, caught completely unawares by my rejection of his great oratory. My outburst seemed to have a deleterious effect on him, and this gave me an idea.

I rode the wave of boldness that had come over me. "I am not interested in your delusions of superiority. Evil is not elevated. It does not even require much imagination, nor does it need intellect. Its only requirement is a soulless heart, and that is not so uncommon."

His smile returned, if a bit stiffly—how human these

creatures could be—as his hands swept outward. "I could tell you of beauty, of pleasure . . ."

I knew at once I was in trouble, recoiling as memory of his physical touch flooded me. Where were Sebastian and Father Luke? I needed to be at my full strength!

Two things saved me. One was Valerian pressing his fingers against my side. Second was my pride, which forbade me to back down, no matter my fears. "You are just a vampire," I told him swiftly, cutting him off, glad my voice did not waver. "In life, your name was George Smythe, and you were a murderer who preyed on young girls weaker than yourself to feel strong and powerful. Even now you are weak, insignificant, filled with the need for others to admire you, revere you."

His eyes grew hard, small pinpoints of hot coal glowing rage at me. The sight of his brewing rage gave me pause. I wanted him agitated, but I knew full well I was prodding a bear I could not tame. The line I trod was a fine one.

"I wonder why you have need for such boasting. I would guess for all your seductions and promises of unsurpassed plea-sure, you never partake of the flesh—not as you are, of course. You used the Irish boy as your surrogate for the consummation of desire. But even as a man, were you ever able to satisfy a woman's carnal demands?"

His facial muscles twitched. I had struck upon it, then. What, I wondered, was I supposed to do now? I felt a little cowed by the madness I saw in him.

"Emma, have a care . . ." Valerian muttered under his breath.

But there was no turning back, and no other choice that I could see. "There is, at the heart of your compulsions, simply the same sickness and evil that ruled you when you were human. You must kill, but not simply to feed. You boast of love, but in truth you despise these poor victims for they cannot give you what you need. No one can."

His mouth curled, and to my shock I saw his jaw tremble. I felt my stomach flip, knowing I'd struck exactly on the truth and wondering what I'd wrought.

The air charged instantly. Valerian grasped my wrist, a gesture of warning. I pressed on. "Now you are a vampire, and since you will never die, you have consigned yourself to an eternity of this cycle, ever coming to the same end. Rejection, terror, disgust—"

"I am a god!" he thundered, but the power of his boast was undermined by a whining, desperate quality to his voice.

"You are a worm," I countered, riding this mad wave of boldness that had taken me over. It was reckless, even desperate; I might not have my Dhampir powers, but I had my tongue. And my hatred. "A very bad man made eternal by the vampire transformation."

"You dare . . ." But it was not fury that shook in his voice; it was disbelief.

"I shall dare much more before this night is out. I am no longer in thrall to your spell. We found the *dracula chimaera* you hid in my room. I crushed it under my heel. It still had traces of blood inside it, the blood you fed it to make the charm. The only question I have is, was the blood yours or your victims? How does this magic work?"

He reared, his face contorting into an expression of horror. It was as if I'd just told him of the death of his beloved child. "You! You have vexed me all along. I should have destroyed you. Damn my ambition, to want you as I did." His eyes glittered malevolently as he studied Valerian and me, and I saw something dawn on his features. "Oh. Oh, look at the two of you. I see it now, why did I not realize it before?" He squinted at me, a chilling leer spreading over his face. How had I once thought him charming? "You already love, my dear," he said, sliding the words out with a sneer. "That is why I could not have you. Of course. There is nothing more mighty on all the earth than love, you know. That is why I use it. But I could not corrupt you. How that perplexed me in the beginning. You were so unattainable."

The vampire fumed at me. Then he grinned. "But you were not completely immune, were you? No. You should know—" he turned to Valerian, "—she was not uninterested."

I flushed, feeling a hot wave of embarrassment. But I had to keep him engaged. "I think you flatter yourself." That was a lie. Suddington knew it and it incensed him.

He leveled a finger at me and squinted as his lips curled in a derisive sneer. "I know I do not. True, you resisted. The night of the dinner party, you were able to rebuke me when I brought you among my orchids and tried to kiss you. Then, when I tried to take you—do you remember, that time on the road?—I wanted to show you what I could do, what I could give, and you would not let me . . ." His voice choked off, as if grief and rage made it impossible to continue.

I waited. I was curious, I admit. I wanted to know why he had singled me out. Valerian's hand on my wrist tensed, but he remained silent as well.

When Suddington spoke again, it was with something of a wail. "Why could you not see how it would have been so perfect? But you fought me. You denied me . . ." His face crumpled with sadness and frustration for a moment. Then he snapped his head up, his mood changed again to renewed anger. "Then I realized what you were. I'd never met the Dhampir before. Little vampire. And I could not have you, not as I wanted, because *he* was there before me." He pinned Valerian with a malevolent glare, then his quicksilver thoughts shifted again and he laughed. "How rich! Marius's half-made brat and a child of Lliam!"

Valerian cut him off, demanding sharply, "Where did you learn of the power of the orchid?"

Suddington threw his head back and glared at Valerian. "Why should I tell you?"

It was the wrong approach, I saw immediately. But I had seen how to get under this vampire's skin.

I angled my head toward Valerian. "Do not bother. He probably stole it. He is no better than a common thief."

I had been right to prick his pride. Suddington snapped his head toward me, his smile melting like wax. "You think you know so much! It was a gift. Long ago, my father—and your father, too!—the son of the great Dracula, picked me. He saw my work. He knew me, and he bestowed his favor on me."

"And how did you distinguish yourself so much that he 'picked you'?" I made the doubt in my voice drip from every word. "He has made over other vampires, surely. I do not think you were so special."

"Ah, but you are wrong!" he announced proudly. "There is power in taking a life, but it is not as simple as mere murder. You will never know how great and important it is what I alone can do. I select these girls, elevate them, take them to heights of passion and love. The sacrifice of their lives is beautiful in the end, joyous even. This is what Lliam understood. It is why I was given the gift."

"He uses you," Valerian cut in sharply, his tone unimpressed. He had picked up on my game, seen how disconcerted my taunts had rendered our foe. "You are merely a tool for him."

"That is not true!" Suddington countered, his lips trembling with rage.

"If he thought so highly of you, why are you not by his side?" Valerian glanced over at me as if we shared a joke at the vampire's expense.

I picked up his lead. "Oh, I have no doubt you are useful. But as to your strange and terribly perverse . . . proclivities, I dare say those have no true admirer save yourself." I cocked my head at him. "That is the trouble, isn't it? No one really has ever been able to understand you. Not even the great Lliam."

"A god, indeed!" Valerian threw the insult with a derisive huff.

Suddington's entire body trembled. Our ability to distract him had finally run its course. He began to change, and as he did so he drew his hands up over his head. I saw his talons grow, glinting in the fast-dimming light, and wondered if Valerian and I had made a fatal miscalculation. What had happened to Father Luke? Had he and Sebastian been waylaid somehow, prevented from the crucial task we'd set for them?

A terrible thought occurred to me. Had it been *we* who had fallen into the vampire's trap? Without the ability to sense, to probe, and the quick reflexes and keen accuracy that were part of my Dhampir nature, I would be no match for the vampire, even with Valerian by my side.

We both watched in horror as the monster took form, turning its wedge-shaped head toward us. Its maw was open, the saliva glinting wetly on the bone-white fangs bared for our admiration.

I looked to Valerian, caught his gaze. He gave me a quick nod, then moved in that impossibly swift way he had when he unleashed the vampire in him. I had not seen that he had opened a vial of holy water he'd secreted in his pocket, but he threw it now. It landed on the vampire, who cried out and flew backward, scalded where the holy water came in contact with its leathery skin. Smoke shimmered on its flesh and the smell of burnt carcass rose to choke me, bringing up bile to the back of my throat.

Valerian turned sideways, putting his back to mine. We

would fight together; I with my stake in one hand and a large silver cross in the other, and he with his scimitar.

The vampire staggered under the effects of the holy water, and turned toward us, smoke rising from its nostrils. Its eyes blazed, dead and black and hot. I cannot say I was unaffected by the grotesque sight of it in its natural form. A vampire is a demon, a monster, unmatched in its abilities to invoke horror. The sight of it was awesome, terrible, and although I was prepared for this, I was not immune to the fear it inspired, especially as I was keenly aware of the orchids all around me, breathing their sickening spell into the air, inhibiting my powers.

That was exactly what it was thinking, for it said, "My precious orchids protect me. You destroyed one of my favorites, my most powerful child, my lovely little *dracula*. But I have others. They are all around me, protecting me."

"That is how you walk in daylight." My eyes darted to the left and the right, searching for any sign of Father Luke or Sebastian. Where were they, I wondered desperately. I kept talking; it was my only chance to delay until help could arrive. "You consume food. Like the *vrykolakas*."

He made a sound, a twisted, awful laughter, filled with glee and pride. "Yes, the magic of the orchids is powerful." He pointed a finger at me almost playfully. "You are not used to it. I have had years and years to learn how to use its gift without sacrificing my strength. You see, you think me mad. But I am far more clever than you know."

It grinned, and my courage all but deserted me. I wrestled with the sudden certainty that Valerian and I were advancing into a trap. But there was nowhere else to go.

And then . . . and then my joy knew no bounds, for the first faint trace of smoke reached my nostrils. I saw with great satisfaction the vampire's threatening stance freeze.

His head jerked, the holes in his skull-like head twitching as it caught the acrid scent of fire. "My orchids!" he cried, the sound echoing through the vaulted room.

Immediately, I felt an infusion of strength, as though I had been released from a choking hold. The cursed flowers must be dying quickly. My limbs moved easier, my mind sprang free, my thoughts no longer encumbered.

I immediately leaped into action, lunging forward and aiming my stake for his heart. The vampire saw me at the last moment and struck out at me, deflecting the blow. The force of his powerful swipe knocked me into a spin. But Valerian absorbed the movement. With both hands gripping the scimitar, he heaved the great sword up and around in a mighty swing. The blow landed perfectly, slicing cleanly through the muscle-corded neck of the monster, and we spun together again, Valerian and I. It was like a ballet, as if we had the ability to predict each other's movements before we knew our own. This time my stake found the heart of the beast and Valerian broke away, raising his foot to plant it squarely in the creature's gut, sending the twisted gargoyle form reeling. It came down with a thunderous crash just as the crisp, crackling sounds of fire began snapping in the air around us.

"Move quickly," Valerian commanded.

"But the fire will get him—"

"No, we cannot trust it. Grab the salt in my bag."

"But I . . ." I stopped arguing as I saw the vampire's body twitch, a clawed hand scrabbling at the shaft of the stake. I had not hit the heart.

I scrambled to do as Valerian bid. I handed him the salt, and as he worked to pour it into the open wounds, both on the body and the neck, the disembodied voice of the vampire rose up around me, laughing. Ruthven—the Cyprian Queen, the man who had lived and killed under the name of Smythe,

the creature whose centuries-old reign of terror was now at an end . . . it laughed.

I grabbed the stake and pulled it out. Taking more careful aim, I positioned it better and readied myself to drive it in. Smoke was gathering around us as the fire devoured the old timbers.

"Hurry," Valerian urged.

But I could not silence the laughter. I stood, looming over the desiccated corpse. "What do you find so funny, fiend?" I challenged.

"Fools!" The words swelled in the laughter, not issuing from the slack mouth on the severed head but coming through the air, in my head, clear and distinct. "You may destroy me, but you shall pay. Oh, my sister, you love poorly in this brat of Marius's line. He will bring you more suffering than a legion of my kind. All your life will be woe."

"Emma!" Valerian's voice was desperate.

I drove my stake into Ruthven's heart and the taunts ceased as a great cry rose into the air, wild and filled with anguish. The vampire stared at me with those horrible, dead eyes of his bulging with shock, outrage, disbelief as it clawed the air to get to me. It bared its fangs and for a moment a sliver of panic pared off a piece of my heart as the thought flashed through my mind that perhaps it had some secret reserve, a trick I had not foreseen.

But the strength went out of the hand that reached toward me and the body went stiff, transforming rapidly into what it truly was—a corpse. The hellish wail was silenced. I let go, and the body hit the floor, as dry and dusty as an Egyptian cadaver.

I felt no sense of triumph, just dull relief. And weariness.

Valerian finished the preparations as the smoke thickened— securing the hands to its sides, severing the head and putting the coin in its mouth, spreading millet seeds around the body and placing the head in a bag tied to its bound ankles. The fire would do the last of it.

Valerian took my hand. I let myself be drawn away, and then we ran. Outside, our three friends awaited us, for Serena had joined Father Luke and Sebastian.

"Come to my cottage," she told us.

The men were of a mood to celebrate. But I was still disturbed. Serena noticed and put her arms about my shoulders. "It is over," she said.

I nodded, giving her a smile. I was relieved—very truly I was. But I could not shake the disquiet left by Ruthven's words.

Chapter Twenty-six

We four—myself, Valerian, Sebastian, and Father Luke—prepared to leave Blackbriar as quickly as possible. There was no telling what the local authorities would make of the goings-on at the school and the fire at Holt Manor, but we wanted to be gone before the wrong conclusions were drawn.

But before we left, we sat down for one last meal at the Rood and Cup. Mrs. Danby outdid herself, with pheasant and a mutton stew that was mouthwateringly tender. The delicious repast allowed us to focus not on all we had to discuss but on the culinary delights spread before us, and we were grateful for it. We concentrated on the food and did very little talking.

There were other patrons in the dining room, so when a

lone woman entered, I did not notice her at first. Then I heard a familiar voice say, "Excuse me," and I saw that Miss Sloane-Smith stood beside our table.

The men immediately leaped to their feet. She waved them back into their seats. "May I have a word with you, Mrs. Andrews?"

Valerian remained standing, partially out of politeness and partially out of protectiveness for me. He glanced at me, silently asking whether I wished him to turn the woman away. I was taken aback at first, shocked to see her. But I was also very curious why she had sought me out. I gave Valerian a nod to indicate I did not require his intervention and turned to Miss Sloane-Smith as I rose. "Of course. Pardon me, gentlemen."

She had aged seemingly overnight. Her face was drawn into lines, her skin colorless. Even her hair looked brittle. But the biggest change was in her eyes, which were flat and wary, devoid of her usual arrogance. "May I speak with you privately?" For all that she looked different, her tone was as imperious as ever.

But I could be haughty, too. "In here," I said, indicating a very small alcove Mrs. Danby kept in the event a patron wished to have a private dinner.

As soon as we entered, she drew the curtain behind us and turned to face me. "I want answers," she said.

"I am not certain you really do," I countered smoothly.

I saw her swallow and realized she was unsure. "The girls—Lilliana and Therese—have been talking. I have made certain they speak only to me, but they are going on and on about this creature. The Cyprian Queen."

I watched her face very closely. "The Cyprian Queen is just a local legend. You know of it yourself. You forbade me to speak of it."

She closed her eyes and shook her head. "It is a disgusting

tale, one almost extinguished and yet not quite. There are still whispers of it now and then. A very *dangerous* story with which to fill the heads of proper young ladies—full of images they have no business entertaining. This . . . goddess is supposed to visit girls in their beds and lure them out to lovers. It is a lurid fantasy, ripe for girls this age and precisely the kind of talk that can kill the reputation of a school like mine."

Like mine. That was the crux of it. She did feel an obsessive protectiveness toward the school.

I told her, "At one point, I suspected you were the Cyprian Queen."

She started. "I?"

"You had the necklace. I searched your office and found it secreted in a box. The dragon necklace, you remember."

"Lord Suddington gave that to me. After the dinner party. But what does that . . ." She blushed and appeared confused. *She knows,* I thought. *She knows it was him—that he was somehow responsible for all of it—but she doesn't understand how or why. And she doesn't want it to be true.*

"He . . . well, I was a bit overset," she said. "Lord Suddington and I have a very special friendship. To put it plainly, I was thinking of letting you go. He persuaded me not to, and gave me the necklace as a token of his esteem. Why do you mention it?" She spoke the words with great reluctance. How adeptly our minds can deceive us, I thought, lead us to comfortable lies and deceits when the truth is too hard to bear.

"The necklace has come up in the past, associated with the Cyprian Queen legend. That was why I thought you were behind what was happening. Vampires can be female, you know."

It was reckless of me, blurting it out like that, and yet what blessed relief to reveal myself at last. Miss Sloane-Smith gaped at me, her mouth finally working to form the word, yet unable to.

"Yes, vampires. It was a vampire who posed as the Cyprian Queen. He has been coming here every second or third generation for the past three hundred years."

Her eyes narrowed, and I laughed. "Now you will call me mad. Go ahead, I am used to it. Victoria Markam was mad when she found those bodies—the ones that did not exist, according to the local authorities. But those bodies were there, I'll wager. She was right about them, just as she was dead to rights about the girls."

To my surprise, she did not rebuke what I was saying. She did not embrace it, either. She seemed made of stone, transfixed with the face of a stubborn child surrendering to the administering of a bitter medicine.

"Do you have nothing to say?" I queried mildly.

"I . . ." She struggled visibly to find words. "I do not think I believe you."

"Yet you do not seem as if you *do not* believe me. Did you suspect something of this kind?"

She drew in a long, shaking breath. "I went to the grounds where Victoria Markam had claimed to see those bodies."

This surprised me. "You did?"

"Yesterday. The girls kept saying things . . . about what they'd done. About what they saw. At the end. Vanessa." She cast about helplessly, as if to find refuge, but the torment was already rooted in her mind. "I went to the place they told me, to see if what they said had any truth. It was the same place Victoria had claimed to see that horrific pile of bodies, but of course they were not there. Nor was there any evidence of them."

"He cleared them away when he was found out," I said with confidence. "No doubt he never imagined the cache would be discovered. He had been so careful to choose victims not likely to be missed so no alarm was raised hereabouts. He wanted to keep his presence a deep secret."

She closed her eyes, squeezing them shut like a child. "Yes. That is exactly what must have happened. But . . ."

"You know something," I prodded.

Her face spasmed and a glimpse of anguish came and went in an instant. "In light of . . . recent events, I had an idea. So I went to the cemetery, where the caretaker keeps a quicklime pit." She opened her eyes and looked at me, her eyes pleading as if she would have me read her mind and save her from having to tell me.

So I did. "You stirred the quicklime?" She nodded. I said, "And you found bones?" She nodded again.

If she had been anyone else, I would have reached out to her and laid a comforting hand on her arm. But with Glorianna Sloane-Smith, I did not. Instead, I kept my voice steady, professional. "Tell me more."

"I was quite near the clearing, the one where the girl from the village was found."

"Janet," I supplied, annoyed by the impersonal reference. Janet might have been a servant, not a paying student, but she, too, had been a beautiful, vibrant life that had been snuffed out too early.

Miss Sloane-Smith didn't register that I had spoken. "I found things there, in that awful place . . . odd bits of clothing and the like, things that belonged to the students. They must have indeed been sneaking out of the school and meeting there, doing . . . unspeakable things."

"Again, just as Victoria Markam had claimed."

She screwed up her face as she shook her head. "How could I believe it, and from her? She was always nervous, fussy, with no backbone. Weak." She said this last word with disgust. "I thought she merely wanted attention."

"Sometimes," I said, feeling as if I spoke to Judith, to Alyssa, to Alan, as much as to Miss Sloane-Smith, "it is not so bad a thing to give someone who needs attention a bit of what they crave."

She didn't understand what I was saying. Her kind never do. She took her leave of me and I followed her out of the room. As I resumed my place at the table with my friends, she continued on toward the door. Then she paused. Very stiffly, she turned her head and asked, "It *is* over, isn't it?"

I nodded. Her gaze rested on each one of the three men at the table. I had the feeling she wished to say thank you, but could not bring herself to do so, and at last, silently, she went on her way.

My companions and I exchanged curious glances. "Pride goeth before the fall," Father Luke quoted.

"Oh, bother," Sebastian moaned. "If you are to begin preaching, I am going to have a difficult time keeping this luncheon down."

Father Luke leveled a daunting glare at him. "What is it you have against God?"

"I have no problem with God, *father*. It is the infernal pounding over the head of *religion*, the aim of which is to make us feel like miserable creatures undeserving to draw a breath. I say if God made us, then—"

"Shall we see what Mrs. Danby has made us for dessert?" I interjected quickly. I was not in the mood for one of their quarrels.

The prospect of Mrs. Danby's cuisine diverted us all effectively and there were no further debates on doctrine or talk of vampires as we ate our cobbler and custard.

Winter was locked tight over the lakelands, but I decided to walk a bit before I closed myself into the confines of the carriage for our journey south. That particular day was crisp and clear, with lemony sunshine like watered silk across the sky. The cold weather here held a beauty that I wanted to enjoy. It was clean. And so I took to the road, striding briskly with my hands stuffed in a fur muff and my breath coming in great puffs of smoke.

I stood aside as a carriage passed coming down from the fell. As it drove by, I saw Eustacia's small face in the window. She stared at me solemnly, her eyes wide, dark circles radiating out from underneath them, but then brightened, sat up a bit straighter, and raised her hand to me. I lifted mine in response. "Good-bye," I called, but I knew she could not hear me above the clatter of the carriage.

I wondered what she would make of all of this, what memories or horrors she'd carry forward with her into the future. Would she ever tell the tale? Would anyone ever believe her if she did?

Then I was struck by a most immodest thought. At least she had a tale to tell, and a future to tell it to. Was it conceit to realize I had saved her life? As in Avebury, there was plenty to mourn. I regretted Janet and Vanessa, and the poor woman and child who still haunted my dreams. But I had saved Eustacia's life, and the lives of the other coven girls. I was going to have to learn to be content with what I could do, and not weigh too heavily all that I could not.

I had hired a carriage to take us south, down through the Yorkshire Dales. I was unsure of where to go from there. I seemed to dither over my choices: I had thoughts of returning to Ireland to see if I could pick up the trail of my mother. Or maybe I should head to Greece to try and see if the alchemist would help me.

I would also have dearly loved a long burrow in an archive to wait out winter. Then again, I knew Valerian was anxious to be on the hunt again for Marius and I wanted to join him to finish that business once and for all.

My inability to make any decision was uncharacteristic; I had always been known for my strong will and stubbornness. But in the end, I decided to go home, to Dartmoor, where I could think, get my bearings, and decide in good time what my next step should be.

When I arrived back at the Rood and Cup, Father Luke was putting his shoulder to the task of securing our belongings. Sebastian had been in an apoplexy all morning about the clumsy Mr. Danby; he did not trust the innkeeper to see to his luggage.

Catching my eye, Father Luke smiled. "Almost done," he said, securing a strap with a powerful snap.

"I am ready," I replied.

I felt someone beside me, and a man's hand rested lightly on my waist. I knew it was Valerian even before I turned to see him staring at me with sober concern. "Everything all right?" he asked.

"Yes, of course."

He smiled at me, and there was a lovely tenderness in his eyes. "You did well, Emma."

"We did," I agreed. "We all of us did."

"Ah, well, they say there is strength in numbers," he observed.

"There is strength in ours," I replied thoughtfully. And I realized that, yes, I had accomplished something, but not simply on my own. I loved these three men. They were my family, more so than those living in Castleton or Dulwich Manor, despite those blood ties . . .

I sobered sharply, the idea of blood ties reminding me of my kinship to those of the revenant world. Lliam. And the

Dracula. A cold, hard knot throbbed deep in my breast as the implications of this relation settled over me. I was so deeply afraid of what it meant.

Seeing the departure time was approaching, I brushed aside the disturbing thought and ducked inside the inn to say my final farewell to Mrs. Danby. As I made my way to the kitchen door, I noticed Old Madge at the hearth. Reversing my direction, I went to see her, smiling tentatively as I gauged her mood. I was in luck. Her eyes were alight with awareness as she stared back at me. "You are leaving," she said.

"I am."

She nodded.

"I want you to know she is gone. The Cyprian Queen. She is gone. Forever."

Her eyes narrowed, and she lifted a palsied hand to her lips. "She is? You . . ."

"It is a story that would distress you to know. Just . . . she is gone for good."

"Gone for good," she echoed, her mouth trembling. "Yes."

"I wanted you to know that. And to thank you for your help," I said.

She did not seem to hear me. The look that came over her told me she had faded into the past, but not in the unfocused manner of her dementia. She was thinking of her sister, no doubt.

A tear slid down her cheek, but she made no sound.

"It's time, Emma," Valerian called gently from the door as he gestured to me.

"A moment, please," I replied, ducking quickly into the kitchen to say farewell to Mrs. Danby. Then, I hurried outside.

Valerian intercepted me at the door. "We are coming with you. All of us. We've talked it over."

This surprised and delighted me. Still, I wanted to be certain they understood that I was not at all yet sure of my bearings. "I am headed home for now. I need some time to think over what the next step should be."

"Then I hope you have enough guest rooms," he said. "And perhaps we can decide together what comes next."

I laughed, feeling a sudden buoyancy lift my spirits.

"What a blasted cold day!" Sebastian announced, coming toward me as I emerged from the inn. I was astonished to see he was dressed more for a drawing room than for travel, in a fine coat and sleekly pressed trousers. I would have suggested the day would be much more tolerable were he attired appropriately, but I knew his answer would be to admonish me that comfort was always second to fashion.

"I am so glad you are coming with me." I cast a contented look to him, the priest, and, finally, Valerian. "All of you."

Valerian raised his eyebrows and smiled, and something secret and intimate passed between us before I cast my gaze down, a bit embarrassed.

Sebastian made a harrumphing sound and inquired, "Why, where else would I go?"

"Back to the city, where the beautiful people are," I said lightly, trying to break the uncomfortable mood.

"I rather think you are the most beautiful person I know," he retaliated with a shrug, "so I will tag along with you, if you don't mind. And besides, we have important work to do."

Father Luke came to join us, giving a nod that we should board the carriage. His face was strained after the exertion of loading the luggage. He was still pale and clearly not at his full strength, and I suspected he still struggled mightily with his desire for the poppy. But he was stronger, and I had renewed faith in him. "What? Who has important work to do?"

"You do," Sebastian said. "We all do. Fighting vampires. Who else is going to do it if we do not?"

The priest gaped, then blinked. Then he grinned, giving each one of us a long look. "I believe that is the first time I can agree with you, Sebastian. Who else, indeed."

"I will," a new voice stated. We turned to see Serena Black standing a few paces off, holding a small valise. Her face was somber, but there was no hiding the combination of hope and fear in her eyes. "I have nothing here," she said feelingly. "I have nothing in my homeland. But with you, what you did, that is something to make a person proud. It is what I wish to continue to do. I could be of use to you; I will cook and take care of you, if nothing else. I promise you will not be sorry." She blinked once. "If you will have me."

No one moved or said anything until I touched Father Luke's hand. "You surely have room for the valise among the other luggage. It cannot take up much space."

Valerian caught my eye. "Five of us?" I knew why he hesitated. He was a man used to working alone, being alone. So was I. And Sebastian, and Father Luke—all of us had been alone in so many ways for all of our lives.

We'd parted after Avebury, tried to go our own paths. It hadn't worked. I needed them. I was convinced I would have failed here in Blackbriar if not for them. They'd aided me, saved me. They had come to me because, I realized now, they needed me as well. *This* was love, I suddenly saw—so much for the promise of the Cyprian Queen. Nothing so glorious, just ordinary people standing together.

We none of us were alone any longer. Serena would not be, either.

"Five is a mystical number as well," I said cheerfully. "Five decades to a rosary, for example."

"Five . . ." Valerian gave me a helpless look.

"Five fingers," I said, showing him my hand, "gripping a stake to strike at the heart of the undead."

He coughed a wry laugh, his eyebrows furrowing in disapproval at my dramatics.

And so it was five of us, then, that headed out of the Vale of Eden that day, taking our time as we travled to Dartmoor to plan, to think, to talk. For, as Sebastian had observed, we had important work to do.

Emma Andrews
Brighton, February 1928

A+

AUTHOR INSIGHTS, EXTRAS & MORE...

FROM

JACQUELINE
LEPORE

AND

WILLIAM MORROW
An Imprint of *HarperCollins*Publishers

An Interview with Jacqueline Lepore

Q: Tell us a little bit about the origins of this book. Why did you decide to send Emma to the Lake District?

A: Pure envy—I want to go there! I did visit England a while back, but I did not make it that far north. For the story, I wanted a beautiful, peaceful, very pastoral setting to serve as a contrast to the dark happenings at the Blackbriar School. I always enjoy my research of England, as I'm a devoted Anglophile. I needed the setting to be isolated—a must for every scary story—and I found the Lake District, long one of my favorite spots, was perfect.

Q: And how did you come up with the "Cyprian Queen" legend?

A: One of the most compelling ideas that has come out of my research on vampires was the idea from a scholarly source that legends of supernatural evil rose up out of the mind of simple villagers and townsfolk who could not conceive that the particularly brutal crimes like serial killing, murder/suicide, mass murder, infanticide, et cetera could ever be committed by a human hand. Keep in mind that these folks lived lives strictly dictated by their religion, so these heinous acts came to be seen as the work of evil. Monsters, like vampires, demons, witches, and werewolves—all of which were vulnerable to holy and spiritual protections—were imagined to be responsible for terrible things people didn't understand. I thought this was a brilliant notion. I looked and found that in the annals of history, you really don't see any accounts of these kinds of crimes. There are two notable exceptions to this: Elizabeth Báthory and Gilles de Rais. But they can't be the only ones, right?

So, I got to thinking, what if a real serial killer found some way to become immortal? Surely, they would jump at the chance—an opportunity to practice their crimes eternally, to really be elevated to "god" status by virtue of being a supernatural being. Therefore, if such a being existed, what would his crimes look like? Like many serial killers, the sexual aspects of the crime would be more about power than sex, so the fact that the vampire cannot, in my world, have sex (I mean the *strigoii mort,* the truly undead) would not present a problem. The appetite to kill would not be abated, and it would complement the vampires hunger for life's blood. And, it would revel in its new powers to dominate and manipulate, which is what the serial killer craves. In fact, when you look at the folklore about vampires, it really seems to mirror our modern understanding of a serial killer. That was the jumping-off point.

In looking to ratchet up the creep factor, I thought a setting where a community of women were isolated and vulnerable would really make matters worse, and I thought of a girls' school nestled in the woods. This is the perfect hunting ground for a predator, protected by the shroud of mythology so that no one really took the disappearance of a dozen or so girls every seventy years very seriously. Really, I was just looking for the worst possible situation that Emma might confront.

As to the term "Cyprian Queen," it came from the Darwin quote I placed at the beginning of the book. The phraseology was kind of creepy—lovely and a bit "off" in my mind. Girls lifting their arms dreamily to their lover, sighing soft "alarms" (what kind of alarms?) It lent the idea of something both beautiful and desirable, and yet dreadfully dangerous.

Q: You must do a tremendous amount of research for your books; the Emma Andrews mythology is rich with a variety of vampiric legends, classic novels and poetry, and—in this book—botany lore. How do you tie everything together, and where do you take liberties to make your vampires (and characters and setting) your own?

A: I love to do research because it always gives me so many ideas. Whenever I'm stuck, I go to good old Google and the next thing I know I've got the plot problem solved.

My favorite bit of interesting material in this book was the legend of Spring-heeled Jack. It came up when I was doing research and I loved it, but it didn't really fit with the timing of the book and the location. Then it just came to me when I was designing the differences between the feuding Marius and Lliam that I could utilize this in a great way. I always knew Lliam would be like the Joker in *Batman*—maniacal, deadly, crazy, and capricious. It was a good fit to designate Spring-heeled Jack as a manifestation of Lliam. I was so pleased with being able to use this fascinating legend, and I hope to develop it more in the future.

I use a great many sources in building my vampire world. First and foremost is the seminal *Dracula*. I use real historical sources, like Dom Augustin Calmet and the many documented instances of vampires in Eastern Europe, and these are often cited in the book. I love how many of these accounts were actually legitimized by investigators in the Catholic Church and other official government agencies. All cultures throughout history had some variation of the dead rising and preying on the living in their mythology. This is certainly curious, and I think it speaks to the archetypal appeal of the vampire as both hero and villain. The challenge I faced, given this wealth of information, came in weaving together all of the different characteristics for the living dead and providing an explanation of the differences. This is where I take broad artistic license, but the root of everything I have created in Emma's vampire world is based in the actual legends and beliefs existing throughout history across the world.

Q: We meet the young Bram Stoker in Immortal with a Kiss. *That must have been fun to play with! How much of what you tell us about him is true to life?*

A: I was inspired to bring in a young Bram Stoker by a historical mystery novel I read a while ago where the protagonist meets a young Edgar Allan Poe, which I thought was brilliant and bold. I loved the idea so much, and was impressed with that kind of historical license. So, I thought, since I'm modeling my vampire world after the traditional Stoker-esque model, that it made sense to suppose that Bram Stoker had been, in Emma's world, influenced by the same things she learns about in the book. And I thought it would be really interesting to imagine they actually crossed paths.

In researching Bram Stoker, I found many fascinating things about him, which I mention in the book. One is that his mother was a pioneer of the early feminist movement. Another is that he had a serious illness as a child, which necessitated him being confined to bed for many years. I wonder how much his imagination kept him entertained during those long, lonely days, and how that affected him and influenced his interest in mystery and horror. (Is that just the psychologist in me coming out?) And finally, he apparently was part of a boisterous, large family. I thought that was interesting, given his dark literary works. But people always surprise you, and fascinate you.

Q: Your books are "vampire novels," but they are also mysteries, with a little bit of romance, and they could be categorized as gothic or historical fiction, too. That's a lot to pack in to one book! Do you have to outline to make sure everything happens as it should, or does that come naturally with the writing?

A: Oh, I'm a planner, definitely. I like having the security of a detailed outline. The process of producing it is quite a ritual. I compile my notes, which I've generated over a period of time, and transfer them on to sticky notes. Then I have a huge whiteboard where I play with the timeline, subplots, character arcs, et cetera. It's actually quite fun. Once I have the plot down, I move the notes into folders and work from them. I usually stick pretty closely to the outline as I write, but I'm not locked in by any means. Having a detailed road map allows me to concentrate on lots of other aspects of the writing and gives me a sense of security that I know where I'm going, what my characters are doing. Given the mystery aspect of the books, I can weave in lots of details and foreshadowing that I'll use later, either in the book being written or a future one. It also helps me keep track of the intricate lore and legends I'm using to make sure I don't leave any dangling threads or pop something out at some point that I didn't seed into the story earlier to give it some heft. Overall, it's much better for me to work with a sense of discipline and focus.

Q: The romance between Emma and Valerian heats up in this novel—but not always in a good way! Can you talk a little about that? And about how the romance in these novels differs from the romance you've written in your romance novels?

A: The romance between Emma and Valerian is completely different from traditional romances. As star-crossed lovers, they cannot be together, but they are each other's one true love, so the conflict is constant. At times, each one of them acts nobly. And, at times, each one acts not so nobly. They are both flawed, but truly and deeply good people who are just trying their best under impossible circumstances.

I modeled Valerian after the traditional gothic hero—brooding, mysterious, aloof, even "cursed," if you will. He's got baggage! But I didn't want Emma to be the traditional mousy heroine of those old time gothics (as if!). It's been a real challenge figuring out ways to bring these two together and pull them apart, but considering the forces moving in the world they live in it makes sense. There is one, insurmountable obstacle they have yet to discover that will throw them into crisis in the future. You actually get a hint at the end of this book of the reason they are star-crossed that will figure more largely in future books.

Q: Though Emma is, of course, the main character in your novels, her supporting characters are just as important to the cohesiveness of the story. Which of your "not-Emma" characters is your favorite, and why?

A: That's like asking a mother which of her children is her favorite!

In this book, I spent a long time developing Father Luke's tragic past, and I really felt my fondness for him grow as I got to know him better. He represents something very personal to me in how he has searched to come to terms with his past. I think I relate him to those with whom I've worked with in my psychology practice who have to wrestle with some awful things but find reconciliation.

On the other hand, I so love Sebastian's wit and fearlessness. He always says the caustic thing I wish I had the nerve to say. I happen to like smart-aleck types, so I really appreciate his brash humor and I like how brave he is to be himself in a world that cannot accept him. And yet, he never goes too far (but only just!). He demands and gets respect. He does his own thing and makes no apologies, and out of all of the characters, he impresses me the most because every one of them has a compelling reason to be there, but he does not. He does it because, and only because, he cares about doing the right thing.

And then there's Valerian. . . . He's so tragic, so earnest, so jaded, and yet so hopeful. I can't resist him and his dark brooding presence—and I can't imagine how Emma ever would, no matter how frustrating he can be. I want Valerian to be happy, but he's got a lot to solve before he can ever achieve that state. And, poor soul, he's been seeking peace for so long and yet he is still as dedicated and determined as ever. He has not lost hope. I can't imagine he will, no matter how hopeless things look. You have to feel the impending urgency in him, knowing as he does that at any time he can be transformed into his worst nightmare, and I know I for one am rooting for him to win out over Marius in the end.

I will say this, however, in reference to favorites: I get strong reactions to Valerian from people (usually women) who appreciate his heroic attributes. I also get a lot of people who love Sebastian. Who can resist someone who makes you laugh out loud?

Q: There are a lot of vampire books out there right now! (And TV shows and movies.) If you could pick one other vampire book, TV show, or movie to recommend, which would it be? And how is it different from your books?

A: I love *True Blood* because it's so out there and shocking and funny. Sookie Stackhouse is an amazing character. I like the way *True Blood* navigates the nature of good and evil, especially in the character of Eric. I also am a *Twilight* fan (team Edward, thank you very much), although you probably guessed that with my romance background. Both of these franchises are very different from my books in so many ways. Namely, there is the time period. I've chosen the murky shadows of Victorian England. Plus, the vampires in my books are the bad guys. Also, religious iconography and church references, as well as the old traditions and folklore play a major part in my vampire world. And all of these others have—so far—not included the most terrible vampire of all—the Dracula! Their take is completely original and modern, and mine is more traditional and rooted in ancient legend and myth, so it's just a different way to explore the world of the supernatural.

One really amazing thing I found out from my research, which might explain the current obsession with vampires, is that all cultures, even ones dating back thousands of years, have some semblance of an undead legend. This indicates an archetypal significance of the vampire, and perhaps this is why those creepy, sexy creatures continue to fascinate and entertain us.

Read on for an excerpt of the first Emma Andrews adventure, *Descent into Dust*

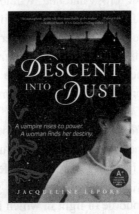

I was twenty-three years of age in March of 1862 when I traveled to my cousin's home in the countryside of Wiltshire. The fifth day of that wretched month found me huddled in my carriage, the drizzly gray gloom outside soaking a bone-deep chill into every aching part of my body, which had been roughly abused by the long confinement and ill-kept roads I'd traveled coming up from Dartmoor.

I did not know then that these would be the closing days of ordinary life. The only suggestion of the monumental changes about to occur was the headache that had come upon me upon crossing the Dart River. The pain, as fine as tiny needles being pushed into my temples, increased as I traversed the chalk downs and approached Dulwich Manor.

At the time, I assumed this was due to anxiety, for my younger sister and her new husband were among the guests invited for an extended stay at my cousin's sprawling country house. As I was long accustomed to contending with Alyssa without anything like this haunting megrim, I suppose I should not have made this rather obvious misattribution. But how could I have thought differently, back then?

The house was a large, ugly thing, squatting low on the land like a spider on a softly rounded hilltop. Stones blacked with lichen and soot formed a plain rectangle of unadorned walls dotted liberally with cross-hatched windows, lying dormant under leaden skies. There was no sign of life about it or any of the outbuildings. Everyone had taken shelter from the rain.

I emerged into a light drizzle and drew the cowl of my cloak over my head. At the top of the impressive set of carved steps, a very correct-looking butler awaited. "Emma Andrews, Mrs. Dulwich's cousin," I told him.

He did not quite meet my gaze, as all good servants manage not to do, as he opened the door wider and ushered me inside to a vaulted hall. I was instantly struck by the feeling of being very, very small in a very, very large place. The gas jets on the wall leaked only a small puddle of light in which I stood, beyond that, I saw only shadowy hints of the rest of the room.

"I shall tell madam you have arrived," the manservant intoned soberly.

Once alone, I quickly checked my appearance in a pier glass hung on the wall. I was decidedly damp. My hair was nearly a ruin. The expensive gown I had donned that morning, thinking it would lend me courage, had been a bad choice. There was nothing to be done about the crushed silk. A smart travel dress would have been better, had I owned one. But such things required seamstress consultations and fittings, all amounting to too much time, time I never seemed to make room for in my ordinary routines. I did take comfort in the fine brushed wool of my cloak which Simon, my husband, had given me for Christmas last year, a month before he died. It was of excellent quality.

A voice brought me up sharp. "I am most put out that the weather is foul," my cousin, Mary, said as she swept into the hall. "I wanted to show the house to its full advantage."

She posed regally in the hall of the Jacobean house, her pride radiating from her. She knew her surroundings elevated her, as wealth is apt to do. She had married well and that is always a woman's conceit.

And yet, it had not been mine. My late husband, Simon, had left me his wealth, something I found made my rather ordinary life a bit more convenient than it had previously been, but little else had changed because of it. I certainly took no pride in showing it off.

"The house is magnificent, Mary. I am anxious to see what you have done with its restoration. It seems very grand indeed."

That pleased her, thawed her a bit. She cocked her chin at me and turned slightly so that I might press a kiss upon her cheek, in a rather pretentious gesture for a woman only three years my senior. But I complied. I have no trouble indulging others' vanities, if they are harmless.

"Come then, Emma," she said, "the parlor is through here. Give Penwys your cloak. Alyssa and Alan have already arrived. I know she is anxious to see you. Penwys will see your things are delivered to your room and the servants will put everything to rights. You'll want to freshen up."

I did, but it would take too much time and I was feeling impatient to join the others. "I can go upstairs after my things have been unpacked. And to tell you the truth, a cuppa right now would be lovely."

"Very well," she said primly.

She was showing off a bit, taking on the same airs Alyssa was so fond of. And just as with my sister, they had the tendency to prick my sore spot and made me wicked.

"But please direct your man to be very careful with my portmanteau," I said. "It is old, and I take extra care of it since it had been my mother's."

The mention of my beautiful, tragic mother changed her expression to one rife with thoughts best left unsaid. "Your belongings will be treated with the respect they deserve."

We proceeded together down a short corridor. Above, a series of large arches stretched across the high ceiling like ribs, giving me the unsettling feeling of traversing the interior of a vast corporeal chest. My eye was caught by some words carved at the apex of the last of these stone vaults, just above the heavy double doors beyond which I could hear the muffled sounds of conversation. An odd place for decoration, I mused. It would be easily overlooked as it was placed high overhead. But I could read the three words.

Corruptio optimi pessima.

I stopped. Something strange and unpleasant fluttered through me. The air went crisp, as if ionizing in preparation for an electrical strike.

Mary saw me staring. "Interesting, isn't it? Those carvings are all over the house. The man who built the original manor was a bishop, back before Henry, when the papists still had the run of the place." She laughed. "It's a curiously religious dwelling as a result, and I've kept it that way through the restoration. These ominous sayings carved here and there are terribly quaint, don't you agree?"

My voice was dry as dust. "Do you know what it means?"

She must have forgotten my unfortunate habit of overburdening my brain with reading, for she thought I didn't know. "I believe it means 'The best of men are incorruptible.'"

It did not. The fact that she didn't know made my unease grow. It felt to me—very strongly so—that it should be important for the owner of this house to understand what was written into its very bones. The correct translation was "Corruption of the best is worst."

Photo by Lindsey Navin

JACQUELINE LEPORE is a native Philadelphian. She holds a Ph.D in psychology from the University of Pennsylvania. She lives with her husband in Maryland, where she has practiced for more than twenty years as a licensed psychologist. For more information on Jacqueline, visit her website at www.jacquelinelepore.com.

JACQUELINE LEPORE

DESCENT INTO DUST
ISBN 978-0-06-187812-1
(paperback)

IMMORTAL WITH A KISS
ISBN 978-0-06-187815-2
(paperback)

"Deliciously macabre . . . The rural Victorian setting is evocative, and the vampire threat palpable. While Lepore's tale does come to a nail-biting climax, her compelling characters are not finished with their missions, and so will continue their vampire slaying in future books, which will surely please readers."
—*Booklist* (starred review)

Something evil is preying on a girls' school in the Northern Lake District, and Emma Andrews is called upon to find out what's lurking. Undercover and underprepared, Emma heads north where she will face a new menace of the night, delve into her mother's vampire history, and edge closer to the Dracula himself.

www.JacquelineLepore.com